COME WHAT MAY
I0770231

By Lexy Night

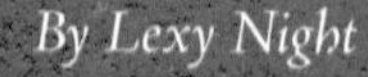

Tales of Forgotten Fae
To No End
Come What May

By Lexy Night

COME WHAT MAY

TALES OF FORGOTTEN FAE

BOOK 2

LEXY NIGHT

Edited by Noah Sky
Proofreading by Rachel Theus Cass
Book Cover Design by Krafigs Design
Illustrations and Font Design by Jade M Design
Map Art by ©Travis Hasenour/To the Moon and Back Design
Interior Design by ©Travis Hasenour/To the Moon and Back Design

ISBN: 979-8-9908638-3-5 (Paperback Edition)
ISBN: 979-8-9908638-4-2 (eBook Edition)
ISBN: 979-8-9908638-6-6 (Audiobook Edition)
ISBN: 979-8-9908638-7-3 (Hardback Special Edition)
Library of Congress Control Number: 2025915054

First Edition October 2025
Published in Overland Park, Kansas
Printed and bound in the United States of America

Under The Covers Publishing
www.lexynight.com

Fate happens.
Destiny is chosen.

If you cannot know yourself in the darkness,
you can never honor yourself in the light.

THE FAE REALMS OF
DEMIR
House Wick
House Tiernan
Elorn Basdie Mountains
House Huxley
House Evenus
House Kasparov
House Brynmawr
CAMBRIA
Tinsilor Castle
ENDLESS TIDES
Haven House
Doorlae Tavern & Inn
Erisas Bay
House Blackthorn
Riverlands
House Corliss
Ledor Canyon
Ledor River
Sadem
Nasallus Castle
Artume
The Ivory Waste
Damas
Caano
Endless Tides
N

CONTENT NOTES

A pronunciation guide can be found by skipping to the back of the book.

This story contains adult themes and the mention of the following that may be concerning to some readers:

- Abduction, Confinement & Imprisonment (brief scenes)
- Acts of War (common theme)
- Adult Murder (common theme)
- Classism (brief theme)
- Consensual Nudity/Sexual Scenes (fully described)
- Death (common theme)
- Female on Male Violence (common theme in the form of battle)
- Grief & Loss Depiction (brief theme)
- Language (infrequent)
- Male on Female Violence (common theme in the form of assault and battle)
- Murder (common theme)
- Poisoning (brief scenes)
- Poverty (common theme)
- Self-Harm (brief mention, brief scene, forced infliction)
- Servitude (common theme)
- Sexual Assault/Rape (brief scene)
- Torture (common theme)
- Verbal Assault (brief scenes)
- Violence (common theme)
- War (reference to past, present and future)

PROLOGUE

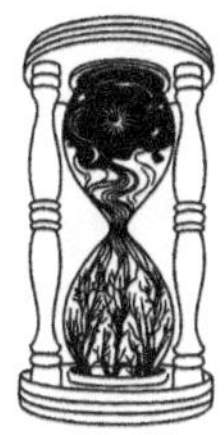

The roots of a tree are as winding as its branches. Sever a branch and another grows to fill the void. Sever its roots and watch it wither.

Proverbs, Lessons in Lineage, Chapter 8. Verse 7.

Unlike the northern kingdom of Cambria, the southern territories of Artume offered its inhabitants little. Harsh winds swept across the desert, shifting the sands across the sun-scorched landscape. And yet, its people endured. Long gone were the days of rampant skirmishes and ransacked villages—the tithes of war. These were the days of peace, ushered in by a pact between the two kingdoms centuries ago. Though the years had not been plentiful, the peace held.

But it could not last.

Treaties and accords proclaim peace through every royal hall, but sedition bleeds onto the page before the ink is even dry. Boundaries are rearranged, and mighty walls, impenetrable for generations, are scaled or reduced to rubble with the innovations of war. The histories remember peace with a sentence; they canonize bloodshed and sacrifice with marble statues and tomes.

To alter the course of history, one must be brave enough to set events into motion that would see it rewritten. A monarch's legacy lives on, not only through the bloodline, but in the chronicles scribed after their reign has ended. And if the current ruler does not pave a bold new path for their lands and people, then like the delicate rose bush, the bloodline can only survive with a bit of pruning…

King Baelin had no male heirs. His daughter, Princess Embry, would someday reign as Artume's first queen—should she remain an only child. Her mother's youth offered her husband some comfort as they continued to try for a son.

Prince Silas, his younger brother, also resided in Baelin's palace, and one might have believed from his cordial and charismatic personality that he was content to live the life of a royal without the burden that his brother shouldered as king. He was unwed till recently, when his brother Baelin forced upon him a betrothal to the daughter of a wealthy master of trade. Silas accepted his fate with little reluctance, but continued keeping company with many ladies of the court and other, more deviant consorts.

One evening, by the dim light and crackle of the fireplace, Baelin played a game of cards with Silas. A common occurrence for the brothers; a hobby they'd shared since childhood. Baelin had always been the better cardplayer and had no tells. He played with honor and a distinct strategy. Silas, on the other hand, was sloppy, taking risks that often did not pay off. After losing a number of hands, Silas was confident he had finally been dealt a round of cards in his favor. He laid the cards down neatly, one by one, to boast certain victory. Baelin assessed his brother's cards, then lifted his chin, a smug smile stretching across his face.

Suddenly, Silas lashed out, lunging across the table to plunge a dagger straight into his brother's chest. He wrapped his hand over Baelin's mouth, muffling the sounds of struggle. Silas removed the dagger abruptly, ensuring rapid blood loss and a swift death. He held his brother in his arms as Baelin looked up into his eyes, the unmistakable gaze of accusation and betrayal. He tried to speak but instead coughed up blood. With no use of his voice, there was only his eyes. A pleading, confused look, as if asking, *Why, dear brother?* Silas' glassy stare hinted at immediate regret.

Yet, he could not bring himself to reply. From a darkened corner of the room, a tall, cloaked male approached. Calm but menacing, he declared, "A new era requires a new heir…"

He crouched down, revealing himself to the dying king. A commotion of screams and ringing of swords echoed throughout the keep. In a quiet, gravelly voice, he spoke again. "Your reign has come to an end."

Silas, distraught at having taken the life of his own brother, could not bring himself to carry out the remainder of the task. Instead, a small militia loyal to Silas and the cloaked male finished the initial massacre, beginning with the slaughter of Queen Islan as she slept. The princess was taken for collateral and locked in the dungeon to be kept under constant surveillance. Any Kingsguard that attempted to thwart the coup were killed, and any staff that did not follow instruction were also eliminated.

That night would be forever known as the 'Silent Eve,' when the Kingdom of Artume fell from within at the hand of the king's own brother. Outside the castle walls, as darkness pushed the last rays of daylight aside, the townspeople tidied their kitchens and sang their children to sleep. Beyond their homes, the night was unnaturally quiet, for somehow even the nocturnal creatures sensed the violence on the wind, and so kept their conversations hushed. By the time the first songbird gathered the courage to sing at dawn, the castle had installed a new regime.

"My liege, it's only been a few weeks and we have nearly rooted out all of the sympathizers to ensure our new court consists only of loyal subjects—whether by true belief or fear. Still more loyal subjects are arriving daily to be fully vetted."

Zarif, the newly appointed Hand of the King, had seen to the effort himself. Though he towered above Silas, he always approached the king with a curved spine and shrunken shoulders, a clear manipulation for anyone who had *truly* seen him. Those that felt his presence fully knew the evil that resided in him. He was what common folk referred to as hexed, having one brown eye and one blue. Those who believed in the lore of the old Gods said that anyone with such an affliction had severed their soul, likely in some dark bargain.

While Zarif's post named him as an advisor for the king's affairs, everyone knew his counsel was law. It was by his hand that Queen Islan took her last breath. With an army at his command and spies paid from the royal purse, Zarif's true lust for blood and power was unbound. Hushed rumors quickly spread throughout the land that he was intent on bringing about the next great conflict.

Silas was, by all measures, inexperienced as a leader. He'd long ago stopped paying attention to the mundane affairs of his brother's kingdom, as he never expected to one day rule. He was a malleable male, especially since he kept himself regularly lubricated with drinks of the vine.

As long as Zarif kept Silas busy with parties in his honor, courtesans at his beck and call, and a full goblet, he was able to enact his own will and call it the king's with little to no opposition.

"Is all of this violence really necessary? The reports I am hearing are disturbing, even for you," Silas questioned his Hand.

"You know the plan, do not waver now. Your people must believe that Cambria is a threat once more. Let me sow the seeds of discontent. It is essential we distract them while we make progress on the other front."

"How are things coming along with the mining operations?" King Silas asked. The sooner their secret endeavor came to fruition, he thought, the sooner the senseless killing of his people could come to an end.

"We've located the pocket of the canyon that is rumored to conceal what we seek. Our people are working on making entry without alerting any of Cambria's border patrol. The risk of detection is high, of course, but so is the reward. I'm receiving regular reports and will continue to share any progress with you."

And so the plan continued as Zarif executed the dark and necessary deeds in the name of the Crown, justifying them as a means to an end. Threaten their safety, show them the cruel face of war, soak their households in the blood of their own, and when it came time to advance on the border, there would only be unwavering loyalty to their cause. By then, their secret weapon would be ready to provide an undeniable advantage. Cambria couldn't prepare if they never saw it coming.

Unbeknownst to them, Cambrian forces had already arrived...

CHAPTER 1

I have a mate.

My logical side struggled to reconcile the notion, pushing back against the new declaration. However, something else—possibly my heart—knew it was true. Suddenly, the irritating hum that had sat beneath my skin ever since arriving at the Offering could no longer be denied. Akin to finding the other end of a long rope that had been tethered all along. But to what? I had no idea.

Varro may not have been forthcoming, but Trace's lack of honesty about his identity seemed calculated. Despite all the time we'd spent together, in many ways, Trace and I remained strangers. He only grew more distant once we could no longer hide behind the facades we had created. I might never understand how he could so easily deny me in these circumstances, while Varro proclaimed our intertwined fates.

Perhaps it all came down to choice. Trace refused to stake claim over my heart. Varro had known all along we were fated, and let me feign choice in the matter. The Gods are cruel indeed. Memories flood the forefront of my mind.

The first time I saw Varro, my keen awareness of his presence and striking features were quickly overtaken by my own prejudice and misinformed judgements. Despite this, he remained completely devoted to patience. Every day he tried to show me something authentic. My inclination was to combat his every remark, remain rigid in my defense of Trace, and write off any minor connection we had to disregard the friendship we were forming. Dare I say, trusting him to the point of relying on him.

When I needed someone to second my cause for Nori, he was the first to take a stance. When I deserved silence, he gave answers. And when the shadow of death came for us both, he embraced me, ready to greet the Gods together. The others only voiced their concerns, or simply succumbed to their own trepidation, offering worried glances now that I was capable of dark magic. But not even that would dissuade Varro from his commitment to me. As a friend. As a member of the Imperi.

As his mate.

But amongst those memories were also recollections of Saryn's flippant, negative remarks about mates and Gia's warning, all now reverberating through me.

"Count yourself lucky you're not bonded."

I had not bound myself to Varro, and yet the idea of suffering any semblance of the pain Gia had endured was enough to deter me.

Lost in a labyrinth of my own thoughts, each turn I took led to another passageway darkened by more questions and doubts. Still, I continued my uneasy daydream, sinking deeper into the maze until Varro's quiet, shaky voice broke through and provided escape.

"Cress..."

I looked up to meet his crystal-blue eyes, swimming with a mixture of emotions, rolling like the waves of an ocean.

Fear. Longing. Concern. Rejection. Hope. Relief.

"I…I need time. Tell no one," I replied, unable to find the appropriate response to convey anything other than a mess of words that would come out all wrong and lack any of the right intentions.

I turned to walk away from him, knowing full well that no matter how far I distanced myself, the pull of our bond was inescapable.

As I turned on my heel, he said, "I won't. This has been my secret since the moment I laid eyes on you—and now it's our secret. Meet me back here tonight? Please?"

I gave him a nod and saw relief wash over him as his strong, broad shoulders relaxed.

Walking back to my room, his words *"since the moment I laid eyes on you"* reminded me how, all of this time, he had been certain of his feelings while I remained completely unaware. Another shameful moment of naivety. One of many I'd swallowed since arriving at Basdie.

I passed Cairis and Nori without a word. They were both lounging in the common room with their noses in books; each glanced up, looking at me with a hint of concern, but said nothing.

In the privacy of my room, I could finally think without the overwhelming presence of my supposed mate hovering nearby. Mates are not that common. What are the odds that I would be destined for one at all, let alone find them after being conscripted to the Imperi? Worse yet, that I might be shackled to the son of my father's sole enemy?

Thank the Gods I'd never have to see the horror on my parents' faces when they discovered their daughter was tied to a disgraced bloodline. Between the rawness of this revelation and the recent discoveries of dark wielding, I was overwhelmed—to say the least. My chest tightened into a familiar knot, constricting my breath as I fought back the emotions welling in my eyes, threatening to escape.

I was determined to learn how to control my anxiety. I'd swallow it whole and find a way to convert that energy into something more useful.

Anger. Revenge. Focus. Strength.

I'd been reading how Dark Wielders, more than anything, had to master their emotions. It was when their emotions got the best of them that they lost control—resulting in unwanted consequences, such as shaking an entire mountain. I'm surprised Saryn wasn't knocking down my door for an explanation. I reasoned that he might as well get used to it if he wanted me to practice this ability.

My clothes were still wet from the mist behind the falls when I dropped onto my bed. I felt the crumpling of paper digging into my leg from my pocket and remembered what Trace had given me before he and Gia left to make their way south.

I ran my fingers along the damp edges of the parchment, nervous to unfold it. Questioning if I wanted to at all. As much as I sought to shut the door on Trace completely, he was like a tiny open wound that refused to heal. Why does my mind find itself fixating on him even when I command it not to?

He didn't choose me.

He betrayed me.

He left me for dead.

These were the things I would repeat to myself any time a modicum of forgiveness crept into the corners of my thoughts. Trace remained my teammate, and we were still Imperi. Nothing more, nothing less. And, now that I had a supposed mate, what did that mean for any predilections I had for another male—past, present, or future?

We shouldn't bond. That was a gift reserved for two people in love that wanted to bind their souls. But, regardless, we were still connected for an eternity, and had no control over it. Had anyone ever sealed the bond as friends? Is that what Varro and I would be expected to do if Saryn or Theory ever uncovered the truth? A forced solution to what would be a tactical advantage. Mind-melding would surely come in handy once we both headed south, but I couldn't fathom doing the 'act' with someone merely for the sake of the Imperi. And what of the people we might have to perform 'acts' with because of the mission… How could two bonded souls possibly navigate the intricacies of such an impossible situation without hurting one another?

My thoughts spiraled down that familiar labyrinth once again until I realized there was a question—possibly the most important one—I'd been avoiding asking myself: Do I have any real feelings for Varro? Would I let myself explore those feelings even if I did? There were too many complications. Gia endured the pain of a severed bond. What would she think of me having a mate? Would Trace even be able to look at us, let alone fight alongside us? Saryn and Theory might exploit the powers we'd gain. At the end of a very long list, what we were really up against was the notion that we'd gain something that everyone else had lost.

Each of us had severed our ties from family and lovers alike. We were all destined for a singular future as the unseen peacekeepers of his majesty, the king. What fairness lay in Varro and I claiming more than that? Having semblance of comfort and safety in the arms of another, the urge to aid each other before all others. Our group dynamic had barely recovered before Gia and Trace departed for Artume.

Varro had not voiced any true feelings for me; only stated what he believed to be a fact. For all I knew, he was just as hesitant as I was to explore our bond in any capacity. But since he'd known about this far longer than I, he'd had much more time to play out the various outcomes, while I was just beginning to wrap my mind around them. Maybe if I met with him tonight as he requested, he would set my mind at ease. What if he had already thought this through, and only meant to assure me that we'd remain purely platonic?

Flashes of those moments consumed me. Countless nights in the healing pools, his strong, skilled hands kneading my skin. Gently removing clothing from my injured body. His refusal to leave my side as arrows rained down upon us, and the occasional stolen glances that he didn't think I ever noticed… I was almost certain that Varro's feelings were not wholly platonic.

And there was the way he had said my nickname all those times. *Moirai…* The words carried an unanswered longing when he spoke them. Why call me "fated one" if he did not believe I would ever fulfill that role? To call me a mate sounded technical, even practical. But fated one… It was teeming with *want*.

I sighed, returning from the fog of distraction, ready to conquer my reluctant curiosity. I unfolded the single piece of paper, my nerves on edge as I braced myself for the words that might make sense of his betrayal. To my surprise, a sketch filled the page. One that was undoubtedly done by his hand. The normal, all-black charcoal, devoid of any other color. It was a drawing of the night sky over the Elorn Mountains. Amongst a moonless scene, there were only stars drawn to exemplify their twinkle. Below it in his handwriting were the words:

Stars shine brightest in the dark.

Written in the script of the old tongue… The cryptic words felt hollow, and yet I longed to uncover his intent. But more than that, my heart sank at the realization of another secret he had been keeping from me. Every lie, every glamour, every layer peeled back, pierced through me with indescribable sadness—and fury. Had I ever really known him?

Rubbing the sleep from my eyes, I grappled with the fact that I did not meet Varro as he requested. I just couldn't yet bring myself to have the conversation. Not knowing what feelings he may or may not convey would have left me unprepared to react with composure.

It wasn't like when I had lured Trace. Much of that had felt like theater…until it wasn't. We began and ended with the belief we'd never see one another again. Despite being my most vulnerable with him, any semblance of our relationship eroded quickly with each passing day spent in Basdie. Many times I felt like all that remained were tightly wound strings of attraction, jealousy, and a myriad of other unreconciled emotions.

But now my mate had been revealed to me. Whatever sentiments he or I had on the matter of our bond, we were already tied, bound to one another for the rest of our days. The will of the Imperi superseded our personal feelings, after all, so having any would distract us if not destroy us completely.

Lost to my thoughts, I headed to a late breakfast, then practically jumped at the presence of Varro standing in my doorway. My reflexes narrowly saved me from running face-first into the center of his broad chest. Hesitantly, I lifted my chin to meet his expression, expecting disappointment but instead finding warmth.

"I...I'm sorry I didn't meet you," I uttered, uncharacteristically bashful.

Varro placed a gentle hand on my shoulder. I relaxed into the warmth of his grasp as he responded.

"I knew you wouldn't come, but it was a relief to me, all the same, to know you would at least consider it. I've waited a long time to tell you. It's a good thing I'm very patient."

I breathed a sigh of relief. Irrationally, feeling slightly defensive, I said, "How did you know I wouldn't come?"

Varro smiled, flashing his brilliantly white teeth, somehow still shining in the dreary light of Basdie.

"I have been paying attention to you for far longer than you realize, Moirai. Let's just say, I know when you're overwhelmed. And I don't blame you."

His words brought back memories of the various times he and I had caught one another's gazes, and how suddenly my feelings of trepidation or anxiety would dissipate with that one glance. Conceivably, Varro had been alleviating my emotions with Siren Song more often than I was aware of. Before his confession, I might have felt like it was intrusive, but suddenly his actions, words and decisions, were all starting to make sense, like puzzle pieces slowly snapping into place. He had been watching me and waiting patiently since the day we all bathed in the waters of Mirtith. So much time had passed, that seemed like lifetimes ago.

How did he ever keep all of this to himself? Had I any inclination of what was really stirring between us, would I have kept it a secret... waited for him to acknowledge me? Part of me wished Gia were still here to discuss this with, especially knowing Nori wouldn't ever engage in these kinds of relations. And…well, Cairis' advice would be worthless. He'd tell me to fuck any handsome or charming Fae that showed interest.

"I'm paying attention to you now." I replied cryptically, mustering my confidence, then pushed my hand flat against his chest and shoved him out of my doorway. "And…I'm starving."

I smiled as he followed me to the dining hall. I felt a tickle along the bond in response to my coy behavior.

"Well, did you think I wouldn't remark on the quaking of the literal mountain, Cress?"

Saryn sipped his drink and eyed me with annoyed accusation, while the others tried to act like they weren't listening in on his interrogation. I knew there wasn't a chance in the three moons of Demir that he wasn't going to bring it up. I tried to conjure some sort of logical excuse, but he cut in before I could get out a word.

"While I'd like to assume this means your studies in that dusty closet are finally starting to pay off, I'm going to wager that was an uncontrolled outburst just like the first time. Otherwise, you would have been at my door to show me such an impressive feat, correct?"

I nodded in quiet embarrassment. This is precisely what the others didn't realize and couldn't relate to. Their magic was confidently summoned, even under Saryn's scrutinizing gaze. My dark magic seemed to evade my grasp, evaporating just as I aimed to call upon it, then roaring to the forefront when I was unprepared to wield it.

I continued to nibble at my breakfast; my appetite ruined by Saryn's judgement and Theory's displeased glances from across the table.

"Everyone, breakfast is over. Join me on the flight deck. I have some experiments I'd like us to explore together."

Saryn's instruction had each of us looking equally concerned. His ideas were seldom enjoyable for us, though it didn't dissuade him from subjecting us to them.

Many of us added layers of clothing before meeting outside. The crisp winds of early winter left a sparkling frost all across the valley, and the temperatures were steadily beginning to drop. The once-vibrant greens were now scattered with hues of burnt orange and deep red, except for the evergreens, who stood proud and tall amongst those that would shed their leaves. Varro stayed close by my side at all times. It occurred to me that he may have been positioning himself nearby far more often than I'd ever noticed.

"Nori, come here," Saryn commanded as he pulled out a rope from a sack he'd carried with him.

We all watched as he stood behind her and told her to move her hands behind her back, then bound them with said rope. Loud enough for all of us to hear, he instructed, "If you so much as singe these ropes with fire, you will regret it. Do you understand?"

Nori nodded fearfully, glancing quickly between him and us and back again. What was he doing? If she couldn't use her elemental manipulation, then what was she expected to do?

He then escorted her to the ledge of the flight terrace and faced her away from us so that we could only see her back and the rope.

"Cress…" Saryn yelled, drawing my attention to him instead of her.

"Tell me, can a Fae unfurl their wings when their hands are tied behind them in a position such as this?"

The question was absurd—and alarming. All at once, the fear overcame me when the answer would not come quickly enough. Maybe? No. Probably not? Was this a trick question?

"Let's find out!" All of a sudden, Saryn pushed Nori over the edge of the cliff, and her high-pitched shriek echoed throughout the canyon.

There was only a single breath before I reacted, sprinting toward the ledge to go after her. The moment I was off the ground, I could see her plummeting without a single white wing in sight. Just the shrill sound of her screams following her down.

I angled my wings in tightly, trying to give myself the speed to catch up with her, fear of the ground we were spiraling towards increasing with each moment that passed. When I reached her, I grabbed her and held the weight of her falling body to me. Or attempted to. She was too heavy for me to hold aloft, and I was immediately pulled down after her. Quickly, I snatched a blade from my thigh and cut the rope, freeing her arms.

"Fly!" I yelled in panic.

We were so close to the ground, I didn't know if there would be enough time for her wings to unfurl before we hit the bottom. As the ground continued to rush toward us, suddenly, large, black wings came soaring quickly past me, scooping up Nori and leaving me in their wake.

I breathed a momentary sigh of relief; it was Cairis. I flared my wings in an attempt to slow my collision with the ground, but achieved only moderate success. I let my body roll into the dirt, trying to soften the blow of the impact. My chest heaved with exhaustion. Varro was at my side in an instant, reaching to pull me up from the ground and steady me.

"Are you okay?" he asked, worry furrowing his brow as he scanned my body.

I took inventory of a few sore spots from the impact, thinking it could have been much worse. "Where is she?" I asked, ignoring his question and frantically searching for Nori and Cairis.

About ten feet away, I saw them both looking uninjured, but no less shaken than I was. As I looked above us at the towering heights of the stone outlook, I could make out the hints of Saryn and Theory peering over the ledge. Fury took over. Without another word, I left Varro in a gust of wind and took flight straight up toward them. The other three followed, landing shortly thereafter. Nori didn't need to concern herself; I was going to kill Saryn for the both of us.

"What the fuck was that?" I yelled, infuriated with his reckless treatment. "Tell me, Saryn, what exactly did we just learn from that little experiment?"

Varro pulled me back, knowing full well I might take a blade to Saryn again. I didn't know if the throbbing I felt was the bond or just a blood-rush from anger and fear coursing through me.

Saryn didn't even flinch. "It proved one or two things. Either fear of losing Nori isn't a strong enough motivator to draw your power, or fear isn't your real motivator."

Before I could spew any sort of venomous retort, Theory added, "I do love to see you all acting like a team again."

I didn't know if I was more furious at Saryn, or at Theory for reminding me of the Canary Veil—when a lack of teamwork almost cost us our lives. Their taunts had my anger boiling over. I glanced at Varro hovering over me and then felt a minor wave of relief wash over me. It did not overly dull my sentiments, but it did allow me to compose myself. It was clear from the look he was giving me that this was his exact intention.

"As with all experiments, one test does not prove a guaranteed result. You should be aware this will continue. That alone might motivate you to understand the darkness that hides within you. Show it to me, or I will draw it from you," Saryn warned, before turning his back on all of us and returning inside.

I turned away from Varro's concerned stare and looked at my companions. My powers, though significant, proved mysteriously elusive. We narrowly avoided disaster today, but Saryn seemed intent on repeating—or even intensifying—his experiments until he achieved the desired result. I cast my eyes downward, heavy with guilt.

I went to Nori's side, where she still appeared shaken from the ordeal. "I'm sorry," I whispered. "This is my fault."

Nori looked up at me, smiling weakly. "It's really not. I just wish you weren't having to leap after me a second time."

I pulled her into my chest, hugging her tightly as the vivid moments of our friendship flashed through my mind. I looked up at Cairis and mouthed *thank you* to him in appreciation.

We ate dinner quickly before returning to the common room; none of us wanted to share Saryn and Theory's company for any longer than was required. Without Gia and Trace, the space felt bigger, emptier, and I doubted I was the only one concerned about their whereabouts. We had no idea how soon Idris would return for more of us.

I opted for another game of Bones and Stones with Nori, which she soon won handily. Varro read quietly in a corner while Cairis entertained himself sharpening his blades, the repetitive metallic scraping providing an unpleasant background noise for our activities. As Nori continued to make a fool of me, scoring point after point, I spun around in frustration and yelled, "Who are all those knives for?"

"I'm planning to make a visit to the Vespers this evening and blow off some steam. Today was tense."

He wasn't wrong. The sore knots across my body were the undeniable combination of stress, anxiety, and strenuous activity. Unlike the rest of us, Cairis did not enjoy the healing waters—or any water for that matter. It was no surprise he had other ways of relaxing. If distracting himself with a little violence and a Vesper was his way, then so be it. There were many times in the early days of training with the Vespers when they also afforded me a welcome escape from the halls of Basdie.

Cairis and Nori had grown close, and I think he thought of her like a little sister as much as I did. He'd probably never admit to how terrified he was watching her fall and me flying after her, hoping neither of us died in the process. Cairis had siblings, ones that probably didn't even know he existed. When his father denied Cairis' identity, it all but guaranteed his younger siblings would never know their older brother in any meaningful way. I had been watching out for Nori since we arrived here, and it relieved me to know someone else was too.

Before turning in for the night, I agreed to join Varro in the healing pools. My aches and pains from the fall were so minimal by that point that I could have probably healed myself and just gone straight to sleep, but it was a good excuse to spend some time getting better acquainted with my mate.

As we made our way down toward the waters together, Varro said, cautiously, "I need to tell you something," and I braced myself for whatever he was about to share.

"Yes?" I replied anxiously.

"Nori has been playing you for a fool," he stated matter-of-factly.

"...What?" I asked in confusion, not expecting the topic.

"She's cheating at Bones and Stones. I can't believe you haven't picked up on her scheme yet."

Varro continued to walk by my side with a playful smile plastered across his handsome face.

"She uses your trust and naivety against you. She knows you only see the good in her. But I assure you, no one wins that often."

"How so?" I inquired further, trying to wrap my mind around sweet and innocent Nori cheating at anything, even a silly game.

"Her elemental manipulation is better than any of ours. You don't think she's influencing those tiny rocks or bones before they land?"

The moment he proposed the idea, I realized how simple the manipulation would be—and how truly stupid I'd been all that time. She had disarmed me with our friendship and cheated without the slightest indication.

My Gods, how could I not have been questioning such a thing? I'm certain Varro thought he was only pointing out something miniscule, but it was in that moment that I learned one of my greatest lessons yet while here at Basdie: The enemy may appear as a friend, someone close to us, and they will smile with joy in their eyes as they move the pieces one by one toward your demise.

I would not make that mistake again. I would not be played for a fool. I gave Nori credit, though. Plenty of it. She didn't have an overwhelming arsenal of magical skill, but she was unexpected, methodical and disarming, radiating feigned innocence. If she were here with us, I'd probably pinch her in annoyance but also pay her a compliment for her efforts. For a moment, I wondered what damage she could pull off if her intentions weren't so simple. A silly game to pass the time is one thing, but when the moment came for us to face our real enemies, maybe she'd prove more invaluable than I ever imagined.

We had finally reached the bottom, and I was about to tell Varro that Nori's cheating was going to come to a swift end, when we were immediately alerted to the sound of deep, roaring screams. A male voice, crying for help. It sounded like it was coming from inside the falls, from the room where Varro had found me shaking the mountain the day prior. I quickly reached for the door handle and entered the room, the deafening crash of the falls thundering around us. I could also hear the frantic, desperate pleas, as if someone were being tortured. That's when we saw him.

Cairis was hanging upside down from a rope tied around his ankles, his hands also bound behind him. His body was tethered to the underside of a rocky ledge so that cascades of rushing water pounded him relentlessly. With each scream, the torrent filled his nose and mouth, causing him to choke and writhe. We yelled up to him, assuring him of our intention to help. How long had he been like this, and how much longer until he hadn't the strength to maneuver for air?

Without further hesitation, I unfurled my wings and flew up to assess the situation, pleading with him to stay calm. The water continued to pour down through the center of Basdie, the noise drowning out the sounds of my instruction. With all the power I could muster, I focused my energy to shift the water away from his body. I pushed strenuously against the constraints of my mind, but moving such a force of nature proved exceedingly difficult. Slowly, the falls began to waver and shift outward, as if a small dome pushed them aside.

My head began to ache, and I felt a wave of exhaustion threatening to replace the adrenaline that had taken me thus far. I wasn't going to be able to keep it up for very long. Cairis hung there, limp and almost unconscious. I yelled to Varro, who was now airborne beside me, hoping he could hear me as I strained to keep up the resistance against the water.

"Get him down!" I yelled through gritted teeth, fighting the pain of my own exertion.

Varro moved to cut the rope, but not before bracing Cairis' heavy body against his. As soon as the rope was severed, the weight of Cairis would be too much. We'd be lucky if Varro could bring them both to a controlled fall. I'd have to keep the water at bay, otherwise it would crush both of them from above before Varro could pull them out of the twisting pool below. The water fed the healing pools, but it also drained out of the mountain through underground caves that fed the valley's river. There was a high risk of them being sucked into the undertow.

Time slowed down as I watched the rope snap and both of them careen downward, Varro placing himself under Cairis as best he could to brace the plunge into the water. In Cairis' powerless state, he could easily hit his head on a rock and drown. When I saw Varro breach the water holding Cairis in his arms, I released a breath I hadn't even realized I was holding, and relief flooded over me. But with that distraction, I felt my strength wavering. The rushing waters inched toward me as I struggled to hold them back. As soon as I could see them both laying safely on the rocky landing at the edge of the pool, I let the waters resume their fall at its center.

Landing at Varro's side, I helped pull Cairis' body across the slippery ground and through the threshold of the doorway into the hall. The first thing I noticed was the difference in the sound. The hallway was so much quieter than inside the waterfall; now I could hear our heavy breathing and the sloshing of our wet clothing. I knelt beside him, my whole body trembling with panic. Cairis lay there, unmoving, looking like a very large, dead fish.

Suddenly the sound of hurried footsteps came towards us, and I looked up to see a frantic Nori as she assessed the scene with two more approaching shadows behind her. Having granted us the minor courtesy of alerting our best healer, Saryn and Theory looked on with apathy.

Nori quickly bent down to Cairis' body, placing her hands on both sides of his chest. Within a few seconds, heaps of water came flowing out of his mouth, followed by deep coughs and gasps for air. Cairis finally opened his eyes and continued to choke out more water as Nori and Varro rolled him to his side.

There was no greater form of torture for Cairis. He despised water, and my throat stung at the cruelty Saryn and Theory had inflicted upon him, all in an effort to get my attention. They were trying to force something out of me that I had no control over. Didn't they know that by now?

Saryn and Theory hovered over us, faces unconcerned. They must have been the ones to string him up. Only, how did they catch him unaware? How could they know he would be rescued in time? It was all absurd. We'd almost lost Nori, and now, Cairis. Anger was raging inside of me. Like always, Saryn could read my every emotion.

"You're all heading into enemy territory soon. Gia and Trace may already be suffering torture at the hands of the Artumians, and who is there to cut them down or heal them?"

I sat there seething, biting my tongue as he continued.

"Cress, you may not like my methods, but you're going to like it far less if you're not prepared. It would be a great advantage to us all if you figured out how to manifest the dark magic. Then I won't need to keep testing you at the expense of your fellow Imperi. We had hoped something other than water wielding would rear its head, but alas, the experiment continues."

The madness of his threat consumed me and I screamed, lunging up at them; Varro reached out to contain me. He held me tightly against him as I writhed and shouted.

"I *hate* you. I hate you both! Fuck you! Fuck all of this!"

They walked away at a calm and even pace, ignoring my outburst entirely. Varro twisted me to face him, and when I'd finally calmed, I looked up into his eyes to see what we both already knew: They'd come for him next.

CHAPTER 6

I spent the entirety of the next day scouring the texts of the former Dark Wielders, hoping I would find some sort of insight that would allow me to achieve the control Saryn desired. If I could find it before he went after Varro or anyone else, then I could bring an end to his ruthless explorations. It's possible he was right, that fear wasn't the key to unlocking my abilities. Thinking back on what happened the night of the Canary Veil, I had been convinced it was fear of my own death and Varro's that led to my power being unleashed. Fear of the pain of a hundred arrows raining down on us. When Nori and Cairis were recently put in harm's way, all of my training and instinct kicked in—but not the dark wielding, even though I'd been terrified. I relied on what they'd taught us first. The two times I *had* displayed dark magic, it felt nothing like instinct.

As I continued to devour notebook after notebook, I happened upon a text containing information that had me fearing my power more than ever—something I hadn't thought possible. The scribbling at the top was messy, appearing as if it had been squeezed in above all the contents below it. It read as a warning for everything that followed.

Beware of the Drift. Some magic is too dark; it will dim the light inside of you, obscure your memories and path. Wield just enough, and it will only consume your energy. Wield too much, and it will consume you instead...

I paused my reading, feeling slightly lightheaded. I realized I had been holding my breath as I looked over the note. My sweaty, shaking hand caused the ink below my thumb to smear. I took a deep breath, then another, trying to calm myself and satisfy my nervous curiosity. There were multiple journal entries tracking this Dark Wielder's findings.

I find myself struggling to remember things clearly. Not the recent past, but moreso the family I left behind. At first, I thought the exhaustion of my wielding would pass and clarity would return, but it has not. Memories of their faces and my home, the lands which I once rode through daily, become blurrier with each passing day. No matter how much I focus and clear my mind, I cannot see them, and I fear I may lose it all completely.

One of the others found me today, staring at a wall. Unmoving, unflinching, lost in a maze of my own thoughts. They claimed they called my name loudly, multiple times, and yet I did not stir. Not until they shook me and physically moved me from my stance. I do not remember how I got into that position, nor how long I had maintained it. I can only trust what they said. They encouraged me to eat, drink, and rest, but I do not find that it helps this new affliction. Each day I train these dark gifts, I feel less like myself. I worry I am becoming something else.

As my training continues, my gifts grow stronger—but I am losing control elsewhere. I have scoured the historical texts of past Dark Wielders, and according to their words, I'm inclined to believe that I am doomed. I must either give up this practice (which the Imperi will never allow) or suffer the culmination of this fate.

To those of you reading this, someday long after I am dead: The "Drift," as I have decided to call it, is the price we pay for wielding such an unholy and tainted power. Where we are given such a force, something must be taken in return. The continued use of dark magic will undoubtedly result in your demise. It seeps into your mind, twining through every vein of your body like a rot, spreading till it's withered you fully. If you are not killed before you succumb entirely to the Drift, then you best end it yourself. As a member of the Imperi, you may be houseless, nameless and forgotten, but there is something worse.

I've surmised there are two possible ways to avoid the Drift: give up dark wielding or anchor to a mate. Like many of us conscripted to a life in the Imperi, it is unlikely you will ever find your mate—if you're even destined for one at all. It is theorized that a bonded mate can serve as a tether to reality, and in some ways, lessen the burden, ease the corrosion of the mind. I have lived many years. I have served the realm. I have never felt the bond calling, and I don't know how much longer I can withstand the Drift. I can only hope that the Offering comes to an end, or that no other bloodlines containing dark magic are awoken to suffer as I and a few others before me have.

My chest tightened, constricting my airway. Fear flooded my entire body as I absorbed the journal's warnings. Now, more than ever, I wanted to render this magic useless, unobtainable. But more than that, it was crystal clear that if Saryn discovered Varro was my mate, paired with the information about the Drift, he'd have every justification to exploit this and hold me to my oath. *My loyalty is bound to you and our cause.*

There was safety in knowing I had a mate that could possibly protect me from this so-called Drift, but there was also surrender. Surely, this would require we seal the bond, and as of now, the weight of that wasn't one I could bear. I'd barely toyed with the idea of having a mate at all before Varro, let alone bonding for the sake of additional power like mind-melding. Now, the decision included protection against a corrosive disease of the mind that may already be coming for me, despite having never dark-wielded of my own volition.

Which path do I take? Learn to control the magic and avoid using it unnecessarily, hoping that would be enough to avoid the effects of the

Drift? Or accept that I am out of my depth, and seek all the help I can get. Should I tell Saryn everything, in hopes that he and Theory would find a way to help me navigate this safely? They had to believe a mindless Imperi was a risk and of no use to the realm, right? What if I told Varro first? Did I even want Varro to know that my ties to him may be more necessary than ever? I still didn't know if he even wanted to seal the bond, or what his motivations were. Added to that, I didn't want to scare him with the knowledge that I might quite literally lose my mind without him.

I paused briefly, closing my eyes, trying to bring visions and memories of my family back into my mind's eye. I felt tears prickling at the edges of my lashes at the thought of not being able to remember them if the Drift ever got me. The journal entries implied that older memories would be taken first, but who's to say that one person's experience suffering from the Drift would be exactly the same as another's? Scattered across pages, the histories chronicled other unique experiences encountering its effects.

I'd read enough for the day, I decided, enough to concern me for an entire lifetime. I made my way back to the common area to see how the others fared in a day of training without me. I had intentionally grabbed breakfast early to avoid seeing them, unsure if I could look Cairis in the eye after what they did to him. Because of me. Varro was no doubt the one who had left a plate of lunch outside my door later that day.

As I approached them, I heard the sound of Nori's giggles in between Cairis' deep chuckles; an unexpected ruckus, considering the events of the previous evening. I rounded the corner and almost fell to the ground as Nori suddenly appeared out of a tiny cloudlike swirl in front of me. Cairis came running towards her, and she quickly disappeared again, re-appearing on the other end of the room. Varro sat on the couch, shaking his head at them with a warm smile.

"As you can see, you've missed out on some very intense training," Varro teased. I plopped down beside him on the couch to watch their games continue, relieved that somehow warmth and color had returned to Cairis' tan cheeks.

"I can't believe they gave you guys the stones!" This was obviously a distraction from what they'd done last night. I felt a bit jealous, wondering where my stone was. As if on cue, Varro held out a stone that looked tiny in the palm of his large hand.

"You didn't think I was going to let them withhold yours, did you?" He winked.

I had no idea if they had actually considered keeping mine from me, but it wouldn't be surprising if they had. They'd spent so much time familiarizing Gia and Trace with the portaling capability before their departure that the rest of us had barely had glances at our own stones. Reaching for the moonstone, I let my fingers gently graze his hot skin and felt a tickle run across the bond. Varro's throat bobbed with a nervous swallow at the contact.

"Will you practice with me after dinner?" I asked politely.

He grinned at the invitation. "Of course! Meet me here."

And with that he stood, a small cloud appeared, and Varro was gone. I quickly headed to the dining hall, hoping that he had left some dinner rolls for the rest of us.

Theory and Saryn were blessedly absent at dinner, which left us all feeling relieved. Cairis converted the water to wine and even convinced Nori to come off her high horse and drink with us. Even still, she kept reminding us that wine was ceremonious and not meant to be drank at leisure. Lecturing us on how easy it would be to lose control of our inhibitions. I reminded her that soon we'd be with our enemies, and that meant we'd likely never risk being drunk again.

Each of us moved our goblets to the center of the table, clinking them with a unified "cheers!"

"To the Imperi," Nori said sarcastically, raising her glass again.

"To almost dying before we're sent to die," Cairis added enthusiastically, giving me an apologetic yet playful nod.

"To fate!" Varro exclaimed, eyeing me meaningfully.

I lifted my cup last and added, "To the cruelest Gods."

Even that one had Nori giggle so hard, she almost snorted her wine.

The rest of dinner carried on with an ease and lightness that I can't recall feeling since before our first mission. Cairis and Nori talked about what it felt like using the portal stones for the first time, and I was eager to conclude dinner so Varro could take me to try mine.

"I guess all that training you did on how to scent-track Nori won't help you if she can just portal away before you find her," I said to Cairis, amused.

He pondered the idea, irritated at the thought of being evaded so easily.

"It's ok, I plan to learn some new tricks tomorrow," he declared.

"And what's that?" Nori asked, her curiosity piqued.

"I'm going to portal *while in flight!*"

"Is that even possible with moonstones?" I asked, just as interested as Nori.

"Why not?" he questioned. "Saryn and Theory said you either have to be able to see your destination or picture it clearly in your mind. I'm going to try to portal from one end of the valley to the other, all while airborne."

He sounded so confident, as if he'd thought all of this through already. Nori looked concerned. He placed his hand on her shoulder reassuringly.

"Someone else will have to cover beverage services if I die…" he joked.

I winced at the persistent mention of death from Cairis, which led me to believe that he was more shaken by what transpired than he was willing to let on. I hardly ever heard Cairis say a serious word, and humor was a shield he knelt behind often.

Varro felt the awkward silence thicken and commented, "Just make sure Nori is on standby for healing during said attempts." He grinned at me before continuing, "If Cress happens to show any promise in portaling tonight, we'll join you on the flight decks tomorrow for one of the most epic games of tag this world has ever seen."

Everyone smiled, our imaginations running wild at the prospect. We should have been taking things more seriously, especially since our fellow members were Gods-knew-where with the enemy. But sometimes, we just needed to permit ourselves these carefree moments to survive our own reality.

Indulging in the fleeting sweetness of the evening, I decided not to broach the topic of the Drift with Varro. That time would come soon enough.

A bit after dinner, I met Varro alone in the common room, holding the portal stone tightly in my hand. He looked delighted to show me what he and the others had learned while I toiled in a closet, discovering that my power would turn me into a mindless shell of a Fae.

"I figured we could walk down to the healing pools together and use that as an excuse to make short portal skips. Sound good?"

"You're the teacher! I will do as you instruct."

There was a slightly wicked look in his eye at my response, and I rolled my eyes at the implication.

"So, your first time might feel...strange..." He continued with a smirk, before growing serious and explaining, "After a few jumps, you could feel a bit nauseous from moving through the loops quickly, so try and keep your sight line steady and your mind clear."

I listened to his guidance intently, worried that if I made a misstep, I'd accidentally portal myself through the glass walls shielding me from the falls. I couldn't afford to be distracted. Not even if Varro was looking particularly handsome this evening.

"They did not want us portaling from memory until we'd mastered jumping from one space to the next in close proximity."

Their concerns were warranted, but my fingers itched with anticipation to try what he and the others had mastered earlier. I put the stone in my pocket and studied the destination in front of me, noting the details of the hallway farther ahead. Varro did the same next to me, and a small circular cloud appeared right before him.

"Concentrate," he reiterated sternly.

I breathed in deeply, and let it out slowly and calmly, focusing on drawing my energy to my core. A small ring like the one Varro had conjured began to form. It hovered, flickering and stretching, but was still too tiny for my body.

He placed his hand on my shoulder reassuringly. "You can do this. Focus on the clarity of where you're going. Let the circle expand. It only has to be big enough for you to step through. Nothing too taxing, Cress."

I let the heat of his hand relax me even more, and slowly the circle widened, bit by bit, till it was large enough to accommodate my size.

"As you proceed, keep your mind singularly focused on where it's taking you. We're going to step in at the same time. I don't want you to become distracted by me arriving before you. On the count of three."

I nodded to him without turning my gaze from the floating portal.

"One, two, three."

We stepped into our own portals in unison. It felt like only a second or two passed, and in that brief flash, I could not see or hear him. Only nothingness surrounded me—bright light, a noiseless expanse—but I quickly braced myself for the next step, almost tripping as I exited. I arrived about twenty or so feet from where I began, looking back with shock as the cloud dissipated. My surprise was broken by the sound of Varro's celebration.

"You did it! I didn't lose you after all," he said clasping my shoulder enthusiastically.

I looked at him with concern—did he think that would actually happen?

"I'm only joking; you're a Dark Wielder. I'm not worried about you and a portal stone."

He meant it as a compliment, but it struck a deeper nerve than he realized. Everyone on the team acted like I was becoming something invincible. How could they even think that, given how little control I'd demonstrated? My power slumbered inside of me, only to occasionally awaken in an uncontrollable outburst.

Even so, I was happy to have accomplished portaling on my first try. Every challenge conquered made me feel more confident, something that I sorely lacked when it came to dark wielding.

Varro looked ahead, farther down the winding hallway, and asked, "Again?"

Together, we portaled the entire way down to the bottom of Basdie, making leaps every visible length of the hallway. Due to the twisting of the halls, my sight line was limited to a few dozen feet ahead, and he encouraged me not to make jumps where the destination was unseen. By the time we had reached the bottom, I couldn't recall just how many jumps we'd made. It must have been at least a hundred, and I was now at ease with the skill.

He was also correct in that I was beginning to feel a bit nauseous from the whole exercise. Saryn and Theory weren't joking when they explained how quickly it could deplete your energy. Even these short, repetitive jumps were a bit tiring and dizzying. Varro noticed my minute swaying and moved to steady me. From his pocket he revealed a small orange, and handed it to me.

"Eat this. It will help, I promise."

Did he bring that for me specifically? I took it from him without question and began peeling it, but he pulled it back from me and finished what I had begun, quickly handing it back to me ready to eat.

I popped a piece of orange into my mouth and relished in the tart, citrus taste and the renewed sharpness to my senses. Varro opened the door to our usual pool, stepping aside for me to enter first.

"I don't think they were lying when they said if you portaled a great distance you might find yourself exhausted and starving. Didn't you see how much Cairis ate at dinner? All that practice with the stones really makes you hungry," I said, while continuing to eat.

The warmth of the room enveloped us, drawing a sheen of sweat across my arms. Varro began to remove his shirt, leaving his loosely-tied pants hanging below the dips of his hips, accentuating the outline of his abdominal muscles and ribcage. If I hadn't been chewing an orange slice, I might have been drooling, but there was nothing hiding my stare. If this was the mate promised to me, I could have done far, far worse than this.

Finishing the orange quickly, I slid off my layers and entered the pool after him. These visits were beginning to feel comfortably routine, like we knew we'd always have this—barring the previous night's missed rendezvous. The moment I entered the pool, the hum of the bond amplified, causing goosebumps to ripple over my skin.

"Do you feel that?" I questioned, my voice echoing in the rocky cavern.

"Yes," he sighed, his back still turned to me. "I always feel it..." His tone was somber.

I made my way closer to him, my body half-submerged. "Why didn't you ever say anything?"

He took a seat across from me and ran his hands through the wet tendrils of his hair. "I didn't know if you knew and were choosing to deny it, or if you really had no idea. I don't know which I was more worried about," he answered earnestly.

"Honestly, I had no idea. I've never met anyone with a mate till Gia, and well...it's a sensitive subject for obvious reasons. But she's how I made the connection; I'd asked her about the humming as she was leaving, mentioning that I'd been feeling it since the Offering. I wish she were here to help us—I mean me, navigate this."

I don't know why I was confessing that to him, but who wouldn't want a friend to confide in, who understood the emotions occupying my every thought?

He spoke up abruptly. "Gia knows I'm your mate?"

"Well, not exactly. She's probably deduced someone here or nearby must be, but the carriage left before I could say any more. For all she knows, it could be anyone at Basdie."

"Do you think she's told Trace?" he asked with concern, a question that I hadn't even considered.

"I have no idea. But Gia is smart and loyal. She wouldn't risk the mission by clouding his mind with such distractions."

I contemplated how Trace would take the news. Would he want to hear it from me or her? Would it eat away at him? If the tables were reversed, I think I'd still be upset, even after all that transpired between us.

Varro glanced away, scanning the room, avoiding eye contact. "That's good. Especially since we don't know what this is anyway…"

I took the bait. "What is it to you?"

"I'm afraid to answer that," he replied gently.

I had never heard Varro say he was afraid of anything. I didn't imagine there *was* much that scared Varro. Not after he decisively wrapped his wings around my body and shielded us from death. Maybe he was afraid to let me down. Perhaps he thinks he wants more than I'm willing to give, and he's holding back for my sake. It was obvious, after I'd thought about it, the way he felt, always putting me first, but I was equally fearful of what those feelings might become.

"Why are you afraid?" I asked.

"We've had everything taken from us, but most of all, our freedom. I don't want you to feel like this bond takes even more from you. I don't want you to feel obligated to me. I'm not my father, but I understand what he did to your family and how you might never overcome those feelings entirely. I do not want to be your keeper or your complication when you are so much more than that to me…"

My breath hitched at his admission. He had finally gained the courage to look me in the eye, and now I was the one shying away from the weight of his words that erred on the side of romantic.

I pressed him for the clarity that I needed to hear.

"What am I to you?"

"You're my Moirai. You're my fated one, and always will be. Whether we seal the bond matters not. For me, this goes beyond oath, duty, and the Imperi. It's so much more. The Gods have chosen to tether us, but I need you to know I am yours in whatever way you will have me. As your friend, your confidant, your protector, your partner…even your lover. Because I don't think I can say no to you, Cress."

Silence hovered between us. Even the water was silent, as our bodies remained still. He was offering me anything.

He was offering me *everything*.

I just had to decide what I wanted to take. How much of myself was I willing to give? My intertwined fingers fidgeted below the waters, twitching with both anxiousness and relief.

"I'm afraid too," I whispered.

Varro stood and moved to close the gap between us, almost as if involuntarily, and cupped my cheek in his hand. "Why?"

I looked up into those icy-blue eyes, more crystalline than any water I'd ever seen, and tried to convey the unending fear within me.

"I'm afraid of what they will do to us, of what I'll do to you. I'm afraid to become each other's weakness."

And although I didn't say it, there was a fear of rejection, of Varro someday changing his mind. Ever since Trace, I was terrified to tie my emotions to another male again. The distraction of Basdie and my duty to the realm made that easier to accept, as I had lost sight of frivolities such as relationships, marriage, children or any semblance of a life of my own.

There was a peace in not having freedom, one that was hard to articulate. As soon as I let myself want for things, I was setting myself up for loss or disappointment. Being a pawn in some grand plan meant walking the line, not drawing my own. I had such a fear of leading myself astray that I had settled into this powerlessness more than I'd realized.

But as Varro held my face in his palm and the bond tingled through every fiber of my being, I began to accept that I, too, was powerless to fight this.

"Then let's be afraid together." He smiled warmly, and it was an invitation I could finally accept. It was a doorway to something more that we'd define together. We didn't have to say it with words, we both just understood.

That night, I lay in my bed with the slightest renewed sense of hope and curiosity. Varro was only a couple of doors away, and though he did not invite me in after the baths, I felt welcome. Unlike Trace, whose door had felt barred to me since arriving, I innately knew all the ones leading to Varro were always open. There was much to fear about my future and what would transpire once we were finally sent to join the others in Artume. Yet knowing Varro had his own fears meant I wasn't alone, and something about that was deeply calming.

During my short time at Basdie, I'd become accustomed to falling asleep alone, dozing off with a head full of heavy thoughts. Praying for dreams, and not nightmares. Somehow, tonight's conversation made me feel ten times lighter. Warmer. Wanted. Welcome. I rolled over to my side, squeezing my extra pillow tightly to my body, letting myself wonder what it might be like to allow myself to feel again. To let the stains of past betrayal rinse from my body and heart. Perhaps in Varro's golden light, something in me could bloom anew.

CHAPTER 24

When I awoke in the morning, there was a striking energy pulsing through me. It bobbed alongside the low hum of the bond, itching for its own attention, aching to be acknowledged and accepted. I reasoned this must be some other side of the bond I had yet to experience. Was it conceivable that opening myself up to the possibilities of the bond had strengthened it? I was alert, which was unusual for me at this time of the morning. Even without windows to herald the light of day, my body buzzed with a sense of purpose and did not yearn to linger beneath my bed linens. Was it the excitement of seeing him?

At breakfast, he slid my plate closer to his, and I glanced around to see if Nori or Cairis had taken notice. Would he be so brazen with his affections? Did he care what the others would think? He said it was our secret now, so I had to believe he'd let me choose when and who found out about our intertwined fates. Though I wasn't particularly hungry, I had filled my plate with a sensible breakfast, reminding myself that the Dark Wielder's texts specifically encouraged proper sustenance. Despite my efforts to ignore it, I still carried the strange energy I'd felt since waking, not sure what to do about or with it.

Cairis did not let us forget about his daring plan for the flight field following our morning meal, and though Varro assured them I had done well portaling, the thought of doing it mid-flight intimidated me.

"Everyone have their stones with them?" he inquired excitedly.

Each of us pulled the tiny moonstones from our pockets where they were stowed, showing them off to each other like children.

"Great! Hurry up and finish so we can get out there before Saryn or Theory ruin this for us."

I looked up at Varro as he shoved two more bites of oats into his mouth, winked, and pocketed a tiny orange which I was almost certain was for me. When we arrived outside, I was glad to have added another layer to my attire. The gusts were chillier than the days prior, as winter's grasp inevitably continued to tighten its icy grip. I disliked the feeling of cold on my wings, but for Cairis I was willing to entertain it.

Without hesitation, he declared, "Me first!"

Cairis unfurled his large black wings, the taloned tips shining in the morning light. He hovered just above all of us, this time making his portal expand wide enough to allow his impressive wingspan to pass through.

"Last one to the far side's a weakling!" he proclaimed before suddenly darting through the portal and disappearing.

Soon after, we heard jovial laughter echoing from the distant side of the valley as a small cloudlike ring appeared and Cairis zoomed out, doing nothing to contain his self-aggrandizing celebration.

"This is amazing!" he yelled back to the rest of us.

Without hesitation, he generated another loop and soared through it, disappearing and reappearing again on the other side. Suddenly, I heard the rustling of Nori's wispy, white wings unfurling beside me, sparkling like water beneath the sun. She let out a small giggle before she was up and through her own portal, appearing at Cairis' side. And so, it began.

He immediately disappeared again, leading her on a chase all across the open valley.

I took a step closer and stared up into Varro's eyes, alight with entertainment. Silently, slyly, I took my hand and slid it down into the pocket of his trousers, letting my fingertips graze his thigh. The only thing separating our skin was the thin lining of his pocket. His eyes widened at the act. He swallowed, and I watched with pleasure as his jaw flexed instinctively.

I grabbed the tiny orange, withdrawing it, and said wickedly, "I'm going to need this."

Then I unfurled my wings, taking flight before he could respond. I focused all of the pent-up energy inside of me on generating a portal. Just as I felt the tickle of the bond, I plunged through the swirl, leaving him alone and speechless while I joined the others.

I exited at Nori's side, an inescapable giggle leaving my mouth from the exhilaration of it all. Cairis' idea was brilliant. Varro arrived quickly after, and what ensued was a frantic game of chase as each of us flitted and darted after one another, trying to guess the other's next destination. We weaved in and out, mixing our skills of agility and evasion with the calculated use of the stones.

We could have done this all day, except that our bodies wouldn't allow it. This was much more taxing than flight alone, and I was fixated on the thought of the orange where it now rested in my pocket. I grew more tired with each portal, and my mouth was parched. When we all landed back on the flight deck, I was practically famished. We headed back to the dining hall to refuel, exchanging spirited remarks and laughter.

We arrived in the sparring room feeling thankful for a meal to recuperate from our nonsensical games that morning. Theory and Saryn stood there waiting, per usual, as if we were somehow tardy. I tried my best to blend in so that Saryn didn't send me back to the closet for further reading. I wanted to train with the others—and be by Varro's side.

"Today, we want to see you mix elements of your magic with combat. Each of you shows strength in different ways, so you'll need to be creative in choosing when and what to wield. If done well, I imagine more than one of you will need the healing pools this evening," Theory explained, looking eager to explore the notion.

We went through the normal motions of stretching and reviewing our weapons. Ever since Idris spent a healthy sum outfitting us for the Canary Veil, most of our weapons were sized perfectly to our stature and skill. I admired the blades as I adhered them to my thighs. They were lightweight, the handles fitted to my grip. The sword sheathed at my back was among the finest I'd ever held, also lightweight, yet still substantial, the metalwork second to none. I had become almost protective of it. My trainer at the academy back home used to joke about naming his swords. I had scoffed dismissively at the time, but the idea had grown on me since this beauty came into my possession. I just hadn't come up with a name worthy of her.

I glanced around the room, taking note of what elements could be used to my advantage. I watched as Varro prepared, beginning to tighten leather straps across his waist and torso to hold his arsenal in place. My cheeks warmed at the sight of his muscular form, and that all-too-energetic sensation rippled across the otherwise calm bond.

Saryn assessed us with his one good eye, the other covered by its usual black patch against the border of his sharp cheekbone. If he weren't so demanding and arrogant, I'd almost describe him as ruggedly handsome. None of us had ever seen underneath the patch, and I doubled my mental shields while toying with that curiosity.

"How about every Fae for themselves?" he suggested mischievously.

I rolled my eyes at the proposal. By now, you'd think I'd be used to his stunts.

The four of us spread out in a square, each of our backs up against one of the stone podiums bracing the ceiling. We glanced back and forth, looking at one another and trying to determine who would strike where and with what.

Nori may have been a pacifist before the Imperi, but I would never underestimate her cunning again. Not after what Varro told me. *Do not let her innocence sway you,* I told myself, remaining alert. Suddenly, she sprinted to the center of the room. As if the fire from the torches were attached to her fingertips, she drew the flame to her, shaping it into a protective ring. The heat of it forced me to step back and shield my face. She remained at the center but continued to pivot, watching for anyone who might try and extinguish the flames.

Cairis pushed the fire nearest him into an archway with a smirk. This brief manipulation allowed him to enter Nori's circle, no extinguishing necessary. He raised his sword and drew her into a duel while the fire raged around them. I began to pace the inferno's perimeter, attempting in vain to make eye contact with Varro amid the smoke and flame.

Before I could make any sense of his location, he was suddenly behind me with one blade in his left hand at my neck and the other hand holding one low to my belly. He could have flayed me from either vantage if he wanted to.

"I so love to feel you writhe against my blade," he said in the old tongue, menacingly. With my body restrained against his knives, the only weapon at my disposal was my mind.

I dropped my mental shields, knowing that he would always be listening, even if we were not mind-melded. I let my thoughts run wild and free. Distracting him with visions of our naked bodies pressed firmly against one another, writhing in passion as my lips roamed his mouth, his neck, his ears. I wrapped my legs around his waist, scraping my hands across his wide, muscular back, unable to satiate the hunger I conjured in this illusion. As expected, his attention was diverted briefly enough for his grip to slacken ever so slightly, allowing me to make my move. I slammed my head into his face, drawing blood from his nose and causing his arms to drop as he instinctively reached toward the injury.

I quickly distanced myself and unsheathed the sword from over my shoulder, preparing for his next move while feeling the scorching flames at my back from where Nori and Cairis still battled. Varro had blood gushing from his nose, and it dribbled across his mouth and down his chin. I knew that at any moment he could choose to render me useless with Siren Song, but he was attempting to play fair. I'm not sure he'd have said the same about me after what I'd just pulled. It was such a pretty face to damage, but everything goes in the midst of competition. Besides, there was an adept healer amongst us.

He swiped the blood from his face with his hand and smiled. The old tongue sounding melodic from his lips—he'd greatly improved his inflections since arriving at Basdie.

"If you wanted a date in the healing pools, all you had to do was ask."

His normally casual gaze turned deviant as he began to stalk toward me with weapons in hand. My lurid illusions from earlier and the idea of us in the healing pools created a warm ache in my core that I fought to disregard. But the allure of the bond could not be ignored.

He had only taken two or three steps toward me with that bloody and gorgeous grin of his when I heard the sound as if it were the only noise in the room. The sound of two *clicks*; plucked strings and soaring arrows; wind rushing down long wooden shafts. Each sound a staccato, like they were frozen in time. I ducked, instinctively throwing my arms out straight, as if to block them with some invisible wall.

The whoosh of air caused Nori's fire to cease immediately. The weapons all along the walls came tumbling to the ground. The only sound remaining was my hammering heartbeat. From where I crouched, I looked up to see Saryn and Theory laying sprawled out on the ground, their crossbows strewn across their bodies.

They had actually tried to shoot us while we were all sparring. Saryn's words, "…every Fae for themselves," now echoed in my thoughts, and I was reminded of why everything he ever said carried far more intent than we realized.

He sat up, dusting off debris, and smiled with excitement. "You did it! And while distracted, nonetheless!"

As the normal sounds of the room came back into focus, I looked around, realizing that those of us in the middle had remained untouched by the blast. The blast that *I* had wielded to shield us from their arrows. Varro was at my side, bracing my arm to help me stand and looking at me in astonishment.

Saryn couldn't have cared less about the disastrous state of the training room; he was at my other side immediately, and I could feel Varro shift into a defensive stance.

"What was different this time? It can't be fear. There was no time. Think, Cress—what did you feel?"

His questions overwhelmed me; I was still preoccupied with the thought that I had actually controlled my dark magic to some degree. It was purely a reaction, but control nonetheless. I chose to protect my friends and my mate. I still didn't understand how I drew it forth, or how I knew what kind of magic would show itself, but it finally did.

In the hours after class, Saryn and Theory interrogated me with an onslaught of questions, trying to determine how I had finally found my control. Despite all of that, I wasn't certain of much more than they were. I wasn't convinced I could do it again, but as I analyzed each time it had occurred, I noticed a growing familiarity. Even the most adept elemental wielders, they discussed, could only hope to conjure a fraction of such displays. And augments, such as pairing a shield with a concussive blast, were a rare combination at that. The pool of magic I was drawing from was as deep as it was dark, and the risks associated with accessing it were bountiful.

I shared with them what little I knew from my readings, figuring the more they knew, the more likely someone would come to understand it. I kept from them any details regarding the Drift, as I was not prepared to reveal that information just yet.

 When it was finally clear that there were no more answers or explanations to be had, Saryn told me to sleep on it, guaranteeing he'd pester me again tomorrow.

My reluctance to see Varro and his likely-broken nose at dinner was quickly diminished as I turned the corner and spotted him at the table eating, looking just as handsomely pristine as before our incident. His bright smile beamed across the room when he saw me.

"Nori is quite the healer, don't you think? I've only glanced in the mirror ten or twenty times, but I think it looks perfect… I mean, back to normal," he teased playfully.

He was so cocky, and yet I was relieved for the excellent work she'd done on the repair.

Saryn and Theory joined us for dinner, and I waited for the topic of my ability to take over the conversation. It did not.

My gaze flicked left, then right, searching for signs of concern or uncertainty on the faces of my companions. I saw none. My inability to control the power had scared them before, but manifesting it today to protect them seemed to have eased their minds.

In any case, I was grateful to not be treated like a pariah. I knew Varro didn't think that way, but it felt good to be treated normally by the others as well. Between games of portal tag and dark wielding a shield, I had developed a massive appetite, which I satiated with second and third helpings of dinner.

All through the meal, I wrestled with the looming thought that I wasn't certain if Varro and I were actually going to meet at the healing pools later that night. His nose was already taken care of, but he must have noticed the minor advances I'd made that day. If I were being honest with myself, I probably owed him some semblance of an apology for crossing that line so brazenly. Though, throughout dinner he showed no signs of displeasure with me, so I was hopeful that I wasn't awaiting a reprimand from my would-be mate.

The hearty meal punctuated the end of a long, exhausting day. Nori and Cairis retired to their rooms while I idled near my door awaiting some sort of inclination from Varro. I was tired too—probably more so than the others after my magical exertion—but I found the prospect of an encounter with him enticing enough to stay up.

When the others were settled in their rooms, he arrived at my door and gestured for me to follow him. I did so eagerly, and without question. When he stopped at the Vesper rooms, I was surprised. I had assumed we were headed to the pools like usual. He grabbed a small torch from the wall, then opened and held the door while ushering me inside. The room was ominously dark, so I stopped and waited for Varro to lead the way. The firelight danced warmly on the cold, stone walls until a fixture for mounting the torch came into sight. That light, however bright though it seemed in the hallway, scarcely pierced the darkness of this chamber.

The scene reminded me of late nights reading by candlelight, turning the pages eagerly near a waning wax taper. Basking in the comfort of those memories, I admired his easy confidence as he turned to me from the torch, and found the atmosphere alarmingly romantic.

I'd become very acquainted with these rooms, though for all the wrong reasons. Memories of the nights I spent tortured, or torturing, flooded back to the forefront of my mind. It had been some time since I visited with a Vesper. I couldn't fathom why Varro had brought us here, apart from the fact that these rooms were some of the few with locks…

"I thought we were to have a date in the healing pools," I declared boldly.

Varro faced me with an enthusiastic smile. "I am still taking you up on the date, but I had a better idea."

He pointed me to the chair in the corner of the room while he took a seat at the edge of a small cot. His confirmation that this was a date made the bond tingle slightly, and I clasped my hands together to continue appearing calm and collected.

Varro turned his gaze toward the Vesper, and within seconds, it began to quake and shift into a tall, slender Fae female. My jaw dropped as I realized he had conjured her in my likeness. She casually made her way to the bed and sat down beside him, remaining motionless as she awaited more instruction from his imagination.

It was like looking in the mirror, but her eerie silence did not sit well with me.

"This is strange, what are you doing?" I asked.

"Hear me out..." he started to explain, reassuringly. "If I know you as I think I do, you may believe all I seek is to seal the bond. And while I would not deny that request—I'd happily fulfill it—I want to give you the opportunity to explore any affections you may have for me without fear of that."

He wasn't entirely wrong, but I still could not reason out his intentions.

"If at any time you feel uncomfortable, we can stop. It's just that..." he paused. "I'd like to show you what you're missing."

His cryptic words were both enticing and confusing, but I let him proceed with his demonstration. He had piqued my curiosity, which pulled me further into the exchange—most likely his intention, proving he knew me even better than I thought.

I sat in the corner of the room, watching as the other Cress—Vesper-Cress—angled her body toward Varro. There was only the crackling fire of the torch and the hushed movements of their repositioning. He leaned into her slowly, and she reciprocated. Varro raised his arm, gently cupping her chin, then ran that same hand down alongside her cheek to the curve of her neck, allowing him to pull her closer. He placed a small kiss on her forehead, holding himself there for a moment longer than expected.

I was frozen to my chair watching this sweet, intimate act unfold, and yet my heart was beginning to race. In my thoughts, I found myself urging his actions on.

After removing his lips from her, they both tilted their faces downward to rest their foreheads against one another. Both closed their eyes, and my mind grappled between feeling guilty for watching their intimacy and fascination at observing my own body engaged in such acts. I could feel the electricity surge between them, and I wanted to see more.

I watched as Vesper-Cress closed in and hovered just in front of his face, waiting for him to make the move, offering him the first kiss rather than taking greedily. What felt like an eternity later, their lips came together, and he parted hers delicately with his tongue.

I realized I had been holding my breath, the tight feeling in my chest constricting more with each passing second. She tilted her head back slightly, and he sucked on her lower lip, biting it teasingly. The Vesper grasped both sides of his face to pull him deeper into the kiss, and I could feel my core warm with desire, along with a tinge of jealousy.

Their kissing became more fervent with each swipe of their tongues, and I saw their hands twitching, anxious to roam freely. I squeezed my thighs together tightly, noting my own building arousal. This charade was as unbelievable as it was alluring. All of a sudden, Vesper-Cress sat up, hoisted her leg over Varro's lap and straddled him, her back to me. I let out a gasp and watched as Varro froze.

"I'm sorry, I've gone too—"

"No, don't stop," I interjected breathily, practically begging him to not end this.

Without a word, Varro continued to show me a raw display of his affections. Using one hand, he gripped Vesper-Cress's rear, pulling her further into him, her hips to his. With the other, he gathered a handful of her long tresses, bunching them together and tugging them back gently, exposing her neck to him. He began to place deep kisses all along it, nipping every so often. I grit my teeth and clutched the sides of my thighs, watching his every move. As his lips continued to roam all along her neck, he looked up at me from over her shoulder, locking our gazes. Though his hands and mouth roamed the Vesper, in that moment, it was only us.

I stood abruptly, lunging in his direction. The Vesper disappeared back into a glowing orb, quickly returning to its position in the corner. Varro stood quickly to catch me and I crashed into him with a feverish hunger. I wrapped my arms around his neck and he pulled me up into an embrace, holding me to him as my legs tightly encircled his waist. He moved me to the wall, bracing my back firmly against it as the feeling of our breaths danced over our lips.

"Moirai," he whispered breathlessly, and without a second of hesitation, I crushed my mouth to his, desperate to taste him. To feel everything the Vesper had. To satisfy everything he had provoked in me. No more showing me what I could have—I wanted it now. I wanted him, and I let myself fall into the arms of my fated one with reckless abandon. When our lips touched, it felt like the Gods bowed before us, etching this moment into destiny.

With each desperate kiss, I felt the thrumming of the bond pound through my veins, as if it wanted to crawl out of my skin and into the body of my mate. It ached pleasurably, and I leaned into the feeling as I drowned in its frenzy. Did Varro's bond feel the same? Could he feel our souls clawing to reach one another and be joined forever? I had never imagined this was part of the bond or having a mate. I should have exercised more caution prior to this escalation, but there was no turning back now.

My body against his felt like home; I was drunk on it. In between our frenetic kisses, he whispered huskily, "I have wanted this for so long."

I intertwined my fingers through the curls of his hair, tugging and tilting his mouth to my every whim, realizing we were each taking breath-less gasps in between kisses. I unraveled my legs and slid them down to the floor, keeping my chest firmly pressed against his. I felt lightheaded, and yet, I couldn't stop myself. He leaned in, placing his mouth at the tip of my earlobe, and whispered, "Moirai," sending tickles down my neck.

All semblance of my control was quickly vanishing, and I needed one of us to show restraint. This was foolish and crazy and right in every way imaginable. Varro cupped both sides of my face and pressed a long, firm kiss to it before pulling away, trying to compose himself.

In the dim light, I could make out a smile. Not his normal cocky or humorous expression, but instead one filled with warmth, vulnera-bility and admiration. He was looking at me like he was astonished I had reciprocated.

"What's wrong?" I asked breathless, still locked in a haze of my own.

"Patience," he replied, as if trying to convince himself of the same. "We should be patient. If I don't stop now, I won't. I want you to be certain."

I understood what he was doing and why. He couldn't understand how much I appreciated it. Thank the Gods one of us had the mind to stop because my body was telling me to keep going.

"You're right, we shouldn't take this lightly." I tried to steady my uneven breaths and come down from the lust-induced fog. It wasn't just lust, though. Yes, it felt uncontrollable in the way lust often does, but there was something primal that had awoken within me—something that would be impossible to ignore.

Parting with Varro the night before was a feat in and of itself. I had fallen asleep with lips still swollen from our kisses; my imagination running wild with fantasies we had not yet allowed ourselves. I awoke from a deep and dreamless sleep to the abrupt appearance of Varro in my room. He had portaled in with zero notice, half-scaring me to death. He laughed at my shocked expression and bent down, placing a small peck on my cheek.

"Morning!"

"I'm not a morning person," I chided, trying to pull the blanket up over my head to hide how disheveled I looked.

"Well then, rise and shine my beautiful night owl," he teased, trying to tug the blanket away from my arms.

"You're awfully brave, to be stirring a Dark Wielder from their slumber," I threatened playfully, unable to stay grouchy in light of his presence.

"Do your worst, Moirai!" He yanked the covers away, making it impossible to delay any further. The chilly air of Basdie prickled across what few layers I wore.

Varro granted me privacy while I washed up and readied myself for another day of training. I met him and the others in the dining hall and noted how the strange, undulating energy from the day prior now felt steady and even. This felt separate from the hum of the bond, like it sat next to it, curling up against it for warmth and strength. Or perhaps the bond was leaning into it. I couldn't be certain which.

Theory directed us to the flight deck after breakfast. An easiness settled into our team dynamic since the departure of Trace. There was no denying my steps were more certain, absent the worry of a tense encounter with him lurking around every corner.

"All of you but Cress, go warm up in the valley. Loosen your muscles and be on alert for drills." Theory pointed out into the valley as Saryn moved to stand by my side. Gods, what did they want from me now?

"Your dark magic is defensive. It's always a reaction to being attacked. It would be more beneficial if you could take the offensive."

Saryn's evaluation wasn't inaccurate, but I wasn't entirely sure how to make my shield more offensive. I had only seen it manifest itself as a shield blast or quaking, which I had deduced was some untamed form of elemental manipulation.

"See that small cliff to the west?" he asked.

"Yes," I nodded, squinting my eyes to bring it into focus.

"I want you to bring it down."

Saryn's instructions were plain, like it was a simple request. He said it as if he'd seen me do it a hundred times before.

He added, "And please do us all a favor—just the cliff, not the entire mountainside…"

His misplaced confidence did nothing to motivate me. I watched as the others practiced their warm-ups out in the flight field, and became nervous at the prospect of doing something wrong, lacking the control that might result in their injury.

There was no fear of the cliff, nor was it attacking me. Saryn and Theory made no threats to my safety. They just stood idle, waiting to see if I could do as instructed. I saw Varro's beautiful teal wings shimmer and flit across the skyline, a beautiful cerulean dotted with puffy clouds of ivory amidst a brightly shining sun. I focused on the excess of energy dwelling within me and sought to shape it into something more tangible. As soon as I could feel it hovering at the surface, I turned my attention back to the rocky cliff overlooking the far side of the valley.

I stared hard, locking my vision on the outline of each rigid edge, imagining that it was not strong, fortified rock, but rather delicate and on the verge of crumbling. Long, deep breaths created a rhythm, allowing me to root myself into the ground and become attuned to my surroundings. The sounds around me faded first into a muffled dissonance, then muted altogether, until only the pounding of my heart beat against the silence.

Soon, I could hear a distinct quaking followed by the sharp cracks of rock breaking. Suddenly, the entire ledge of the cliff fell away from itself, causing a landslide of boulders and debris down the mountainside. My concentration was broken by the sound of Nori shouting Cairis' name. I whipped my head in her direction. She wasn't near the cliff, but Cairis came to her side urgently, both of them looking back toward me with concern—except for Varro, who was still looking at the result of the destroyed cliff.

"Perfect, well done." I heard Theory say to me, and I couldn't recollect another time she'd ever complimented me.

The entirety of the morning, Saryn commanded me to dismantle parts of the beautiful mountainside. Each time he seemed more impressed, as if trying to understand the limits of my power. I did not let him or the others see it in my expression, but on the inside, I did feel powerful, my pride bubbling with every fulfilled request. Once Cairis and Nori were certain that I had some semblance of control over what I was doing, neither of them feared being in the flight field while the experimentation continued.

By lunchtime, I had caused multiple rockslides, and even managed to send a shield blast far enough that it created rocky explosions across the side of the mountain. Any remaining wildlife in the valley below had scurried to the other end of the river, along with flocks of birds that had become too frightened to remain hidden in the trees that skirted the mountain's edge.

I swayed a little, exhausted, and within seconds Varro was by my side, holding my arm.

"She needs food and rest!" he chided Saryn. "You know that."

He sounded displeased at the way Saryn had pushed me with little regard to how it was taxing my energy levels. It wasn't until Varro interrupted that I realized how truly drained I was. Though the warmth of his touch sent new energy fluttering through me, it would not be enough. He was right. I needed to sit and recuperate.

As we all began to traipse back to the dining hall, Theory shouted, "Portal, you fools!"

It had almost been a week since Idris escorted Gia and Trace to the border, and there was no word yet on whether they had been successfully installed. We had no idea how soon he'd be back for the rest of us, but I wished we could somehow receive a status report sooner than later. My nerves were uneasy thinking about the two of them alone without the rest of us to lean on. A foreign land, new culture, strangers and enemies at every turn. The thought made me queasy, yet also grateful they hadn't sent me first. Gia and Trace were so strong, each of them mentally fortified in their own ways. I had confidence in them—but I'd have more if we were by their side.

I was beginning to lose track of how long I'd been away from my home. I wondered if Versa had started to suspect anything from the lack of letters. What sort of excuses had my parents made? I was feeling particularly nostalgic after draining all my energy this morning in the flight field. Maybe it was fear of the Drift that had me trying to focus on them and ensure my memories were still intact. By now, Versa would have been wed, perhaps even with child. Were they going about their days normally, following their routines?

There was something wild and untamed about all of this compared to the life I once had. Sometimes, I wondered if I would have chosen it, knowing what I do now. But I also recognized the naïve side of me that always learned the lesson too late, and didn't truly understand the horrors that lay ahead.

If I hadn't been offered, would I ever have run off and met Trace, allowing me to learn so much about myself? I knew I'd have never explored my magic. Never gotten to break free of the manicured customs and etiquette of not showing my wings and flying. Obligations as High Fae exchanged for obligations to the Imperi. I would have never made these friends that I now treat as my family. Certainly, I'd never have gotten the chance to go beyond the borders of Cambria. Would the dark magic that runs through my veins ever have shown itself otherwise?

And lastly—but possibly most importantly—would I have ever encountered my mate? Things were starting to feel like a strange twist of fate, like a blanket woven with patterns I could not see until I stepped back to view it at a distance. But if this was where the weavings of fate began… where did they end? What future could I hold with so little freedom?

There would be no wedding, no children or celebrations with my family. I may never see the sprawling orchards and gardens of my home again…but I would see the world instead. I'd see its vast cruelty and magnificence. I would help paint the veil that kept our kingdom safe, however thankless that role may be.

How do you weave the threads of two lives spent in servitude to the Crown? The brilliant hues of a journey made more authentic through experiencing the world as it truly is. Intense. Captivating. And above all, a sense of purpose, protecting the people I loved and preserving the realm so that others may bask in blissful ignorance and routine. The pale strings of their lives would continue through obligations of marriage and family, their entire worlds stretching only as far as their eyes could see. I was once content to live that life. But no more. The richness of my existence, however brief, would be meaningful.

I spent the day eager to be alone again with Varro. I wanted to continue our illicit activities, but I desperately needed time in the healing pools before making any advances. The waters reinvigorated my energy levels on a day when even a good meal or two could not. When I arrived, he was already there waiting for me. I admired his body, slick and glistening, the white curls of his hair in tight, wet ringlets. My mate always looked his best in the water, and I hoped to someday truly witness him in his element, aboard a ship or wading amongst the seafoam of the Endless Tides.

I wasn't ready to seal the bond, no, but I was interested in continuing to explore this more intimate side of Varro. I began disrobing down to my undergarments, and with each item of clothing I removed, Varro stared shamelessly, even biting at his knuckle while he appraised my body. I wasn't going to reprimand him, since I'd been doing the same. I made my way towards him and took a seat, submerging my body up to my shoulders.

"I want to show you something, but first I need you to turn out the lights," he said, nodding in the direction of the torches along the walls. In the dark, alone with Varro; the possibilities were absolutely wicked, but I did not question his request. With a simple flick of my magic, all the torches went dark, except for one that I kept dimly lit.

My eyes struggled to adjust to the lack of light, and the only thing that kept me alert to his whereabouts was the sound of water moving. All of a sudden, there was a bright green and blue luminescence fanning out above the water in the shape of…the shape of wings! The glow of which was bright enough to illuminate the small area around Varro. I was astounded and speechless upon seeing the absolutely magical display of his wings. They were gorgeous in the sunlight, yet nothing compared to what I was witnessing here in the water and darkness.

"Wow, that's amazing," I whispered, still caught up in the shock, the awe of it all.

He made his way directly in front of me, the light of them now creating a glowing circle around us both. He lowered his body slowly into the water, and his wings continued to glow even after they were partially submerged.

"Everyone has seen our wings, Cress; I cannot change that. But… this, this is for your eyes only."

My eyes scanned each serrated tip in amazement and, almost instinctively, I reached my hand out to touch the glowing wing like a moth drawn to a flame. The second my hand brushed its surface, a single teardrop blurred my vision as a ripple of luminous color flickered across the entire panel.

I heard Varro's breath hitch at the same time I let my hand run gently across it again, and his wings continued to pulsate colors of light. Surrounded by nothing but his illumination, I wrapped my legs around his frame and pulled him to me. Our bodies were now skin to skin, with only thin pieces of clothing to separate us. I could feel the outline of him becoming rigid against me. I was overcome with gratitude for what he'd shown me, for what he had saved for just us, in a place where nothing was truly ours.

Varro lowered his splayed wings and curled them inward, wrapping them around my back to cocoon us within the green and blue hue. I leaned in, initiating the kiss, and pressed my body tight against his so he could feel my hardened nipples and know the pleasure, the reaction he drew from me. My hands roamed, trying to memorize every angle of his Gods-like body. His tongue danced lightly in and out of my mouth, switching back and forth between sweet pecks and deeper kisses. I pulled my mouth away and pressed it along his neck, lapping up droplets of water. I didn't know if it was inappropriate, but I gently flicked my tongue across the gills behind his ear, then released a cool breath over them. I felt goosebumps blanket his skin, and a shiver went up his body, causing him to twitch between my thighs.

"Gods, Cress, what are you trying to do me?" he said with a restless groan.

"I don't know," I said breathless. "Everything feels so natural, so right when I'm with you. Sometimes I don't even know if I'm in control."

Varro pulled away at my words, resting his head against mine.

"I have to be careful with you. Our bond calls us to each other. It wants nothing more than to be consummated, to be made whole. I must ensure it does not influence your decision."

There was so little that I understood about having a mate, but every word he said made sense. I trusted that he had my best interests at heart, even when my body had other ideas. I just wasn't sure how much longer we could walk this fine line.

Looking up into his eyes I saw nothing but unwavering devotion, and I was frustrated with myself for how long I'd gone without noticing.

"Cress?"

"Yes..." I replied softly.

"I've had far too long to think about all the things I want to do to you. We could do everything but seal the bond, and I promise that will only ever occur when you are certain. No matter how much self-control I must exert, I swear to you, that final decision is yours."

I gave him a gentle kiss on the lips to show my appreciation and acknowledgement of his vow.

"However, it wouldn't hurt if you could demonstrate some self-control too," he teased playfully, letting out a laugh that reverberated through our cavernous surroundings.

"But tempting fate is so much fun…" I replied wickedly while running the tips of my fingers along his glowing wing.

CHAPTER

6

In the days and nights that followed, Varro and I made a routine of portaling in and out of one another's rooms, surprising each other while keeping these brief visits a secret from the others. Our hushed whispers and giggles felt akin to a childlike crush, and there was an innocence that surrounded it. We shielded our budding relationship from the dangers that otherwise consumed us as members of the Imperi.

We fell into a natural rhythm, taking note of each other's preferences, nuances, and flaws. His optimism balanced my rooted sensibilities, creating a more hopeful counterweight. He was a light piercing the darkness that wanted to eclipse my soul, and our bond somehow caused my power to flourish more than ever before. The regular and dark magic, alike, felt simpler, easier and more obtainable in his presence.

His unwavering belief in my power gave me confidence to push harder. During our days of training, Saryn and Theory's critiques lessened, and I had no more fear of them using the other members' safety as a means to provoke me. My time spent reading the other Wielders' journals had transitioned into time spent documenting my own journey. Part of me wanted to avoid it altogether, out of defiance. I wanted the Offering to come to an end. I secretly hoped Basdie would collapse in on itself, and the Order and Imperi would be lost to time so no other families would be torn apart. But the part of me that knew it was unlikely felt the need to carry on the tradition. For the others coming after, whoever they may be.

Centuries after my soul had returned to the Gods—if they'd have me—my words and experiences would help guide someone else who was just as lost as I was the day I sat down before these texts. While many of the journals read like academic notes, I tried to write in the style of a diary. I leaned into cataloguing the emotions I felt, and the details around the event that had awakened me. And though no one else within these walls knew Varro was my mate, I wrote about us. None of the others had the luxury of their mate being present. While I could not speak to the sealing of the bond yet, or how it might help me avoid the Drift, I still wanted to write my truth.

In these confessions, I expressed how my power felt more present and tangible since accepting my mate as being a part of my life. With each flick and curl of the quill, I had no fear of revealing myself. Saryn and the others would not be able to open these texts without the gift of dark magic.

Varro never complained, but it was impossible not to notice how inflamed his poor gills had become. The absence of salty air and sea water was doing a number on his otherwise luminous skin, but his gills were taking the brunt of it. Sea Fae weren't meant for the dry, cold weather that characterized the Elorn Mountains. I made it my mission to prepare for him a healing salve that he could rub on his gills to lock in moisture. In between experimenting with new poisons and antidotes, I was determined to put my talents to better use. It took me a while to convince Theory that I needed the ingredients, but eventually my persistence—and possibly her irritation—convinced her.

While he could use a small expenditure of his power to heal himself daily, or even enlist Nori's assistance, there was nothing shielding the sensitive flesh from the elements. This salve would help protect his skin, creating a barrier that limited the damage.

He was bashful when I'd pointed out what terrible shape they were in, so I made sure to gift it to him privately. I placed the small jar of salve with instructions by his bedside table and signed it *Moirai*, as if he wouldn't already know who'd prepared it. He later thanked me with a small bundle of holly. Given it was now winter, the valley in the Elorns that once flourished with abundant wildflowers was now mostly lifeless and dusted in snow. The bright red berries reminded me of holiday celebrations back home, and I was appreciative for those memories.

Nights with Varro were my favorite. He'd sneak into my room and hold me while he told me stories from his childhood, ones that all Sea Fae grew up hearing from their parents. The sound of his smooth voice lulled me to sleep, and oftentimes he'd have to repeat passages of the tales from the night prior because I had drifted off. He'd tuck me under the covers and make his way back to his own room. On even rarer occasions, I could convince him to sing a quiet lullaby. His singing voice was even more hypnotic, and I told him I wasn't absolutely certain he wasn't a Siren himself.

My dreams were something else entirely. They had become detailed sexual fantasies of Varro and me. Experiences we'd not even approached yet. Sometimes I would wake up sweating from the intensity of it all. So many of them felt real, and I was too embarrassed to ask him if he'd experienced anything similar. Was this just me or some side effect from sleeping in such close proximity to my mate? Did our bond call to us so strongly that it even sought to bind us in our dreams? Each morning I'd wake, I'd have to give myself a moment to shake off the memory and remind myself it wasn't real.

Sometimes at breakfast he'd let his hand graze mine under the table, interlocking our smallest fingers, testing the boundaries of our secret. There were many sweet moments, rivaled only by the encounters where our control unraveled into wild passion.

Most often these acts took place in the privacy of the Vesper rooms. Though anyone with decent elemental manipulation, or even a good swift kick, could make their way through the measly lock, it brought us a minute sense of privacy.

One of those evenings, Varro pulled a small orange from his pocket and began peeling it. This had become routine, him providing me with small snacks in between trainings to keep my energy up. He pulled the orange apart and instructed me to sit on the cot while he leaned casually against the wall across from me.

"Cress, let your shields down, and I'll do the same."

I did as he instructed, but with a bit of hesitation. It had become the norm to guard our minds at all times, even from each other—especially from others. One slip of our true thoughts and feelings to anyone listening in would leave us exposed, so we'd become very good at fortifying them.

He walked over to me and knelt down to the ground, placing himself between my feet, resting on the stone floor at the edge of the cot. The position was already beginning to make my stomach tighten in knots with anticipation.

As if he were saying his thoughts aloud, the vivid illusion he began to draw with his imagination painted clear pictures of his true desires, playing out in refined detail as I connected my mind to these thoughts. In his fantasy, he wasted no time, untying the drawstring of my pants. Plucking the laces through each hole and loosening the waist. My breathing became unsteady at the suspense of Varro's next movements.

Before me, the real Varro placed a small piece of orange in his mouth, the juices glistening on his lips as he gave me a devious smile. He lifted my shirt up slightly, exposing the bare skin of my belly, and he took another small piece of orange and crushed it in his strong grip, letting the juices dribble down my skin. The cool sensation of the droplets made my muscles taut, and I became even more eager to reach out and touch him.

He projected images of him sliding my pants off, exposing my sex to him as he remained on his knees between my thighs. In reality, he leaned in and, at the same moment I felt him lap up the citrus from my stomach, he sent me visuals of him diving between my thighs and assaulting my core with his rigid tongue. Flashes of images where my thighs rested over each of his shoulders; both of his hands holding me firmly against his face; my fingers intertwined with his white curls, tugging tightly.

My body was on fire with want, eager to experience these images he conjured. Varro leaned up and cupped my chin with his hand, running his thumb gently across my lower lip.

"Do you want to taste?"

His finger still pressed firmly against my lip; I nodded as I continued to grow more restless for him. He gently slipped two fingers in my mouth, sliding them across my tongue as my lips closed tightly around them. I sucked, tasting the sweet, orange flavor combined with the saltiness from his skin. As I savored the taste, he continued to fill my mind with images of me riding his face, grinding my hips and sex against him.

My eyes began to close, letting myself sink deeper into his fantasy. Suddenly, Varro stood, his frame still placed solidly between my thighs. I had become so wet with arousal from this torment. He tilted my head back to look up at him.

"Open your mouth," he instructed.

I was pliant in every way for this male. I parted my lips again, ever so slightly. He held another small piece of orange above me and squeezed, letting the liquid drip from his fist into my open mouth. The tart droplets fell against my tongue, and I licked them from my lips, noting the wanton look in Varro's eyes. I watched as his chest rose and fell rhythmically, matching the intensity of the energy between us.

It was becoming too much. "What are you doing to me?" I questioned breathlessly.

He bent down to my ear and whispered, "Every time you so much as look at citrus, I want you to think of me. I want the smell to make you long for my touch, and the taste to make you remember me devouring you…all of you."

The moment he finished speaking, he knelt once more. My lips crashed into his, and he tugged and tore at my pants. He began to place rough kisses all down my stomach, looking up at me from just above my slick sex.

"Focus on your feeling of pleasure in your mind, and I promise you, you'll never have felt anything as good as this."

He ran his tongue down my center, beginning to work me with his fingers simultaneously. My legs tightened around him, and I groaned in deep satisfaction at how well he knew my body and what it wanted, without my ever having to say a word. I tried to do as he instructed, focusing my thoughts on the way his actions felt, unsure of why he asked this of me. Weren't my moans and gasps enough to show him my adoration?

Instantly, every sensation seemed heightened. My legs began to tremble, and I tried to cage my moaning through clenched teeth. My body was hot all over, like ticklish flames dancing across my skin. There was a strange, deep numbness that balanced against the most intense orgasm I'd ever felt. They glided back and forth along one another, both refusing to let the other take over. Waves of profound pleasure, surging and waning.

My eyes were shut tightly, and though I could still feel Varro doing amazing things to my body, I also felt as if I were on another plane of existence. My chest heaved as I fought for release. The feeling could only be described as the sound of a violin string hitting a higher note with each draw of the bow. The notes unending, the bow unyielding. It felt so good, but I could not sustain it.

I writhed against his mouth as I felt his hand reach up; my fingers clutched around his as I sought to fall into the final crescendo of this deafening symphony. One final note, and there it was…the descent into quiet nothingness, following a single, gasping cry that I could not contain.

Tears began to stream down my face, yet I was not sad. I almost felt a giggle leave my mouth. I was in a dizzy fog from lack of breath. He pulled me into his lap on the ground, and I wrapped my naked legs around his waist and rested my tired head on his shoulder.

"What in the three moons of Demir was *that?*" I panted.

He ran his hands through the sweaty tendrils of my hair and pulled a piece back, exposing my ear.

"That, my fated one…is what Siren Song feels like alongside your orgasm."

I gasped in surprise at what he'd done. I'd never imagined his gift could be used in such a way. He was an artist with what he'd done with the instrument of my body.

I clung tighter to him and whispered back, "I will never hold that kiss against you again."

Varro let out a small chuckle, and I had no idea how I was ever going to make him feel half as good as he'd just made me feel.

CHAPTER

7

The next morning, there was an unexpected knock at my door. Varro quickly kissed me on my cheek and portaled away from the room before our secret could be discovered.

I answered the door with a passable yawn, attempting to act like I was still sleepy and had just awoken. It was Nori. She requested a private audience so, after peering into the hallway and looking both directions, I ushered her in and shut the door.

She sat on the bed opposite mine and bit at her nails, a tell-tale sign of her nerves.

"What's going on?" I inquired, anxiety creeping in.

"Please don't be upset with me," she said, looking more bashful than apologetic.

Before I could ask why, she continued, "You know how I don't have the best control of my ability, and sometimes I just slip in and out of others' dreams without even trying?"

"Yes…and?"

"Cress, I didn't mean to, I promise, but I feel so intrusive I have to tell you. I know you dream about him…"

I knew exactly who she was referring to, but in an effort to protect mine and Varro's secret, I played naïve.

"Who?"

"Varro. You dream of him often and quite explicitly. I was embarrassed to say anything because it's so unquestionably…private."

I kept my breathing calm and steady, attempting to avoid revealing anything with my facial expression.

"Oh, Nori, don't worry. You know how dreams are; we don't have much control over them. Varro is very attractive after all," I explained, trying to downplay the notion entirely and see if she'd let me get away with the excuse.

"You need to know something else…" she continued shyly. "He's dreaming of you too—and I don't mean his own versions. I mean, he's having the *exact same* dreams as you."

"What?" I said, unable to quell my surprised reaction.

"I've been slipping in and out of both of your dreams, and they are identical, just sometimes through your eyes and others, his."

"That's impossible," I whispered, unable to reconcile what she was saying with anything I'd ever heard.

"I know," Nori said. "I don't know what it means, but it has to be something, right? That's why I had to tell you! I couldn't just stay quiet; it's no longer just a coincidence. Though, I don't think you could ever call it that to begin with."

I sat in silence, trying to accept that all my fantasies had also been happening to him. How come he never spoke of it? After giving it a moment of thought, I realized that, of course, he didn't for the same reasons I hadn't. How foolish could we be? And with an inexperienced Dreamwalker sleeping just a few feet away from us…

There was an answer looming in my mind, but I had to know if she had come to any similar conclusion.

"What do you think it means?"

"I don't know, I've never encountered anything like this; I've only had the ability since arriving at Basdie after all. I have to believe it means you two are connected in some significant way though."

"I think you're right," I said dejectedly, feeling bad for withholding the truth about Varro and I being mates. I just didn't feel right telling her anything without first aligning with Varro. I wouldn't do to him what Trace had done to me when he'd outed us to the others.

I rose to my feet, trying to indicate to Nori that we wouldn't be discussing the matter further.

"I appreciate you telling me this information. I'm sorry that you've been exposed to us in such an intimate way. I will discuss this with him at the earliest opportunity."

A soft smile overtook Nori's features, replacing the nervous expression that had been plastered across her face since arriving at my door. "Cress?"

"Yes?"

"If this does mean you two are connected, or perhaps feel for one another... I want you to know that your secret is safe with me. There hasn't been much room for love and compassion since we were all delivered to the Offering. I don't think we should have to lose those parts of us just because they take everything else."

Nori's sincere words almost moved me to tears. I grabbed her hand, giving it a tight squeeze.

"I appreciate that sentiment more than you know."

Once Nori left, I got dressed quickly and made my way to Varro's room, anxious to tell him about my encounter with Nori. When he shut the door behind me, I began to accuse him in an urgent whisper.

"When were you going to tell me you've been having dreams about me?"

He let out an amused laugh. "How do you know I've been dreaming of you? Though, I'm not going to pretend I haven't."

"Did you forget we have a *Dreamwalker* in our midst?" I asked sternly.

Varro's golden cheeks warmed with embarrassment, his smile only accentuating his dimples.

"Well, did she enjoy the show?" he asked teasingly. "And why did she come to you, if she's been sneaking around in my dreams?"

"She came to me because she's been slipping into my dreams as well—accidentally—and she discovered we're having the same dreams. Not dreams just about one another, but literally the *exact same dreams!*" I exclaimed, throwing my arms up in the air.

"Really? Some of my dreams have been pretty, well, let's say… untamed. She's seen all of that? *You've* seen all of that?"

Varro began to stitch together the pieces of what that meant, and his cheeks grew redder.

"Now is not the time to dwell on the unchaste nature of those dreams. Our bond is connected even when we sleep, and now Nori knows something is going on. I played it off well enough, but I think we need to tell her."

Varro's silence filled the room as he pondered what it would mean to let another member of the Imperi in on our secret.

"We can't control our dreams; this is only going to continue!" I added, trying to convince him that this was the right decision.

"If you want to tell her, I support you. But you have to decide if you can trust her. That means Gia knows you have a mate, even if she doesn't know who, and now Nori would know everything. And we'd be keeping Cairis in the dark if we go this route."

"You're right, but I am worried that the more people who know, the more we run the risk of Theory and Saryn finding out. We don't know what stance they'll take, and I haven't even told them about the Drift."

The words left my mouth before I could catch myself, and I instantly realized my mistake. Varro's expression quickly turned to one of confusion.

"The Drift? What is that?"

Gods be damned, this morning was unravelling with each passing minute. I couldn't lie to him. Withholding information was one thing, but a direct question was something I was unable to dodge.

I hung my head, disappointed with myself for keeping him in the dark this long.

"It's something I've read about numerous times in the journals of the Dark Wielders that trained here before me. It's some sort of affliction or corruption of the mind that happens from practicing dark magic."

I could see Varro holding his breath, his gills motionless, with not a single bob of his throat. Fear was already beginning to pool in his eyes, and his brow furrowed in concern.

"What do you mean, 'an affliction'? What happens?" he questioned demandingly.

I continued with some hesitancy, trying to quell his concern, but knowing nothing else I said could accomplish that. It would only exacerbate things further.

"Some of them began to lose their memories, unable to remember the more distant past. But others…they began to lose themselves entirely. The word 'mindless' is referenced a lot. Like daydreaming, but worse."

I had intended to continue, but Varro interjected, "And this is guaranteed to happen if you use your gift?"

He was already connecting the dots so quickly.

"It seems likely, at some point… They speculated that there are only two ways to avoid it. Stop dark wielding altogether, which you know the Imperi will never stand for."

I stopped my explanation, hoping, praying he wouldn't ask about the second.

"And the other…" he prodded, my silence having gone on for too long.

"I don't want to tell you," I admitted dolefully.

Varro now stood before me, hands grasping both my shoulders.

"Why? We must find a way to stop this from happening to you. I'll do anything to help you!"

I took a deep breath, then uttered shakily, "It is presumed the only other way is to find a tether to reality, to share the burden…through an anchor. Through a bonded mate."

The silence between us following my confession was palpable. Both of us held our breath, fearful of what might be said next. I couldn't stand it a moment longer.

"I didn't want you to know because I cannot tie you to this fate. I won't. All along, you've let me have choice in the matter of our bond. Telling you that I might need you in this way could consume you with obligation. Steal away the freedom I want for you. I can't ask you to do something like that when we don't even know the risks. We don't even know if it will actually protect me—and, Gods, can't I just believe the Drift may never come for me at all?"

Varro pulled me tightly into his chest, squeezing me into a protective embrace.

"You should have told me sooner. I can't believe all this time, you've kept this from everyone. I had hoped you knew you could, at least, tell me. Don't you think we can handle it?"

"I want to believe that," I whispered back.

"We will, I know it. And it begins with letting others help us. Remember, survive as a team or perish alone."

Together, we trained as usual with Theory. Working our bodies to the brink of exhaustion, leaving little energy to spare in the flight field. There was no avoiding the frost in the air as each peak, now fully blanketed in snow, succumbed to the blustering winds that scattered flurries along the craggy cliffsides. Each of us, having come from more temperate climates, despised the harsh weather in the Elorns. We yearned for the warmth and sunlight that awaited us when we finally ventured south to join Gia and Trace.

Varro and Cairis' warm-colored skin tones would fit in naturally amongst the Artumians, but Nori and I would need to glamour a hint of a tan until we actually appeared sun-kissed. No one would believe we had resided anywhere near our destination if we arrived as pale as we were. From all my readings, the sun lingered in the lands of Artume, creating longer days and shorter nights. There were endless sand dunes as far as the eye could see, lush tropical trees and flora flourished along the coastline.

I shared everything I had read with the others, trying to prepare them for what would become our new home. With what little downtime we were granted, the part of me that always sought to control things felt compelled to find ways we could all benefit.

In the late afternoon, Saryn continued to push each of our abilities, finding unique ways to test our endurance, creativity, and quick wits. Saryn and I agreed on one thing—there wasn't anything subtle about my dark wielding. Our acts of espionage would need to be calculated, and above all else…quiet.

My unique abilities would need to be kept hidden until a time when they were of the utmost value. Embedding our team within Silas' court and kingdom was an act that would require meticulous strategy and adaptability. Any outward act of aggression that could be traced back to Cambria would likely result in immediate, all-out war—the very thing we were trying to avoid.

After dinner, Varro and I told Nori and Cairis to meet us in the healing pools to speak in private. Cairis put up a fuss about the location, but I rolled my eyes and told him he didn't have to *actually* get in the water; we just needed somewhere that prying eyes and ears couldn't find us. He acquiesced with a grumpy *humph.*

A short time later, we were all gathered; the empty, restorative pools at our side. The echoes of the cavernous room and our idle chatter soon gave way to silence as we tiptoed around the crux of our impromptu council.

"I can't believe you come all the way down here for healing almost daily. You really ought to get a friend like Nori." Cairis winked at her and nudged her shoulder playfully with his large fist. Nori blushed, a faint sheen of sweat forming across her cheeks from the pervasive steam.

"What did you want to discuss," Nori inquired, bringing the conversation into focus.

Varro looked at me, nodded, and gave me the floor. I inhaled deeply, knowing that no matter how many times I had practiced the words in my head, they were unlikely to come out the way I hoped.

"We're a team, right?"

Cairis responded quickly, "Of course!"

Nori nodded her head in agreement.

"Well, teams shouldn't keep secrets from each other. Not unless it's mission-critical. I've kept things from you all in the past, like knowing Trace before the Offering. I don't want to make that mistake again. Especially now that each decision I make could impact our well-being and safety."

My voice echoed off the cave walls, but the others were mute, waiting with bated breath for me to explain myself.

"Through my readings, I have discovered that dark wielding comes with risks. It is written that a sort of mental corrosion is likely to occur with its use." I heard Nori let out a small gasp. "I am fearful for myself; I won't lie to you about that. But I also will not deny us this advantage should we need it."

Cairis studied my expression intently with a furrowed brow, genuine concern spanning every one of his sharp features.

"Do Saryn and Theory know about this?" he asked.

"They do not."

"Why?"

"Because once I tell them about the Drift, as the texts refer to it, they will want to know how to avoid it or control it—and I'm not ready to share what little I know about that."

Nori looked up at Cairis in confusion, before turning to me. "What do you know? You can tell us."

I swallowed hard, trying to let the anxiousness in me recede, but the room was becoming unbearably warm. I felt the hum of Varro's bond seeking to comfort mine.

"The Drift can only be avoided by ceasing use of the magic altogether, or possibly anchoring to a bond, a mate."

Before I could get another word out, Cairis shamelessly chimed in.

"That's shit luck! There're better chances of me bedding the queen of Cambria than you finding a mate now that we're all stuck here!"

Under normal circumstances, I would have let out a snort of amusement at his ever-dramatic commentary, but I just stood there smiling warmly and waiting for my moment to break the news to them.

"Well, Cairis, I'd say your chances of bedding the queen of Cambria are quite high, then…"

He squinted at my joke, looking perplexed, and suddenly, Nori's high-pitched voice startled us all as she yelped, "You're mates! That's it. You and Varro are mates, aren't you?" She quickly covered her mouth, startling herself by the volume of her echoed enthusiasm.

"What?" Cairis coughed out in disbelief, looking back and forth between me and Varro.

Varro spoke for the first time since I began tip-toeing through this explanation.

"We are mates, but we are not mated. We have not sealed the bond."

He said the words flatly, not with distaste, just a curt assessment of our situation.

You could see Nori practically hold in a squeal as she did everything to quell the fidgeting of her hands and feet. Only someone as delightful as her could see joy in these circumstances. For that, I envied her.

I continued Varro's admission.

"It's true. I have only known for a short time, and we are navigating the predicament together. We didn't want to keep it from you, but we needed time to figure out what this meant and determine if we're safe. We have no idea how Saryn and Theory will react if they find out about us, or when they learn of the Drift. Saryn could see it as a risk to have us together and send Varro away, or worse."

I had never let Varro hear me say those thoughts aloud. But I had thought through them many times in private. Saryn would want to keep my power, and if he spared one of us, it would be me, undoubtedly. Theory might jump to the conclusion that our loyalties to one another would be too strong, even un-bonded, and be a risk to the mission and the team as a whole. And then there were the other scenarios; the ones where they forced us to seal the bond in order to protect me from the Drift, along with the added leverage the gained power of mind-melding would bring. With my mental shields momentarily down in distraction, the others had already understood every scary thought racing through my mind, and now looked at me with deep understanding of the severity we faced.

Cairis was always the first one to speak his every thought without a moment's hesitation. This time was no different.

"Would you even be willing to seal the bond, for tactical advantage or otherwise?"

It was a fair question and I did not begrudge him for asking it, though I could feel Varro's irritation at the notion as he answered first.

"I care deeply for my mate in ways that can never be explained with words. I would never do anything Cress wasn't okay with. Though I am sworn to protect you and our kingdom, I will always protect her first— and that is why we are a liability. One you deserve to know about."

Varro had never said those exact words to me, but I knew them to be true. I think I'd known since the moment he demonstrated he'd rather lay down and die with me than save his own life. We *were* a liability to the team.

"Fuck that, we are all liabilities!" Cairis' voice grew louder and more passionate with each declaration. "Yes, the mission comes first, but if you think I wouldn't put myself in jeopardy to protect Nori or Gia from harm, you're wrong. You think Nori wouldn't put us all at risk if it meant protecting some innocent kids? Every day they try and grind us down to see if we'll come to heel. We let them believe we are perfectly pliant monsters, but this is a mask. I wear it every day and I know you do too. I do it to survive. So we all survive. But they are never going to change that hearts still beat here!" he said, pointing to his chest. His words reverberated off the walls, punctuating his resoluteness.

My cheeks warmed with gratitude for Cairis' honesty. His words were ones I had wanted to believe so deeply about both myself and the others too. That no matter how many terrible things I'd practiced with a Vesper, no matter how many lives were lost at the Canary Veil...hearts still beat in the chests of monsters. Someday, the Gods would determine if my cause was noble, but until that judgement came, I would protect my home and all its people as the Imperi had done before me. The future of the realm was entrusted to us, and I did not take that obligation lightly.

"We won't say a word to Theory or Saryn," said Nori. "Thank you for trusting us. I believe things happen for a reason, and it cannot be a mistake that your gift has also come with the arrival of your mate. Cress, the Gods take, but they also give..."

Although I didn't quite share the same belief system as Nori, her optimistic perspective brought me solace.

Days passed in a blur. The sparkling snow that covered the flight field in the valley only grew deeper. With Nori and Cairis now aware of our dilemma, it felt more relaxed, despite continuing to prepare for a secret infiltration of the southern kingdom.

Varro and I were sitting in the common area, surrounded by books, trying to appear as though we were discussing what we'd read. In actuality, it was the Drift we were talking about when an unexpected messenger arrived. I was on pins and needles, anxiously hoping we were finally receiving word from the south, but also nervous that we were finally being called forth to join the mission. I wasn't ready...although, I wasn't sure if I'd ever be truly ready.

A large scroll sealed with thick, bronze wax was passed to Saryn, and with a silent nod, the cloaked figure departed as quickly as they'd arrived. It was always jarring to see someone new in Basdie, just like when the tailor had briefly visited to take our measurements. How were these strangers allowed to come and go freely? Were they blood-sworn?

Were they even who they appeared to be? If the Imperi had taught me anything, it was to be skeptical and untrusting, particularly of strangers. Deception was an instrument of the deadly.

After breaking the wax seal, I witnessed a smaller piece of parchment rolled inside the larger one fall to the floor. Saryn bent down and lifted it to inspect its contents. He made his way toward me with a displeased look on his face.

"I do not appreciate our darling Gia using official Imperi communications to send personal correspondence."

He tossed the small scroll in my lap and turned on his heel, carrying the larger scroll over to review with Theory. The two of them headed down the hall, and I began to thumb at the curled parchment. Varro gave me an intrigued look, but I scurried away to the privacy of my dormitory, eager to see what was so urgent that Gia would risk enraging our mentors.

I sat on my bed, holding the paper close to the candlelight to illuminate the words on the page.

> I am safe. Everything is going to plan. We are awaiting your arrival. If what you implied was true when we parted ways, please take care of your heart and use your head. You need to know he is not okay. His role is more…violent than mine. I am concerned for him. Tread lightly when you see us again. We need him. I cannot do the things he's been forced to do. I think he is the only one among us who can endure it.
>
> —G

My heart raced as I reread the short but intense letter over and over. Her need to warn me about the state of Trace's wellbeing was so strong that she risked sending this, and through formal means of communication no less. This couldn't be good. While I was glad to hear she was safe, and that whatever plans they'd put into motion were on track, I couldn't ignore the foreboding tone in her warning. Saryn had already read the letter; no doubt he'd be questioning me soon enough. And while I could rationalize a warning about Trace due to our intertwined pasts, there was no excuse for the other part. Gia was vague, but I suspected Saryn would be obliged to pry the truth from me through any means he deemed necessary.

I made my way back to the common room and gave Varro a look that hinted at a later discussion. Theory and Saryn joined us in the dining hall. It was obvious we were eager to hear whatever news they'd be willing to share with us, but our silence indicated we were all unwilling to be the one to make that curiosity known. I stirred my food, trying to appear uninterested, thinking maybe they'd be more open with us if we didn't seem desperate for information. Our mentors played this game often. Whether it was being part of this life for so long, or simply who they were, they found amusement in toying with us.

"Well, they're not dead if that's what you're all wondering," Saryn said with a smirk towards Theory while he slurped at his bowl of soup. There were some days it took everything in my power not to go after him. I'd like to cave in the roof above his head right about now. I gritted my teeth and eyed the others as if to encourage them to stay quiet. Don't let him bait us into a confrontation. If we were silent and didn't react, he'd be more inclined to share. Instead, Theory continued while Saryn returned to his meal.

"Gia has successfully managed to embed herself as a lady of the new court. The king has taken a keen interest in her, and this will provide opportunities to ensnare him further. She remains on friendly enough terms with the queen, who is no stranger to her husband's many consorts. We are very lucky to have one of our assets this close to their inner circle; she's done well in setting the stage for your arrivals."

Theory provided me with even more insight about Gia than her own letter had, but there was a reason that her note to me was short and cryptic. She had to have known any worthwhile detail would have been included in the larger update regarding their status. Now I was anxious to hear about Trace, given Gia's grave warning.

"While Gia has been enjoying the lavish lifestyle of the court, Trace has also been embedded successfully—but under quite different circumstances. His short time amongst their Kingsguard resulted in the acknowledgement of his skillset, along with a unique propensity for violence. It's going exactly as we hoped. This has led to a quick promotion, and he is now commanding a small militia of Artumians. Moreover, we've learned that this group has been tasked by the Hand of the King himself to run secret operations. They've been impersonating savage Northerners who've illegally crossed the border and are wreaking havoc across small villages in the south."

Theory's review of Trace's progress had me squeezing my hands into tight fists, my pulse beginning to race. I could feel Varro's bond attempting to soothe mine, but to no avail.

"Why are they pretending to be Cambrians?" I asked.

"It can be assumed this is part of some larger plot to build a coalition against Northerners and incite the next Great War."

Saryn interrupted before Theory could expand any further, "King Aeon has tried to get word to the South and vehemently deny any involvement in this group's actions, but they've been unsuccessful in quelling the lies. Tensions are beginning to boil as the citizens of Artume are unable to ignore the brutality they've seen in the name of the North."

"Brutality?" Cairis prodded.

"Yes, it seems they are targeting smaller villages on the outskirts. Ones that cannot easily defend themselves, conveniently absent of Kingsguards. The atrocities committed thus far are unspeakable. The mere fact that they are inflicting them upon their own people to drum up support for another conflict is a sign that their agenda is not to be underestimated."

Gia's words began to make more sense, and I shuddered at the thought of what those atrocities were and just how Trace was being forced to play his part. It seemed that while Gia's hands were forced to grasp at silk sheets, Trace's were being covered in innocent blood. Nori was chewing at her nails again, her soup cold and untouched.

"Send us south already!" Varro said.

Cairis nodded in eager agreement.

Saryn took a bite of his dinner roll, speaking while chewing obnoxiously. "Soon enough. Don't be so eager to leave the safety of your training. Idris will be back for you all in no time."

"What parts will we play?" I asked, trying to understand if more of us would be forced to join Trace on the front lines of these horrific acts.

"Lucky for you, Cress, I'll be joining you. Idris doesn't feel comfortable sending a particularly volatile Dark Wielder into the mission without some oversight, so I guess you can say I've been fully reinstated. Theory will serve as our messenger, helping us get information back and forth across the border."

He saw me about to interrupt, raising his hand and continuing.

"Cairis will be embedded as another Kingsguard, but one that is stationed in the castle itself, sworn to protect the royal family, along with any other important nobles residing there."

I saw mild relief flash across Cairis' face as he realized this would allow him to be close to Gia and protect her if need be. Additionally, I sensed a feeling of solace that he was not being sent to aid Trace in those endeavors. Hearing Cairis say that he wore the mask of violence like we all did was a brief insight into how he really felt about the Imperi and its purpose.

"And me...?" Nori whispered.

"You, my little Dreamwalker, will also be stationed in the castle in the hope that we find use for that rare talent. You'll be working as a healer in their Order of the Oscillius. This will be a more than adequate place for you to blend in, which is exactly what you'd better do. Keep your head down. Their healers are obviously imbued with special gifts, so they are often sequestered and untouched. Which, lucky for you, means you won't be fucking your way through the kingdom like Gia."

Nori's eyes widened at Saryn's crass remarks, but beneath that surprise, I knew there was also relief. Her biggest fear had been mitigated…for the time being.

"And what about Cress and I?" Varro asked with just as much interest as I had, especially as the topic of "fucking" had been mentioned. I could feel the erratic pulsing of his bond against mine.

Saryn turned to face us.

"Cress is going to be placed in service of Gia, as a lady's maid. The current one will meet an untimely illness, leaving the position available."

I exhaled a sigh. Being close to one of the other team members was everything I'd hoped for. I would wash Gia's feet if it meant staying in close quarters to her. I grew up with ladies' maids in our household, so I understood the job well enough to pull off these duties convincingly. I awaited Varro's assignment, hardly breathing, while my thoughts ran wild with horrible ideas ranging from those of sexual slavery to abhorrent violence.

"Varro, you will be working in the shipyards—you and your gills can thank me later. There has been a peculiar increase in ship production in the bay outside of Nasallus. We are assuming King Silas has demanded the creation of an armada. We need you to find out what's going on, and since many of those already employed are Sea Fae, you should fit in especially well."

I had no idea how far the bay was from the actual castle, but knowing Varro would be laboring near the water was a best-case scenario, as far as I could tell. I hoped the distance between us would be minimal and attempted to conceal my worry for his sake.

All in all, the plan sounded solid enough. We were well-suited for the roles we'd been given, and beginning to understand the details surrounding our enemy's actions meant we could mentally prepare ourselves.

That night, we each scoured the texts available in the common room, seeking information that might help us in our individual assignments. There were minimal texts on the etiquette of servitude for house staff, but I read what was available to me. The tasks involved usually ranged from helping the Lady dress and bathe to general tidying and delivering meals. Knowing I'd be serving Gia and not some spoiled Lady meant the margin for error would be generous; that is, if I were only assigned to her.

Gia was fully capable of doing her own hair, but to keep up appearances I would still need to be seen styling her. Nori's short, choppy hair wasn't the most ideal for me to practice with. When I approached Cairis, I began by stroking his ego, offering pleasantries and compliments about his long, beautiful locks. He ate up the blatant flattery—until I asked him if I might practice on him.

Cairis was none-too-pleased about the request, but after much protesting he finally acquiesced in the name of the mission. I swore to him there wouldn't be any ribbons or bows...for now. Once I got him to agree, I made Varro promise me there would be no jokes or quips at Cairis' expense. If he cost me the chance to practice, I was going to stop visiting the Vesper quarters with him. Just the mention of that threat ensured his lips were sealed.

Within a few days, we arranged for additional texts to be delivered to Basdie. From that point onward, Varro spent most of his time reading up on the mariners in the south. He studied meticulous drawings of the differences in how their ships were constructed compared to Cambria's, making note of even the most minute things—such as how they tied their knots differently. He'd bore all of us at dinner recounting how the building materials used to construct Southern ships varied greatly from those in the North. His enthusiasm for the subject was endearing to me. The drastically different climates meant the availability of suitable timber was at a premium. This was notably why what little trade that went on between the North and the South came at such a high price to the Artumians. We had strong timber in abundance, and that gave us the upper hand in negotiations for such goods.

It was well documented by Cambrian scholars that the Great War was largely due to resource constraints that the Artumian people had brought upon themselves. Because of this, the Northerners were firmly against letting them migrate any farther north, for fear that they would do the same to our lands. The Ledor River became a natural border between the devastation they had caused, separating it from our still resource-abundant territories. Artume, now an arid desert, had once teemed with natural resources. Centuries of overgrazing and deforestation in the name of expansion and trade profits meant they had left nothing for themselves.

Before they knew it, the land became rife with shimmering heat and desolation. The sun arced slowly across the sky, blistering the region relentlessly, with few trees or foliage to grant the relief of shade. Instead, the endless sparkle of fine sands and twinkling mirages on the horizon became the new normal for a people that had once flourished. I had read about it at the academy, seen paintings and drawings, but never thought I would someday feel the sands of Artume between my own toes.

If they were, in fact, building an armada of ships, then the king was likely spending inordinate amounts from the royal purse to acquire the timber—that or the illegal smuggling trade was at an all-time high. Kingsguard were usually spread out along the Riverlands, but it was impossible to cover every mile of such an expansive area.

It was also common practice for villagers in this region, who were not wealthy, to aid the smugglers. After all, to them it was just wood, something that flourished in their lands, and if it meant putting food in the bellies of their children, who could blame them?

But the stakes were higher now. They had no idea they might be contributing to a fleet of war ships intent on bringing bloodshed to their shores. Unfortunately, King Aeon could not alert them of their missteps, as this might set off a chain of panic within his own kingdom, so the illegal trade routes remained active.

We continued to ready ourselves by studying and training, awaiting the arrival of Idris. Nori and Cairis guarded our secret as promised. Varro and I had not broached the topic of sealing the bond since we'd last spoken with them. But each time we met in the late hours of the night, practicing self-control became increasingly difficult. Our bodies called to one another in a way that could never be denied. His skin felt like home against mine. When we were entwined, we were of one body. Now, after waking from my dreams, I felt extremely self-conscious during our time alone, knowing he had the same torrid fantasies rushing through his head. How much longer could I keep the bond at bay when even our unconscious minds would not let us rest?

Despite additional private lessons with Saryn, utilizing my dark abilities did not yet materialize symptoms of the Drift. Just abject fatigue. Winter was officially in full force in the Elorn Mountains, but there was one particularly chilly afternoon where Saryn insisted that I join him privately on the flight deck.

"You're not a Wind Wielder, that I know for certain," he stated once we'd made it outside, pausing only a moment before continuing his assessment. "The simplest execution of wind magic has evaded you, no matter how many times we've explored it. Yet, there must be some innate form of it within you. The sheer force with which you've executed the dark wielding must be intertwined with the elements. I see no other alternative."

His logic made sense, but each time I'd reached for this particular element it had evaded my grasp. With fire, I focused on the flame; I imagined I could feel the heat, even smell the smoke. At times, all other sounds would deafen around me except for the slight crackle of the fire, whether it be from wood or wick. I could *feel* fire; I sensed it, and thus I could bend it to my will.

It was the same with water. Any time I attempted to manipulate it, I would focus on the change in temperature; the cool relief of it washing over me. Water magic always felt fluid to me. It was safe and comforting, and I had no fear of it.

When I was outside, I could feel the wind. I could see its effects, swirling strands of my hair, cutting across my cheeks, causing chills and raising goosebumps along my skin. But it never felt tangible. No matter how much I focused, I couldn't mentally touch it. There was no way to reach out and grab it in the same way the other elements had lent themselves to me. And once I was inside the stale and motionless air of Basdie, it seemed impossible to even detect its presence.

I shared this sentiment with Saryn in hopes that it would help formulate a theory as to why I couldn't master it.

As if the idea quite literally struck him, he exclaimed, "Wait, have you tried to *see* the wind?"

"What do you mean 'see' the wind? It's invisible. I can see the *effects* of it," I replied, motioning my hand at the small flurries of snow cascading down the mountainside.

"It's not invisible!" Saryn disagreed. "Or, so I've heard. Those most gifted in wind magic don't need to feel it, because they can see it. That is why they can wield it even in the stillest of airs."

I looked at him, confused and awaiting additional information. I was pretty sure I'd know if I could see the wind…wouldn't I?

"I've read that Wind Wielders can see the normally imperceptible aspects of the element. It's been described as a small glimmer or ripple, other times a shine. It's about seeing the way light bends through air, and witnessing how it interacts with the other elements around it."

I stared down into the valley, scanning my eyes across snow-covered treetops. Vast, endless white. The occasional bird soaring across to break up the monotony. I squinted, tilting my head, trying to see some indication of what Saryn described, but I detected nothing of the sort. Everything was crystal clear. No glimmers, shimmers, ripples or otherwise. I loosed a frustrated sigh.

"Saryn, I don't see anything like that."

"Give me your coat." He held out his hand, impatiently.

"No, it's freezing out here. I need it."

"I won't ask again."

Knowing it was more than just a threat, I reluctantly began to remove the fur-lined coat from my body and placed it over his arm. The frigid chill quickly sucked most of the warmth from my frame, and I hugged myself, trying to contain what little was left.

"Gloves."

"Are you serious?" I asked through chattering teeth. Saryn just stared at me.

"Fine!" I said, removing the gloves angrily and handing—or practically throwing—them to him as well. "What now?" I asked, impatient.

"Until you can see the wind, you will sit out here every day from after breakfast until lunch. Freeze for all I care, but you will do this without question."

Briefly, I thought to myself, *How in the three moons of Demir would he even know if I lied?* I could just tell him I saw it.

"I will know if you're lying," he snapped, clearly reading my mind, "and praise the Gods that Artume is a desert wasteland, since apparently a moment of cold has you forgetting your mental shields entirely. You're going to get yourself fucking killed."

I felt my jaw clench, frustrated at myself for having lapsed my shields, and at Saryn for being such an ass at every opportunity.

"Complete this task alone," he said, turning on his heel, as if he were keenly aware that Varro would make an attempt to join me once he found out about this torturous assignment.

I found myself persistently glancing up at the sun, willing it to move swiftly—but to my utter dismay, it only shifted the minutest of degrees while I sat there freezing to death. Saryn's antics were bound to kill me, long before I ever got myself killed. I despised the cold. I switched back and forth between sitting on the side of a rock—which only made me colder—and pacing while mumbling to myself. Mostly, I thought of ways I'd like to hurt Saryn. I might just grant myself that exploration with a Vesper if I made it through the remainder of the day.

I did everything from staring blankly at a single area for an extended period of time to intermittently scanning across the expanse. I searched the landscape for signs of the wind's color, but there were only hints of dark green trees amongst whites and grays.

Half of the time I was distracted by the incessant sound of my own teeth chattering. My once-pale skin was now irritated and red. Rubbing my hands together had quickly become pointless. I couldn't feel my fingers, even if I shoved them into the bottoms of my trouser pockets. My leather vest barely shielded me from the cold, and below it, my nipples were fully erect and beginning to burn in pain from the frigid air. I removed any daggers fastened to my legs and laid them on the ground beside me, shedding the cold, unwelcome metal. When the sun finally reached its destination in the sky, I trudged back inside, the sting of failure the only thing more biting than the cold.

Six days of excruciatingly long hours in the freezing cold. Hours after spent defrosting by a fireside, with Varro bringing me hot cups of tea and cocoa to distract me from my anguish. My skin dry and irritated, my lips chapped to the point of bleeding. My once enjoyable trips to the healing pools now became required therapy to survive Saryn's impossible task. Varro was frustrated past the point of reason, knowing he could not assist with my endeavor. Saryn would know if

Varro tried to get close enough and used his Siren Song to relieve me of the discomfort.

Six days wrestling with my own mind, my own memories, and only the rustling of leaves, whistling of the wind and the occasional call of a hawk as it made its descent. The isolation led my mind to wander places I had not allowed myself to for a very long time. Comforting memories of my youth with Versa, turning the pages of our favorite books in the library; Chef's extravagant desserts; Father's cologne; Mother's latest finery.

The longer I allowed myself to sink into the depths of those memories, the less I felt the numbness taking over my extremities. They wrapped around me like a heavy blanket, protecting me, even now. And it was in that moment, when I allowed myself to stare off into the distance thinking of the short life I had with my loved ones, that I saw a small glimmer cresting along the mountainside.

I blinked my eyes, thinking they had become dry from staring, but no matter how many times I tried, I could still see that vague glimmer. I jumped to my feet and widened my eyes, trying to ensure they weren't playing tricks on me. Had I wanted to complete this task so badly that I was seeing things that weren't real?

I scanned to the left, following the glimmer as it moved down the mountainside and up across the canopy of treetops. The sparkles twinkled like tiny diamonds on the tips of each branch. Patterns in the wind began to reveal themselves to me, detailed spirals weaving fluidly around every object that stood in their path. The sight was distinctly harmonious. If land was the staff on a sheet of music, then the wind were the notes, placed delicately and intentionally.

"I see it!" I yelled in excitement. "I can see it!" I continued to shout into the void, no one there to hear me but the birds and hibernating creatures below. Quickly, my sluggish limbs began to pump with blood from my elation. All my screaming must have caused a commotion, because

Saryn and Theory came running outside. I grabbed Saryn by the shoulders, exclaiming, "I did it! I really can see it."

Never in my time with Saryn had I ever touched him this way. Our only physical encounters were ones of training and sparring. I couldn't contain my excitement, though, and I shook his shoulders as if trying to shake him into believing me.

"How am I supposed to believe you? How are we to be certain you haven't just tired of the cold?" he asked, prepared for me to spin some elaborate lie.

Already irritated with his disbelief, I snapped back, "Fine, I'll let down my shields and you can see for yourself, but I'm not lying!"

He looked at Theory, nodding a silent agreement to determine if I was telling the truth. Ignoring their distrust, I turned back to face the snow-filled valley.

I looked for the same signs, but they had dissipated, making me annoyed and even more frustrated with myself. I tried staring blankly into the spot that it had formed the first time I noticed it, but nothing appeared. Wracking my brain, trying to think how I had done it, I could tell Theory and Saryn were growing impatient with me. But while they sifted through my thoughts of irritation and failure, they also had to see there was complete and undeniable belief in myself.

Trying to recreate that moment, I sighed, knowing the thoughts I was about to grant myself were not ones I ever wanted to share with the two of them. I inhaled deeply, closed my eyes, and began to let a whirlwind of memories unfold and wrap warmly around me.

The day my father walked back through our front doors from the rebellion at Erisas Bay, my sister and I running to hug him tightly. My sister presenting me with our matching bracelets on our tenth namesake; the anticipatory smile on her face as I pulled the ribbon from the box containing the dainty braided metal. My parents laughing as they waltzed by the fireplace after a solstice party, thinking no one was around to see it. Riding Rain after a summer storm; his unbridled vigor pounding the wet earth with every stride, the wind cutting sharply across my face as he and I descended into a feeling of complete freedom, if only for a moment.

I could have basked in the warmth of those memories forever. If only the winter of the Elorns could keep those moments perfectly formed in my mind, I'd settle for nothing more than becoming a frozen statue, caught permanently in the bliss of my former life. A perfectly imperfect life, whose value I couldn't see until it was no longer mine to keep.

I opened my eyes, staring out into the wide-open space before me, and blinked back the tears that had formed behind my eyelids. At the far end of the mountain range, I could see the glimmer again, shining brightly only for my eyes to see. A sly smile spread across my lips; I'd show them where they could shove their skepticism.

The west winds carried strong gusts from the shadowed side of the valley to the slopes bathed in sunlight. The dustings of snow billowed in the same direction, causing the tall trees to bow as they caught the brunt of it. Except now, the patterns that tethered these elements together were mine to control. Turning to face east, I began to visualize their circles switching direction entirely. The tree trunks made loud creaking noises and the rustling of branches now twisted wildly against the sudden change. As I began to create a strong east wind, I sought to push its limits. The rotating breeze swelled in intensity as I narrowed my focus to create a gale of wind so powerful that it blew away the snow from each treetop, leaving them trembling.

The tempest approached us and a rush of snow flew past Saryn and Theory, coating them in frost before scattering a layer of fresh powder along the mountainside. As they shook off the chill, they too gazed out upon the vibrancy of a dark green forest below, one we had not seen since the first snowfall at Basdie. Tall, strong trees, some of which had been born long before our ancestors, stood heads above the younger saplings surrounding them.

After the swaying of the trees settled, I considered summoning another windstorm from the other direction just to make my point, but instead I turned to Saryn and said simply, "I can see it now."

Theory smirked, one raised brow at Saryn. I retreated from them both, making my way inside, wondering how I'd ever be able to tap into the power they'd just witnessed should my memories fade. Fate might decide that someday I would be drained of the very thing that seemed to feed the essence of my power.

CHAPTER 10

The others were in awe each time they witnessed my power, whether unleashed in its raw, destructive form or guided with finesse by my every whim. I stood idle in silence, summoning all my strength and control. On the inside, I focused on the calm that only fond memories of my past could grant me. Varro tended to my needs closely, ensuring I wouldn't be overcome with fatigue.

As the tenacity and predictability of my powers grew, so did the concern in Varro's demeanor. Though he beamed with pride at my achievements, a subtle fearfulness clung to him, blossoming like the white mushrooms that flourished on the trunks of the forest trees near my home. I saw it lurking behind his eyes, felt it when he held me just a fraction tighter in our embraces. We both knew why, but did not speak of it.

After dinner, Saryn found me journaling in the cramped confines of the Dark Wielder's room. He knocked and waited for me to open the door. I pushed it open with one hand till he could see me sitting there, writing by candlelight. He walked in and our bodies immediately encroached on one another, so closely that I could now make out his distinct peppery scent as he hovered behind me. He reached down and gently pulled back the hair that was hanging in my face, tucking it behind my ear. The encounter felt strangely invasive. If Varro had witnessed it, I'm certain there would have been a quarrel or, at the very least, an exchange of very heated words. I sat frozen, trying not to react to his actions.

"This marking…" he said seductively, languidly running his fingertip across the tattoo behind my ear. It caused a ticklish feeling and I leaned away from his touch, feeling more uncomfortable with each passing moment.

"What are you doing?" I spat out in irritation, rotating my body away from him to put distance between us in the tightly cramped space.

"Only the very wealthy have tattoos in Artume. You should know that. A poor lady's maid could not afford such a luxury, don't you think?"

I drew in a deep breath, overwhelmed with the information that I had not yet discovered in my studies of the southern kingdom.

"Handle it," he said, emotionless.

"But I can glamour it!"

"You expect me to believe that on top of keeping your mental shields up at all times, you're going to suddenly be adept at maintaining a constant glamour?" he scoffed in disbelief. "I already have my doubts about your plans to address that pale skin of yours. Let's hope your body responds to the sun's radiance before long, or we may have to change your backstory."

"Trace does it!" I snapped back.

Saryn leaned down, making himself eye-level with me. I could feel his hot breath on my face.

"Trace has been glamouring far longer than you! He's been glamouring those despicable tattoos since the day they appeared on his skin.

He hides them because he is ashamed, as he should be. You think I approve of a fucking black cloak on this team? Be glad that savage is off doing what he was bred for. You are not him."

Saryn's disparagement of a fellow Imperi hit me with such force I wasn't sure whether I was more appalled at his choice of words or the conviction with which he delivered them. I'd heard Saryn's sharp tongue say many things to us, some of the worst directed at Nori, but there was an edge to his tone when he spoke of Trace. One that I'd never heard. There was also truth buried between his spiteful remarks.

Saryn removed himself from the tiny room, leaving me behind with the door open, and as he disappeared down the hall he called back, "Deal with it—or I will."

His command upset me so deeply that I immediately went to Varro's room seeking comfort. I couldn't hold the tears back any longer as I entered his room. I practically fell into his embrace as he cupped my wet cheeks, trying to understand what had caused my unravelling.

Through sniffles and upset gasps, I explained, "Commoners don't have tattoos in Artume."

Varro looked at me with a knowing expression, and I continued, "If I were going to be installed as a noble like Gia, maybe it would be different. But I'm not. Saryn has commanded that I deal with it before he does."

My mate stared at my tear-soaked face, trying to discern how he could bring me some sense of comfort. With our shields already down, he knew not to mention a glamour.

"Will you help me?" I looked up into his crystal-blue eyes, watching me with so much emotion, begging for him to walk with me through what felt like torture.

"Of course," he whispered. "What will you have me do?"

I looked at the knife sheathed on his leg, then pulled it from the safety of its strap. His eyes followed mine as I glanced over at the candle burning brightly by his bedside.

"I need you to burn it…deep," I clarified.

His breath audibly hitched at the idea of holding a scalding hot piece of metal to the thin, soft skin behind my ear, at causing me any ounce of pain. I placed the small blade in his hand, as if to give him permission. Letting him know, without words, that this was what I needed from him.

He took it from my palms reluctantly. "I promise you there will be no pain, simply let my Siren Song soothe you."

"No," I interjected immediately. More tears began to form in the wells of my eyes. "This is a tattoo my twin sister and I got before we parted. She has a matching one."

I paused, trying to compose myself and convey my feelings to him. Trying to show him how desperate I was for him to do this for me. "It's supposed to guide me back to her," I said between sniffles. "I'm so afraid of losing her, Varro, of losing it all to the Drift. This tattoo could have helped me remember her."

"Then at least let me get Nori in here to help us; she will ensure there is not a single scar."

"Don't you get it?" I snapped at him, finally breaking. "I *need* the pain. I *want* the scars. I must have something to remind me of what I've lost. Please, let me have this."

Accepting my outburst, only a soft, understanding expression remained. He never wavered, no matter how upsetting my anger had become. He understood my pain. He knew the same grief of being a twin, a triplet, and what that kind of loss felt like. It was akin to the idea of losing each other now that we had discovered we were fated to one another.

I nodded at him, letting him know I was ready, and turned my gaze back to the flickering candlelight. He removed his leather belt, laying it on the bed. I sat down beside it, watching as Varro held the blade over the flame for a long moment, letting it get as hot as possible. The hotter the blade, the more likely he would succeed on the first brand. Time seemed to slow as my patience dwindled, wanting to get it over with. Sensing my rising anxiety, he spoke without taking his eyes off the knife. "Patience, Moirai, one burn needs to be enough." *I can take it*, I thought, steeling my will. Then, it dawned on me: *But, can he?* As if he heard me speak aloud, he added, "I have the strength to do this once, but perhaps not twice."

When he was certain it was hot enough—as much as he could be—he walked to my side, tilting my head to expose the area behind my ear where three tiny crescents sat; the moons of Demir. The marks he had once said reminded him of his gills.

I grabbed the belt, already knowing its purpose. I placed it between my teeth, tasting salt on the sea-stained leather.

"Do not put up your shields, Cress. Let me know your pain alongside you."

I gave him an accepting nod, knowing that while I needed this from him, that was what he needed from me. My palms began to sweat and I reached for his free hand to squeeze when the inevitable, unbearable pain would begin. I'd burned a Vesper many times during the darker parts of my training. On occasion, I'd let a Vesper burn me back, but each time, I would heal myself and ensure no scars remained. I braced myself; bit down on the leather, looking up at my partner, my mate, while blinking away tears. Then nodded, so he knew I was ready.

No one could have prepared me for this. The deafening sound that rings through you till it feels like it's coming out of your eyes. My whole body writhed against the unimaginable pain Varro was inflicting on my skin. The smell of my own flesh burning swirled in my nostrils and made my stomach turn. I squeezed his hand so hard I was sure his bones would break. I knew that in that moment, the single hardest thing for Varro to do was resist using Siren Song to ease my agony. Had he given in, his power could have transformed my experience into that of a feather brushing along my skin.

Instead, I closed my eyes and let the feelings of agony sink deep into the forefront of my mind, beginning to weave the sensation with memories of my sweet sister, Versa. They braided around one another so tightly that soon my memories were stronger than the torture I'd inflicted upon myself, eventually turning into a manageable numbness. The loud-ringing sound that had overtaken me now seemed as if it were off in the distance—more of a low keening knell. I could feel my body covered in perspiration, my teeth aching from biting down so hard on Varro's belt, but now I was afraid to let go. Afraid to descend from the heights of pain to accept what was done—gone.

Each memory of Versa spilled over into the next, like watercolors splashing into each other, painting vibrant images of my past and our youth together. I could hear Varro's voice faintly in the distance, but I willed myself to ignore it. To stay right there with her in this dream-like place that I'd created, to survive having another piece of my heart wrested unwillingly from my chest. The Imperi takes and takes far more than it gives. I'd give it all up—everything—to see her again. A wish I repeat in my heart, so quietly with hopes that my mate cannot hear it.

My grip eased from Varro's hand, and my jaw slowly unclenched from the worn leather; my eyes fluttered as candlelight came back into view. The blood rushing to my ears caused a steady thrum now, much easier to manage than the ringing sound during the act itself. My muscles were so tired from contracting against the pain that my body went limp, and Varro gently laid me on my side. He pulled a salve from his bedside drawer and began to dab it along the back of my ear. Each time his fingertip touched the wound, I winced, until the cooling effect began to do its work and offset the irritation. I didn't need to see a mirror; I knew it probably looked awful.

I lay on my side and Varro crawled into the bed behind me. It was barely big enough for the two of us, but I didn't mind the closeness as he laid an arm over my waist, wrapping it around me and gently tugging me in tighter. We lay there in silence. I could feel it as he grappled with what he'd just put me through, while I tried to hold back more tears—both at what I'd lost, and at the torment I'd caused my mate in asking him to do it.

"Varro," I whispered.

"Yes, Moirai?"

"Will you listen to my stories?"

"I'll always listen to you."

"But I need you to remember them," I pleaded gently. "Someday, there is a good chance I won't remember where I came from—my family, my sister…any of it…" I trailed off.

"I promise to remember for you, Cress."

And so, it began. Mornings, nights, hours in the healing pools—any chance we could be alone, I would recount the stories of my life to Varro. Never in any particular order, as I had a habit of jumping from one excited tangent to another, each memory reminding me of something else important. Some stories would fill us both with laughter, others with shared sadness. There was a simple joy that came from telling my mate every possible thing I could remember about my life prior to the Imperi, and it served two very meaningful purposes.

Hopefully, there would be time for Varro to tell me more about his life before arriving at Basdie, too, but for me, time was not promised. Each day he selflessly granted me all those hours of listening and committing my stories to his memory as if they were his own. Emblazoning them on his heart as if they were his to protect. So, when Idris finally returned for us, it meant the sands of my hourglass had finally run out, and I hoped I'd told Varro enough to keep my histories intact.

To keep Cress Blackthorn alive.

Each of us went through the same preparations that Trace and Gia had received. New clothing, becoming of the roles we'd play— and I had to say that Gia's wardrobe was far more interesting to peruse than mine, yet I was still surprised to see how little clothing even the servants were expected to wear. On one hand, less clothing and light fabrics would keep us cool in the extremely warm climate of Artume, but on the other, it left few places to hide weaponry, and was the farthest thing from protective. I was reminded again how much of our role was theater and espionage when I riffled through these costumes.

My garments were restricted to shades of blue, as apparently it was the color all servants were expected to wear at Nasallus. Most pieces were a thin muslin fabric; typically sleeveless, with panels crossing over the chest and flowy skirts allowing me to move freely. The slits along my legs seemed absurd and useless for a commoner in servitude, but were in accordance with the styles I'd seen in Gia's nicer wardrobe.

Nori's attire was much more elevated. All of her outfits were red, and unlike mine or Gia's, hers covered almost every inch of her body. The fabric was still a thin cotton, but it was long-sleeved with full-length skirts and layer upon layer of fabric. The sleeves and hemlines were embroidered with intricate gold patterns of filigree. I had a hunch the red was specifically chosen to represent and even conceal the color of blood. The thought sent shivers up my spine.

The God, Oscillius, was said to have walked a cursed city at night, placing a bloody hand print on the door of every innocent. For those that awoke to an unmarked front door, they would eventually suffer a great plague, bringing about countless deaths. The Order that Nori was joining had adopted the God's name, believing that healers gifts would only work on the innocent, and that efforts to heal those judged by Oscillius were futile.

The red hues clashed with her scarlet hair, but it was barely detectable when she donned the required cowl with a scarf wrapped around her neck. The healers were honored, revered, untouchable. It was improper to gaze upon their flesh, and her uniform embodied those sensibilities. I admired the subtleties of the outfit, and while I presumed it would be unbearably hot, I thought Nori had been granted the best possible reprieve.

Cairis' package was similar to Trace's in that it contained heavy leather armor with the insignia and designs of the Artumian Kingsguard. Each article was tinged a rich shade of brown and smelled of a smoky-sweet oil, ornate with dark, bronze-colored buckles. While the pieces Trace received had appeared weathered, perhaps even hand-me-downs, these were pristine, almost ornamental. Cairis would be stationed inside the castle itself, and though they were placed to protect the occupants, the king and his inner circle would not subject themselves to odorous, battle-worn uniforms.

The most notable difference between the northern and southern Kingsguard attire was coverage. Cairis had straps and panels of leather armor across his chest and back, but it was still bare skin everywhere else, showing off his exemplary tan, muscular frame. His physique was a close second, only to Varro—but I *was* biased.

A brief flashback of Trace's body came to the forefront of my mind. I had easily suppressed such memories since his betrayal, but there they were. Trace's pale skin, a stark contrast to Varro and Cairis'. He, too, was all muscle, but he was lean where they were bulky. His slender body allowed for the leathers to hug every dip and curve perfectly like a second skin, whereas Cairis always looked like he might burst through his clothing at the seams. I inhaled deeply, trying to push the memories of his body far from my mind.

Varro's attire was something more akin to a well-traveled wanderer: worn-out, brown trousers, and an assortment of lightweight crème-colored shirts. The only unique item was the silver band that he was to wear around his bicep, a clear indication that he was a member of a shipbuilder's clan, similar to the northern guilds. The armband was a marker of who worked for whom in the shipyards, and designated each individual back to its group's leader. Idris didn't have to say it, but I'm absolutely certain there had been Sea Fae who'd met an untimely death off the coast of Nasallus for us to acquire such a band.

As we continued to pack our things, my nerves began to set in as I realized I would need to leave behind anything from my past: the bracelet from my sister, the small handful of books I'd brought with me from home, the notes and sketch from Trace—even my dark wielding journal. These items would be safe inside of Basdie, but there was a looming notion that I may never see them again if we did not succeed in our mission. I packed them all away into a bag, committing the nostalgia of each item to memory and reasoning that, if I didn't return, they'd be easily disposed of that way.

My journal remained safely tucked away with the others in the room that no one other than another Dark Wielder could access. My story, my *truth*, was unfinished, but I'd recorded what I could before leaving it behind.

Most importantly, we each needed to find ways to transport our moonstones with us and carry them undetected on our person. They were small, but this wasn't easily managed for those of us who were given roles with so little clothing involved. I wondered to myself where Gia had hidden hers, particularly when she was engaged in any seductive activities.

Before leaving, it became obvious that I wasn't going to depart the premises without demonstrating my latest capabilities to Idris. Saryn pored over the details of my progress with him and Theory. My mentors were visibly impressed, but Idris, on the other hand, didn't show the slightest sign of appreciation. Instead, I was met with glances of skepticism. It was unmotivating, to say the least. Idris was very old and very powerful; I shouldn't have been bothered by the fact that he was unimpressed. But something in his demeanor made me wonder if there was a hint of jealousy there. Did he covet the idea of being a Dark Wielder? If he knew the possibility of it decaying the mind, I wonder if he would envy it so deeply?

With so few remaining hours at Basdie, I expected we'd have increased our training and discussed detailed plans, but instead, we mostly just lounged about the common room, trying to do normal things that would distract us from what lay ahead. I played one last game of Bones and Stones with Nori, and now that I could see the air, it was too tempting not to pay her back for all those times she had cheated. This resulted in tie after tie, until she realized I'd discovered her secret and matched it with a deception of my own. She smiled at me knowingly, packing the small pieces into a pouch one last time. Instead of taking them with her, she placed them on the shelf near the books, perhaps for some unfortunate, future member of the Imperi to find.

On our final night, Varro and I met privately in the healing pools. The tension of every unspoken word was palpable. If I let my mental shields down, he'd have been bombarded with questions, many of which I had no answers to. Should we have told our mentors about us? Should I have confided in Saryn about the Drift? Are we making a huge mistake in not sealing the bond now, or would that be an even graver mistake? How was I ever going to explain any of this to Trace? Did I owe him that?

Varro could see I was lost in a well of thoughts, moving behind me and wrapping his strong arms around me like a protective cage. I sank into the feeling of safety, not knowing when I'd feel that again. He rested his chin atop my head, and the heat of his body radiated more warmth than even the waters. I lolled my head back into the crook of his neck, and he gently kissed the tip of my ear. A small shiver ran down the back of it, and though there wasn't any pain, it was still a reminder of the scars that resided there.

"Do you think we should?" I said just above a whisper, nerves already spreading goosebumps over my skin.

Varro tucked my hair behind my shoulder, not needing me to expand further. "Cress, you're not ready. I know this, and I'm okay with it."

I turned abruptly from his grasp to face him, frustrated with myself. "Maybe it doesn't matter if I'm ready or not, maybe this should be about survival, and I'm just being reckless."

"You know I would give myself to you freely if you just wanted a chance to avoid the Drift, but I know your heart. I know you don't want that to force your decision." And though he didn't say it, I knew he didn't want that either, that he wanted me to *choose* him—not out of fear, but out of a want, a need, a desire to.

He said the words so calmly and confidently, like he had thought it over many times and come to a clear conclusion…unlike me. Every time I wrestled with these thoughts, I found myself making a different choice. I knew he was my mate. I was grateful for our connection and his unwavering support, even going so far as to lay down his life for me. But this had been given no time to bloom. The way Gia spoke about her mate, there was a deep devotion…there was love.

I had learned my lesson the hard way, to not confuse lust and limerence with love ever again. Whether the Gods conspired to bring us together, or if it was just mere chance, one thing was certain: I was his Moirai and he was my mate. The depth of those words certainly implied love, though neither of us dared speak it by name.

It felt like home when I was in his arms. In a world where I would now forever be a stranger, severed from my family ties, taken from my home to be a servant of the realm, he was the only one that truly knew me. We were supposed to have forever to get to know one another, to explore each other, to share what made up our very souls. But life in the Imperi felt like a matchstick, ignited with friction and then burning furiously until one could no longer hold on. Our lives, normally so long, felt unbelievably short in service to the king. Despite my efforts to keep them at bay, a tangle of doubts and fears crept into my mind.

What if we were separated by death? Could either of us ever feel whole again? What if our souls were blackened by the choices forced upon us in Artume? Would the weight of those trespasses fracture the bond between us?

If, Gods willing, we survived the mission, what sort of life would remain for those commanded to serve the realm forevermore? Could we ever truly be at peace when every approaching hoofbeat or unkindness of ravens could harken the call to the king's service once again?

Saryn and Theory were called back years later to serve as mentors, but we didn't know what they had endured or the lives they'd led before. They never shared a single intimate detail of their pasts with us. Were they both living separate, alone and isolated from creating any identity for themselves? Were they settling for brief dalliances with strangers to feel some semblance of normalcy? Perhaps the king had sent them off on smaller, solitary missions.

A long life that constantly felt short, filled with the threat of endless unknowns. How could love survive that? How could Varro and I endure? Maybe we'd already committed ourselves, simply by entertaining our feelings, and there was no turning back. My mind continued to race out of control, yet he just waited through all the silence and unspoken words. The Gods had truly created a mate with immeasurable patience just for me. That's when I asked him the question I'd been wanting to all along.

"Do you promise you will always be my fated? No matter what happens in Artume or elsewhere, no matter what we're forced to do to survive…will you be there at the end?"

When I finally said the words aloud, I realized I was also asking myself the same thing. My parents and Versa were taken from me, and Trace had made his choice, but what I feared now was convincing myself we could survive anything only to have the other leave. A flash of what Gia had done to her mate came to mind. Loss and heartbreak, trials and tribulations. These could be navigated, perhaps overcome. But the severing of a bond? The anguish was unimaginable.

The loss of a bond through death had to be different. Still painful, yet there must be a peace in knowing your other half was at rest, no longer in pain or suffering. That the bond was still intact, just waiting until the Gods allowed two pieces of a whole to meet again in the afterlife.

But to suffer a life of unbearable grief was not something I could choose. I needed to know we were strong enough to prevail, or death take us both!

Varro's deep, warm voice broke through the silence created by my thoughts. "I will only be parted from you in death. I've known that for some time. I would have never told you that I believed you to be my mate unless I had accepted the full meaning of our circumstances." He reached for my arm, gripping it gently to pull me closer before taking my hand in his. "It's why my one wish for you would be freedom from all of this. Our journey to one another was an unconventional and unfortunate beginning, but I am not so naïve as to believe our journey to stay together will be easy. Fate simply won't be enough for us, Cress. We will have to fight the odds—perhaps forever—to choose this life. That is why I will wait. You must choose it for yourself, Cress, because our great love is a duel with destiny…not a dance."

I could feel tears pricking at my lashes, hearing the conviction in his words; it made me want to say those three simple words—and yet, I couldn't. I searched for the words, but still found only hesitation. I was well aware I was being a coward. But the look in Gia's eyes as she had stared out at the sunset, then turned to face me…I'd never seen anything more broken in my entire life than what I saw there. In an attempt to break free from the undertow of my fear, I extinguished the only flames lighting the room and threw myself into Varro's arms, our lips crashing together as we were enveloped in darkness.

I wrapped my legs around his torso, like I so often did, and he submerged us farther under the water. Our hands moved fervently and recklessly across one another's bodies, desperate to seize the moment. Before our skin became tainted by the touch of others, or marred with scars from missions ahead. Not just in Artume, but on all paths the king would have us follow.

Our bodies were uncorrupted, our intentions true, but soon we would be thrust upon a narrow road with consequences at every turn. Our adversaries would darken the way and prey upon our insecurities and doubts. But we would not let them. The fires in our hearts would at once be both a beacon to one another and a devastating inferno, reducing any who came between us to ash.

In between rough kisses and the writhing of our wet bodies, I mouthed the words of my promise to him.

"Tonight, make me forget tomorrow. And one day, when I come to you seeking to seal our bond, know that it will be without reservation.

I would give my heart fully and with conviction, with you its constant guardian."

In the dark, with our cheeks pressed against each other, I felt a smile curl across Varro's chiseled jaw. As he sank our bodies even deeper into the water, he unfurled his wings—and suddenly, we were surrounded by glowing hues of aqua and green. His stunning display lighting up our intertwined bodies.

"Let me see every angle of your climax, Moirai, so these memories can serve me until the day you give yourself to me in every way. I will wait."

At that, I was completely undone. He spent the next hour singing his Siren Song in and out of the depths of each and every sensation he wrought from my body. Our bond vibrated so strongly, I could imagine ripples pulsating across the top of the water from the intensity. The fact that I didn't give myself to him right then and there was a miracle of Godslike proportions. Varro meticulously covered my body in kisses, as if trying to claim the entirety of my skin for his own. And I *was* his. Entirely. I just had to overcome my fear of sealing the bond that was holding me back from showing him my true devotion. But I knew where he stood, there wasn't a doubt within me that Varro was mine as well.

CHAPTER 12

The journey from Basdie to the Artume border would take us five days. Our small caravan was meant to look inconspicuous, for thieves occasionally patrolled the main roads searching for easy targets. Despite our carriages being well-armed, they did not appear well-maintained. Unfortunately, the drab appearance also meant a less-than-smooth ride. Unlike the carriages of the High households I was once accustomed to, these were outfitted with large, thin wheels that seemed to magnify every rock and rut. There were moments I almost told my companions I'd rather just fly the whole way if it meant avoiding the nausea. But a group of Fae flying overhead was certain to draw unwanted attention, since the everyday Cambrian would never do such a thing.

Each night we'd make camp deep in the woods, setting up portable, lightweight tents and cooking meals over an open fire. Idris travelled ahead of us, while Saryn and Theory remained with the group. The experience travelling south was strange. Not only because we had finally departed the mountains, but also because the last time we were transported, we had been asleep thanks to some elixir Idris had provided. There was a strangeness to watching the lands of Cambria recede through the carriage window, knowing it was home, longing to take in the scent and scene of it, but also knowing it was goodbye. Hopefully only for the time being. The farther south we went, the signs of winter began to disappear. If I were honest, I was grateful to be rid of the frigid chill that made my bones feel like they were chattering.

While making camp, Varro and I maintained our façade. When it was just us in the carriage, or even when we cramped ourselves in with Nori and Cairis, they did not make an ordeal of our handholding or miniscule flirtations. They knew it was all coming to an end soon, and we knew it too. We cherished the small gestures as long as we could.

Riding with Saryn, however, was exhausting. His constant prying about the Dark Wielders that came before me was never-ending. Part of me felt that if the tomes were bound by blood magic to only be read by someone who shared the power, didn't that imply the knowledge wasn't meant for others? But he was not going to relent, and I wasn't about to tell him anything about the Drift, so I shared innocent tidbits here and there just to get him to shut up.

Though a Dark Wielder had existed amongst his Order's class, it became abundantly clear that she did not speak of it often or share details with him. I wondered if it was frustration or intrigue that motivated Saryn's interrogation of me. Perhaps she had shared truths with other members of his class, like Theory, and did not include him for some reason.

Theory never spoke of their Order, either. It could be reasonably assumed that, since they did not return to Basdie to train us, they were all dead. The possibility of some of them being alive but deeply embedded on other missions sat at the tip of my tongue nearly every meal together, but I never got the courage to ask. Theory and Saryn were so plainly private people that I feared they'd react unfavorably to my prying. Varro and the others knew I had these questions—we all did. We'd speak of them quietly during the long, bumpy ride to our next destination. We joked about flipping a Lorc to see who'd be delegated to ask—well, anything really, about the former members of the Imperi. But each time we settled into a silent embrace of unknowing. That silence was the black cloud of our own realization that the Order of the Imperi meant death. Death was the only way out.

On the last evening before our arrival at the border, Saryn explained that he would be setting up a safehouse just outside of the Nasallus castle walls, within the bustling village that surrounded it. The word "safehouse" sent me down a spiral of memories from the treehouse with Trace, and everything we'd done there in the days leading up to us both being delivered to the Offering. I swallowed the anxious feeling in my throat and tried to listen intently to Saryn, but he had created an unwelcome distraction I couldn't seem to escape from.

He noted that once we had set our sights on the surroundings of our safehouse, we might be able to portal to and from, as long as we were careful not to get caught. If we could not portal, we'd need to find a way to make passage there undetected. In some cases, like Gia's, it would be more difficult. Playing the role of a noble lady meant she couldn't be seen wandering about the poorest parts of Nasallus without an escort.

Varro would need to make sure he did not cause trouble amongst his clan and bring about any unwanted attention. Trace would likely face the most difficulty getting to us, and suffer the worst consequences if he were to be caught wandering far from his militia's encampment. If there was one group of people they'd be watching for treachery from, it would be those in armed positions. The purpose Silas' Hand had bestowed upon Trace's group meant they were impersonators; separated from the conventional military. If too many untrusted individuals found out the attacks on Artume were staged by the king himself, a coup might unfold.

We were instructed to deliver regular reports to the safehouse and, if we were able, hold small meetings as a team to plan our next steps. Though the idea of getting to and from the safehouse without getting caught sounded intimidating, it also brought me relief to know there would be an opportunity to see Varro and the others. Saryn was in charge of relaying information to Theory, whose clandestine maneuvering between borders allowed her to pass along reports from Idris and, effectively, the king himself.

On the last night of our journey, Varro and I both pretended to head in opposite directions of the forest for some privacy to relieve ourselves, but our true intention was to walk in a circle until we were reunited. When we finally arrived, our handheld lanterns created pillars of light amongst hundreds of smaller glows flitting about. Fireflies swirled and swarmed, illuminating the winding branches and leaves of the forest surrounding us. Their beauty was arresting, not only for the wondrous acrobatics their tiny, frail bodies performed, but also a distinct reminder that this lush landscape would soon be left in our wake. Creatures as gentle and fair as the firefly could not survive the harsh climate of Artume. Slowly, deftly, I waved my arms through them, their magical glows spiraling with my movements.

Varro approached me and hung his lantern on a nearby sturdy tree branch, while mine sat on the mossy forest floor. I inhaled deeply, mesmerized by the complex aromas of our setting. We were in the Riverlands now, just a few days ride to the west from House Blackthorn. The possibility and temptation prickled at my eyelids as I fought back thoughts of my family being so nearby. Varro's bond was ever still, just hovering beneath mine. Steady and gentle. He knew the grief of the moment I was processing, and he let me have this silence. His steps toward me were quiet and even until I could feel the heat of his broad chest radiating against mine. He slowly lowered his forehead to mine, resting it there, and as our eyes closed, he intertwined our fingertips.

We breathed each other in, committing our scents to memory.

Varro's was complex. It ebbed and flowed like waves, carrying with it a faint mixture of elements hiding amongst the more powerful features wrapped up in a hint of the sea mist. If I closed my eyes and relaxed, I could imagine the feel of the breeze, the sand between my toes, the whipping of the ship's sail catching the wind and the creaking of the wooden frame as it bobbed against the Endless Tide toward its next destination. There was a slight hint of lemon intertwined with the sea breeze, as golden and bright as he was.

"We're apart only moments and you've adopted a flock of fireflies," he said.

"Sparkle."

"Hm?"

"A sparkle of fireflies. Not a flock."

"Well, you're native to the Riverlands. I am but a humble servant of the sea."

"Only the sea?" I said coyly.

He drew me closer. "And uniquely gifted Fae," he added.

"That's better," I teased, my mood turning from playful to sincere. His smile faded as he met my gaze; we searched each other's eyes for what to say next. I had not yet found the courage to seal the bond, or to say the words my heart wanted to but, in the morning, there would be no time for words such as these.

"Just know that I do…Varro, I really do," I whispered, so close that my lips brushed against his between each syllable.

"As do I," he said back without a moment's hesitation.

He pressed his lips to mine, enveloping us both in a long kiss that needed to last us a lifetime—because it might be our last.

CHAPTER 16

In the morning, we were split up. Varro and Cairis would be transported separately, not only due to their size, but also their destinations. Nori and I were small enough to be paired together and were both headed toward the castle. Idris prepared trade wagons to be fitted with small hidden compartments beneath the floor boards of the main storage. We would have to lay flat for the entire journey, while remaining perfectly quiet and still, regardless of the bumps and jolts we'd feel along the way. There would be checkpoints requiring proof of official trade alliances for us to be allowed across the border. Along with official paperwork, random inspections were often carried out to deter smugglers and tariff-crooks. There were many wagons in our caravan, but which ones would be searched was anybody's guess, so all had to be ready.

Once nestled in our secret holding places, there would be no opportunity to make unscheduled stops of any kind. With this in mind, many of us did not drink or eat much at the morning campfire. We took special care to relieve ourselves, knowing the journey would be many hours and that lying along the thin chassis of the wagon would be a horrible combination for one's full bladder.

I watched on with nervousness as they loaded Cairis and Varro into their separate wagons, placing wood planks over the full length of their bodies. You'd never know they were there, not unless they made a noise to give away their locations. Nori and I moved quickly and anxiously into position. I gasped for air like it might be my last breath as the rays of light from above disappeared. I grabbed Nori's hand tightly in mine, squeezing it for both luck and to fight back my anxiety. Although we would not be able to converse verbally, I was grateful to have a partner for the trek.

We devised a crude form of communication by blinking our eyes and lowering our mental shields briefly to share our thoughts. I could tell we each struggled to mask our own fears, and that these short exchanges brought us both some comfort.

The activity was tedious and reminded me of the idea that, someday, if Varro and I sealed the bond, we would also share *Fideli Cœur*, and that mind-melding connection would allow us to speak freely to one another without words. I knew, being stationed in vastly different parts of Artume, there was a high likelihood that the sensation of our bond would be stretched so thin that I might not even be able to detect him. But with mind-melding, the proximity of the mated mattered not.

As the hours passed by, the temperature beneath the floorboards became stifling—an indication we were nearing the border. Nori and I closed our eyes, squeezed hands, and worked to keep our breathing in sync, creating a rhythm of deep inhales and exhales as we attempted to fight off the nerves that preyed upon us.

When the wagon came to an abrupt halt, we heard the hooves and nickering of the horses as they shifted impatiently. This had to be the official trade corridor. The time had arrived for our first major risk of discovery. Though we each felt powerful and strong with a number of physical and magical abilities in our arsenals, this was not about destroying everyone and everything in sight. If we did that, we would sound alarm bells that might close the trade corridor entirely and force us to entertain riskier or more time-consuming alternatives. Each of us was equally committed to getting our aid to Trace and Gia as soon as possible.

We heard the likes of Artumian Kingsguards shuffling about outside as they walked along the caravan, inspecting for any signs of misconduct or discrepancy in the shipments. We heard the inspectors chatter, but from where we hid, we had no way of knowing which wagons concealed Cairis or Varro. All we could do was stay silent and still while praying to the Gods that they would not be discovered. Never in my life had I wanted to be blanketed in Varro's Siren Song more than right then. With his gift, he could calm my very essence to the bone, perhaps even lull Nori and I into a deep slumber. I could hear two or three guards conversing nearby, then a boisterous laugh. Nearer to us, another guard cleared his throat, startling me. Were we next?

The deep, guttural yells in the distance resulted in the slow creaking of the wagon wheels as they began to turn once more. We had done it; we'd managed to get the seal of approval without detailed inspection of our own wagon. The movement of the caravan caused thick dust to bluster through the cracks in the wood. The second it began to swirl in the small, tight space we were hiding in, I could feel the heave of Nori's chest. Just as she was about to let out a giant sneeze, I slid my hand across her mouth and nose as fast as I could to muffle it.

The wagon's forward motion slowed momentarily.

Oh Gods, had they heard her?

Was this it, the moment we unraveled into chaos?

Nori and I lay there motionless, my hand still covering her face and my palm wet with her spittle. We both kept our mental shields firmly in place, waiting to see if the wheels would begin to turn again. After the momentary pause, the wheels began to shift and the caravan continued ahead. Once we resumed a steady pace, I slowly pulled my hand from Nori's face and wiped it on my pant leg. She lolled her head to the side, looking at me with tears welling and thoughts of deep apology practically screaming at me. I grabbed her hand and squeezed it again, letting her know we were going to be okay. The unpredictable jostling of rocks and ruts beneath the wagon suddenly gave way to hollow clacking and the roar of rushing water. Normally, water brought me comfort, but this time, the dreadful feeling of passing over the Ledor River reminded me we had officially left the northern kingdom.

Within the hour, the underside of the wagon was sweltering hot; my skin was moist all over with sweat and my hair was beginning to feel sticky against the back of my neck. I was already thinking of intricate braided hairstyles to wear in order to keep my hair from becoming a bird's nest. What I wouldn't give for a nice refreshing dip in the sea, or an ice-cold bath. Thoughts of water were beginning to race through my mind, which was a bad idea for multiple reasons. By then I had to pee, regardless of how little water I'd had before the start of the journey. But I was so Gods-damned thirsty all I could think about was indulging in an entire jug of water, or any liquid for that matter. I knew Nori felt the same as I watched droplets of sweat roll down her forehead and into her matted red hair.

In an attempt to distract myself from the irritations of the journey, I let my mind wander with thoughts of seeing Gia again and how much we needed to catch up on. Primarily her letter and its cryptic warning, followed by everything that had transpired with her and Trace while we were apart. It felt like so much time and yet none at all since I had bid her farewell at Basdie.

Memories came rushing back of me anxiously jumping from her

carriage in realization that the strange sensations I'd been feeling meant I had a mate, and my unwillingness to reconcile with it. Even as my hurried footsteps descended into the depths of Basdie, I could not escape, could not outrun the truth. Anger, fear, and embarrassment all exploding out of me in a literal shaking of the mountain. And later, when I confronted Varro, demanding an answer to the question I already knew, I had searched his face for hesitation, doubt. There was nothing but unwavering assurance, and perhaps a hint of sorrow for the pleading tears that shimmered on my lashes. *The Gods are cruel.* His words echoed through me. I squeezed my eyes shut tightly and sent out a prayer to those same Gods. Protect us. Protect him. Please.

When the carriage stopped, I froze, holding my breath for fear that we were at some sort of secondary inspection point. Then I heard the familiar voice of Saryn. As he lifted the plank of wood from above our heads, sand and dust spilled over us, and I squinted to refrain from getting any in my eyes. Every part of my body ached from lying flat all those hours. Our poor muscles had taken the brunt of every bump and turn. When we finally crawled our way out of the hidden compartment, I felt the dirt everywhere, coating our skin like a fine powder. I felt it in my ears, my nose, and every crevice of my body.

When I exited the carriage, the bright sun felt as if it was scorching my vision, forcing me to shield my eyes and wait for the splotches of green and orange to subside. Soon, the sun became less harsh and my surroundings came into view, but I could not remember ever encountering such abrasive daylight. In Cambria, daylight was always filtered and cut into shadows, whether by canopies of trees or mountains. Even on the open sea, where the sun's rays came not only from above but also the surface of the water, I couldn't recall such an adverse glare. Nori stepped down beside me, and I could hear her bones cracking as she crooked her neck to the left and right. What I wouldn't give for a fucking bath!

Nori and I looked terrible, there was no way we could arrive at the castle looking like this. We'd need the chance to ready ourselves, or we'd be turned away at the gates, effectively ending our mission before it had even begun.

When I looked up, I saw that what lay before us was a modestly-sized, unassuming house of bright orange clay with very few windows. The roof appeared to be made out of straw thatching matted together with even more clay. I looked around, assessing my surroundings. The house was a short distance from the next one, but the sprawling arrangement of houses and huts, though varied in size, were constructed of the same material, interconnected by narrow corridors and what could generously be called streets. There was sand everywhere, mostly colored a burnt orange. The air was dry and there was the occasional pungent odor of livestock. Saryn continued to unload our packs from the carriage and moved them in the front door one by one. There wasn't a doubt in my mind this was the safehouse, which meant we had successfully accomplished step one.

I looked around, hoping to see Varro, but he and Cairis had already departed to their next destinations. I longed for him—to see his face and seek comfort in the crystal-blue depths of his eyes. And…to possibly ask for a back massage, I thought to myself humorously.

Artume's landscape was stark and utterly foreign. Saryn looked up and down the streets skeptically, as if taking note of any onlookers who might suspect this was anything more than a delivery of goods to trade. He ushered us both inside quickly. The house was dimly lit and lacking in just about everything. Only Saryn would be staying here, so I doubted he'd lift a finger to put any sort of effort into making it feel like an actual home. In typical Saryn fashion, he began ordering us around.

"Both of you need to bathe and get into your intended attire, then we will transport you to your stations."

"Gods, can we get a drink of water first? Perhaps, even relieve ourselves?" I muttered in irritation.

"Do what you must, Cress, stop asking for permission."

Saryn began to mill about the room unpacking his own things while I reached for the pitcher to pour Nori and I large glasses of water. We both chugged them quickly but not carefully, the water spilling down our chins and out of the corners of our mouths as we satisfied our thirst. Nori emphatically held her cup out for a refill, and we laughed for a moment at the absurdity of looking wholly unrefined. Our High Fae etiquette was now a distant memory.

Once satiated, Nori made her way to the wash room. When she was finished, she carried out her disgusting bathwater, murky and brown from the dirt and dust that had previously coated her tiny body. I could finally see the vibrancy of her hair returning as it fell in thick wet locks to her cheeks. Now, in her garment, she truly looked the part.

I refilled the tub with clean water and began to work on myself. Washing away all the silt and grime felt luxurious, and I began to dread that our time in Artume meant my skin might always feel like it was covered in a fine powder. Another part of me thought perhaps it would help me to see and bend the air more easily should I need to exercise my abilities.

I wrung out my hair as best I could and patted it dry with some thick cloth. Then I braided it into a crown around my head, keeping it off my skin entirely. I left a few strands down and loosened my braids enough to hide the scar behind my ear. I didn't want to draw attention to it, but I also knew anyone wearing their hair down in weather like this would stand out. I put on my uniform—if it could be classified as such. It felt more akin to lingerie, only covering my most salacious areas. I left the dirty clothes we arrived in on the floor in a pile. I hoped Saryn would wash them for us before we returned, but knowing him, they would probably never be seen again.

When I came back into the living area, Nori was seated at the large table in the middle of the room, nibbling on an orange. She turned to face me and handed one over. Couldn't it have been any other fruit? Flashbacks of Varro sparked through my mind. Him squeezing the citrus all across my flesh then lapping it up. His sensuous reminder of how he devoured me… I began to peel the orange, trying to put him from my mind and focus on the task ahead. If I let these distractions consume me, I'd miss him even more and we hadn't yet been parted a day.

"Nori, you will wait here while I handle delivering Cress. Do not leave, do not stand in the street, do not even look out the windows. Do you understand?"

"Yes," Nori said in quiet subservience.

"Before you leave, you're each going to look out the back door and the front window. You will then walk slowly through the first floor of this house. Take in your surroundings and make note of the most minute details. Commit them to your memory. You must be able to remember this place clearly, no matter how new or strange this environment is to you. If you are to make your way back here using the portal stones, you must know this place like the back of your hand."

The ask seemed simple, yet it was loaded with pressure. Using our moonstones to return to the safehouse would be the fastest way back here, but would I be able to do it? How far would we have to portal; how much energy would we need to expel to do it successfully? Nori and I had been here less than an hour. The place was so plain that there were hardly any notable details to remember. I began to follow Nori at a measured pace around the first floor of the small building. I committed the shape and approximate size of the living room and kitchen to memory. I noted the dusty round rug laying in front of the hearth, covered with intricate patterns unlike any we displayed on northern tapestries. I breathed in deeply, noting how the fragrant remnants of pipe smoke clung to the few pieces of furniture, likely from its previous tenant.

The floor did not creak or groan. The wooden beams were embedded deep into the dry mud below them. There were no pictures hanging about the space, only the endless texture of clay walls; a monotonous sea of indistinguishable swirls.

Nori and I stood side by side in silence, staring out the back door of the modest home. There was an abandoned alleyway with what appeared to be a few run-down homes or shops, but their exteriors were scorched black, having clearly suffered some sort of irreparable and catastrophic fire. There were broken clay pots strewn about the street, and nothing but silence—not a person in sight.

With the lack of surrounding commerce, this dwelling was probably acquired at a sizeable discount and provided suitable refuge from onlookers or prying eyes. The implications had Imperi written all over it. I had to remind myself that nothing was ever coincidence…not when we were involved. Saryn and Theory could only hope that one day we all aspired to that level of planning and espionage. Killing a ship worker for their silver arm band, burning down a neighborhood for privacy—these were all calculated and meticulous decisions by a ruthless Order that had existed far longer than I could imagine.

I breathed in the scent of the alleyway through the window, committing to memory the smell of ash and burnt thatch when I heard Saryn say, "It's time."

The ride to Nasallus wasn't as I'd hoped. I did not get to sit up front with Saryn, which would have given me not only a view of the city surrounding the castle, but have also allowed me to take in more of my new—hopefully—temporary home. Instead, I was forced to stay concealed in the wagon, sitting with my trunk and doing my best to keep as clean as possible. With each bump along the way, it was as if my muscles remembered the exact feeling of being hidden below it, and I felt them tense and spasm with each unpleasant shift. I kept my breathing slow and steady, forcing myself to fortify my mental shields. *Soon you will be reunited with Gia*, I kept telling myself.

When we arrived outside the castle gates, Saryn looked at me with his one good eye, nodding at me to proceed with the plan. No farewells or well-wishes, just silence and a gesture. I already knew he'd be checking for my mental shields, and I wasn't going to fail that test. When I stepped up to a small side gate, I was greeted by a Kingsguard in a uniform just like the one Cairis would be wearing.

"What's your business here?" demanded a gruff voice.

I reached into my bag, steadying my hand for a moment to settle the shaking, and pulled out a piece of parchment. I handed it to him confidently, ignoring his gaze that had obviously fallen to the exposed curves of my flesh. *Gods,* I thought to myself, *this is what it's going to be like all of the time, isn't it?* The Kingsguard unfolded it and scanned the note informing him I had been summoned as a replacement for Gia's lady's maid who had fallen ill and taken to an untimely death. He looked it over a moment longer, and I feared his scrutiny might lead to the realization of its forgery, but he folded the note and handed it back to me, then began to unload my belongings from the carriage. Saryn sat still and quiet, as if waiting to go about his day as a driver and on to the next errand or delivery.

"All done," the guard yelled up to Saryn, and with that, the horse began to trot away. Now I was alone…alone in Artume and on a mission.

The husky male picked up my things and led the way through the gate and into a large courtyard of the castle—one of many I suspected. Inside the walls of the castle was a much different experience than that of the outside. There were ornate stone ponds and fountains at every turn. It was full of lush, tropical vegetation. Tall palm and fruit trees, spiky plants, and exotic flowers were littered about the place. So many shades of green. The walkways were a light beige stone and absent of sand, except for the bits I dragged in on my sandaled feet. It was a stark contrast from what I observed near the safehouse. It seemed one side of this city consisted of scavengers, survivors, and pilgrims trying to make ends meet, while the other half reveled in the trimmings of luxury and excess. Did the people of Artume know what was on the other side? Would they have reduced it to rubble if they did?

Having no answers to these questions, my mind sought perspective and wondered if this was how the commonfolk in Cambria felt about the High families. Our lands were sown just before the season of renewal, tended and nursed to maturity, then plowed and harvested with great effort to maximize yield. Our markets teemed with an array of artisans from the brawny metal workers to the delicate weavers, stitching their linens and tapestries with equal measures of skill and grace. Cambria presented its inhabitants with the occasional drought or disease, but the lands—like its people—were resilient, and those who persevered, prospered. Perhaps the Honored Fae, like myself, held more prestige with our sigils and banners and seasonal balls, but our coffers were filled in much the same way as every commoner—through tenacity and toil. In what little I knew of life in Artume, hope seemed as scarce as their resources. The land was barren and desolate. They were surviving, but there was little opportunity to thrive.

While we walked the short distance toward the castle doorway, I kept my face straight and emotionless. I did not want to appear astonished or perplexed by my surroundings. My job was to keep my head down, be subservient, and not ask questions. I was a low-born now, lucky to be in service to the Crown and to have the opportunity to send my wages back to my loved ones. I continued to repeat the story of my false background in my head, focusing on becoming the character that I would play until we succeeded in our mission. I steeled my mental shields. One thing our training taught us was to carefully assess our surroundings and consider all elements that could be manipulated as an instrument in our survival. I considered every ornamental fountain, every flame-lit torch in that courtyard.

Once inside, the guard approached an older female, busty and full-figured in a gown similar to mine, but in a deeper, richer shade of blue.

"Who is this?" she questioned him with some authority. Her thick accent made my ears perk as she made familiar words seem somehow foreign.

The guard set down my trunk and looked at me, waiting for me to present my summons paperwork. I did not bow to her, but I kept my head and gaze low as a sign of respect while handing her the same parchment I'd provided him. She, too, scanned the paperwork, eyed me up and down, and then continued to read. After a moment that felt like an eternity, she said, "Cress Talok, is it? Here to serve Lady Gianna?"

It sounded like a question, but was it? I nodded, unsure if I was permitted to speak. She then inclined her head at the guard and escorted us to what I presumed would be Gia's chambers. It was strange hearing my fake name aloud for the first time. Blackthorn was not a surname used in the southern kingdom, so I had adopted the name Talok which was common of low-born people from the Artumian city of Caano. I also hadn't heard Gia referred to as Gianna since our first day at Basdie. Was she calling herself that while here? Luckily, Artume's diversity of heritage and dialects meant there was no need for me to speak with a particular accent. My dialect sounded like that of the Kingsguard and I breathed a momentary sigh of relief, knowing my acting skills only had to go so far.

She motioned us to follow her, the Kingsguard pacing slowly behind with my belongings. She offered her introduction while walking forward, making no attempt at eye contact. Her demeanor made it all the more difficult to tell if she was a friendly face or someone to fear.

"I am Shira, and I am the matron of ladies' maids that serve His Highness' court while they reside in Nasallus. I have held this position for many years..." She paused, as if to correct herself from accidentally exposing that she once served King Baelin.

I made a mental note, as it was likely that anyone serving the previous regime only remained employed as an act of survival.

She continued, "My servants are held to the highest standards, and if I see or hear otherwise, I will not hesitate to replace you with haste."

She proceeded with a speech she had clearly repeated more than once as we made our way up staircase after staircase; if I hadn't been so well-conditioned from training, I might have been out of breath. That's when I realized I probably *should* be out of breath, and began to let out little huffs to create a bit of a charade.

"Our dear king, Silas, appreciates the finer things life has to offer, and while you will find that many revelries occur here, you'd best keep in mind that you are here to serve and not be seen. You will follow all the standard etiquette of the training you received that made you eligible for such a position here at Nasallus. We only accept the very best."

Shira rattled off a list of instructions and rules that I took note of while continuing to assess my surroundings during her pauses. I tried to prepare a map of the castle in my head, and would continue to do so over the next few days.

When we reached the fourth floor, she turned to lead us down a long, carpeted hallway rather than continuing up to the fifth level. As we rounded a stone column, a very tall male walked briskly toward us. He was wearing all black, except for his accessories. Layers of fabric draped over his lanky frame. His gaunt appearance would have convinced me he was another servant if it weren't for the fact that he was wearing a rather large, ornate gold collar around his neck, embedded with expensive stones, the likes of which surely cost a fortune. No, he wasn't a servant at all, but perhaps a noble. I cast my eyes down and continued to pace closely behind Shira hoping I could just get to Gia before encountering anyone else, but that would have been too easy.

The male stopped before us and Shira immediately went into a low bow and I followed suit without hesitation. The Kingsguard bowed his head and held his hand over his chest, above his heart, the salute of someone who is in position to guard and serve with their life.

Out of the corner of my eye, I could see a disturbing, unnatural pallor to the newcomer's skin, along with unusually spindly fingers. Though the Fae aged slowly, the hands revealed the passage of time to the keen observer. His wrinkled hands showed deep, striated grooves, indicating he was *very* old. His skin was so pale I might have questioned whether or not he was ill. He did not have signs of the sun-kissed, natural tan that most citizens here presented.

In a rough, gravelly voice, the noble stranger asked Shira, "And who might this be?"

She stood from her bow now that she'd been addressed directly, and I mimicked her actions. Glancing up but keeping my head low, I tried to take in more of his features, the most alarming of which were his two different-colored eyes.

Shira replied confidently, but there was a hint of fear threaded through her response that one would expect from anyone who'd survived the Silent Eve.

"This is Cress Talok of Caano. She has just arrived to serve Lady Gianna."

He didn't even glance in my direction. "Ah, yes…Silas' favorite plaything. And what of her former maid? Or am I to believe Lady Gianna requires two servants to tend to her whims?" He lingered on each syllable of her name mockingly.

Hearing them speak so openly of the king's affections for Gia could only mean she had been extremely successful in her efforts thus far.

"She succumbed to the sickness. We feared she was quite contagious, so we had her removed immediately before a spread could occur." Shira's words were brittle, as if they might crumble from any rebuttal. Frantically, she continued, "She was so young; it was most unfortunate. We are glad to have secured a quick replacement; King Silas would never stand for Lady Gianna to be without." She wrung her hands in contrition, waiting for any sort of indication of the formidable figure's acceptance.

The male grabbed my chin abruptly, squeezing it tightly between his cold fingers, pain spreading across my face as the sharp edges of his nails dug deeper into my skin. He tilted my head up to face him and turned it from side to side, inspecting me as if to give his approval. I was worried that he might have seen through my glamour. I fought my instincts to react defensively. Being grabbed in such a manner had my muscles tightening and ready to fight, but I resisted the inclination and forced my body to slacken and cower in fear. He dropped his hand from my face and finally made an introduction.

"I am Zarif, Hand of the King. You will mind your position and serve his court well. We have welcomed many newcomers since the rightful ascension of Silas, and we value loyalty above all else…"

While his words trailed off menacingly, I did my best to penetrate his mind to see if I could find any ill intent. Something about him made my skin crawl, and I learned long before my training at Basdie to heed that warning. His mind was blank and well-fortified, which meant one thing—he had something to hide.

I nodded respectfully and meekly said, "It's my honor to serve King Silas' court, my Lord Hand."

The interaction must have sufficed, as he walked away with no other remarks. I trotted behind Shira, who attempted to hide her trembling fingers by clasping them in front of her. Now I had the confirmation I was seeking—the Hand of the King was someone to fear.

Shira and the guard led me to a giant set of double-doors framed with detailed carvings and patterns, gilded and shimmering. Unlike so many of the designs we saw in Cambria, these were rigid and geometric, with sharp angles. It made me miss the romantic, flowing embellishments in my former home.

She knocked twice and stepped back, awaiting permission to enter. The door opened and another young female in all-blue attire welcomed us into the room. It was giant and luxurious, adorned with fine fabrics and a giant four-poster bed. There were already two servants tidying things and hanging dresses in an armoire. When Gia turned around to face me, I held my breath, concerned the faintest expression of familiarity would betray us. But she did not falter. In fact, she looked right through me as if I was nothing and turned to Shira for an explanation.

"What's this?" she said coldly.

Shira bowed, and I did the same, orienting my body toward Gia as a sign of subservience. "Lady Gianna, this is your new lady's maid, Cress. We have been fortunate to find a replacement so quickly, don't you agree?"

"It's taken days. You're lucky I haven't made any formal complaints," Gia replied, scolding the matron.

Then with a sneer, she pointed at the young brunette standing by her writing desk. "And her, whoever she is, is useless at doing my hair. Thank the Gods I've been graced with such beauty, otherwise the king might have found me unsuitable."

The female before me commanded attention and respect. Her outspoken disdain for the servants portrayed entitlement and callousness, but also her status as someone the king wished to please. I watched as the poor girl shifted back and forth nervously at the reprimand from her lady, my lady…Gia. Gods-damned she was astounding! I knew she would be, but seeing her embody the character of Lady Gianna was a sight to behold.

Shira began to utter an apology when Gia snapped again, "In fact, I am in need of assistance right now if I am to be ready by this evening's party. Let's see if what you've brought me will suffice. The rest of you, leave! You…" she pointed at me, "You can stay. The rest of you, get out. Now!"

The two young ladies scurried away quickly, and as Shira made her exit, Gia said sternly, "If she doesn't suffice, we *will* have words." The matron closed the door behind her, Gia's threat still hovering above us like a storm cloud.

With the two of us finally alone, there was so much to be said. Which Gia I'd be dealing with remained to be seen.

I waited for her to indicate what kind of interaction this would be. The last few minutes were unlike anything I'd ever seen. Gia had become an entirely different person, based on what I'd just witnessed—one that, for a moment, I'd feared. Feared that she might not embrace me warmly after all of this time. There was silence, too long of a pause for comfort, but then she marched toward the door and, after the click of the lock, turned to me and pulled me into a firm and abrupt embrace. My body collapsed into hers with relief. She wasn't Versa, but everything about this hug felt like a homecoming. We clutched each other sincerely with the joy of our reunion and the reassurance that we were both safe. It was the type of hug I'd greeted my father with after long voyages, or the kind Versa and I shared on many occasions, including our final farewell. Tears pricked my lashes as I conjured the images in my head.

"Finally," she whispered, nuzzling her face into the crook of my neck like someone longing to inhale a sense of familiarity and comfort.

"I know," I said, squeezing her tighter. "I'm so glad you're okay. More than okay, it seems."

Gia released me but stayed close, as if putting too much distance between us might mean I'd disappear, like a mirage.

"I thought being a bitch on occasion was amusing at first, but this is exhausting, Cress. You really can't imagine. It feels as if my soul is being firmly corrupted from the inside out."

"I can't even fathom it. But you're so convincing, they practically cower in your presence."

"Yes, well, I've been pushing my status a bit recently."

Gia took my hand and tugged me to the edge of her bed, where we both sat down. The divine texture of velvet sheets beneath my fingertips was yet another reminder of home. There was nothing of the sort at Basdie. It had been many months since I'd encountered a bed this grand. Suddenly, flashes of the ordeal with Nix inundated my mind, threatening to escape the black pit I'd created to trap all the bad memories I'd acquired since the Offering. I placed my hands on my lap to free myself of the distraction.

"I'd say you have the king wrapped around your little finger. When we ran into Zarif, he made no secret of your station with Silas, Lady Gianna…" I said her name with a long drawl.

I heard as much as saw Gia's breath hitch.

"You met Zarif?" she questioned, concern rampant across her stunning features, which were on full display with her hair pulled back in typical Artumian fashion.

"Yes, just before we arrived at your door. I don't have a good feel—"

Gia cut me off, almost in a panic. "He's evil, Cress, in every sense of the word. I had hoped you would remain off his radar as long as possible, but he knows everything and everyone. The only reason he lets me be is because I'm Silas' pet, and whatever pleases the king, pleases Zarif."

She paused and looked to the door, as if it being locked was not enough to protect us. She lowered her voice.

"When I arrived, he did not treat me as kindly as he does now. Avoid him at all costs. He is one of the few individuals here who guards his—"

This time, it was I who cut her off. "His thoughts, I know!" I exclaimed. "He had his shields up, and I'm betting that's not the only ability he is capable of."

Gia shushed me, then lowered her voice. "Yes, he is one of the rare few in Nasallus who keeps up their mental shields," she confirmed. "And I suspect it's not just because he is the Hand of the King. I think it has everything to do with the heinous shit Trace is involved with."

Something about his name on her lips gave me pause. We hadn't talked much about Trace after they departed Basdie. It's not like Varro and I were avoiding it—except, maybe we were. Or perhaps he was just confident that my sentiments toward Trace had been solidified after he left me for dead.

My interest was piqued, though; this was the conversation I had wanted ever since her letter arrived, warning me.

"What has Trace been made to do?" I was intrigued to hear more details after Saryn's vague account. But nothing could have prepared me for what Gia said next.

"He is part of a secret operation tasked with committing atrocities in the local villages while disguised as Northerners. It's creating a stir of false hatred towards Cambria. Even though we would never commit such acts."

"Like the kinds of things we practiced with the Vespers?"

I thought back to all the hours I practiced the art of torture in those tiny rooms at Basdie.

Gia looked at me with deep concern.

"Did you practice leaving heads on pikes with the Vespers, Cress?"

I cringed at her question. I shook my head in silent response.

"They'd all be dead if Trace hadn't found more creative ways to appease the bloodlust of whoever is behind all of this. I'm almost certain it's Zarif."

Setting aside the fact that she was pretty sure Zarif was the mastermind of these war crimes, I couldn't help but prod further, morbid curiosity welling in the pit of my stomach.

"What do you mean 'creative ways'?"

"Trace somehow convinced them to spare the females by only cutting out their tongues, so they may never recount what they've seen or speak ill of their Northern enemies."

I felt my hands begin to sweat at the idea of Trace not only beheading innocent males and putting their heads on pikes, but also separating Gods-knew how many females from their tongues, blood pouring from their mouths alongside muffled, indistinct screams. I could almost taste the blood in my own mouth.

"And the children…"

"No!" I interjected, not wanting to hear anymore—morbid curiosity, or not—my heartbeat now standing on edge at the mention of innocent youths.

Gia ignored me and proceeded anyway. "He has resolved to cut off their fingers…so that they may never grip a sword against the North, nor ever send an arrow into the Cambrian sky."

Every detail from Gia's mouth was more gruesome than the last.

"The beheadings were reserved for the leaders of the villages, but the rest did not fare any better. Trace and the others who partake in this secret regime have been taking one eye from each grown male."

With every word she spoke, I was fighting back a bombardment of images of Trace covered in blood—real blood, not the tattoos that scattered across his pale skin which held the same meaning.

"The Artumians really believe that Cambrian rebels did all of this?"

"Yes," she said. "They've been dressed in Northern attire, leaving behind Cambrian flags coated in the blood of the villagers. No one suspects this is coming from within. How could they?"

Trace must be so tormented by the brutality he's been forced to deliver. I don't think any of us would have been capable of doing what's been required of him. Yet, even in the face of such vicious tasks, he still sought ways to minimize the damage inflicted.

But how can one look at a village full of speechless mothers, maimed children, and blinded fathers, and interpret anything but abject cruelty and torture? I couldn't help but think Trace wasn't really sparing them if that was the life they'd now endure.

"With so much damage done, how are any of these people even surviving?"

Gia looked utterly infuriated. "Because they've allowed the king's healers to swoop in and mend the wounded, like a miraculous act of heroism from their savior, Silas. Don't you find it suspicious that there were no Kingsguards protecting the villages? They were primed for the taking. Even when they sent reinforcements to aid nearby towns, they sent new recruits, poorly skilled, and too few to be of consequence."

The silence stretched between us. She'd had time to absorb all of this, but the way she spoke of it, it was clear she hadn't become calloused to the information. For me, it was raw, brand new. I felt silly sitting here at the castle playing spy games when there were people dying. All I could think was that if they were willing to do this to their own citizens, Gods protect Cambria should they ever cross the border. An entire kingdom enraged by those sadistic acts would lead to even more unreasonable acts of revenge.

Zarif, if he was behind all of this, was an opponent we could not underestimate. He and the king had already demonstrated there were no lines they were unwilling to cross. If we were not successful in our mission to thwart their efforts, the next great conflict would surely follow. My resolve to protect my homeland steeled completely in that very moment. Like Trace, I would try and take as few innocent lives in the process, but I would not let this thirst for blood reach the shores of my kingdom.

Gia glanced at the window, admiring the setting sun beginning to cast shadows over her room.

"The hour is growing late. Come, we must primp. It's okay if you don't know how to do my hair, I've taught myself. Because…well, that girl from earlier really does do a terrible job," she giggled, adding an air of lightness to the conversation. Her stunning smile was sincere, and it made me wonder how rare this expression had been since her arrival.

Gia sat down in the chair and I stood behind her, beginning to pull pins from her hair.

"I'll have you know that I've become an expert in braids…thanks to Cairis."

Gia swung her body around to face me. "Cairis?" she said in tickled surprise.

"Yes, Nori and Varro's hair is too short, and I wasn't about to ask Theory if I could touch her locks, so he was the only option. Don't tease him when you see him again, or he'll kill me. I had to make Varro swear not to in order for Cairis to let me do it to begin with."

The sound of Gia's laughter warmed the parts of me that had become cold and frightened after her recounting the details of Trace's time in Artume. I needed a break from the topic while I braided her hair, so I tried to think of other things I wanted to know about her time here. And how in Gods' names she happened to rise in favor so quickly.

"So, how did you manage to capture the heart of the king, besides the fact that you are impossibly gorgeous?"

She smiled at me in the reflection of the mirror in front of us as I began to separate her soft blonde hair into sections and pieces.

"You're not going to believe this! Remember how you told me about the trick you taught yourself—falling safely from a horse?"

"Yes," I said, looking at her with intrigue as I pinned pieces of her hair in place.

"Well, one day there was a party of lords and ladies out riding, and I figured if I didn't pull it off, the worst that would happen was falling in some sand. But I executed it flawlessly. All the king saw out of the corner of his eye was a wild horse on its hind legs and poor little Gianna, plummeting to the ground, gown and all. Of course, I yelped, writhing while clutching my wrist and letting the waterworks begin."

"You didn't!"

"Before you knew it, he was off his horse and on the ground by my side to aid me. The queen was still on her horse; I'm almost certain she suspected the fall was an act. She's very skeptical, but I would be too if my husband bedded as many whores as he has. Silas helped me to my feet and escorted me back to the healers on his horse to ensure I was taken care of properly."

"I cannot believe you tried that without having practiced it before."

I thought back to how many times I'd failed, falling into soft hay before I ever attempted it at a trot or a gallop, and against hard ground. But Gia was fearless, and I'm convinced she would have settled for a broken wrist or hand if it meant getting the king's attention that day.

"It was the perfect opportunity for me to lean into the warmth of his strong, protective arms, and perhaps graze his leg with my good hand," she recalled in a seductively, sly voice.

Just as I was beginning to wrap the final tendrils of curls into the intricate updo I'd concocted, there was a knock at her door.

"One moment!" she yelled in the tone she had when I first arrived. All command and no grace.

"While I'm at the party, stay out of trouble. Get settled into the servant quarters and do not wander, Cress."

I gave her a look that said, *I promise nothing.*

"I mean it, I have more to share with you. Return to my room after the party to help me undress for the evening. We still have a very important topic to discuss."

Her interrogative glance in the mirror meant one thing—she wanted to talk about the bond.

CHAPTER 16

U pon exiting Gia's suite, we were greeted by another young female in all blue. She dipped into a curtsey at the sight of Gia. "My lady, they are expecting you in the Great Hall. I am here to escort Miss Talok to the servants' quarters."

Gia scoffed. "I will arrive when I'm good and ready, and I don't care why you're here." She stepped around the poor servant like she was nothing more than furniture. I watched as she moved swiftly down the hallway, the soft fabric of her gown swaying delicately behind her. As soon as she was out of earshot, the servant turned to address me.

"Hi, I'm Eladir, but you can call me El."

In a completely unexpected gesture, she held out her hand to me, palm facing up. It was a greeting I had not encountered in such a long time. Maybe not since initially meeting Gia. It was a friendly and welcoming Fae custom, usually recognized in introductions amongst friends. The gesture was a sign that the female before me was perhaps gentle and good-natured. I lifted my hand and placed it atop hers, our skin barely grazing. Her hand felt warm and clammy, but soft like it had not been forced to perform manual labor.

"I'm Cress Talok of Caano."

"Yes, I know! I'm from Damas—not that it matters, the whole of the kingdom is just a bunch of sand anyway."

Her practical attitude further reinforced that she was comfortable in my presence. Was she like this with everyone, or did she just innately trust me? Either way, I was content to have a friendlier face at my side.

"Shira instructed me to escort you to the servants' quarters when Lady Gianna was finished with your assistance, and to show you the ropes. Well, actually I offered…since I'm your roommate!"

She said the last part like an excited child. Her use of the old sailing adage left me nostalgic for conversations with my father.

Her zealous expression led me to believe she was younger than me, perhaps even more so than Nori. Her optimism and joy seemed a strange thing for someone in servitude, hailing from a poor village like Damas. As she paced us away from Gia's door, I followed closely behind but continued to make note of my surroundings.

"The guard already delivered your belongings to our room," El prattled on, like the two of us were old friends, dishing the dirt about this and that. "It was silly of Shira to make him carry them all the way up to the fourth floor when we're all housed in the lowest levels of the castle. I'm not sure if she likes to abuse her power and watch them sweat, or just finds it amusing to make someone perform pointless work."

Her penchant for gossip would benefit me, as she seemingly had no filter in sharing her observations. I would not have expected any of the servants to question Shira's intentions aloud, and the others probably didn't. I'd wager this was unique to El, and I wondered if it had already gotten her in trouble once or twice before. She led us farther down the torchlit corridor until, finally, she stopped in front of an unassuming wooden door.

"This is a servant's door. All of them look like this, so you're safe to open them. Just make sure they look exactly like this!"

She reemphasized the point to warn me, making me think she had already learned from that mistake once before. When we entered the doorway, it was nothing but stairs in both directions. Narrow halls dimly lit by torchlight with no windows. She began to make her way downward, and I followed.

"These were built all throughout the castle to allow the staff to move freely and quickly between their duties. Some of us are given very little time between shifts, and don't get me started if one of the guests has an emergency."

"Why did Shira and the guard take me up the grand staircase if this exists?" I questioned, trying to understand the rules of the castle while still getting as much information about these hidden stairwells as I could. El continued to make the trek down and answered my prying questions thoroughly, but also with a twinge of annoyance.

"You weren't in the middle of duties, so the main staircase is acceptable. Do you think the nobles want to see us servants carrying around dirty bedsheets, linens, and chamber pots at every turn? We use this staircase to hide the existence of our work here in Nasallus."

Now it made sense. It was not considered beautiful or luxurious to witness the labors, so they largely took place behind the scenes.

The air was warm and thick in the stairwell, and soon a sheen of sweat broke out across my skin. When we finally arrived at the bottom, there was a maze of hallways and doors that made up the servants' quarters.

El continued on like an enthusiastic tour guide. "This is the basement; we are below ground level, so there are no windows. You'll have to get daylight and fresh air during your breaks, should you so choose." As we moved toward our destination, I could hear chatter and movement behind every door. "The males are down that hall." She pointed while continuing past one hallway.

"At the end of that corridor and to the left is a mess hall. The staff who live along that strip have the fortune of getting to smell everything coming out of our kitchen—and that's not a good thing. Lucky for us, we're nowhere near the wafting scents of day-old stew and fermenting fruits."

I breathed a sigh of relief, although my stomach was beginning to grumble now at the mention of food.

"What of the Kingsguards?" I prodded, trying to determine if there was any chance in the three moons of Demir that I might run into Cairis, or by some stroke of luck be in close proximity to him.

El came to an abrupt halt causing me to almost crash into her backside. She turned to face me; her nose already scrunched with displeasure.

"What concern do you have with the Kingsguards?"

This was the first reaction out of El that made me feel the need to tread lightly.

"Oh, I just always feel safer when they are in close quarters. I had a good friend who was a Kingsguard and promoted recently. Will they be stationed nearby?"

She let out a snort of disbelief. "You feel safer when those smelly barbarians are around?"

"I guess so," I muttered.

"They are on the same floor as us, but located on the far west side of the castle basement. They have their own dormitories and mess hall."

I dropped the subject, unsure of why El had taken issue with the Kingsguards, but not wanting to hit any sore spots. We arrived at a door that looked like any of the countless others we'd passed, and I was almost certain I was going to struggle to remember which one was ours. El must have seen the concern in my expression.

"They aren't numbered, which is a bit silly, don't you think? I made this little mark on the doorhandle with a dinner knife so you'll always be certain it's ours; just look for this little scratch here," she pointed at the blemish on the brass knob. Perfect, I thought to myself. Friendly and resourceful. I already liked my roommate.

The cramped dormitory was not unlike those in Basdie. There were two beds, likely better suited to accommodate children, one of which was laden with my belongings. Most disappointing of all, however, was that there was no private washroom.

"Well, it's small but it's ours, and I've missed having someone to talk to since…"

El cut herself off, recoiling into silence.

"Since what?" I pried.

Her expression turned somber.

"Since they took Kaya. My former roommate. She became sick, and they were convinced she was contagious."

The sad silence sat between us. I was unsure what comfort I could offer her, since I was almost certain Kaya fell ill at the behest of the Imperi.

"Since you're here…" she continued flatly, "I'm guessing that means Kaya did not survive her ailment. She was good at her job, truly. I miss her. That extra blanket was hers. But I guess it's yours now."

El's confession was a confirmation of her soft heart. That, paired with her unguarded words, had me concerned. But, if someone like her could survive in this role, then certainly someone as meticulous as me would be fine. Taking the chance to endear myself to her and make a quick friend, I placed my hand gently on her shoulder.

"I am sorry about your friend. I appreciate you volunteering to meet me and show me around. I hope my banter will live up to Kaya's."

El gave me a warm, watery smile and nodded as she tried to keep in a sniffle.

Trying to sway the subject toward a lighter topic, I asked, "So, what's the special party this evening?"

She let out a small snort followed by a giggle, discreetly wiping away a tear. "I don't know what household you served before Nasallus, but

Silas doesn't require a special occasion to throw a party. There's usually a dinner celebration, or something even more extravagant almost nightly here." She paused, catching her train of thought, "At least, until Silas is hungover and needs to nurse himself for a couple of days."

In the hour that followed, El showed me more of the quarters, ensuring I could recall which staircases led to each wing of the castle. The mess hall was modest, what you'd expect. Rows of long wooden tables and benches, not even individual chairs. A large hearth and fireplace for warmth, with a long chimney running up through the very top of the castle. Not like Basdie, where every fireplace was imbued with magic. Idris would never have signs of smoke over the Elorns giving away his secret stronghold.

She occasionally introduced me to a few other servants, whose names I struggled to keep up with, especially because we were all dressed in similar shades of blue, making distinguishing each other limited to our faces. One male eyed me longer than necessary, and his unguarded thoughts made it clear he found me attractive, a fact I might later need to exploit. Almost every single servant was thin, some rippling with the sinewy muscle that came from heavy labors. It seemed they were fed just enough to keep them capable of doing their duties. Shira, as the head of lady's maids, must no doubt be given extra portions and liberties to be as shapely as she was.

When El finally became distracted from being my tour guide, I took the opportunity to make my way back to the main castle with every intention of getting my eyes on that dinner party and witnessing Gia's interactions firsthand. I also hoped that I'd somehow get eyes on Cairis, too. I'm sure he was fine, but I'd feel more at ease seeing him safely installed in his position. My mind wandered to Nori, who was unlikely to be at this event since healers would only be called upon when needed. And above all, I thought of Varro finally reuniting with his beloved sea and hoped it would bring him comfort in my absence.

The ballroom was a bustling scene of loud music, Artumian banners hanging from every archway, and golden platters filled with decadent displays of gluttony. Wine flowed from every goblet, and at the head of the table sat King Silas. To his left was a stunning and regal female with deep ebony skin wearing a luxurious, all-black gown. She was dripping in heavy golden necklaces and braided metals adorned in rubies, emeralds, sapphires, and other bright stones. Atop her head was a similarly-fashioned crown. The accessories appeared heavy enough to topple one of the Kingsguard, yet she sat there statuesque and unyielding—the picture of a queen. Her expression was cold, unimpressed, certainly not one of revelry and joy.

The reason for her sour demeanor…Gia, the king's consort who sat directly to his right. Gia was wearing purple, a stark contrast to many of the king and queen's inner circle of nobles who all wore black. Had she worn the color to stand out? Was it a protest, or was it an order?

The dining hall itself was as long as it was wide, similar to the estate at the Canary Veil. The level above served as a balcony, allowing for a full view below. I paced slowly through the upper balcony, occasionally pausing to stand behind a column and peer down inconspicuously. I studied the dynamics of the other nobles who sat at the head tables. Which ones eyed Gia with judgement? As I continued to scan the room for my bulky, long-haired friend, I was startled as the band suddenly picked up tempo, followed by a troupe of dancers that came rushing into the center of the room.

They moved in synchronous steps, performing a choreographed dance for the onlookers. The lightweight fabrics of their costumes covered very little skin, and you could see the curves and dips of their flesh with each seductive movement. The queen stared forward, unflinching. Her mouth set into a rigid line while Silas smiled gleefully, even letting out a whoop and a holler in between large gulps of wine. His posture relaxed lazily into his towering chair. Gia nudged him playfully, pointing at certain dancers to draw his attention. She leaned her body into him, offering a full view of her exposed cleavage, and even was so bold as to place her hand atop his. Silas' already warm-colored skin flushed. Perhaps from the wine, maybe from the exotic dancers, but I'd wager it was Gia's attention filling his ego to the brim.

In an unexpected shift of events, the dancers began to writhe and sway with one another, the dance becoming more carnal, the music fluid like their bodies. Gia stood from her seat at the dinner table and made her way to the dance floor; the only noble to do so while the performance carried on. She imitated their movements, and slowly, gracefully, eased her way in between two of the female dancers. I continued to pace my way toward the next podium, trying to ensure that no one would catch me staring at the events of the party rather than attending to my duties.

Gia's skill blended in with that of the professional dancers, the rich violet standing out amongst the green-clad performers. I watched on, mesmerized at her bold act of seduction. She stared Silas down with each swish of her hips and wave of her arms, pulling him into a trance like they were the only two people in the room—as if his wife weren't seated directly next to him. It was abundantly clear that Silas made no secret of his playthings, and at the expense of embarrassing his wife in front of the entire court. What a miserable existence she must have, but mentally, I was applauding Gia.

Even with the loud music echoing throughout the room, beneath the melodies I could hear the chaotic buzz of people's unfettered thoughts. The music drowned out any clarity, so I'm certain even if Silas was listening, he couldn't make any of them out or be certain of who might be thinking ill of Gia's impromptu performance. In a complete lack of restraint, Gia clasped a dancer's face in her hands and pulled her in for a sensuous kiss. To some it may have seemed brief, but to those of us really watching, that suggestive act, in front of the king and the rest of the court, was the longest kiss we'd ever witnessed. The dancer seemed to be in a fog when Gia pulled her mouth away and then looked over her shoulder back at the king with a flirty smile. The queen's posture stiffened, revulsion pulling at the fine features of her face.

So much tension swirled in the room below. Fury from the queen. Desire without restraint from the king. Envy from the other ladies seeking the affections and favor of Silas. But there was one male who did not bear a single hint of expression—Zarif. He sat at the far end of the king's table, his meal untouched and his goblet still filled to the brim. Zarif was unreadable, but I feared for Gia's safety as his icy gaze fell upon her and the other dancers.

When the festivities died down, nobles began to give their parting gratitude to one very intoxicated king and made their exit for the evening. The queen had long since gone to bed, leaving Silas with a handful of his most roused and obnoxious friends, who had taken up seats at the head table. They nibbled on leftovers while drinking every last drop of wine from the former occupants' cups. They should thank the Gods they were still surrounded by a number of well-armed Kingsguards, because none of them stood a chance of defending themselves in their current state. Gia whispered something in the king's ear and ran her hand along his chest before making her way toward the staircase. I took that as my sign to quickly make my way back to her room to await her instruction.

Gia entered the room looking a bit sweaty and disheveled from her antics. Once again, she locked the door behind her and scurried to her dressing table.

"Help me get my hair out of this braid, it won't be long before the king calls on me."

I began to loosen sections of hair quickly while she powdered her face in the mirror.

"You're really incredible," I whispered, trying to tell her everything I felt about what I had seen her pull off at dinner.

She was so much better at this than me. Her deceptions and manipulations seemed to come easily to her. She fell into character with a natural grace I envied. And not because we wanted to be the kind of Fae we were pretending to be, but because we knew it was the key to our survival and, therefore, the preservation of our kingdom. But while I envied her ability to fully submit to the mission, I knew there were parts of this, the part I was now preparing her for, that I did not envy at all. Tasks that I feared I couldn't bring myself to do if called upon. As I helped Gia into a set of lingerie and a lightweight silk robe, I began to feel my insides twist with regret for the act she had to perform—one she'd already been performing.

Gia was quiet and focused, steadfast on her task. I had so many questions for her, and I'd love nothing more than to get to spend all night with her in that room going over everything each of us had missed. Her time in Nasallus, my time at Basdie. Our time apart, so different, and yet, she was the only one who could understand or relate to what I'd been going through with Varro.

"I can't believe you have to dress up like this for him," I muttered in annoyance while continuing to help lace her up. "He doesn't deserve you."

"Stop!" Gia snapped. "I prefer it. It's my costume. My armor." She paused a moment. "It's a reminder that none of this means a fucking thing."

I lowered my gaze in regret for having clearly struck a nerve. It was so easy for me to forget Gia had been going at this alone all this time. Without another familiar or friendly face. Forced to bed a stranger…an enemy. I should have known better. This was a ritual for her. Something that allowed her to disassociate from herself.

"You're right. I'm sorry. I—"

She interrupted me before I could continue with my apologetic ramblings. She turned to face me now that I had tied off her corset, reaching for the robe to tie around her. Her expression intense, etched into her face like stone. She was a warrior dressed in delicate armor of lace and silk, strings and bows. A deadly snake, ready to slither up next to its prey, wrap itself gently around it and squeeze ever so slowly, beginning as a cool embrace and ending in bone-crushing constriction.

"Tomorrow is the sabbath. Make sure you bring your moonstone."

"Wait. What?" I asked trying to understand what that meant, but Gia began to make her way to her door. Before she unlocked the door to make her exit, she glanced at me over her shoulder; a devious, penetrating gaze staring back at me.

"In the morning, we discuss how we're going to kill the queen."

CHAPTER 17

That night I lay in my small bed across from a soundly sleeping Eladir. My mind was restless, and my body too. It was accustomed to the rigors of both physical and magical exertion, which brought sleep swiftly at the end of the day. But today, I hadn't done anything remotely comparable, so I itched to find sufficient release. I pulled the blanket over myself, hiding underneath to attempt small forms of magic to exhaust energy. Inconsequential things like glamouring, even going as far as to briefly shapeshift myself an additional finger. While this proved to be an amusing oddity, it did not bring me any closer to sleep. I'd stare at the small torch hanging near our doorway and focus on trying to make it burn brighter and then dimmer. Hoping that toying with my elemental magic would lead to a reprieve of this restlessness, but nothing worked.

I hadn't realized the day of sabbath was already upon us until Gia said something. The mention of the moonstone had me on edge. Saryn had said we'd be more likely to be able to visit the safehouse when everyone was preoccupied with ceremonies and private prayer related to the sabbath. I ran my fingers along the smooth, polished sides of the stone in my fingertips. What if I failed to successfully portal back to the safehouse? How many times had Gia already made the jump?

With my eyes closed, I thought of every detail I could remember about the safehouse. The charred alleyway behind it, the sunny and sand-filled street in front. The barren, unassuming interior. I let the images surround me like a gallery of paintings. Before long, the gentle swirls of pale cream, ochre, and sable lulled me into a dreamless sleep.

I awoke extra early, once again hid my stone away in my undergarments, and made my way to the servants' kitchen to grab a biscuit to scarf down so I could meet Gia first thing upon her waking. Each of the ladies' maids were on different schedules, dictated by the noble they served. Some of them wanted us there first thing in the morning, others preferred to be left in solitude until they required assistance. When I arrived at Gia's door, I encountered a young male carrying a tray of breakfast who was just about to knock on her door.

"I'll take care of that," I said, while grabbing the tray out of his hands. He looked at me, bewildered. My commanding expression left no room for negotiation, and he quickly went on his way.

I knocked on the door politely and heard Gia groggily reply, "Come in!"

She sat up in her bed, looking tired with her long hair a tangled mess. I put the tray down on her bedside. She grabbed a piece of fruit and began eating it like someone starved. She relaxed back into her pillows and continued to shove food in her mouth.

I paced back to the door to lock it and ensure our privacy. "You convinced them you're a noble, eating like *that?*"

"I am a noble!" Gia grabbed a plum and chucked it at me from across the room. I caught it one-handed and laughed. Sometimes it *was* easy to forget we were once High Fae.

Once she was done eating, I began to tidy her room while she perused her overflowing closet trying to decide what to wear for sabbath.

"This is my favorite day of the week," she explained. "And not just because it's the best opportunity to visit the safehouse, but because Silas will be tied up all day with services, prayers, and then the Gifting Ceremony."

"What's that?"

"The poor and destitute come to plead their cases to their king. Some asking for family members to be forgiven of their crimes, others begging for handouts. Let's just say listening to these depressing requests all afternoon does nothing to ignite Silas' desires. He usually likes to sleep alone after the sabbath."

"I'm sorry that you're in this position." There was no plainer way I could state it.

"Don't be. Half the time he's too drunk to get it up, and I just have to fool around a bit till he rolls over, passes out, and begins his incessant snoring."

"It's still not fair," I grumbled while pulling up the sheets to finish making her bed.

"Speaking of not fair…" she teased, and I already knew where she was headed. "A mate at Basdie? Well, it can't be Saryn; you two despise each other. And I'm guessing that our whorish friend Cairis isn't pining after you. So, if Trace wasn't your preferred flavor after all, that leaves…"

"Varro." The feel of his name on my tongue allowed me to let out my first big exhalation since arriving inside the castle walls. My muscles relaxed at the thought of him and finally being able to tell Gia.

"All that time you never mentioned the call of the bond; I could have told you immediately what it was. It's so distinct, unlike anything I'd ever felt before," she explained.

"I thought it was our powers growing since the waters of Mirtith!"

Gia shook her head at me like I was an immature child who should have known better.

"The first time I felt it, I was so young," she recollected. "Something kept drawing me back to the stables. I couldn't understand why, since I despised the smell of them and how it dirtied my dresses."

Gia was so melancholy at the time we spoke of her former mate, that I feared mentioning it ever again. Even now, I felt the need to tread lightly.

She continued, "It's so strange once you realize that the sensation is an actual tether to an individual, one you can't ignore. The closer you get, the stronger it thrums. The farther away—you fear its absence." Gia looked lost momentarily. I contemplated my response, but then the moment was gone as Gia's tone shifted. "Of course, that is until you seal it, and then that whole mind-melding business becomes intrusive as ever."

She stripped off her night gown baring her nude body once more with zero embarrassment. I envied her boldness, I really did. She slipped a dress over her head and then began her interrogation. She wanted to know how I'd confronted Varro, and his subsequent reaction. Had he known before I did, or was he equally surprised? Did the others know?

I explained to her why I hadn't yet sealed the bond, adding the information about my dark wielding and the Drift. Gia was now as informed as Cairis and Nori, which was a relief since I would need her help keeping this secret from Saryn.

"That's some serious self-control," she remarked, to which I informed her that we'd done plenty else to occupy ourselves at Basdie. And then she asked the question that had been buried in the back of my mind ever since receiving her note.

"Are you going to tell Trace?"

"I have to. Somehow…" I trailed off. "He lied so frequently, and I hated it; I won't be such a hypocrite."

Unsure of exactly how and when I'd confront Trace, I turned the conversation toward more important matters, lowering my voice to a whisper.

"Why do we need to kill the queen?"

"Because there is someone being kept prisoner in the cells below the castle, someone important, and the only way we're going to get to them is to cause a little chaos. We'll discuss more once we're safe to do so."

What followed was a clear list of instructions from Gia. She was going to head to the atrium of the Prayer Hall to ensure she had been "seen", but shortly after, she would step into a more private area and portal to the safehouse. Sometime after she exited her room, I was to do the same so that I would be last seen exiting the dormitory of the lady I served. She looked at the leftovers on her breakfast tray and encouraged me to eat some fruit before making my attempt, acknowledging the distance between the castle and our safehouse.

My nerves caused me to fidget. While I'd much rather make the attempt with her by my side, I trusted her guidance that the stones offered the best chance to leave the castle undetected. When she left me alone, the quiet of her room began to feel haunting and only furthered my feelings of dread. I anxiously chewed on a piece of fruit, noting how ripe it was compared to the half-rotted ones they provided the servants. I slipped into the hallway and made my footsteps as soundless as possible before reaching an empty corridor. I'd practiced this many times at Basdie and tried to think of Varro standing by my side, comforting me and radiating the confidence that I could do anything I put my mind to.

I removed the stone from where it was tucked into my undergarment and inhaled deeply, slowly exhaling while reminding myself of all the detailed pictures of the safehouse I'd painted in my mind the night before. I rubbed the smooth stone between my fingers and channeled its power until the familiar swirling cloud appeared before me. I reassured myself, saying, *Do not fear the destination, know the destination.* And with that, I stepped into oblivion.

CHAPTER
10

When I stepped out of the portal, I landed square on my rear in a pile of hot sand, the sun beating down from overhead. Raising my arm to shield my eyes, a hand intercepted the light and offered to help me to my feet.

A hand I knew well. Trace's hand.

Clasping my grip tightly around his, he yanked me to my feet. The moment I was up, I jerked away from him. Jarred by his presence after so long, I offered no greeting while patting sand off my clothes. I was grateful that I'd somehow managed to land in the correct place, but I still nervously glanced around the back alley to the house, Gia nowhere in sight. My head ached, and the exhaustion from the portal jump was beginning to set in.

"She's inside already." His husky voice was low and calm, utterly unaffected. "Your mental shields have always been questionable."

Realizing I had dropped them when I took an abrupt tumble from the portal, my nose scrunched and brow pinched in irritation at Trace's remark. *Nice to see you too, ass.*

Our meeting couldn't have been more unlike mine and Gia's. She and I practically ran to one another. Trace and I stood across from one another, silence lingering between us like two swordsmen waiting to see who would draw first.

"I always have you to remind me of my weaknesses," I said bitterly.

Trace looked utterly weathered. Dark circles encompassed his once-stunning hazel eyes. His pale skin was darkened from days under the Artumian sun, though his deeds have been executed under the cover of night. The curly locks that I had once twirled in between my fingers were now cut short, trimmed tight on the sides with a bit of length still on top. It was not a glamour. Even as close as I stood to him, his distinct scent was undetectable. No tattooed markings, no scar through his brow; a near constant glamour that I'm sure factored into the exhaustion that now blanketed this once mysterious High Fae male.

His eyes were tormented, and I didn't conceal the pity from my expression as I assessed him.

Eager to leave the encounter, I began to glance around looking for others. Specifically, Varro. Frustratingly, I was unable to detect any vibrations from our bond.

"He's not here."

Trying to play it off with nonchalance, I redirected my intent. "Where's Nori?"

"She's inside. Are you mated?"

His question showed no restraint in its directness. And so, I mustered the courage to respond in equal measure.

"We are mates."

He tried his best to conceal some emotion I couldn't decipher. Anger? Anticipation? Jealousy?

"But are you *mated?*" he repeated, gritting his teeth through the question.

I couldn't believe he was asking me this. This was not how I had planned to discuss the matter. I would have used more tact, for one thing. I would have also had more respect for our past—but he, of course, wouldn't have it any other way.

"No, not that it's any of your business," I replied, nearly seething.

Why did I say 'no' instead of 'not yet'? I was going to seal the bond someday, wasn't I?

I'd tired of this conversation already and turned on my heel to enter the back of the safehouse, but before I could go anywhere, he grabbed my hand and pulled me back to him.

"We need to talk."

"Do we?" I answered him with wide-eyed annoyance, trying and failing to pull away.

"Please. Afterwards."

His words softened like a plea, and reluctantly, I gave him a nod.

He finally released me, and as we entered the space, I saw Gia, Nori, Saryn and Cairis surrounding the small kitchen table laden with a spread of food and pitchers. Varro was not among them, as Trace had said. Panic at the lack of my mate's presence immediately began to settle in as I approached them. If something had happened to him, would the unsealed bond somehow alert me to it? Would I know in my heart if he was in danger?

"You're a Gods-damned genius, Nori!" Gia squealed in excitement, and a blush of embarrassment came over Nori's cheeks.

I pulled out a chair and took a seat next to Gia, Trace taking a spot directly across from me. I was so relieved to see Nori and Cairis there, but it only made me worry more about why Varro hadn't yet arrived.

"Varro may have more difficulty finding opportunities to return to the safehouse. It's the nature of the work he's involved in," Saryn explained, having noticed my constant glances toward the door. "They have the shipyard clans working day and night."

I breathed a sigh of relief that there was at least an explanation, but that would never fully settle my nerves. I needed to see him, to touch him…

"We're lucky Trace was able to make it here," he added.

"So, why is Nori a genius…? I already knew she was special, even when everyone was treating her poorly. But do tell!"

My comment was meant to sound like a joke, but it was clear that it didn't land. Nori gave me a warm smile, but Saryn huffed in contempt.

"Because she has helped us determine how we are going to kill the queen," Gia added gleefully, clearly recognizing what I was trying to do and working to clear the tension.

I tilted my head to the side, assessing innocent little Nori. "I leave you for a day, and you return a cold-blooded assassin?"

Out of the corner of my eye, I saw when Trace turned his head quickly at my remark, and I winced inside as I realized how that must have sounded. He'd been embroiled in the mission long before our arrival.

"Go on," Saryn said, "tell them quickly so we can get to some actual planning while we still have time."

Nori began to recount a short but elaborate fable she'd read during her time at Basdie. The story chronicled how a comely, low-born maiden used her powerful gift of shapeshifting to become a courtesan worthy of legend.

She managed to take the form of all six of the king's mistresses at one point or another. But the role of a mistress was not her intended position. She bathed the king, massaged his aches and pains, and pleasured him with the sinful methods that only the most desirable courtesans practiced. This close proximity to the king granted her a familiarity with the queen as well. And the courtesan studied her meticulously. Her mannerisms, her speech, her interactions and friendships.

The art of being a courtesan of such status required the ability to indulge the male fantasy, which comes in many guises. And she was truly gifted in her art. So, as she accumulated the habits of the queen, it became easy for her to mimic them. First in private, before the mirror, then to one of the servant girls. She was so convincing that, when she shapeshifted, she was indistinguishable from Her Royal Majesty.

When it came time to seize her prize, she murdered the queen in secret and discarded her body, assuming her position for the rest of her days. It is said not a soul knew, until she lay on her royal deathbed and a healer witnessed her final shift back into her true form. By then, she had already ruled alongside the foolish, greedy king for hundreds of years. Beloved and feared.

We were all enraptured by Nori's storytelling, but I had failed to make sense of how our plan would unfold. Were we now going to install Gia as queen?

Saryn did his typical, unimpressed slow clap.

"Thank you, Nori, for the colorful inspiration. But we have a lot to cover, so I'll take it from here."

He looked across the table at each of us, demanding our attention.

"The queen's death will be a decoy to create panic and chaos within the castle walls. We will use this to get to the prisoner so we can extract whatever information possible."

"What prisoner? Gia had mentioned something along the lines of needing to get to someone in the cells, but who is it?" I interrupted, trying to determine if I was the only one without this information and playing catch up.

Gia said, "We believe Princess Embry—King Baelin's daughter and rightful heir—is still alive and held beneath the castle."

"So what if she's alive?" Cairis chimed in. "Why do we need her? She's as good as dead."

"Because if anyone has information about the king's plans and is willing to help us, it's her," Saryn responded, trying to hide his annoyance.

"What's the course of action?" Trace said dryly, always trying to keep us focused on the task at hand.

Gia began a methodical explanation.

"First, we must set the stage. Gossip spreads like locusts within the walls of Nasallus, that we can count on. I will shift into various forms and assist Cress and Cairis in spreading rumors of the queen having taken her night guard as a lover. In a week's time, the castle will be abuzz with whispered accusations."

Each of us listened intently.

"Cress, this is where your skill set comes in. I will introduce you to the king's Grim Garden, where I'm certain you'll be able to ascertain the proper ingredients for a strong and effective sleep potion."

At the mention of sleep potions, my mind began to race through various ingredients and concoctions to achieve such a thing. My train of thought was interrupted as Gia continued.

"During the next sabbath's supper, Cress will make certain the queen's usual maid has fallen ill, giving the opportunity for a substitute to deliver her nightly tonics. She will then prepare to intercept me, appearing as the queen's servant during the conclusion of dinner."

The thought of being the one responsible for drugging another servant *and* the queen in the same night made my palms slick with sweat. Trace tilted his head with an almost imperceptible expression of concern that only I noticed. Humorous how someone who left me to die would even feign concern.

"Since I will be needed for these next steps, it's important the king does not call on me that evening. I will ensure Silas is aware I am feeling unwell during dinner and excuse myself early. Perhaps it will even solidify my innocence if people think myself and the lady's maid fell ill on the same evening of the queen's murder."

I watched as the others took in Gia's plan with bated breath, trying to assess if it would actually work. Could we pull it off? What risks were we not accounting for? The climax of her plan had to be executed flawlessly.

"The queen will return to her quarters, and the night guard will begin his watch shortly thereafter. I will take on her lady's maid duties and carry the tray of her usual tonics and such handed off to me by Cress. The guard will show no signs of concern upon my arrival, as this is the nightly routine."

"How long will it take?" Nori questioned, realizing as I had that this would all need to happen quickly.

Gia answered with precision, like a mastermind who'd been contemplating this for weeks—which, I supposed, technically, she had.

"Once I witness her drink the tainted tonic, I will exit the room and inform the guard the queen has asked for something additional and that I will return shortly. This should allow enough time for the queen to put herself to bed and fall into a deep slumber."

"What's my role in all this?" Cairis interjected.

"Patience!" Gia chided. "We're getting there. As the guard expects, I will return, and once inside, I'll move the queen's sleeping body underneath the bed. During that time, we need Cress to create a distraction. Across the hall, I need you to accidentally trip and spill everything in your arms to draw the guard's attention."

"Then what?" Saryn inquired.

I was actually shocked to see how silent he had remained. Had he and Gia already worked out some of this plan prior to our arrival, or was this all really from her own imagination? It had the decisiveness and creativity of someone with a great deal of experience. Had Artume already hardened her resolve that much?

"Enough time will have passed, allowing me to shift into the queen's form and garments. In an unexpected series of actions, I will open my door and request the night guard enter my quarters. At first, he will insist against it—propriety and all. But who can deny a queen, and one with such beauty?"

"Won't he ask where your lady's maid is?" Cairis added.

"If he does, that only requires a simple insult of his duty: *'Didn't you see her exit a moment ago? You must not be very good at your job…*'" Gia demonstrated her acting skills in a perfect imitation of the queen.

"I will offer my loyal night guard a drink of wine, which he will also refuse, but I will persist until he is nicely lubricated with a lack of inhibition, defenseless against my pursuits."

Cairis smiled wide, flashing his teeth at her. "You're positively wicked."

"And, if Cress is any good at her job, that foolish male will be snoring before I even have to attempt a more formal seduction."

Saryn gazed out the solitary window, noting the sun moving across the sky as time passed. "Gia, get to the point. We haven't even discussed the prisoner yet."

She scrunched her nose at his impatience, but spoke more quickly, still covering each detail thoroughly.

"I will move the queen's sleeping body beside him into her bed. The night guard's blade will make its way across the queen's throat, delivering her demise. I will shift back into the maid and make my exit with no guards as witness."

I held my breath, my pulse racing at how nonchalantly Gia implied she'd be the one to take the queen's life. An innocent pawn in our games of espionage.

"In the morning, a Kingsguard will arrive for shift change at the same time a servant will be delivering breakfast. Concern will set in and, upon entering the room, they will find a slain queen and a night guard in her bed, covered in irrefutable evidence of an assault and struggle turned deadly."

Cairis wasn't the brightest amongst us, but when he interrupted her with almost the same thought as me, I knew he'd been keeping up.

"The guard is going to be in a state of confusion and complete denial! He will never admit to this crime."

Gia cocked her head predatorily in Nori's direction and pointed at her with one slender finger. "That's where you come into play. Our

Dreamwalker's first assignment is to visit the night guard during his drug-induced slumber and plant dreams, false memories of his interactions. While he may awake confused, there will be no denying his own twisted memories—or should I say nightmares of a tryst with her majesty turned violent…"

Nori's sweet face contorted quickly into one of fear and concern. She hadn't yet attempted to plant false dreams or memories to my knowledge. Asking her to do so, especially ones that consisted of sexual assault and murder, was a tall order for someone so chaste. Saryn wasted no time in pressuring her.

"Remember, Dreamwalker, the Imperi has no place for those who waste their gifts."

Nori shot a defiant glare at him. "I'll do it."

A mischievous smile crept across Gia's face as she watched the pieces of her plan fall into place. "Good, because if I'm going to murder her, the least you could do is take a night walk."

Gia had definitely hardened. Maybe she hadn't committed the same kinds of atrocities as Trace, but she'd spent so much time obsessing over the mission that it was clear her duty was beginning to outweigh her morality. I knew not to judge her. That would be all of us, soon enough.

She bridged the plan into act two by instructing Cairis to be with the Kingsguard on hand when they undoubtedly arrested the night guard. They would make every attempt to quell the scene and avoid further embarrassment for the king.

"You will be asked to escort the guard to a private cell until his punishment is determined. In doing so, we are hopeful you'll get eyes on our target within the same prison."

"How am I supposed to know it's the target? I've never even seen Princess Embry!" Cairis complained.

Silence befell the room as we each thought on the truth of his statement, as none of us had seen the princess before.

"There can't be that many females in the cells. She may look dirty, emaciated, but you should be able to recognize the beauty of High Fae royalty, regardless of her state. Or you could listen to see if anyone addresses her while you're down there," Trace tried to reason.

Suddenly, Saryn stood and went to a drawer in the kitchen, pulling out a very small but detailed painting, tossing it onto the table. "This is Princess Embry."

Each of us looked abruptly at him with accusatory glances, all except for Cairis who began to study the image.

"How did you get that?" Gia demanded.

"You guys have your jobs, I have mine. Regardless, it doesn't matter how or where I got it. But that's what the target looks like. Got it, Cairis?"

Each of us accepted his explanation without question. Saryn was always up to his own mischievous behaviors, so the fact that he had somehow acquired a tiny painting of our intended target didn't surprise me in the slightest. And if it helped the mission, then who were we to question it?

I'd not seen a single portrait of the royal family anywhere in Nasallus thus far, and I'm sure that was done intentionally to avoid any reminders of the Silent Eve.

Cairis quickly repeated the plan, like a young student trying to capture their instructor's lesson. "…I am likely to be accompanied during this time by another Kingsguard, but at this point, all I have to do is get confirmation of our target being present?"

Gia let out a sarcastic laugh and replied, "Well, if you really wanted to be helpful, Cairis, you could report back to us about where you see her, how many prison guards are stationed there and their positions—you know, anything that might actually help us try to get to the target ourselves!" Gia rolled her eyes. "You know, being a spy…the whole damn reason we're in this Gods-forsaken sand pit."

Cairis and Gia were always playful with one another; sarcastic, direct, and even crass at times. Their relationship was that of good friends with thick tension that they may have once explored—had the whole being blood-sworn into the Imperi not happened.

"This is what I have to work with," Saryn muttered to himself.

"What if they decide not to execute the guard, or Nori's attempts fail?" I pondered to the group.

Gia laughed. "Oh, Cress, you haven't been here long enough. Zarif has a penchant for violence, and a trespass like this against the king would cause an embarrassment they'd never allow to spread. There *will* be punishment. A grave one, I assure you. And while that's unfolding, we make our next move."

Over the course of the hour that followed, we worked out the details of exactly what that next move might look like, should we be successful. Trace mostly sat in silence, since none of these plans involved him directly.

When the planning concluded, various attendees needed to portal back according to different schedules based on when they'd be required at their specific stations. Gia was the first to leave, as she was expected for dinner with the king. With a knowing look, she said she could ready herself if I needed extra time here.

Nori hugged me and, giving her a squeeze, I whispered into her ear, "You can do this."

She assured me everything was going well in her position and that she wasn't seeing much action as an apprentice beyond some basic wound-mending. Since the healers were kept mostly sequestered, her time was spent reading up on the art of salves, tonics, and other such relevant topics in between appointments. She made no mention of accidentally slipping into anyone's slumber—an improvement, granted.

Cairis quickly departed after Gia, and Trace made his way to the alley, with me following close behind. Before exiting, I turned, looking over my shoulder at Saryn who was tossing Embry's portrait back into a drawer. Words hovered on my tongue—the desire to inquire about Varro. But I wouldn't give him any reason to question my particular interests in the Sea Fae.

CHAPTER 19

Outside, the sun had turned from brilliant white to crimson as it made its way toward the horizon. I would welcome the cooler temperatures that came with nightfall, but even then, the dry heat still sat heavy all around me. Trace continued to walk farther down the alley, making a turn into one of the houses abandoned after the fire. I followed silently, entering behind him. He continued onward, up a dilapidated staircase to the rooftop of the house. I chose my steps carefully, trying to ensure I did not fall through what remained of the stairs, while also trying to keep soot off my uniform.

When we reached the rooftop, I gladly greeted the gentle breeze that threatened to pluck a few sweaty strands of hair that were matted to my forehead. We walked aimlessly along the flat expanse of sand-colored clay and charred thatch, avoiding what came next. Finally, when there was no more roof to traverse, he sat down, his legs dangling over the edge, and I took a seat beside him facing the opposite direction. I noticed the way the sun highlighted tiny, almost imperceptible lines on his face.

Ones that should not be there for as young as we were. Ones easily glamoured away, if he cared to. Signs of the wear and tear on his body from all he'd been made to endure—to carry out.

The silence between us no longer felt uncomfortable. It felt like surrender. There was an eerie calm to it now that we were alone, playing strangers in a strange land. His voice shattered that silence, breaking it into pieces like shards of glass with a confession I couldn't deny him.

"You know they sent me first because I was already a monster, long before arriving at Basdie."

The Trace I'd met and once knew wasn't a monster, but I didn't know anything of his true past, so I found I couldn't argue. My words would be placating and hollow, at best.

Instead, I said, "To protect the realm, we must sometimes do unspeakable things. That is clear to me now. The realm is in your debt, and you will be forgiven."

He turned to face me, his expression swarmed by so many emotions, none of them indicating agreement with what I'd said.

"*Forgiveness?*" he laughed in disbelief. "Do you remember the Bath of the Four Mothers? '*Within these waters, there is no past, there is no shame, there is no regret. You are forgiven before forgiveness is asked.*'"

He quoted the words so succinctly, it was almost as if I could hear the priestess's voice again. His hands balled tightly into fists resting on his thighs, and he clenched his jaw as he continued.

"I was never forgiven, and I never will be. I have nothing but shame and regret from my past, my present, and what little my future holds. What forgiveness exists for me?"

The sorrow in his words lingered on every syllable, and he clearly believed them to be true. Recalling the ease with which we used to care for each other, I dared to push the conversation further.

"Before Basdie, why did you choose the life of a black cloak?"

Ever since finding out about his past, I had wanted to understand what could make anyone fill their days with such vile acts by choice.

He scoffed at me. "You think I *chose* that life? It had been bred—no, burned into me…" He raised his voice, pointing to the scar on his brow he had briefly stopped glamouring. "My father, my brothers, theirs was the only life I'd ever known. It was the only life expected of me. Did you think I could just abandon them without consequence? That my own father wouldn't hunt me down and put me to the blade for such a betrayal?"

His voice quieted a bit as he tried to articulate his emotions in a way I could understand.

"I am drawn to duty the way fate draws you to *him*." He nudged his chin into the unseen distance, the direction of the Endless Tides—where Varro was stationed. "I am bound to my allegiance the way you're bound to him. While other children were taught table manners, I was instructed to serve my commander. My mother's fables were soon replaced by my father's recounting of revered generals and sickening war tactics not meant for children's ears. I did not choose the life of a mercenary. But it is all I know. All I am."

"Is that why you left me to die?" I said quickly in retort, baiting him with my use of the old tongue. And when he began his reply, I gave him a knowing look and interjected. "For all your upbringing and talk of duty, no one made you a liar! All this time, you spoke the old tongue?"

Trace shook his head, realizing what I'd done, but quickly prepared his retaliation in our verbal sparring. "Did you think I would suddenly forego secrecy upon entering a secret Order?"

As if that excuse made a difference, or even addressed the question!

"All you ever did was lie to me… I can't trust you. I was ready to accept you, if you had just fought for it. For me. If you had just found a way to trust me, I would have spent my days trying to heal your broken heart. To mend your tainted soul. But you are unmendable!"

The words left my tongue before I could polish them with any sense of consideration. Tears bordered my eyes, because this conversation had been fighting to explode from my insides since his betrayal. Admitting to him aloud that I had seen a chance for us, even while at Basdie, incited feelings of guilt toward my mate. But Trace needed to know that *he* was the one who lost *me*.

"And what would you have me do, Cress? Fight fate? Bend the will of destiny? You're his fucking mate! His *Moirai*..." He elongated its pronunciation in mocking. "I knew that long before you ever did. I could smell it on him since the moment he saw you. Every day I let myself believe I could still have you was delaying the inevitable. The Gods took you from me; there was never any choice in the matter!"

The tears were becoming harder to fight, and my teeth hurt from how badly I had been clenching them, listening to every word of his admission.

"I was worth fighting fate for."

I said the words plainly, confidently, wanting him to know my conviction. The Gods could plan whatever future they wanted, but *I* would decide who claimed my heart—something Varro understood. He insisted that I not fulfill the bond out of duty or responsibility, but because I needed him, wanted him...because I *chose* him.

"I can't fight with you anymore," he pleaded.

"And I can't trust you," I replied.

"What can I do? Yours is the only forgiveness I seek."

I thought on the question in silence. Could I give him forgiveness of any kind? Did he even deserve it?

"You promised to right your wrongs. But that's not good enough. Mark it with magic. Make me a bargain."

The demand left my mouth before I even considered the ramifications of such a request. How would Varro feel about me binding myself in any way to Trace? Would I come to regret this decision? He was the only one in our Order who had outright showed me that he would put the mission above our safety. While that was the intent, I did not believe the others would so easily risk their comrades' lives.

He held out his hand to me. Before I could question it further, I clasped my hands around his, noting the rough, calloused texture and scars that had not been there before. His gaze stared into mine, seeking any semblance of my approval.

"Swear to protect the lives of the Imperi at all costs, putting their safety above your own. Forsake this bargain, and you will meet the Gods a coward, by my hand or that of another. Only they will hear your sorrowful pleas."

My words were sharp and grave. Both a command and a promise, all in one. Trace lacked what the rest of us had understood inherently when taking the oath of the Imperi: Our loyalty wasn't just bound to the cause, but to each other. Trace, however, required explicit instruction. It's all he ever understood. He was not raised to judge nuance. He was not raised to have empathy or question orders. If he had never known a higher authority than duty or the mission, I would give him one. He had now bound himself to me, to us.

With his life.

I would have no problem delivering him to the Gods myself if he ever betrayed one of us again.

Trace clutched me hard enough that his nails pressed into my hand, looking me in the eye and binding himself to me with magic.

"I will. You have my word, on my life."

Trace did not pull his hand back from mine as we stayed that way a moment longer, understanding this was likely the last time we would ever touch this way. His hand felt so heavy in mine, like it held all the weight of our past in it. As if we held them long enough, we could disintegrate all the bad memories, or somehow go back in time and do things differently. Not that it could have swayed my heart. He did not flinch or turn away from my assessing gaze as I studied his face, my reflection in his eyes. Had I ever truly known this male? Did *he* even know his true self? Or had he only ever been what was expected of him?

I imagined dark charcoal on his fingertips, solitary moments of him drawing beautiful landscapes, a haven from his harsh reality. Flashes of the soft Nightwing feather grazing my skin. The safety I once felt in his embrace, inhaling the scent of pine and sandalwood. Five questions. A gloved hand. A knife at a gambler's throat. A whole timeline of memories that now seemed like a means to an end. There was a path the Gods had laid out, and our time was merely a detour. I closed my eyes and tucked away the tears of what might have been, feeling the closure of this moment take hold in my heart.

When I opened my eyes again and looked into his, he knew. We both did. That I belonged to someone else. That I chose that person, and he chose me. Trace would spend the rest of his days making up for what he'd done, a loss I was sure he'd feel in more ways than one. Haunted by his decisions. And that was all the revenge I could ask for.

CHAPTER 20

In the days that followed, we spun an intricate web of lies about the queen and her night guard that spread like wildfire, just as Gia had predicted. El was particularly chatty, taking every chance she got to inquire if anyone had any updates or had seen anything with their own eyes.

As is the way of gossip, it took on a life of its own. Gia and I found ourselves giggling at the absurd things we'd heard, like one servant who swore they saw the guard's head under the queen's skirt on the terrace one evening, and another who claimed she had taken two lovers. The first part of our plan had worked superbly.

However, acquiring the right ingredients for the sleep potion was a little more complex. Gia knew nothing about plants, so we had to find a way for me to see the gardens myself and make an assessment of what was available. When I asked her how she even knew of this private garden, she'd said that the king was a reveler in every sense of the word. He liked to experiment with extracts and oils that caused erotic hallucinations and sensory enhancements. When Gia acted dim-witted but curious, he was elated to give her a tour of his gardens and educate her on such verdure.

This was how Gia was able to first inquire about the roped-off section of the garden that housed his precious collection. In the distance, she noted that every single plant was black, a clear indicator of a peculiar origin. King Silas was quick to brush her off, noting that it was simply his Grim Garden, and she should not concern herself with such dangerous things. He had carried on with the tour, pointing out the more colorful and exotic arrangements.

So to set the next part of the plan into motion, first, I escorted Lady Gianna on a walkabout through the solarium, which was a giant glass dome. The temperatures inside were even more sweltering than we'd grown used to, but unlike the castle exterior's dry heat, this was thick and humid. Moisture filled the air and left sticky residue along our skin. There were old statues covered in moss, and ivy crawling up lattices along the wall. Giant, leafy plants surrounded small fountains and a never-ending array of bright florals littered every corner of the gardens, creating a maze of rainbows. Many of these plants could not survive outside the protection these glass walls provided.

If I had known the option existed, I would have requested Saryn and Theory install me as a gardener. The sheer size of it compared to the castle was breathtaking. We quieted our speech with each stride, trying to ensure our voices did not carry. Once I had sight of the Grim Garden, we took many passes of it. Some days, we would take a rest and seat ourselves on the bench closest to the roped off areas. Other times, Gia would stand watch or flirt with the guards while I perused behind her back and pretended to pick a floral arrangement for my lady. It wasn't long before I had spotted the Black Delilah. In small quantities, it could be used to relax the muscles, slow the heartbeat and induce sleep. A slightly heavier dose invited minor paralysis of the body. Only in large quantities did it become lethal. The Black Delilah was commonly extracted to treat sleep disruption, and only when prepared by a healer.

After spotting it, I drew its unique shape on a piece of paper for Gia so she'd know exactly which one to grab and how much. We burned that piece of paper to conceal any evidence after confirming she knew what to look for. Later that week, Gia visited the solarium, shapeshifting into one of the gardeners and, using gloved hands, carefully collected my materials.

I had no way of preparing the items while sharing a room with El, who had become central to the gossip ring down in the servants' quarters. Therefore, after dinner, I would work in secret in Gia's bedroom. Pretending to cater to her needs while I was actually carefully extracting the essence of the Black Delilah, I prepared a healthy dose of sleep tonic. I would have preferred to have my books to guide me, but I relied on memory to the best of my ability and followed standard practices for handling such delicate materials. Separately, I had prepared a much simpler concoction of other ingredients that would induce a fit of vomiting, keeping the queen's lady's maid occupied in the washroom for hours.

As the weekdays passed and the night of our mission approached, my thoughts were consumed by Varro. Had he made it to the safehouse even once? Had Saryn kept him informed of the plans? We would not have the luxury of returning to the safehouse on the next sabbath, since that would be when we'd carry out the plan, which meant it would be an additional week before I even got the chance to see him for the first time since leaving Basdie. I just needed to see his face to be certain he was alright. During the day, I kept my mind sharp and focused, but at night when I lay in bed next to a snoring Eladir, I struggled to keep my thoughts from wandering to him. On more than one occasion, I considered giving myself a tiny dose of the tonic to remedy this.

There was also anxiety about whether or not Nori could pull off her part. I imagined the dreamworld was not like reality. Did proximity matter? What did we all look like inside our dreams? How would she find the night guard? I reasoned she knew where the royals slept, like all healers would. Once she located the queen's quarters in the dream plane, there would only be one sleeping mind to enter—Gia would make sure of that.

For a castle that had recently undergone a coup, it was surprising how relaxed their procedures had become. Zarif was the only individual who truly struck fear into me. He was always watching, always assessing, and his silent manner made for an eerie presence. He had not spoken to me since our first encounter, but he'd glanced at me on more than one occasion, gazing too long for comfort. He was the only reason I constantly looked in the mirror, checking my appearance. Making sure the burn behind my ear was covered by my hair, that my skin appeared to have a natural tan and, most of all, that I was as inconspicuous as the rest of the staff. Since Gia had made no complaints about my services, this kept Shira out of my way. I'd made acquaintances with a few more servants thanks to El being particularly friendly.

Gia did share that she had learned early on that Zarif suffered from what is known as "Ever Autumn," a type of colorblindness, but that the servants referred to it as a hex and claimed it was the mark of a severed soul. This only heightened the staff's fear of him. Typically, I found myself erring on the side of science, placing no significance on a simple sight disorder. But there was something to the gossip, if I were being honest. Zarif appeared soulless, even lifeless at times. A husk of a Fae. Everything I'd read of dark magic meant there was a price, a consequence. Though he had never displayed anything other than an unpleasant aura, nor revealed any skill with magic, I secretly feared there was more beneath the surface.

The night of the mission passed in a blur. I walked through the motions almost mechanically, in disbelief of my role in it. The Canary Veil was never planned to hurt anyone, let alone murder someone. It just played out that way because of inexperience and mistakes. This *was* well-planned and intended to result in the death of more than one individual. My vials of sleep tonic were like props being carried onto the stage of a play where this tragedy would unfold. Any unnecessary loss of life was regrettable, but I continued to tell myself that every person in Nasallus was complicit in what was occurring.

I kept convincing myself as I handed the tray to a young lady's maid—who looked identical to the real one, now puking up her guts in the basement. I would never tire of seeing Gia's magnificent capability, both in awe and envy. The moment the tray left my fingertips, it all began, and we each played our roles flawlessly.

The queen in her bedroom.

The guard at her door.

The crashing noises of the tray falling from my arms.

Pieces moving quickly, like pawns across a chessboard to sacrifice the queen.

And in the early morning, while tending to Lady Gianna's hairstyle, we heard the sweet sounds of our victory ensue in the form of a shrill, high-pitched scream.

Checkmate.

I dared not peek my head out the door to watch Cairis' part, though curiosity itched at us both to do so. All this would be for naught if he wasn't there to escort the night guard to the cells. All we could do was wait. And wait we did. One long week of silence, waiting for answers that would only come when we could return to the safehouse once more.

The queen was dead. That we knew. King Silas may or may not have been pretending, but he appeared somber and grieving nonetheless. Silas did not seek the comfort of Gia's flesh even once that week. Either he was smart enough not to, or had been advised against it. The buzzing gossip that had clamored amongst the servants and Kingsguards the week prior had come to an immediate halt. No one dared breathe a word of it for fear of being implicated. Especially the queen's maid, who did not want to explain why she hadn't been at her duties that evening, nor could speak as to who was, in her absence. Everyone had turned their focus to preparing for a royal funeral. Zarif moved about the castle with more haste than usual, brow deeply furrowed as he wore a look of intense calculation.

About midweek, Gia made the risky move of eavesdropping on King Silas and Zarif. She assured me that she'd share what she had learned when we were together in the safety of each other's company.

When the sabbath came, we each departed for the safehouse, unsure of who would be able to make it. Gia and Cairis' attendance was critical, since they carried with them the information required to plan our next moves. I entered the safehouse through the back door, brushing sand off my hands, scolding myself internally for my inability to stay on my feet when portaling. The hum of the bond began to pulse rapidly beneath my skin in a flurry of excitement, indicating my mate's proximity. My frustrations from portaling quickly waned when I saw his glorious golden skin and curled white locks seated at the table across from Saryn. Praise the Gods, he was there.

His shoulders moved forward abruptly, as if to propel him to greet me until recognition of our surroundings sobered his actions. My pace quickened toward the open seat next to him, but I reinforced my mental shields, settled my feelings, and calmed my expression to greet him like any other member of the Imperi. By now, Saryn was the only one in the dark about our true affections. I had almost forgotten about the others entirely until I glanced around looking for Trace, who was nowhere to be seen, but every other member of our Order was now contained within the small dining area of the safehouse.

"Trace will not be joining us as he has been sent away on more raids in the name of the North," Saryn said.

Thoughts of Gia's stories about what Trace did during those raids made my stomach begin to roil. I took a cup from the center of the table, and Varro reached for the pitcher and handed it to me, brushing his fingers across mine subtly. Trying to conceal my blushing, I turned away. I filled my cup and sipped at the refreshment to distract myself.

"We succeeded! She's dead," Gia exclaimed with more joy than I'd expect for someone who had offed a fairly innocent individual.

"You sure did…" Cairis snorted out. "I saw the bloody mess you left in that room when I apprehended the night guard."

"She didn't feel a thing, thanks to Cress. I had to make it look like a real struggle occurred," she declared, trying to rally us toward some declaration of modesty in her handling of the situation.

Saryn interrupted impatiently, "Did you get eyes on Embry…I mean, the princess?"

A smug expression came over Cairis' face. "I did. She's down there. She looks like shit for a royal—but anyone would, given the deplorable state of the prison."

There was a collective sigh of relief from the lot of us after hearing that the mission was successful on all fronts. Although Gia would not let it show, I think she was especially relieved to hear she hadn't knifed a female for nothing.

"The night guard kicked and wailed at first, shouting his denials, but by the time we got him to the cells, he had shriveled up in shock and horror. I think it took a minute for Nori's work to settle into his memory," Cairis surmised.

I turned to look at Nori, who did not at all appear proud of her involvement. Meekly, she said, "It will haunt him forever, what I did. Or at least what's left of his days…" Her words trailed off in regret.

"It doesn't matter what he does or doesn't admit to because I've managed to uncover exactly what they're going to do with that poor soul," Gia said proudly, and I was certain she was about to share the results of her eavesdropping. Something I had been curious about since the moment she mentioned it back in Nasallus.

"What will his punishment be?" Varro asked in an even tone.

It was the first time I'd heard his voice upon entering the establishment.

"Zarif, in typical conniving fashion, will never allow the kingdom to believe she had an affair, nor that she was murdered on their watch; it makes Silas and his regime appear weak." Gia's expression turned angry. "They are prepared to announce that her guard was a Baelin sympathizer-turned-insider for the North, and that he committed the act as revenge. They will connect it to all the false activities Trace and others have been up to, further stoking the fires of Northern hatred."

Cairis' hand clenched into a tight fist, and everyone around the table grew frustrated with the idea that our plan had backfired. Now they would have the citizens of Artume believing that we Northerners had gone so far as to assassinate their new queen. I dipped my head in regret for not demanding alternate paths to access the prison cells. It was now abundantly clear to me how far Zarif would go to paint the picture he wanted the kingdom to believe.

"That's not all…" Gia said, and I could tell from her tone that something truly terrible was coming. "They claim she was with child!"

"She was pregnant?" Nori screeched in disbelief, horror written across every line of her face.

"Of course not!" Gia declared angrily. "He never touched that frigid female. Me and the others he actually fucks would know. They're just saying it to make matters worse, to squeeze every last bit of outrage and sympathy out of the situation."

"If they're not careful, this alone could incite a war," Saryn declared. I had never seen Saryn worried, but his current expression conveyed an emotion not far from it. "We have a dead queen, a soon-to-be-dead night guard, and falsehoods that only create more pressure on our timeline."

"There is some good news..." Cairis interjected. The rest of us waited in silence for him to deliver any semblance of the sort. "Princess Embry's cell is somewhat secluded from the others. They don't keep many guards there because she's weak and docile, unlike the other prisoners who require more of the guards' attention."

"I fail to see how knowing she is still guarded is helpful to us," Varro said dismissively.

"Because there are empty cells on both sides of her; it's the female's quarters within the prison. She is the only female down there, currently, to the best of my knowledge. From what I heard, no one stays down there long. They're either sent away for judgement and execution, or quickly moved to manual labor. Sometimes even worse...banished to the Ivory Waste."

It was clear Cairis had been doing his job, paying attention to the prison operations and taking note of Embry's surroundings. It wasn't a ton to work with, but it was enough to at least put a plan into motion. One that would involve much more risk for Nori this time around.

In the few hours that followed, we discussed a means to reach Princess Embry, but we also spent time allowing Varro to share his intel. They were indeed building a large armada of ships in their bay. It wasn't clear yet to Varro why so many ships were needed or what they would carry. Everyone knew that attacking Cambria from the sea would fail. They could never transport enough Fae on ships to offset the siege awaiting them. King Aeon would defend his shorelines with an arsenal of weaponry and infantry within moments of seeing the ships' approach.

This was perhaps the most frustrating part of everything we were doing. It seemed there was a larger picture at play that had not yet been revealed to us. I could only hope Embry's information was correct, as she would be a valuable ally to our cause. Did we owe it to her family to try and free her and restore the kingdom to its rightful heir? That wasn't necessarily the mission we were tasked with, but none of this would have happened if the bloodlines that aimed to keep the peace ruled, rather than the puppet of a deviant Hand. From Gia's reports, Silas wasn't smart enough or particularly interested in pulling the strings. He was under a very manipulative and meticulous kind of control that boiled down to one male—Zarif.

Varro rose from his seat, indicating that he needed to return to his clan. He would continue to try and uncover what the plans for the ships entailed, and report back as soon as he had something. Internally, his exit made me frantic. There was no time to talk, no way to spend an extra moment in private with him the way Trace and I had weeks ago. I followed him to the doorway, pretending to escort him out, and told the others I'd keep watch while he used his moonstone. We were still within earshot of the others, so all I could do was lower my mental shields to him and offer a silent message. The small cloudlike ring appeared behind him and he gave me a nod of acknowledgement, returning my silent affections before I locked my shields again and watched him disappear into the misty portal. It was mere crumbs of what I'd hoped for, but he seemed well enough and that was the best I could ask for given our circumstances.

CHAPTER

21

The next step in reaching the princess entailed another trip to the Grim Garden, with Gia standing watch while I gathered the necessary ingredients. This time, I'd be concocting a potion that wasn't deadly but whose manifestation was not subtle. As soon as it was ready, I tested it on my skin, and within an hour the boils began to appear on my forearm. They blistered and oozed, the pain akin to a sting or a burn, but I had only dabbed it on my skin. If ingested, this same affliction of the flesh would spread all over the body. It would appear much worse than it felt.

Root of Woodsworth was something most Fae were allergic to. It flowered in the spring and created a beautiful display for onlookers, but was not to be handled without gloves. Its pollen was also quite messy. Woodsworth flowers were only valuable to its keepers because they attracted hummingbirds.

I channeled my energy into healing my wounds, which stopped the spread and left no scars. I felt guilty delivering this to someone I'd never even met. The tonic I had made for the queen led to a painless slumber—before her untimely death. This would result in a more drawn-out type of discomfort, but we had to set things in motion, regardless of my conscience.

Over that same time period, I tried to make my presence in and out of the kitchen feel natural by grabbing extra fruits and nuts at the behest of Lady Gianna. I timed the dinner bells with precision, noting when the nobles' meals were prepared, when leftovers arrived for the servants, and, most importantly, when what little remained was plated for prisoners. One time El questioned me on it, having watched my movements a little too closely that day. Her interrogation insinuated that I'd pocketed these items for myself and others. When I acted appalled at her accusations, I asked her if she would like to go question my Lady directly as to why she had certain cravings during her bleeding.

That shut El up rather quickly, and I moved past her with a derisive scoff. She later apologized for the intrusion and explained she just didn't want to be associated with any thievery; the last servant caught sneaking food had their hand removed in punishment. Since I'd never seen a handless servant in Nasallus, I presumed they were also relieved of their position immediately. Ever since the death of the queen, the staff were more tense, focused on fulfilling their duties and keeping low profiles.

The other prisoners were served a disgusting slop of combined leftovers and three-day-old bread; you could barely call it food. It was amusing how obvious it was which plate was intended for Princess Embry. Her meal contained a fuller and fresher variety of sustenance. I poured the liquid I'd created into a few bowls of the stew, as well as her drink. I had taken extra time to prepare the ingredient to make it flavorless. We couldn't just inflict the sickness on Embry. I had to make sure some of the other prisoners caught it too, so it would seem like a small plague had broken out. I watched a few of the servants carry the trays away, which would eventually be handed off to Kingsguards who would then deliver them to the cells.

All we had to do was wait. From there, complaints by the prisoners covered in hideous lesions would alert their captors, causing panic. Eventually, they would realize something was happening and summon a healer. They would need one to make a determination about if this was harmless or more dire in nature, requiring a full immunization of the situation. This typically meant eliminating the carriers, burning anything they'd touched, and sanitizing the space to protect everyone else in the castle from the spread. A very similar approach to what happened after El's original roommate grew ill.

The next part relied on Nori being convincing enough in conveying her experience working in plague settings, and therefore was comfortable handling such cases. She would make note that she'd developed a routine of tonics that strengthened her immunity. If that wasn't enough to convince them, then she'd remind her mentors that their skills were much too valuable to waste on the health of lowly prisoners. They would need to protect themselves, should a spread occur, and their skills be required for the royal family and other members of Silas' inner circle.

Nori wasn't the best liar amongst us, but her innocent appearance helped offset those weaknesses. It was very difficult to look at someone as sweet and kind as she appeared and think that there might be something more manipulative beneath the surface of her kind eyes. But I'd seen those eyes once, when they'd turned pitch black at the threat made against her parents. I'd also seen the ease at which she played me for a fool, time and time again during our games. That was the Nori we needed, and I knew she could do it. My next job was to sleep.

Sleep did not come easily to me in Nasallus. Perhaps it was because I had a roommate that constantly kept me on my toes with her watchful eyes and obnoxious snoring. Wondering about Varro and his safety may have also factored into the equation. Too many times, my thoughts drifted to Trace and the heavy burden he carried on this mission. The look on his face from the rooftop haunted me still.

Nori had accidentally slipped in and out of my dreams before, which meant she'd know how to find me in the dreamscape. We determined I'd be the best candidate to await her messages. If she was able to make it back to the safehouse, she could relay what she'd learned herself. As backup, she was instructed to send her memories through dreams. That would allow me to know everything she'd learned, if she succeeded but was detained from reaching the safehouse. This, perhaps, wasn't the most foolproof part of the plan, given I was the one prone to a potentially deteriorating memory.

Two nights passed since we had sent the tainted food and drink into the prison cells. Gia incessantly checked in with me, asking if I'd learned anything, even going so far as encouraging me to take naps in case Nori was looking for me in the dream plane. Napping while on duty as a servant was an impossible ask. When I awoke on the third morning, I wrapped my arms around my chest trying to quell the tight feeling in it. A familiar feeling. Anxiety. Dread. There was a memory itching at the forefront of my mind from a dream. A memory that felt foreign and not my own. I closed my eyes under the covers trying to tell my body to accept it and not fight it. Is this what it felt like when Nori meddled versus watched? Is this how the Kingsguard felt when he awoke to memories of a slain queen?

The images were fuzzy, dark, and a feeling of cold flushed across my skin. The viewpoint was mildly obscured and seemed to lack vision on the periphery. I realized I was viewing the scene through Nori's eyes. It wasn't like she was floating above herself and seeing the interaction as it played out, instead it was exactly how she'd seen it herself.

Before me was a sickly-slender female in a dirty, tattered dress, sitting on the stone floor of a cell. Her attire, though well made, was raggedy and clung to every inch of her delicate frame. Even in the dim light, the warm undertones of her infected flesh were a sign that she had much lighter skin than her father's side. Together, their pairing had created a stunning Royal Fae whose energy radiated outward from her, generating an aura of warmth despite her distressed state. All her striking features complimented her beauty. She had long, dark, curly hair cascading down her back, cocooning her shoulders in messy tendrils. Her short-bridged nose sat atop full lips, and when she gazed up at Nori, her eyes were a brilliant amber, like honey-colored diamonds. They sparkled despite the despair of her circumstances that threatened to kill the light within. Princess Embry's beauty captivated me as the memory continued to play.

Hushed whispers, exchanges of information flowed quickly back and forth between the two of them, and I did my best to commit all of it to memory. An incredible amount of focus was needed to retain the information, for a stray thought could cause the dream to slip too far from the waking mind and disintegrate into the depths of the dreamscape. There was no way to notify Nori that I'd received her message. She was relying on me to carry this information forward and know what to do with it.

When we were alone, I relayed the visions to Gia to ensure my fragile memory was not the only place storing such crucial information. She and I patiently played our parts as lady's maid and mistress in the days that followed, biding our time until the next sabbath when we could more easily depart. Shortly after the funeral, Silas resumed seeing Gia in the evenings. His mourning had been short-lived. *Was someone still referred to as a mistress if the wife was deceased?* I pondered.

Nori had not sent any additional messages in my sleep, but it was clear her first attempt had resulted in establishing contact with Princess Embry. She had gained her trust and retrieved valuable information that we would soon share with the rest of the Imperi. There hadn't been any murmurs of plague throughout the castle, so she had either convinced them the incident had been contained, or they'd all been discarded by now; their bodies sent away for cremation. I worried every day about

Nori's safety and if she'd be treated as one of the sick ones and made to stay down there.

My job throughout the week involved routinely lacing the prisoners' food with small doses of the Woodsworth to prevent their ailments from resolving fully. This would keep a healer in visitation if they hadn't stationed Nori or someone there permanently. Plagues were not to be taken lightly. Entire bloodlines could be wiped out in a fortnight. Any signs of such would be met with extreme measure. In fact, there were some days when I wondered why Idris didn't just give me the go-ahead to take out the entirety of Nasallus Castle. With the right set of ingredients, it could be done. Was Cambria intentionally showing restraint? When I let my mind wander to darker, more deviant means, I had to remind myself we were here to avoid something more catastrophic occurring. So, sleight of hand it would be, until they gave us a compelling reason to conduct ourselves otherwise.

We waited over an hour at the safehouse to see if Nori would arrive. When she never showed, and the rest of us had all arrived, I was forced to convey everything I'd learned from the memory shared with me, as Saryn's impatience was wearing extremely thin. I did my best to ignore the shaking of my hands as I considered her unknown whereabouts.

Varro's face was the only thing that had brought me any sense of comfort. As I felt a calm wash over me, I met his eyes, knowing that he was using Siren Song to settle my nerves enough to get through the debrief. My side of the bond always felt soothed when in close proximity to him, and I needed to control my desires to satiate the bond.

"Nori successfully engaged our target. The princess is being treated for the skin ailment that afflicts a majority of the prisoners. Upon gaining her trust, Nori has made it clear she is a sympathizer and stands with the now-deceased King Baelin."

Cairis interrupted me before I could continue. "She should be careful; both of them. Nori could get herself killed admitting to something like that. I've heard about what they've done to others who shared those sentiments."

Trace's response was filled with skepticism. "The princess trusts her already? This female is either an idiot, or she's luring traitors to keep her own head."

Saryn pounded his fist on the table, directing all our attention to where he sat at the head. "She's managed to stay alive all this time; does that sound like something an idiot could do?"

Trace rolled his eyes and tugged his folded arms closer against his chest in an even more defensive posture than he normally displayed.

"She's alive because of something to do with the Ledor Canyon," I announced, thinking about its placement on the map. To the far southwest, the mouth of the Ledor River formed a canyon of great depths from years of erosion and, according to historians and scribes, massive land quakes. The Ledor River was a natural barrier between Cambria and Artume, but the canyon was meaningless to Artume for all I knew. A majority of it sat on the northern side, belonging to Cambria. I couldn't fathom what interest the Artumians would have in it.

"What about it?" Trace grumbled.

"Her father knew something about the area he had been keeping a secret. Not even Princess Embry truly knows why her father had a fascination with the region."

"That's not helpful," he replied, and I wanted to smack that smug look off his face so he'd give me a damn minute to finish sharing everything Nori conveyed.

Giving him my best I-will-stab-you look, I took a deep breath and continued: "Zarif knew Baelin had secrets, so he put his daughter through an interrogation until he was able to get her to utter the words *Ledor Canyon*. He tried his best to pry more from her until he was resigned to believe that she had no other information to share. But Zarif is untrusting, and he keeps her alive just in case there is more to be learned or gained by her eventual execution."

Silence hovered between us all as we sat contemplating what little information we had. Were we at an impasse? Would Nori eventually make contact again and have something more valuable to share? Did Embry have more resolve than we all expected and harbor more truths about her father's secrets? This seemed like a meager amount of intel, and the Ledor Canyon was far from Nasallus, so it wasn't as if it were an easy there-and-back mission to scope it out.

At the end of the table, I watched as Saryn's one good eye narrowed.

"I know what they are after," he finally said through gritted teeth.

"What is it?" Gia demanded.

"No one is supposed to know about this. Not even I have clearance for this information. I only know because Idris made the mistake of unknowingly confirming my suspicions."

Each of us hung on his every word, sitting at the edges of our seats, waiting to see if Saryn would unveil this hunch he'd stitched together. What could it be if we weren't supposed to know, let alone him? This did confirm one thing I'd always wondered: The king does keep secrets from the Imperi. We may have been privy to a lot, had access to his treasury, and been given the freedom to carry out his will without retribution, yet there were secrets kept even from the Order of Forgotten Fae.

Saryn pulled a small object out of his shirt pocket and placed it in the center of the table. We looked down at the familiar item, smooth, polished and milky white. His moonstone.

"This is what they seek."

"I thought these are rare and few," I inquired, eyeing the stone with new speculation.

"They are." Saryn's brow furrowed in deep consideration. "But there is believed to be a vein buried deep within the canyon walls."

"What are they going to do with a few portal stones?" Cairis asked, sounding unconvinced that this posed any true threat, especially when said source resided on the Cambrian side of the border. Would Zarif really attempt a mission across enemy lines?

"A few stones? Try thousands. A mine like that in the hands of our enemy's military…who knows how many they could already have?" he said, exasperated. "Whatever the amount, it's too many. We must cut them off at the source."

Once more Saryn appeared visibly concerned, and that was alarming indeed. Sure, I'd seen him surprised, proud, annoyed, impatient—a whole slew of disappointed and judgmental emotions, but there was real fear emanating from him now. Because of that, I knew to take his grave conclusions seriously.

Saryn's certainty of Zarif and the king's intent set into motion a plan that had my unique gift at the center of it. Everybody had quickly resolved that he was right, and our next move should address whatever was going on in Ledor Canyon. Whether because Saryn had already known of these secret mines or because Embry's words somehow corroborated it, we all surrendered to the process of building a plan that would have Saryn and I making the long journey together.

There was no way we could all abandon our posts for that long and then easily return to them. Plus, there was still more to learn. Varro had yet to uncover the details of the ships they were building. Gia couldn't be away from the king's side for long, and if Trace wasn't out committing atrocities, then that might get back to Zarif. To account for my absence, a letter would be delivered to Shira informing her that one of my family members in Caano had been murdered during one of the night attacks from the Northerners. I would be granted leave to tend to funeral arrangements in my home village, so long as my Lady gave permission.

Much of the rest of our time together was spent discussing travel arrangements and how my gift might come into play. The thought of being on a mission *with* Saryn and not *for* Saryn was intimidating, to say the least. I had never thought of myself as his peer, certainly not his equal. Yes, we were both blood-sworn Imperi, but he was from another Order, and his demonstration of shapeshifting alone made me feel like his power had always surpassed mine. He had much of what I lacked. Discipline. Control. Years of experience. And, if I were being honest with myself, ruthlessness. Saryn was what I'd describe as cold-blooded. Every Fae in his path was just an obstacle to be dealt with in whatever manner suited him.

He was hardened from years of performing the duties required of him. He was compliant in the same way Trace was, except Trace still bore the agony of his misdeeds, whereas Saryn wore them with ease. Saryn had surrendered to the inevitability of the Imperi, whereas our youthful optimism still believed that there would be an end. The end of this mission. The end of our time in Artume. We hadn't yet accepted the harsh or inescapable truth that he, Theory, and Idris lived by.

Cairis made his exit to return to the Kingsguard, as many would be making their way back from prayers to prepare for the dinner hour. Before I departed, he squeezed me tightly and wished me luck, unsure if he'd see me again. I tugged his hulking shoulders downward to lower his ear to me and whispered, "Get eyes on Nori, make sure she's okay." It was a plea, and we both knew it. He looked me in the eye and nodded, then portaled back to the castle. Gia exited shortly after without a goodbye, knowing we'd meet again in her room later on.

I looked over my shoulder to see Trace and Saryn in what seemed to be a quiet argument. "Her power isn't infinite," I heard Trace warn him as if he somehow knew the cost.

"Not your concern," Saryn replied, as Trace turned his back on him to make his exit.

Trace and I were alone in the alleyway as Varro stayed back to discuss more with Saryn inside the safehouse.

As he conjured his misty window to portal through, he looked back at me and said, "I pray to the Gods you are not too late. And I pray the cost is not too high," before disappearing.

Just as I had planned, Varro was the last to exit the safehouse. I wasn't about to travel even farther from him, so far our unsealed bond may not even feel one another's existence, without speaking with him. We walked a ways through rows of charred houses and buildings until we reached a patch of dense, tropical forest. Under the leafy canopy, I breathed a sigh of relief, its shade cooling my skin. It was the first time I had heard the buzzing and hissing of insects since arriving in the desert kingdom. The king's solarium was absent of sounds that indicated abundant life, even in its tiniest form. I closed my eyes, trying to remember the forests back home: different plant life, different shades of green, soil not sand. I breathed in the scent, but it was so vastly different from home. Tears threatened to break through the barrier of my lashes as I recalled memories of that place. A place I may someday struggle to remember. Somewhere I might never return. A short life, minuscule in the shadow of time.

Large, strong arms wrapped around me from behind, enveloping me protectively.

"Moirai," he whispered against my ear, his lips brushing the sensitive skin, sending a shiver down my spine.

I exhaled at the sound of it and turned to clasp his face between my hands, desperate to feel those lips against mine. I pressed him to me; his hands moved fervently across my body in response. It had been so long—too long—since I'd felt his touch. He tilted my head with his rough, calloused hands, kissing and biting all along my neck, angling my pliant body to his will.

Before long, I realized he wasn't just passionate, he was frantic. Desperate. He was trying to mark me with his mouth. He inhaled my scent. He ran his fingers through my hair and across my soft flesh like he may never touch it again. He let out a breathy plea:

"Please, Cress. Please let our bond protect you."

Without even waiting for my answer, he dropped to his knees before me, resting his head against my navel and holding me tightly against him. He was begging me to seal the bond because of his own fear. His fear of losing me. Whether to the mission or the Drift. He wouldn't look up at me, instead, he continued to stare down at the forest floor, shaking his head against my stomach in frustration.

"If only for protection, *please.*"

His words practically broke me. With his mental shields down, his mind was racing with thoughts. Among them, the clarity that he would not force me to see him as his mate romantically, so long as I sealed the bond to protect me from harm. His plea was not sexual in nature, though the act required making love. He wanted the bond sealed for every other reason—putting me first, above all.

To anchor me from the Drift. To meld our minds and thoughts. To formally tether the bond, no matter the distance. He couldn't bear sending me away without any of those assurances. His palpable fear alarmed me. Was I being foolish to not give in? I felt his hands grasp my legs harder, and when I grabbed his face and tilted it up to look into his eyes, I saw within them an ocean, a storm swirling in endless circles of desperation. I released him and lowered to my knees as well, taking Varro's hands in mine.

"His loyalty was born of desire," he said, nudging his chin back in the direction of the safehouse. "Mine is born of devotion."

His need to separate himself from Trace and what we had was unnecessary, and it broke something in me to know he still felt the need to do so. Trace had left me when Varro laid down his life. They were not the same. *This* was not the same. In any way, shape, or form.

"I love you." His words were exasperated but clear. His gaze locked onto mine when he spoke, searing his words into my heart. Silence descended between us.

"I love you, too, and because I love you, I will not let fear be the reason either of us completes the bond." I paused, trying to speak the words with a quivered lip. "Fear will not win; let love conquer."

A tear of surrender rolled down his cheek as I fought back my own.

CHAPTER 22

hen Shira arrived at mine and El's doorway with parchment in hand, I knew it was time to pull off one of my better acting jobs. I had the benefit of knowing what was coming, so I'd thought long and hard about what it might look like if I had been notified that someone I loved had died…a brutal death, at the hands of an enemy, no less. Though I loved Varro, I chose to picture someone much closer to me, someone that it would feel like my very heart was being ripped from my chest should news like that arrive. Versa.

"Cress, dear. I have unfortunate news to deliver," she said in a tone I had never heard leave her mouth toward me or any other servant. Did Shira have a soft spot after all, or was she simply that affected by delivering news of the North's continued devastation to one of her own?

I walked calmly over to Shira and grabbed the note from her hand, opening the parchment in front of them both because I wanted multiple witnesses to the act. I appeared to be scanning the words, and as my eyes went down the page, I allowed my hand holding it to tremble. Then

I performed a small glamour, making my skin appear pale white with shock.

"No, no, no…!" I dropped to my knees, crumpling the letter to my chest.

"What?" El squeaked. "What happened?"

She was down on the floor by my side almost immediately as I began to rock back and forth clutching the news to my chest before letting out a shrill scream of "*Why?*" followed by a desperate cry of absolute mourning that echoed all the way down the hallway. As I imagined news of Versa's untimely death, I let myself fall deep into that emotion and the feeling of utter helplessness, a tether since birth cut in half, a loss so unbearable I could only gasp for breath as my lungs felt like they collapsed inward.

Tears streamed down my face, my nose wet with moisture and my eyes bloodshot from the strain of expelling such hurt, a physical manifestation of my pain. I pretended to be incapable of speech and shakily handed the letter to El, unsure if she could even read. She read the letter silently, gave a look of horror to Shira and placed her hand on my back while beginning to rub it in small, comforting circles. I continued to rock back and forth, now clutching my own chest in disbelief.

Shira tried to get my attention in between my muffled cries of grief.

"I will ask Lady Gianna if she would grant you leave so that you may attend to your sister's funeral in Caano." She paused in concern. "It is not common practice to grant leave for such things, but these acts happening to our citizens are unspeakable. Surely, she must understand."

El chimed in, "Tell Lady Gianna I promise I will help tend to her needs in Cress's absence. Please, Shira, convince her just this once!"

I continued the charade of tears and sobs, beside myself while both of them attempted to work out how they'd influence Gia to grant me leave for funeral preparations. Little did they know, Gia was already waiting for the request.

That night I did not eat dinner, and when I returned from tending to

Gia, El could see my eyes were still puffy and bloodshot. Pretending Versa was dead to keep myself in a believable state of distress was exhausting.

Exertion from the day sent me into a quick and deep sleep, which I had hoped for in case Nori sought to find me again. I'd feel much better heading out with Saryn just knowing she was okay, or of any other details that would help us in our effort to curtail whatever was going on in Ledor Canyon.

I awoke the next morning with no feelings of foreign memories awaiting my interpretation or recollection. My sleep was restless and dreamless. When I went to the dining hall with El, Shira found me and was pleased to inform me I was granted leave immediately. El breathed a sigh of relief, and I displayed a numb but grateful expression.

"My Lady is most kind." I nodded as Shira walked away, and El promised she was going to take the best care of Gianna while I was away. She ate every last crumb of her breakfast while I moved the food around on my plate with fake disinterest. Afterwards, as I was packing up some of my belongings for the trip, El grilled me with questions about Gia's preferences and how to best serve her in my absence. Humorously, I thought about misleading El to perform my duties in ways I knew Gia detested. I decided against the idea, though it was tempting.

I had finished packing and was prepared to make my exit when El stopped me and asked me a question that gave me pause. So much so, that I was concerned to be leaving without seeing Gia so I could relay it to her.

"Why do you use mental shields?" she asked, with an edge of innocence to an otherwise provocative question.

I had been keeping mental shields up since the day she'd met me. Why was she just now concerning herself with this? I answered a question with a question.

"Why do you care?"

There was a slight flinch in El's expression, like my response seemed combative, challenging her.

"I-I-" she stuttered, "I was just wondering if you were trained to do that? Is it proper where you're from?"

She sounded insecure in her response and I let the silence build between us. I'd been taught the first person to speak relinquishes their advantage in these types of conversations.

"Almost everyone…except for maybe Zarif, seems to be a buzz of pointless thoughts, but you're not."

"Do you think after something like the Silent Eve you should be so open and reckless with your thoughts, however innocent they may seem?" I questioned her.

El began to utter an excuse, but I interrupted her.

"After what the North did to my sister, I'd burn their people to ash if I had the chance, but does that prove my loyalty? No one needs access to my unfiltered thoughts; is that a good enough answer for you?" I leaned into her, using the proximity of my body to hers to exert a sense of dominance. With such a statement, I'd solidified in her mind that I hated the North with a passion, but also that I trusted no one. El wasn't dimwitted, but she was naïve. I was once like her. In some ways, I still was. But every passing day while serving the Imperi, I learned how trust should never be given, but earned.

Saryn had prepared everything for the three-day journey to Ledor Canyon. The first part of our trip would be on camelback. They were more suited to the desert climate, while also capable of carrying our supplies. The plan was eventually to transition to horseback as we got closer to the Ledor River, where the terrain was more accommodating. I had never ridden a camel before, only read about them and seen sketches and paintings. After securing my packs to my animal's sides, I saddled up and squeezed my thighs tightly as it leaned forward, almost tipping me over its head before standing to its full height. Sitting atop a camel was much higher than riding a horse, and their steps rocked and swayed the saddle far more, creating an uncomfortable experience.

Saryn, on the other hand, looked like a natural, and it made me wonder if he'd had prior missions in Artume that had provided him the opportunity to ride them more frequently. He and I were not the type to make idle chatter, so this wasn't a question I intended to ask him. On any other occasion, I might have found this to be adventurous, being around a new animal and riding it through an unknown landscape. But this time, every step that giant animal took was one towards a task I was dreading down to my very core.

Being alone with Saryn was its own adventure. He was my mentor, so I shouldn't fear him, but he had always trained me with unforgiving authority, and that tension remained between us at all times. As we made our way out of the city surrounding Nasallus, I reminded myself that I was saying goodbye to civilization for at least a week. Three days there and three back meant I'd have nothing but the company of Saryn and the silence of the desert as my companion. I was less than thrilled at the notion, secretly wishing another one of us had been made to join us, but Saryn had insisted we needed to keep a low profile and appear unthreatening if we encountered anyone along the journey. The others being away from their station too long could also cause a slew of other problems for us upon arriving back at the safehouse. None of us argued with him, but Trace was the one who looked particularly displeased with the arrangement, and his concern alone had me on edge.

Trace had been in and out of these lands for some time now, wreaking havoc between villages. Why did the idea of me travelling alone with Saryn concern him?

As the hours passed, the red and orange sands of Nasallus slowly transitioned to light brown as the city itself became blurry, like a mirage in the far-off distance. Eventually, it was no longer in sight, and the sands below the camels' feet were now a powdery cream. This is why the southernmost parts of Artume, the lands where no one dared to go, were referred to as the Ivory Waste. Miles and miles of bone-colored sand in all directions could cause an inexperienced traveler to get lost easily. But we were not headed south, we were headed west, keeping the Ledor River to our right and ensuring we wouldn't become disoriented by the dunes of this strange and vast place.

Much of the ride was silent except for the sounds of the camels' bodies shifting against our leather packs of supplies and the occasional gusts of wind creating flurries of fine sand in the air. Both Saryn and I wore light muslin fabric wrapped around our heads and faces to both shield us from inhaling the dust and protect us from the sun beating down overhead. There weren't exactly roads leading us to where we were headed, but there were clear paths formed by the prints of other hooved animals who had recently traveled in the same direction. I felt a slight moment of panic at the idea of a sandstorm eliminating them and Saryn having no idea which direction we'd come from.

With the silence of the ride, I was left with the solitude of my own thoughts. I kept my shields up despite only Saryn being around, because that is what he taught me and—unlike El—he'd see them being down as a lapse in my judgement for which I'd be chastised. I'd been so busy with the mission and my act since arriving in Artume that I'd had very little time to be contemplative within my own mind. It was eerily uncomfortable, as I was an overthinker by nature.

This is something I might have once cherished. A quiet moment for introspection and reading. Letting my mind wander with the words across the page, being swept into a different world and becoming the characters within the story. But now the feeling was foreign, and I wondered if it nagged at Saryn the way it did me, or if he had somehow found a way to turn that part of himself off. The part that craved peace and quiet with no obligations. Did he crave socialization? Were words sitting at the tip of his tongue like they were mine, just aching to hear the sound of another's voice and take comfort in not being truly alone? Saryn was an enigma to me.

Theory was exactly what she always claimed. She was pragmatic. She was straightforward and sincere. Unlike Saryn, her words were not as calculated and cryptic. For however scary Theory was, she wasn't quite a mystery. Saryn, though, was aloof and vague in a way that made his intentions and loyalties just as elusive. We'd been tied to one another in this Order for less than a year, and I wondered how long it would take until he trusted me or any of us. What would we have to do to earn that? Was it even possible?

My camel seemed content to follow his, so there wasn't really an opportunity where we were side by side and I could perhaps engage him in conversation. I settled for the situation as it was and watched time pass as the sun's shadow of our caravan moved across the sand.

When the sky began to dim, Saryn led us a ways off the main trail and established camp. There wasn't anything around for miles in every direction. This left us vulnerable, but also able to see oncoming danger. It was only the first night, and I already wished that I'd seen Ledor Canyon with my own eyes before now so we could portal there rather than spend two more days like this. I also toyed with the idea of flying to cover the remaining distance to our destination. How high would we need to fly in order to avoid detection? I didn't bother suggesting this, knowing it would be met with immediate criticism, so I just accepted my circumstances.

We unloaded our heavy packs and began to set up our separate tents. Though I tried to keep the interior of my tent free of the intrusive sand, I soon realized that my efforts would be in vain. I despised the sand. It was such a nuisance. I hated the texture it left on my skin and how my lips always tasted salty. I disliked the dry air and the harsh sunlight that caused me to squint my eyes and, subsequently, my head to throb from keeping my facial expression set unnaturally.

As I continued to make camp for the evening, I realized what a petulant child I sounded like, even in my own head. These were the types of moments where Varro, on more than one occasion, had counseled me to count my blessings rather than focus on the negative and uncontrollable circumstances of my situation. I rolled my eyes because he always sounded wise and in control, whereas I still hadn't found a way to stop my emotions from getting the best of me.

I kicked at the sand in frustration and helped Saryn set up a small fire to prepare our meal. He started it with flint stones, and it was an odd thing to watch, remembering what my father had taught Versa and me. With no flame to draw upon, this is how it was done in the natural way. The fire would be essential to keep us warm. I found it fascinating that the desert could be so unbelievably hot during the day and so drastically the opposite at night.

The sun had almost set fully, and we gathered by the fire to eat our dinner when Saryn said, "Are you going to be able to pull this off?"

Nothing like some light dinner conversation. "Why are you bringing me if you don't think I can do it?" I replied snarkily.

"I'm bringing you because you're a more subtle means of thwarting Silas' plan. The alternative, a garrison of northern troops, would present great risk."

"Isn't the fact that they snuck across our border and are essentially stealing from our lands enough to warrant a response? Why would we be at fault for defending our borders?" I asked, honestly wondering why a more covert solution was even necessary.

Saryn took another bite of his food and chewed through his response, but no one was around to judge him but me.

"I agree with you, but our king has always been too hesitant, and Idris fails to counsel him otherwise. He prefers Cambria does not appear as aggressors, and taking down an entire group of indentured miners would go against that strategy."

"But we *are* taking down an entire group of Artumians!" I argued back indignantly.

He snapped his head in my direction. "No, we're not. A landfall that caused a portion of the canyon to collapse on itself will take the life of those miners. That is why you're here." He smirked before taking a drink.

Hearing his summary of how the events would unfold solidified my opinion that Saryn was a truly callous male.

"Oh, how timely," I said sarcastically. "A canyon made of some of the strongest and oldest rock in our world suddenly caves in on itself, how strange that is."

"Very strange," he said back dismissively, continuing to eat his meal. "You know what your problem is, Cress?"

"What?"

"You still believe everything is as it seems. You take things at face value. You think history is as it was written. I wonder how long it will take you to truly shed yourself of such naivety." He paused. "That is, if you live long enough to find out."

Silence hung between us for a long time after that remark. I did not expect him to be the first to speak again.

"Do you think Aeon wants people to know that there may be moonstones in that canyon? Or do you think he'd rather scholars and commonfolk spin tales of how treacherous and barren the landscape of Ledor is so that no one ever bothers to even think about going there. Do you think the lessons in your little books at your highbrow academies teach you the truth or what they want you to believe?"

I'd never thought about doubting a single word of any text I'd read until Basdie. When they told us to read every book with scrutiny and question which side had written those texts. What did they benefit from having us believe their histories? I watched the light of the fire between us flicker shadows across Saryn's rugged face. His facial hair, trimmed tight, showed the sharp angles of his jawline, leading up to his eye patch and more silvery hair atop his head. I always wondered how old he was. How long had he been carrying out the will of King Aeon or those before him? What was the story of his bloodline? Was he Honored or Royal?

"When did you learn to distrust everything?" Of all the questions racing through my mind, this was the only one I felt brave enough to ask.

"Not all of us were given a beautiful life like you. Some of us, like Trace and myself, have known evil since a very young age. Some of us learned it was better to distrust those around us, those closest to us. We didn't have to shed our naivety; we were never privileged enough to have it in the first place."

His truth cut through me like a dull knife as I reflected on the fact that all High Fae, which I had always believed to be privileged and blessed, were not. Wealth, beauty, standing…these did not always beget a fortunate existence.

Perhaps Saryn despised me for the time I was granted those things. Maybe his handling of me was misdirected jealousy.

The sky above had finally turned pitch black, except for the brilliant sparkle of the endless starscape above, where large clusters of stars appeared almost like clouds. I'd never seen such a thing of wonderment. No fires or Fae light in the distance to distract from its vastness and enormity.

Saryn noticed me staring, mouth agape.

"Even when you look up from a place as desolate and scary as the Ivory Waste, there is beauty. I hope to go there someday…"

"To where?" I asked.

"To where the stars hold dominion."

We sat in the silence of his answer, knowing the weight of his response. Wherever that was, the gateway to the Gods or worlds beyond, we hoped it was ruled by fairer, kinder, more peaceful minds. For our world felt destined to be tangled in conflict for eternity, cursed.

The next day, I was anxious to resume our dinner conversations. The prospect of telling him about the Drift had been eating away at me all day. If he and Cambria were counting on my ability to take down the Ledor Canyon, what else were they counting on me for? What if this single act destroyed my mind?

Halfway into the trip, I realized fantasizing about a bath the entire journey wasn't going to improve my attitude or concentration. Instead, I focused my sights on the dunes in the distance, studying the patterns the wind created in the sand. The lines etched like waves, proof of the element's influence over it. I began to focus my energy on creating small whirls of sand in the distance. To any onlooker it might appear as something naturally occurring.

"You're going to have to do better than that!" Saryn yelled from a few camel strides ahead of me.

When would he ever stop provoking me? I was intentionally keeping my meddling small and discrete. Of course I was capable of more. Frustrated with my mentor's prodding, I narrowed my focus and breathed in deeply while thinking of home, of the taste of the fruits harvested from our orchards. The memory of it alone made my mouth water. What I wouldn't give for one of Chef's candied dessert trays. The warmth of those memories collided with the power welling within me, and the sand began to slide from one side to the other until it swirled into a maelstrom. I'd read of these occurring at sea but never in a desert. Anything that got close would be swallowed up into the center, incapable of escape.

"That's better!" he shouted. "But still not impressive enough."

He was baiting me. He had to be. Why else would he want me to demonstrate the true strength of my dark wielding out here in the middle of nowhere? Wasn't he at all concerned this might drain me before the actual mission, or was this actually some semblance of Saryn having faith in me?

I doubled down on thoughts of my loved ones, anchoring myself to them. I then began to weave in the recent memories of mine and Varro's kiss. Each memory created another spark within me. My vision of the wind around us became clearer, and my focus quieted the surrounding noise till it was nothing but me, silence, and energy preparing to explode out of my body.

Saryn cocked his head abruptly toward the south, where sounds akin to thunder began to roar. The unexpected vibrations brought both of our camels to an abrupt halt, and he stared at the artistry of my magic as it unfolded. Waves of sand rushed towards us, creating enormous clouds of dust. A sandstorm a mile high and wide rushed along the horizon line, visibly covering everything it touched. I commanded the rolling sand to crash downward and then splashed up again like the crest of a wave in the Endless Tides. A torrent of air and dust engulfed us, and I shut my eyes tightly to protect them until I heard the rustling of the camels and opened them slowly, watching the sand settle and Saryn come back into view.

He glanced back at me, pulling down the cloth covering his mouth so I could see the wide grin spread from one pointed ear to the other.

"Perhaps there is hope for Cambria, after all." He covered his mouth again, faced forward and pulled his reins, commanding our caravan onward.

His approval brought me a sense of pride. It was rare, and something I coveted much too desperately.

My display of power left me incredibly hungry and thirsty. I quietly fumbled to reach my pack to satiate myself, hoping to avoid a lecture about my lack of endurance. Every time I performed this level of magic, I drained myself completely. So much so, that I found myself struggling to keep a grip on the saddle through the bouts of dizziness that threatened to unseat me. Saryn wanted me to believe that with enough practice I could achieve some semblance of tolerance, but in my heart, I felt that was impossible. Not with this much power.

It's not something I had shared with Varro, or even really wanted to admit, but each time it felt like I was losing a tiny part of myself. That feeling was how I knew the Drift was real. Why I believed it was coming for me if I pushed myself too far. Idris had once said *'Magic, like all things, is finite.'*

Dark wielding always took from me; I felt it in my bones. I felt the consequences of it winding its way through my insides, navigating the honeycombs of my mind to have its way with me. Sometimes I wondered what would happen if I just pretended I was no longer capable of it? What could they really do?

But the stubborn side of me that secretly enjoyed how special I was refused to let it be taken from me. It was my secret weapon, hidden and ready to draw on my enemies at a moment's notice.

The day of travel was exhausting. Neither of us had much sleep the night before. We slept in shifts, the other keeping watch just in case. Staring into the nothingness with only the company of resting camels and a small fire was an act of torture in and of itself. The sounds of crackling flames and the cold desert air were enough to lull even the strongest into slumber.

I was pleased with myself that I was still capable of wielding my dark magic, even after an unrestful night, but I knew what lay ahead would require me to be in peak form. I just had to find a way to convince Saryn to let me sleep longer without sending him into an uninvited tirade. I could almost hear him lecturing me about some prior mission that he completed on three whole days without sleep…

As we sat around the fire eating our abysmal meal, I paced myself so he wouldn't notice how truly hungry I was. Tomorrow we would make our transition to horseback, and I wondered how those horses would be made available to us when and where we needed them. Was Theory handling the arrangements, or Idris? Would we get to see either of them? I didn't pry because there were more important things to be discussed.

The words stuttered from my mouth in an uncollected jumble. "I…I need…to tell you something. It's about…"

He raised his hand to silence me, and shook his head, already exuding irritation. I hated when he did that. Writing me off before I could even get a damn word out.

"I know about you and Varro," he said plainly, taking another gulp from his canteen.

I tried not to let him hear my gasp, but it was impossible with only the vastness of the empty desert as our background. Had that been confirmation enough for him? Did he really know, or was he playing games and probing? With my mental shield solidly in place, my mind raced and my heart pounded. He knew Varro was my mate? Who had told him? I leaned into my training, refusing to be the next one to speak. I would give him nothing. I would force him to show me how much he knew.

"Did you think after all the years I spent studying my enemies and their every movement, knowing them better than they knew themselves, I could be ignorant of a couple of frolicking bunnies beneath my feet?" He shook his head in disbelief, taking another sip. "Nothing happens at Basdie that I don't know about."

I decided to play this differently.

"So what? There are no rules about fooling around with other members. Plus, Trace doesn't count. He and I fucked beforehand; we had unfinished business."

I tried to feign confidence and cockiness all in one. Treat these like meaningless trysts, just sex. I eyed Saryn, hoping I seemed convincing.

"You are correct, there are no rules against fucking anyone. That doesn't mean there won't be complications."

"Like what?" I asked, pretending not to care.

"Like putting the mission above all else. Like leaving people for dead," he replied coldly, knowing exactly what he was doing. Trying to twist the knife in further.

"I'm well aware," I said through gritted teeth. I pretended to have ascended to a place of maturity and ambivalence adding, "It's not like he was my mate; it's just sex."

Saryn cocked his head assessingly, trying to see through my lies. "Mates..." he said with a scoff. "What a particularly sentimental and highly detrimental circumstance."

I could feel the disgust radiating off him. I already knew this was his attitude, which was why I would not be telling him about the true relationship between Varro and I.

"Now that I know you spy on us while at Basdie, I'll make sure we put on a real show for you next time. But I have something more important to discuss with you."

I shot him an insolent wink. My words were sharp, intended to embarrass him—or at minimum make him feel uncomfortable for his intrusions. Instead, he sat stone-faced and unflinching, focused on me. Waiting for me to direct the conversation to where I originally intended before he'd made assumptions. His jumping to conclusions meant he'd made a mistake and spoke too soon. One point for me.

"Since you are asking me to use my dark wielding, you need to know there are implications, ones I have not shared with you."

"What implications?" he snapped.

"It's called the Drift. And I think it's what the wielder in your Order suffered from…"

"Why do you suppose that?"

"You mentioned, when we first discovered my ability, that she'd seemed absent, like she wasn't always there, and I believe her mind was corroded from the Drift."

"And you didn't think to share any of this with me before now?" he scolded.

"It is my burden to understand and navigate, not anyone else's! It's not like you would have stopped pushing me anyway!"

It was one of the first times I had been truly honest toward Saryn. He was callous, cold, and calculated in every way. I had no reason to believe, despite being my mentor, that he would not sacrifice me if that was what it came down to.

"Remember, the mission above all else," I said deliberately.

"It is my job to train and wield you all as weapons of the North, not destroy you… If I can help it."

His words did not align with his actions, and I didn't believe him.

"You would discard of us easily; what about Nori?" I argued, finally having the discussion we never fully addressed.

"If Nori was going to get the rest of you killed with her childish actions, it was my job to protect you all from what would distract you from your purpose and hinder your ability to become dedicated members of the Imperi."

Our voices had become so loud in our heated exchange that anyone nearby would've been alerted to our presence, but that did not stop us. "And what will become of us when we are no longer useful to the realm? What higher purpose will you have for me when the Drift defeats me? Where is *your* Order's Dark Wielder now?"

"She's gone!" he yelled; the first time I'd witnessed him lose his composure. "Likely dead. And she was gone long before that, probably succumbed to this supposed Drift, as you call it."

You could cut the tension between us with a blade, and all that separated us was the flickering of flames.

"Don't speak of things you don't understand. She was more powerful than anything I'd ever witnessed. She was a Seer and a Dark Wielder; she was a Dreamwalker, too. But she meddled, and everyone knows there are lines one should not cross. With so much power amassed in one tiny female, she was arrogant and unruly. She believed the mission was not her calling but something beyond that. She sought to unravel the future entirely." He paused; his hands were both clasped in tight fists at his sides. "Don't make the same mistakes, Cress. Don't assume you are more important than the mission. Don't pursue your own desires, or you will corrupt yourself long before this Drift comes for you."

Every word that left his mouth made the fire glow brighter and burn hotter until I began to sweat. He was spiraling out of control, his magic spilling off him as a result. Saryn was exasperated, taking another drink to punctuate his grave warning.

"I believe you're capable of what is being asked of you. I will not pretend this isn't your most difficult task yet. Every step we take now is treacherous, no deeds meaningless."

This was his version of showing concern for me. I thought he was done speaking and I stood up, turning to head toward my tent when he added, "I will convey anything of concern to Idris, should it come to that."

I didn't know if he was referring to my own safety or the mission. But knowing he'd lost a member to this same affliction and it silently ate away at him was enough for me to have some small belief that he'd look out for me.

That night I lay in my tent while Saryn took watch. He had agreed to let me sleep longer since I told him that I needed it to regain my energy for the task ahead. For once, he didn't argue with me. I think his mind was far from sleep anyhow. His thoughts had been pulled deep into a past he had seemingly not spoken of in a very long time.

I couldn't help but reason that Saryn disliked both Nori and I because we reminded him of her; my dark wielding, her dreamwalking, and our combined upbringings made us prime targets for Saryn's anger and jealousy. But I would not let him forget we were on the same side, fighting for the same things. Never had a single selfish thought about my power crossed my mind until he told me of the female in his Order who had intentions of her own.

I wouldn't even begin to know what to use it for if I wasn't under direct orders of the Imperi. Everything about my power seemed destructive in nature. I let the exhaustion of our journey send my body into a deep slumber; tomorrow we would make the final leg of the journey north, then along the Ledor River until we reached the canyon. Was it asking too much to hope for a peaceful culmination to our expedition? That our arrival would scatter the miners or, better yet, that they had scouted our approach and retreated to safety somewhere deep within the desert? I prayed there would be no need to end the lives of so many.

CHAPTER

24

As the hours passed, the sand beneath the camels' feet slowly turned to soil, indicating we had finally reached the small portion of land bordering the Ledor River. It gave way to more green foliage than I'd seen in the entirety of our stay in Artume. The sight of it sent my memory swirling with thoughts of my homeland and the sounds of rustling trees like a thousand colliding whispers. Across the rushing river was the southernmost Riverlands. Just a bit farther northeast, and we'd reach House Blackthorn territory. Home felt so close, the temptation of it being within reach had me mulling over absurd ideas of fleeing the Imperi altogether.

We trotted beneath the canopy of trees. Their leaves and branches were sparser than those on the northern side of the river, but the nearby water source allowed them to flourish. The shade, while intermittent, was a much-welcomed reprieve from the sun. In the distance, I was alerted to two individuals and instinctively grasped the small dagger attached to my hip, looking to see if Saryn was also on guard. His posture remained casual and relaxed. The closer we got, the more my vision gave way and I could make out a face—and a familiar one at that! Theory.

Her long dark locks framed her bare shoulders. She was wearing a sleeveless leather vest, and her ebony skin glistened with a sheen of sweat. A sword lay sheathed across her back, and the sun glinted off daggers strapped to her thighs. Why was she so heavily armed? Is this what Theory looked like when she wasn't instructing at Basdie? While many of us attempted to blend in, Theory looked like a bandit, making no attempts to conceal she was well-armed.

What was more concerning, though, was the young male at her side. Next to that stranger were three strong horses. He was busy feeding one of them an apple while nonchalantly stroking the mane of the one beside it. Was he another member of the Imperi I'd never met? Since I was uncertain, I decided to follow Saryn's lead before saying anything. We halted our camels and began our dismount. Theory greeted Saryn with a hug, and while I was excited to see her, we had never developed the type of relationship that warranted hugging, even if we were blood-sworn to one another.

Theory approached me and placed a hand on my shoulder in greeting. "Hello, Dark One," she said with a warm smile.

I was a bit taken aback by her demeanor. She had never referred to me as that before, and it wasn't just that, but the fact she did so in an almost playful manner.

"Uh…Hi," I sputtered out, offering a smile in return so she'd know I welcomed her presence. "Who is that?" I whispered to her, jutting my chin in the direction of the stranger tending to what I assumed were our horses.

"Don't worry about him," she answered, dismissing that someone else was amongst us, despite the clandestine nature of our encounter.

Saryn led both our camels to the river's edge, allowing them to drink for the first time since departing Nasallus. Camels were such fascinating creatures to me. We did not have them in Cambria, but they were well-suited for Artume, able to go days upon days without requiring water. But I was not a camel; between thirst and the desire to drench myself in water, I joined them. Moving upstream from the animals, I dipped my hands into the water, letting the cool sensation of it send shivers down my spine. I cupped my hands, cradling the liquid, and scooped it to my mouth.

Before I knew it, I was undressing down to my undergarments without a care for who was watching. If I didn't submerge myself in this water and get all the dirt, grime and sand off my skin, I would continue to fixate on it. No one warned me that my service to the Imperi would be so glamourless and coarse.

The water was surprisingly cold for this time of year, but I more than welcomed it. I slid down the muddy marsh's edge, holding on to the side to avoid being pulled into the center, where the current was strongest. My skin finally felt clean, free from the plague of sand in every unmentionable crevice of my body. I dunked my whole head underwater briefly, then breached the surface, tossing my hair over the top of my head. I was determined to get every grain of sand off of me if it was the last thing I did.

Theory watched me bathing, amused, and hollered to Saryn, "Guess you can't train the privilege out of High Fae, even those that are only Honored..."

Saryn smirked back at her, and I gaped at their acknowledgement of our true identity in front of the stranger. Why would they risk such a thing? I was so concerned by her remark that I didn't even bother to take offense. It was all so bizarre to hear them acknowledge the past in such a manner. After all, they were constantly reiterating that our past selves were as good as dead.

I hadn't thought of myself as High Fae since arriving at Basdie. Yes, I thought of my family and the life I'd had often, but very little of my focus was on my former status. I just missed my loved ones and home. They could keep my family medallion and rank if I could just have back the pieces that truly mattered to me. Thinking this way was useless and would only serve to frustrate me. My circumstances were permanent, but I couldn't ignore that Theory's personality away from Basdie was not as I expected. Sure, she was regularly warmer than Saryn, but usually by no more than a degree or so.

After drying myself off from my dip in the river, I was eager to understand the next leg of the journey. Would Theory travel with us? With three fresh mounts, I could only assume so. The canyon was now only a half-day's ride away, so we'd likely be arriving during twilight. Saryn and Theory had worked quickly to transfer any relevant supplies from our camels' packs to the smaller ones already adhered to the horses' saddles. The stranger worked with both sets of animals comfortably and knowledgeably, displaying no signs of fear toward any of us. I was not comfortable with Theory's instruction to essentially disregard him. It seemed against my better judgement and our training.

I sat on the ground, leaning up against a tree while my hair dried and indulged in a piece of fruit that may have been meant for the horses. I didn't care, and the stranger did nothing to stop me when I snagged it. Sitting there, I watched Saryn and Theory's interactions, trying to determine if she seemed more playful and sarcastic with him, too, or if it was just her interactions with me. She did seem generally informal and unceremonious compared to our previous times together. Maybe this was how she treated peers while on assignment together, and it would simply take some getting used to.

The more I watched, the more I became confounded by what was occurring. Between almost every task, the young male companion walked back over to Theory and she would touch her hand briefly to her temple and then lower it before giving him a new set of instructions which he would then carry out without question. Each time he returned to her it was like a baby animal or child seeking praise. He was young, but still clearly an adult, so why was he constantly seeking instruction and praise for otherwise simple tasks? I folded my knees into my chest, resting my chin on them, and continued to watch it unfold. Task, praise, instruction. Task, praise, instruction. It finally clicked. I jumped to my feet and marched over to them both.

"You're *coercing* him," I declared with accusation. I had no recollection of seeing Theory perform mesmerization before, nor had she ever discussed it while training us at Basdie. But I was more than certain that was exactly what she was doing to this male.

She looked at me with amusement sparkling through her silver eyes. "Should I be interested in doing all of these chores myself?" Theory reeked of dismissiveness, but I pressed my line of questioning. Meddling with one's mind using that kind of magic increased the likelihood of them losing their sensibility permanently.

"How long have you been doing this to him? Look at him!" I demanded angrily. "He doesn't even know where he is or who he is, does he?"

Theory's nostrils flared with irritation. "You listen here," she chided while striding toward me. I took a step back as she closed in. "When I start questioning you about your abilities, you can question me about mine. Until that day, I will decide who and what serves me."

Saryn was now leaning against a nearby tree, watching the altercation with anticipation, almost like he hoped I would provoke Theory to such an outburst. Backing down from an unwanted fight, I stepped away, creating space between us to show her I would not engage her any further. Anger still swirled in me. Saryn spied on those at Basdie, Theory concealed her true gifts…What other things had they been keeping from us? What, if anything, did they keep from each other?

It wasn't long before Theory provided clear instruction to the male regarding the handling of the camels in our absence. It was safe to assume we'd make a similar rendezvous when we returned from the canyon. Would he be under her influence the entire time we were away and, if so, what effect would that have on him?

The entire journey to the mouth of the canyon, Theory and Saryn rode a small distance ahead of me side by side, speaking quietly, proving that he was capable of idle chatter—just not with me.

Soon the landscape began to change again, grass and soil becoming clay and rock. While my two mentors seemed unsuspicious of our surroundings, I remained on constant alert. If Nasallus was performing a secret operation, who's to say they wouldn't have travelers on these very same roads? Were either of them concerned about such an encounter? Were we going to play ignorant and pretend to be part of the cause, arriving to do the very same work already underway? Knowing my companions, they would be content to engage in more violent activities if necessary. I, on the other hand, was not looking for a fight of any kind, knowing I would likely need to muster all my energy to deal with whatever was going on in the canyon itself. I especially didn't need to attempt such a feat while injured, so I kept my wits about me. The only positive thing about this portion of the journey was the absence of sand.

But there was an absence of something else that was causing me anxiety: I could no longer feel the bond. There was no hum or vibration. I had lost sense of it more than a day ago, and until now, had kept my concerns suppressed. The absence of it made me fearful. I kept telling myself not to be distracted by it, but I was. If I had only sealed the bond, I would know he was okay, and he would be comforted by knowing the same of me. Our souls and minds would be bound to one another in a way that transcended the tangible world. In many ways, he had become my best friend. Our simple conversations and laughter centered me. There was a serenity to our relationship that made me feel firmly rooted, even now, so far away.

For someone who had two travel companions, I felt extremely lonely being so far from anyone I could call a true friend. Theory and Saryn were mentors; they were brethren in the Imperi, but I did not believe there was true friendship between us. Sometimes I wondered if we would always feel such apprehension toward our mentors in the Order, and if our group would be able to surpass that relationship with subsequent recruits.

I had my suspicions regarding Saryn's feelings towards Idris. There was understanding, respect, and loyalty between them, but no semblance of friendship. Idris had only ever presented a calm demeanor in my presence, but one could imagine his vigilance in training new members of the Order. Something like vicious repetition came to mind. In reflection, I promised myself that if I was ever given the opportunity to train and swear-in new members of the Order, that they would be met with more understanding and warmth than I was granted. A sword may be forged beneath a hammer, but an arrow does not fly without the delicate fletching.

The sun was retreating toward the horizon as we arrived at the gorge of the canyon and began our ascent on horseback. Saryn had indicated a desire to assess the situation from higher ground, and we were unlikely to encounter anyone upon the elevated cliffside. He also declared that if we happened to run into any scouts keeping watch, they'd be handled expeditiously. This confirmed my earlier suspicions about how they'd manage such an encounter. Theory instructed me that should any sort of scuffle occur, there should be no hesitation on my part to take flight. I hadn't unfurled my wings since Basdie, so I spent the remainder of the trek centering my thoughts on what it would be like to need them abruptly while in a saddled position.

When we reached the canyon rim, we found a vast plain of rock laid out before us. Only the occasional tree or shrub clinging to life dared disrupt the barren landscape. Shades of orange and hues of red were the only colors as far as the eye could see. Later, when the pale, violet shadow of twilight overtook the horizon, we rode along the edge of the gorge, studying the Ledor River as it narrowed and carved out the jagged shape of the canyon below.

The swaying of my saddle ushered forth a wave of nausea as I gazed upon the intense and insufferable depths of the canyon. I held my hand to my head, trying to relieve myself as we continued on, looking for signs of mining activity.

"There." Theory pointed, drawing our attention.

Evidence of Artume's efforts were finally made apparent. On the Cambrian side of the river there were clear indications of attempts to make entry into the rock walls along the river's edge. At some of their entry points, they appeared to dig deeper than others, but each of them was abandoned with none fully breaching the exterior. If there were moonstones, did they expect to find them so close to the surface wall? Saryn had implied that these stones took centuries to form. From what I knew of the sciences, moonstones, like all precious stones, needed two things to flourish: time and immense pressure. Why did they choose to dig there, and what made them stop?

Every hundred paces or so, there were signs of more attempts. Though it was clear they hadn't found anything worthwhile at these dig sites, it confirmed the rumor—they *were* looking. Which meant the odds of needing me to resolve the issue had increased dramatically. I winced as this dreadful realization took hold.

The land above and within the gorge was treacherous, but not entirely unmanageable. King Aeon hadn't needed to do much to convince his people that this area was not worth settling. Even its exploration posed risks that seemed to outweigh any reward. But if our king did have an inclination about what was in the canyon's crust, why was the area not guarded? How were Artumian thieves able to travel across Cambria's border and pillage resources so easily without repercussions?

I squeezed the horse suddenly with my legs, prodding him to catch up with Saryn and Theory. Now that we had seen signs of their activity, we couldn't risk the echoes of our voices. When I caught up to them, we exchanged whispers.

"Why is this canyon not guarded?" I asked.

"If a place is guarded, it implies there is something of value," Theory explained.

"Isn't the border reason enough?"

"The rest of the Artumian border consists of more obvious resources to trade and is populated by Fae who are willing to break the laws of Cambria to trade illegally."

Saryn added, "Official trade means taxes. Those who have no interest in sending wealth to the Crown, both Northern and Southern, will avoid it even if it makes them a criminal."

I pondered my father's business for a moment. Most of his trade occurred among the northern territories. I vaguely recollected some negative remarks about taxes on occasion, but I did not think he would have engaged in illegal dealings directly. The longer I thought on it, the more I wondered if my father was aware of the illegal trade going on in the southernmost Riverlands. This would have been his territory to oversee, after all. He had shared nothing of this with me if he had known. If I had someday taken over for him, would I have been exposed to those sorts of dealings? Which then begged the question: Would I have allowed it to continue, knowing it typically benefited the far less fortunate?

The inequity I had seen in my own village after a day of handing out Lorcs brought visions of a world where their survival did not hinge on lawlessness. My life at the academy was far behind me, but I was becoming increasingly frustrated that none of this was being taught or explained. Not in courses of history, finance, or any other academics offered to us. If we were the wealthiest of our lands, privileged to be educated, how were we to rule, govern and guide others, when were all being kept in the dark?

Since the Imperi had torn the veil of naivety from my eyes, every day I saw people and their interactions differently. I think it's why Theory and Saryn were as bitter as they appeared; they had been exposed to the dynamic truth of our world for far longer than me. My world, once captured in the narrow space between a thumb and forefinger on the map, now seemed impossibly vast and incredibly complex.

Nightfall had finally arrived, making our travel along the edge of the gorge even more intimidating. Saryn lit a small lantern, the only light to guide us along the precipice at our side. I could fly, and therefore wasn't fearful for myself, but my horse could not. I wouldn't wish that sort of death upon any living creature.

I hadn't thought of Rain in such a long time, and it amused me to think of him on this foreign terrain. I'm pretty sure he would have refused the climb, never mind trotted on hard rock with an ominous drop-off. He was a spoiled, pampered horse. His hooves had only ever galloped the lush green forests near the estate, fueled by an everlasting reserve of grass, hay, and the rosy apples that littered the orchard.

"Lights ahead," Saryn whispered to Theory and I, keeping his lantern low. We were probably too high up for anyone down in the canyon to see the glow of a single lantern, but we couldn't be too careful. The three of us brought our horses to a quiet halt and studied the scene below. Hundreds of tiny lights were scattered about the canyon floor, with the occasional large fire pit sprinkled throughout. No doubt this was an encampment of sorts, and we had discovered what we sought.

With so much darkness, we could not make out many of the details of their operations. How far into the rock had they breached? Were they already successful in finding and extracting any of the moonstones?

"Are we doing this in the dark?" I questioned.

"No," Saryn answered. "We'll make camp a safe distance from here to ensure they don't see our fire or hear our restless horses."

"Are you sure?" I asked, thinking it would be far easier to attack when they were unaware and mostly asleep. Secretly and selfishly, the idea of ending so many lives made me feel less guilty if they just went to sleep and never woke up again. There was something guiltless—maybe even merciful—about ending their lives in such a way. I didn't want to see their faces. I didn't want to count the number of my enemies. I would have rather brought down a rocky landslide over their heads in this moment than be forced to brandish my destruction in vivid daylight.

"Yes, I'm sure. Don't argue with me. I need to evaluate the situation when I can see more…" he paused briefly, then continued, "which allows me to report more accurate findings to Idris."

Theory turned to me and reiterated patiently, "We must know if they've already acquired what they seek."

I nodded in understanding and began to lead my horse away from the ledge, not wanting to think any longer about my victims gathered around their campfires, blissfully unaware it would most likely be their last.

We made camp and, to my surprise, it was far colder high up on the plateau of Ledor Canyon than even the chilly nights in the Artumian desert had been. I wrapped a blanket tightly around my body and shivered beneath it, sitting as close to the fire as possible without setting myself aflame. Theory took a seat on the ground next to me and rested her body against her pack. She was still in her sleeveless attire, yet I didn't see a single goosebump along her skin.

"How are you not freezing?" I inquired with jealousy.

Theory let out a small snort of amusement. "You are so young. So new to all of this. All of you are, really."

"What's that supposed to mean?"

"It means that your magic is still so foreign to you that you haven't found a way to make it serve you, and not just the Imperi."

I stared at her, silent, trying to understand her cryptic remark. She looked at me with disappointment, knowing her point had evaded me.

"Saryn told me about your little showcase in the desert. Don't you think if you can wield a sandstorm that you could simply levitate sand off your skin or shield yourself from it?" She pointed at the fire in front of us. "That fire is radiating far more heat for me than it is you." She smiled knowingly.

Saryn, who had been eavesdropping on our conversation, chimed in. "You see magic as something external, a specialized tool to employ on complex obstacles. But your view limits the possibilities."

Saryn turned his gaze from the fire to face me. "Your magic is within you, Cress, as mine is within me. Its endless applications to everyday life could alter your reality to such a degree that ordinary life becomes unrecognizable."

Theory interjected, placing her hand briefly on my forearm as to impress upon me her meaning, "So we can feel *something.*"

"Not being able to wield every element or every ability within the spectrum of magic is the only thing that keeps us humble and grounded," he added. "Idris once told me it's the only thing that stops us from thinking we, ourselves, are Gods."

That night, I lay in my tent wrestling with everything they had imparted to me. Had the others in my class already learned this lesson? I felt silly and naïve, thinking of every possibility I'd ignored or not even considered.

A canteen with little remaining…

Water now filled to the brim.

Cold, frigid air rattling my bones…

A shield from the harsh winter winds.

A tiny flame, too small to emit enough heat…

A fire powerful enough to warm an entire room.

A bleeding cut, deep and painful…

A wound healed with no trace of a scar.

A task of traveling with 3 horses…

An assistant pliant to every command.

An enemy rushing toward you with blade in hand…

The feeling of suffocation, sending them to their knees.

An ancient stone canyon, strong and still…

Crumbling and tumbling like a tower of blocks touched by the hands of an errant child.

Magic itself was neither incidental nor grand. It was made that way by the intensity of how we conjured it. How we viewed the world and our tasks; how creatively and quickly we could think to solve them.

Saryn and Theory had spent so long letting their magic mask how they lived. Had they forgotten the irritating sensation of sand on their skin? Or the feeling of a dry mouth parched for water? Had they forgotten what it was like to live like mere Fae?

Lying there, I ran my hands across the rough dirt clinging to my skin, experiencing their textures and sensations on my fingertips, committing to memory what life felt like without the ability to alter it at a whim. But not all things would bend to our will—if they could, *he* would be here with me, holding me close to his chest the night before I took on something unthinkable.

The intoxicating smell of meat cooking on a skillet wafted into my tent and woke me. I had almost convinced myself I was still dreaming and Chef D'eliar was preparing brunch for Versa and I...but then I felt the unfortunate results of sleeping on the hard ground radiate down my back, and was abruptly reminded I was no longer dreaming. I sat up and crossed my legs, leaning over, trying to stretch when Theory and Saryn's words from the night prior came to mind. I hugged my arms around myself and closed my eyes, letting my magic send healing and relaxation deep into my muscles, travelling through my blood then encapsulating my bones and, within minutes, the aches and pains dissipated. I opened my eyes and smiled to myself, relieved.

Exiting the tent, I saw my mentors sitting around our breakfast chatting leisurely like it was any other day. When I approached, Theory handed me a plate with bacon.

"Figured you could use a good breakfast to give you strength for the task ahead."

"Thank you," I said, grabbing the plate eagerly and sitting down beside her. It smelled delicious, and I let myself inhale its divine aroma before downing each piece quickly. I always ate fast when I was anxious, and my nerves were already setting in. With the sunrise well overhead, I was fearful of inspecting the gorge below and seeing those who would soon fall victim to my abilities. I was certain Saryn and Theory had already done so at first light. Since they hadn't awakened me, I assumed there was no direct threat to us, but that didn't mean everything they saw wasn't of concern to me.

"So…what's the situation?" I asked, jutting my chin in the direction of the ledge a bit behind us.

"Unfortunately, they've fully breached to the interior. Consistent mining operations are well underway, but for how long, we can't be certain," Saryn replied, looking concerned and frustrated that our enemies had already made such progress.

"How many?"

"About 100, maybe 150 I'd wager. With the movement in and out of the mine, it's difficult to ascertain."

Over a hundred Fae would die by my hand today. I sat frozen, staring down at the empty plate in my hand, my mind quickly trying to reconcile Saryn's assessment.

Theory gently grabbed my chin, angling my face to meet her gaze. I felt hollow and disassociated from her presence.

"Killing the unarmed, the unprovoked, the unaware…it is a treacherous truth we must endure. Others might call it dishonorable, but we do not live by their code, we live by our own, that of the Imperi."

Theory's words seemed to play out in slow motion, the sounds of everything beyond her voice were silenced.

"We are preventing something much larger, much worse. Sacrifice the few to save the many, or the next great conflict will be upon us."

I nodded silently, still trying to find my own belief in her sentiment when Saryn interrupted.

"If you're thinking of holding back, keep in mind that any left alive will be mine and Theory's to confront. It will be far more painful and slow. Choose wisely."

Theory shot Saryn an agitated look, but all I could do was dip my chin at him in silent acknowledgement.

"More bacon, please," I said, almost mechanically, agonizing over which method would put them out of their misery, how much energy this would take, and what it would cost me. I chewed the bacon, its distinct saltiness turning to ash on my tongue, thinking of how each of those in the canyon had tasted their last meal this morning.

"There is no innocence in their actions," Theory reminded me, recognizing I was still struggling with what was to come. "They know they have crossed into Cambrian territory; they know they are stealing. And though they may not understand the full picture of what is being demanded of them, they have chosen this."

"Like we…chose this?" I said, looking back and forth between them. Theory and Saryn knew full well the intent of my remark and did not respond.

Many more moments passed by before Theory stood and held out her hand to aid me, "Come, Dark One, lest you waste time in showing them the darkness."

Fear ached in the back of my throat, making me painfully aware of my conscience with every swallow. It took me far longer than they would have liked to get the courage to walk to the ledge and look below, as was made evident by Saryn's pacing and deep sighs. I crouched, then eventually crawled forward, hoping to avoid the gaze of any lookouts. Laying on the hot ground, the sun beating down from overhead, I rested my chin on my hands and surveyed the area. Below, the encampment at the mouth of the mine consisted of a well-established pocket of tents and some smaller, sturdier structures built from driftwood.

Though the accommodations were meager, the tents were arranged uniformly. It seemed the workers were organized and purposeful in their movements. There was a cook running a makeshift kitchen, providing the workers with hot meals. Scouts walked attentively along the bank of the river, armed with bow and sword.

Small pockets of horses and a few unhitched wagons indicated supplies had been brought with them. As I observed new intricate components of their camp, I began to justify what must come next. They may not know what master or purpose they served, but they worked diligently and thoroughly. There were no females or children to speak of, which only brought me a moment's comfort about my own involvement.

The mouth of the mine yawned somberly, cloaking most of the workers in impenetrable darkness. Infrequently, I witnessed several workers emerge hefting a large covered box. They'd bring it into a tent and presumably sort the moonstone fragments into large leather satchels, which would eventually be attached to horses for transport. I could tell by the rustling behind me that Theory and Saryn were growing some-what impatient. I needed confirmation with my own eyes that they had gained access to moonstones before I acted. I couldn't bring the whole of the cliffside down upon them without knowing for certain.

I scooted backwards, then stood up to walk back to where my mentors awaited me.

"I can't do it. Not unless I have proof."

Theory threw her arms up in frustration. "You need more proof than seeing over 100 Artumian trespassers steal from your own king's land?" she said, exasperated.

Saryn pulled something small from his pocket and tossed it abruptly in my direction; it landed at my feet in the dirt. I kneeled down to inspect it while he chided me.

"I knew you were too sentimental for something like this, so I took it upon myself to portal down there while you slept, infiltrate their camp and bring you back evidence of their treachery."

Between my fingers, I held a rough, raw moonstone. Still jagged and dirty, having been plucked from the place it had slumbered, hidden from daylight, until Fae hands disturbed it. I pulled my own moonstone from my inside pocket and marveled at their differences. Strange to see it this way, like it had just been birthed from the crusts of Demir. I glanced up at Saryn skeptically.

"You swear you retrieved this from down there?"

"By the Gods, I swear it."

I gritted my teeth in frustration that there were no more excuses or warranted delays. Today, I decided their fate; tomorrow, who would decide mine?

"Take the horses farther away. If anything goes wrong, we fly. I'm uncertain what further consequences may result from my actions."

They both nodded and began to pack up our small camp, loading our supplies safely onto the horses. While they led them away, I went back to my previous spot and continued to monitor the mining operations and study the wall of the canyon. I closed my eyes and listened to the faint breeze. I smelled the air, inhaling tiny bits of dust, licking my lips to taste them. I lay there, flat on my stomach, quietly attempting to become one with this foreign land. My eyes scanned from end to end, taking note of each jutting ledge and deep crack in the rocks that could be used to my advantage.

The Ledor Canyon was strange to me, unlike the Elorn Mountains, which I could still picture with absolute clarity. I feared that if I did not study it well enough, I would not be able to bring it down as artfully as Saryn desired. There was a definite possibility that I would destroy far more than King Aeon had bargained for. During our travels, Saryn instructed that it was important not to stop the flow of the Ledor River. The goal was to take down the mine so it appeared like a natural rockfall and not garner unwanted attention.

Saryn and Theory returned from leading the horses to safety and I informed them of my plan.

"I'm not comfortable performing this while laying down. I've never practiced it as such, so save your lectures. I need you both to keep watch while I prepare."

They nodded at my instruction, and as we began to make our way toward the ledge, I turned to Saryn. "Remember what I told you."

Reminding him of our conversation about the Drift did not bring me any real sense of comfort, but I did it anyway.

When the three of us reached the ledge, I stood there looking out over the encampment below. This must be how the Gods felt, I told myself, looking down on so many unsuspecting victims. Would they pray to me in their final moments or shake their fists in defiance? I used the belief in this power to fuel my courage. The creators fed the mouths of rivers and raised up the mountains. They both gave and took life. Today, I would play the hand of fate for the souls at my mercy.

Anger and power over the weak would not be capable of drawing out my magic. It never had. It gave me courage to take these lives, but not the strength to wield the darkness. I drew in my breath completely and closed my eyes. I thought about the first time I felt the bond. The way it rippled and tickled delightfully under my skin. The warmth in my belly I felt when I first saw Varro's wings on display. The relief of his fist kneading into the arch of my foot. The admission of him being my mate. The jealousy of him kissing the Vesper until I claimed him myself. The distinct pleasure he drew from me as his Siren Song danced across every inch of my body, and the feeling of his whispering lips at my ear saying, *"You can do this."*

When I opened my eyes, the canyon was a blur of rust-colored rocks set against a blue sky until my vision narrowed, and tiny, small waves of lines floating across the wind came into my sight. I could see the breeze that others could only feel. I could see the light of the sun bend and reflect off each mote of dust. And then the clanging, banging and buzzing of the sounds below silenced for a brief moment, giving way to a deep, thunderous crack, followed quickly by another. Screams echoed off the canyon walls in a cacophony, and the ground below them began to quake.

More bellows of horror threatened to penetrate my concentration, but I carried on, watching the canyon walls break off into shards, one by one, sliding down the cliffside and crashing into the hard ground below. They shattered into thousands of pieces and destroyed everything they touched. Dense clouds of dust engulfed the scene below as more rocks began to tumble down the side of the canyon. I felt the trembling below my feet and compelled the event into a climax. I commanded the mouth of the mine to collapse, sealing it shut before more boulders fell from overhead, making it appear as if nothing Fae-touched had ever existed there.

Horses screeched, fleeing in a panic as more large stones tumbled into the flowing river. The screams ceased quicker than I had expected. When I was done, the only sounds below were the rushing waters of the river and the occasional rock or pebble falling into place.

From my side, I heard Theory sing my praises to Saryn.

"She really is *magnificent.*"

"She will not see it that way," he replied to her sullenly.

Their commentary awoke me from my concentration, and that's when I felt the tears begin to stream down my cheeks. Silent, grieving tears for strangers.

Saryn approached me cautiously, unsure if I would have an outburst that would result in him joining those strangers below.

"*You* did not decide their fate." He paused. "You only introduced them to their makers."

I turned to face him when retorting his logic. "I am the reason they did not have a chance to atone. How will the Gods judge me for that?"

Walking away from the ledge, I turned my back on the devastation I'd committed. I began to cry in earnest, walking till my legs would no longer carry me. The exhaustion of what I'd done finally overcame the shock and denial of it. I sat there and sobbed till my eyes burned like fire and couldn't spare another tear. Neither Saryn nor Theory came for me. They gave me the space to mourn my own actions. My body ached and my head pounded. I had exerted myself beyond my limits, and with each passing moment, I felt the implications expand like a poison spreading throughout my insides.

Over and over in my mind, I could hear myself screaming that I'm a murderer. A killer. I had attacked and destroyed those with no chance of defending themselves. I took hundreds of years of life away from those who became my victims. Their bodies, buried so deep beneath the rubble, were not likely to be uncovered before they disintegrated into nothingness. Their families would be delivered no answers and granted no peace. All because of me. I had wielded darkness before this day, but today I had become it. I lay back on the ground, staring at the empty cloudless sky, and let the numbness wrap around me. I let exhaustion pull me under.

I did not recall falling asleep, but when I awoke, it was pitch black and I was slumped over Saryn's shoulder. My body was limp and too tired to fight; he carried me back to our camp without a word. When he sat me down next to the fire, he placed a canteen in my hands and ordered me to drink, which I did without argument. I felt like I hadn't drunk in days; the liquid poured over my tongue like the very essence of life.

Theory passed me a plate of food and I assessed my surroundings, noting our tents were pitched and our camp reinstated for the evening. I had no idea if they had intended to start the return trip already and I was the reason for the postponement, but I didn't really care, either.

"Did you mourn those that you killed at the Canary Veil?" Theory asked, patiently awaiting me to stop gorging myself on food and answer her.

"I don't think so, not really. I mean…barely," I said, trying to remember. I think I was too concerned with mine and Varro's injuries and Trace's betrayal. I recollected falling apart in Varro's embrace after the whole mess, more overwhelmed with fear of what I'd done than who I'd done it to.

"You will mourn less when you're defending yourself. You will mourn more when they're defenseless. And you will know real grief when they come for those you seek to protect," Theory said before taking a bite of her meal.

Saryn added, "Do not confuse guilt and grief. Guilt festers when we assume responsibility in the matter. Grief is heightened when we have no control. They both feed on every wretched thought you have, and the only way to defeat them is to starve them."

Their weathered words, however wise, were riddled with callousness from years of service committing the unspeakable.

After they explained the plan for the return trip, I dragged my sluggish body back to my tent, already on the verge of sleep before my head could hit the blanket. Saryn peeked his head in and asked me the strangest set of questions.

"What is your name?"

"Cress," I replied in confusion.

"Your full name," he commanded.

I paused, realizing he was testing me.

"*Your full name,*" he reiterated.

"Cress Blackthorn," I whispered back, fearful of acknowledging my born identity to him.

"And where do you hail from?"

"From the Riverlands."

"And you're a sworn member of what?"

"The Imperi," I answered, nervously, as he continued a barrage of simple questions.

"What did you have tattooed behind your ear?"

I paused for a moment and touched my fingertips to the back of my ear, feeling a scar. *What used to be there?* I thought to myself. Saryn began to look concerned as I thought hard on it, when finally, it came to me. I blurted out the answer.

"M-Moons," I sputtered. "The moons of Demir."

Saryn looked at me suspiciously and told me to get some rest.

I lay there, rubbing my fingers along the scar. Now that I had answered him, it seemed so obvious to me. Why had I not been able to respond faster? I think I was just overwhelmed with the impromptu interrogation and the fact that Saryn actually allowed me to say my given name.

I was beyond the point of exhaustion and plagued by what Saryn had declared was guilt. I attempted to fall asleep, but I kept finding myself touching the scar, trying to think about when I had gotten the original marking. Where and with whom? The memory continued to evade me as I finally fell into a deep, heavy slumber.

The return to Nasallus was filled with quiet introspection. As I suspected, Theory's "assistant," for lack of a better word, was awaiting our arrival, camels in hand and the same hollow eyes as the day we'd parted. A piece of me wanted Theory to return with us, but she insisted on delivering the moonstones she'd acquired after catching up with the horses that fled the canyon during the landslide. She would escort them safely into Cambria's borders and reconvene with Idris to account for the mission's details.

The remainder of the journey consisted of mostly silence in between Saryn's suspicious glances. Our procession trotted one behind the other, and occasionally, he'd yell out some trivial question just to see if I'd answer correctly. He had concerns that perhaps some degree of the Drift had set in since I'd exerted myself so fully in taking down the mining operations. After a night's rest, I did not feel particularly exhausted, but I still carried with me a heavy guilt that weighed on my shoulders every minute of the ride back. I distracted myself with small magic. There was no longer sand irritating my skin unless I allowed it to. My canteen never fell below half full. My thighs never ached from the strain of the saddle. I replayed Saryn and Theory's words in my mind, trying to see the world through their eyes and somehow make them my own.

Since ending all those lives, I felt changed. My peers knew what I was being sent to do, but would they look at me differently when we reunited? I did not look at Gia differently for bedding the king. The only reason I looked at Trace differently was because he was unable to conceal the weariness that his own duty had caused him. If I had a mirror, would I appear a cold-blooded assassin? Or would I still look like me? Would I look braver and fiercer? Perhaps our own misdeeds were not evident in our reflection, pooled calmly behind a dam of rationale and responsibility, the resulting guilt slowly seeping through the seams.

The feeling of the bond had felt more present as we neared Nasallus. Rounding the corner, the sight of the safehouse felt like the closest thing to home since we'd departed Basdie. My excitement quickly dwindled when I discovered none of the other members were there to greet us. Not even *him*. I surmised they could not have known our exact arrival time and, since it wasn't the sabbath, perhaps our presence would have been unexpected to begin with. Over the next hour, I bathed, made myself look presentable for servant duties, and changed back into my blue uniform. Saryn returned from exchanging our camels for horses, and I loaded myself up into the same wagon that had previously delivered me to the castle.

I found it particularly ironic that I'd need to trade my emotions of guilt for ones more comparable to grief, since everyone else believed I was returning from a funeral. The Gods were cruel, indeed, as I had only just delivered death myself… How long would it take for their families to receive notice, to plan the deserved ceremonies? Would confirmation of their passing ever arrive, or would answers of their loved-one's whereabouts evade them forever?

"See you on the sabbath," Saryn said quietly, handing me a small bag of my belongings as I dismounted the carriage. I nodded and followed the familiar steps, greeting the castle guard.

El leaped from her bed and squeezed me in a strong, enthusiastic embrace. My body felt rigid in her arms.

"I'd ask if you missed me, but you've already made it obvious," I tried to jest.

"I managed as best I could without you, but Lady Gianna is so difficult to please."

I set my bag down next to my bed and smiled at the thought of Gia giving El an absolute runaround while I was away. Some days, I think Gia really enjoyed acting out the role of a bratty and demanding noble; eventually prying her away from this would be more difficult than we bargained for.

"Worry not, I've returned so you no longer have to juggle Lady Gianna's high expectations."

El sat back down on her bed, looking thoroughly pleased to be relieved of her temporary post. That night I joined her and the others in the dining hall, and she was delighted to see that my appetite had returned. She and the others respected my privacy and did not question my family's funeral. They ate their day-old bread and squabbled about the typical castle gossip: security being upped with a number of additional Kingsguards; the former queen's parents vacating the castle entirely and returning to their home estate; the king's continued infatuation with a particular blonde-haired Lady—and most importantly, the rumors of a disease of the flesh continued to run rampant throughout the prison.

With the mention of a possible plague, the staff remained on high alert, knowing that if they showed any signs of illness they'd be "discarded." This meant that, somehow, the others had kept up the charade while

I was away; hopefully, Nori had been able to convene frequently with Princess Embry. With the moonstone operation completed, Saryn would be itching to understand what other activities required our attention, or even intervention.

That night, I crawled into my cot, thankful for the first night's sleep in some approximation of a bed in almost a week. A servant's cot was nothing compared to the luxurious mattress that Gia was lucky enough to rest her head on nightly, but I'd take this rickety thing over a blanket on the desert ground any day. In the morning, I would awake early and greet Gia with the sunrise, anxious to tell her about seeing Theory and everything else we'd done.

Unimaginable dread invaded my body. It pushed down on me with such force that I could not lift myself up, no matter how much I tried. My arms and legs were of no use. Flashes of light attempted to obscure my vision and, as I writhed against the pain, I could see angry eyes boring into mine. So much chaotic fury in them, and yet, something cold and calculated also swirled within their depths. *This is a nightmare*, I told myself. *Just a nightmare. Stay calm and you will wake up soon.*

Shrill screams of terror echoed in my head, causing my ears to ring, their rapid, overlapping cadence deafening. I felt a hand fighting to cover my mouth and muffle my cries. I had to be making some sort of noise in my sleep from this assault; if I made enough, maybe El would wake me. Strong hands ripped at my clothing, baring my skin. Horrid thoughts of Nix came crashing into the forefront of my mind, but nothing compared to the violating penetration that tore through me and into me, invading my body. I reached for my magic, any form of it that would rise to the surface, but it evaded me completely. There was the burn of unmistakable pain in between my legs. My nails and hands scraped against hard, cold stone, and my fingers began to bleed from my will to fight against the excruciating agony. The hand held firmly across my mouth continued to muffle my screams for help. I again reached for my power to bring me some semblance of healing and relief from the torment, but the magic within me was dwindling quickly.

I felt the sharp edge of a knife pressed firmly to my throat, forcing me to restrain myself—and yet, a part of me craved so desperately for all of this to end. My chest heaved with exasperation, my adrenaline spiking. My mind unable to reconcile if it should fight or succumb. Which would hurt less? Would I survive either? My erratic pulse began to slow as the heathen above me failed to meet his release and slumped across my tiny body, broken and bloodied.

In a strange twist, the scene transformed into a vision where I could no longer see my attacker. Instead, there was a female, not yet in focus, but with long, curly tendrils and bronzy skin—it was Princess Embry. I was startled at the sight unfolding, as I had only seen her in Saryn's painting back at the safehouse. And what had been shown to me in a dream. Only...Nori had seen her.

Embry was standing in front of a tall male whose arms were wrapped around her from behind, and he was nuzzling his face into the crook of her neck. She smiled and giggled at his playful flirting. The male behind her had silver hair, and when he lifted his chin, I gasped with recognition when suddenly, I was plunged back into the darkness of the former nightmare.

Tremendous pain flooded my entire body as I felt the knife, once again at my throat, lift momentarily and then slice deeply across my flesh. My airway began to flood with warm liquid, causing me to suffocate as I struggled to find breath. I tried to lift my hand to stanch the flow of blood, but my arm felt too heavy, and I knew I would not make it in time. Memories of the mere scrape from the ceremony of the Imperi flashed quickly through me and were soon replaced with the feeling of my body becoming incredibly cold and limp. The fear of this nightmare felt like a boulder on my chest, pinning me to the cot. In the pitch-black silence, there was suddenly a whisper:

"Ilithyia, forgive me."

My chest heaved as I awoke gasping from the nightmare. My body was covered in a cold sweat; my nightgown soaked through, and my hands were shaking. She was gone. I could feel it the way I could feel the return of Varro's bond shivering against mine. Something was terribly wrong. Nori had come to me in a dream, but this was not a dream for her. Panic began to settle in, and I had to hold myself back from letting out a sharp cry of disbelief. I clung to that disbelief as I quickly slid on shoes and threw a cloak over my back, making my way to Gia's room in the middle of the night to warn her of the horror I had witnessed. I prayed to the Gods I was wrong and that these were nothing more than night terrors of my own twisted making. Maybe a punishment for the deaths I had caused.

Gia notified her Kingsguard to bring the one named Cairis to her, and while she waited, I portaled to the safehouse awaiting the arrival of them both. When I landed in the alleyway behind the building, there was nothing but shadows cast by moonslight. A cloudlike circle formed before me and a half-awake but startled Varro came running through it, immediately gathering me into his arms.

"What's wrong? I was sleeping, but I could feel your fear through the bond."

I began to gasp for air, trying to get words out through my sobs into his chest.

"I-I think…something h-has happened…to Nori!"

Varro caressed the back of my head, holding me closely to him in an attempt to console me. Gia arrived next, wearing nothing but a silky negligee and a cloak.

"Where is…Cairis?" I asked, trying to speak through my weeping.

"He's coming, I promise," Gia assured us.

Saryn burst through the back door, looking at all of us like we had gone insane.

"What is the meaning of this? Have you lost your mind? Get inside, now!" he commanded.

Varro ushered me inside under his arm, keeping the comforting warmth of his body close, then seated me at the dining table and took the seat beside mine.

"You all better have a very good explanation—" Saryn fumed before I cut him off.

"Nori's been hurt. She...she came to me in a dream. S-Something terrible has happened... We have to help her!" I pleaded.

Saryn's angry expression softened into deep concern. His brow furrowed as he glanced around at the lot of us.

All of a sudden, Cairis came barreling through the back door. His skin looked pale and his face distraught. His eyes appeared bloodshot.

Gia gave him a look and Cairis shot her a slight, almost imperceptible shake of his head in reply, and her features transformed quickly from exhaustion and confusion to fear and heartbreak.

"Where is Nori?" I cried to Cairis, demanding answers.

His throat bobbed, choking as he tried to find the words. I had never seen Cairis distraught until this moment, and I knew. He needed not say the words that confirmed my worst fears, but my impatience with him reached a sharp climax, and I had to hear them.

I gritted my teeth through the tears streaming down my cheeks, and ground out, "Where. The. Fuck. Is. Nori?" Varro placed his hand on my shoulder, reassuring me of his presence. But nothing could comfort me in this moment.

Hunching over the table, Cairis braced his hulking frame with both hands and lifted his head, unable to meet my gaze. Instead, he delivered the news to Saryn like a soldier to his commander.

"There was an attack in the cells from a male prisoner. She's…"

Hearing the crack in his voice nearly sent me into a wild frenzy as he struggled to say the words.

"Nori is gone; she-she's dead. She's dead…" he repeated, his voice breaking on the final word.

In that moment, I felt my ribcage split in two and my heart pound with a deafening rhythm that caused my ears to ring. I held my breath like I had forgotten how to breathe, certain my lungs may never take in air again. My hands trembled, and memories of the landslide came to mind as I questioned taking the whole of Nasallus and everything surrounding it to its demise.

But I would never truly be happy again. Never whole again. Maybe now my dark powers would be lost to me, as Nori was lost to this world. Time stood still as I realized I had been with her, my friend, my sister in all the ways that mattered, in her final moments. As this evil stranger tore her innocence from her, he showed no mercy for the brave and tiny warrior below him. He took from her the only thing she refused to give the Imperi. I would take much more from him in return. My resolve hardened into something monstrous.

"Bring him to me. Alive."

CHAPTER 27

It made no difference to me, the truths that were uncovered in the hours that followed. Nothing could change what was coming to the Fae male who had taken my friend's life. Another deception, an attack from their own, disguised as retaliation from the North. I knew better, and yet, I did not care what his reasons were, nor the duress he was under to commit such a heinous act. I cared not for how Cairis managed to bring him to me, and I had little interest in whether Saryn approved of my methods or if the others would join. He would pay with his life. And just before drawing his final breath, he would look into my eyes and feel the undertow of grief that had swept away any mercy, any hope he had of his life being spared.

Saryn sent for Trace, and when he arrived, I barely acknowledged his existence. I was acutely and singularly focused on one thing—the arrival of our guest.

Cairis proved efficient, and within hours, he was hauling a bound, struggling prisoner dressed in tattered rags to us. I motioned for Cairis to take him to one of the burned-out homes behind our safehouse. Saryn understood my intention. There would be no need to soil this place with blood, and since I planned to take my time, it would be better if we created some distance between the sounds of my meticulous work and any townsfolk.

Cairis dragged the limp and gagged murderer into the room, lit by a handful of lanterns. It was sundown on the sabbath, and I couldn't help but think it was the perfect setting for all things ceremonial. Trace assisted in tying him to the table, following my instructions. Saryn looked on with anticipation, sensing I was about to become what he had always hoped I would.

Cold. Callous. Calculated. Most of all—bloodthirsty.

Gia yanked the gag from his throat, none too gently, and his pleading began instantaneously.

"Please…please, take me back. He promised me my family would be protected. I only did what I was told."

I knelt down and squeezed his mouth between my fingers, pinching his traitorous lips together to shut up the drivel he espoused.

"I don't care if the Gods themselves promised you. Tonight you will witness the North's retribution and my wrath."

I stood and turned to face my companions and stated myself plainly.

"Let me assure you all that our friend, a sworn member of this Imperi, died alone, in pain and afraid. This sorry excuse of a creature took from her the only thing she guarded above all else, her innocence. He assaulted her and showed her no mercy."

My peers stared down at the captive rendered defenseless before us. Each silent, but their eyes teemed with rage waiting to be unleashed.

"All of you once judged me for my late hours spent with the Vespers, but tonight, I will show you everything I learned. You can look away, or you can watch, but I will relish every minute of what is coming to him, and you will not get an ounce of guilt from me."

Saryn listened intently, a sly smile spreading across his face. Tonight, I would savor my revenge, and he approved.

"I invite you to partake in avenging our friend. There is only one rule—I will deal the final blow. Take him to the brink of death as often as you wish, but you will heal him each time. If you take that from me, you will be next."

In the hours that followed, we took turns unleashing ourselves to the fullest extent our imaginations could conjure. The most reluctant of us was Varro. His kind and optimistic heart did not have a place in moments like this. His killing was always precise, intentional, and merciful. His Siren Song created forms of torture none of us could see, but I knew by the writhing and contortion of the prisoner's body that Varro was doing his absolute best. Not for himself, but for my appeasement. He cared for Nori, but he loved me—and what hurt me, pained him greatly.

By now the rest of us had clothes soaked twice through with blood, and I was shocked there was any of it left to mend our victim with each time the next resumed their craft. He reeked of his own urine, but the scent did not deter any of us.

"No mercy," Gia said to me as she approached the table.

Her punishments were impressive. Part of me knew that with every slice, strike, and burn she was doing to him all the things she wished she could do to the king. For all the times he placed his sweaty, drunken hands on her nude flesh. I did not care what personal motivations each of them had, so long as this individual continued to suffer.

Each time the male passed out from our exhibitions, he was forced to return to consciousness. He would not sleep through a minute of this. He would feel every moment of it, just as she had.

I looked over at Saryn, wondering when and if he'd partake, but he just stood there, arms crossed, watching us like a proud father. He never once flinched at the sight of the blood, or at any of the actions we took. Like he'd seen it all before. Likely done it all before.

Trace practiced the gruesome methods he'd been forced to perform during his assignment. He removed fingers with ease and blinded him repeatedly—the only activity of the evening where I may have caught a flinch from Saryn.

Blind, heal, repeat.

I refused to meet Varro's gaze, as I knew each decision I made saddened him, even frightened him. He'd prefer to console my grief in other ways and put this wretch out of his misery, but he'd just have to love me despite what was about to transpire—what had been transpiring—even the side that was capable of all this. He had to understand that had it been him instead of Nori, something far worse would come down upon this world.

It was well into the morning hours, and the exhaustion of our efforts had begun to set in. I directed Cairis and Trace to rotate the prisoner's body, placing him face down on the table. Once he was fully secured, I climbed up on the table and straddled both sides of his bloodied lower back.

"Blade," I commanded Trace.

He pulled a clean dagger from his thigh and placed it in my palm, giving me a nod of approval. It was then that I knew I was no better, no different than him. I had just been delaying the inevitable of what my future looked like.

This.

Until now, we had only been playing at the cleaner parts of our roles, but tonight we had all changed—and perhaps not for the better.

I leaned down and pressed the full weight of my body against his.

"How does it feel? Being hopeless, helpless, death whispering into your ear?"

The vile stranger could do nothing but whimper into the bloodied rag shoved into his mouth. I cared not for his words or pleas anyway.

"Do me a favor, close your eyes, think of flying..."

My instructions, like a hypnotizing song, was the last thing he heard before I plunged my dagger deep into the small area between his shoulder and spine. The nest of the wing, as most Fae called it. This is the place where our wings lay dormant before the magic allowed them to unfurl from our bodies.

"Show me your wing!" I yelled, demanding that he summon the one not pinned against my blade.

Sweat poured from his brow onto the table below and he winced from the immense pain of my weapon digging so deeply into his back.

"Show me your wing," I demanded again, twisting my hand against the hilt of the dagger, causing him to writhe against it.

In this state, it would be a shock for him to have any magic left to summon them, but I felt the shift of his bones finally make way for his left wing. A white set of feathers adorned it. Blood was smeared across it and dripping from the tips, marring the beauty of it.

"How fitting," I said. "She had white wings too. They were far more beautiful than yours."

Abruptly, I grabbed his wing, yanking it back toward me at an unnatural angle, then tearing the dagger from his right shoulder. I began to slice the muscle from the bone, flaying his wing from his limp, almost lifeless body. Feathers scattered into the air and I tossed the bloody wing onto the floor where he could see it. Some say there was no more painful way to die than having your wings removed. The first few times I tried it with a Vesper, I threw up before getting the wing fully detached. Something about the tension of the knife against the muscle and bone always made me sick before I could complete the task at hand. But tonight, there was no hesitation, no restraint. My stomach and nerves were calm despite the sight of it on the floor.

I could feel the life draining from him as blood seeped endlessly from the wound. Finally ready to send him to the divine creators, I grabbed what was left of his hair and yanked his head backward to meet my hollow gaze. I held my dagger tight against his throat and basked in the smell of fear wafting from every pore on his body.

"Tell the Gods I am not sorry."

I slid the blade slowly across his throat, ensuring he met the same ending he granted my friend. For the first time since his arrival, my body relaxed into the feel of the warm blood spilling over my hand. I held his head firmly in place, watching every last trace of his existence disappear from this world. The sound of his gurgling turned to silence, and all around me, the others stood in mournful silence for the one fate we could not stay. My dearest friend, the purest amongst us. The most undeserving of a cruel end.

Mother Ilithyia, please send her back to me, even as a shadow.

Even as a dream.

CHAPTER 20

I don't know how long I laid crying atop the male's lifeless, blood-soaked body. My hand clutched the dagger, unwilling to accept that there was nothing more that could be done. The pain in my chest was still unbearable. The distraction from my grief was a temporary bliss, because the rage had felt manageable. But the grief still came in uncontrollable swells. I had never felt anything like it in my short life. I had never lost anything or anyone that mattered until this moment. Time stood still and nothing felt real. I lay against the lifeless corpse so long, I felt my skin turning as cold as his. My perspiration had now dried on my skin, causing me to shiver.

My companions conversed around me, but the ringing in my ears obscured their words. They moved about the cramped, charred interior as if I wasn't there. Eventually, I felt a warm hand rest gently atop my back, and Varro crouched down till he was eye-level with me. Tears burned my eyes, blurring my vision until I was able to focus on the unmistakable vivid blue of his uncertain gaze.

"Cress," he whispered, his tone soft, gentle. "It is done."

My mind searched desperately for another foothold of anger, a toehold of vengeance. But only anguish, like a cold, unyielding stone wall, remained. My entire body felt sore now that the adrenaline of my actions had subsided.

"Let me help you down," he offered, giving me his other hand for support. I slid off the body and steadied myself before fully standing upright. My nightgown was soaked crimson; the others did not appear any cleaner—except for Saryn, whose attire remained pristine.

He stepped forward, making certain to avoid one of the puddles of blood beneath his feet.

"I will handle this mess. Tomorrow…more precisely later today, is the sabbath. Each of you needs to return to your stations before your absence is noted. If you are able, we should reconvene as soon as possible."

One by one, they exited in silence. My mind had already begun to race, frustrated with everyone's aversion to discussing the possibility of retrieving our friend's body and giving her a proper funeral. Wasn't anyone else concerned with getting to the bottom of who caused this and what we were going to do with them? How was Gia going to make it safely back to her bedroom looking like she had murdered someone? I'd need to help her dispose of our compromised clothing. And what of Cairis? His uniform was fully soiled. And now he needed to account for a missing prisoner? It seemed like the best course of action was for everyone to remain at the safehouse and resolve these matters, but no one showed the slightest bit of interest.

In the alleyway, each portaled away to their own unique destinations in sullen silence, resigned to handle these mounting questions and concerns on their own. I didn't want to be alone, though; I didn't want to be without any of them. Why was I the only one that wanted to stay? Having lost one of our own had put me on edge. We were stronger together. Varro took notice of my antsy fidgeting that grew worse with each departure, till only he and I remained. Our reunion after the Ledor Canyon was meant to be so different, but now those events were far from my mind.

"Come with me," he asked in a tone that sounded more demand than question.

"I can't, I've never seen the bay. I can't portal there," I argued.

"I know. We'll walk. A change of scenery will do you good," Varro proposed, taking my hand before I could respond.

My hand was sticky, still covered in dried blood, but he took it without hesitation. He led the way at a slow, steady pace down winding streets I had never had permission or reason to wander. The sky above was still aglow with stars and moonslight, but it wouldn't be long before it became a soft blue-gray from the encroaching sunrise. Had anyone actually been awake at this hour, they might have been confused and shocked at the sight of us strolling hand-in-hand, covered in blood.

Varro walked confidently, like he'd always known these roads and this city outside of the castle walls. I imagined someone peeking their head out a window and him waving jauntily, wishing them well before we continued on our way. His calm demeanor was a stark contrast to mine, which was still coming down from the night's deviant activities. He did not speak the rest of the way to wherever he was leading me, but instead of being uncomfortable, the silence was contemplative and welcomed—there was just something about being in his presence, our two humming pieces of the bond seeking refuge in one another.

When we arrived at the street's end, the three moons of Demir sparkled on the bay before us and small waves flowed into the sandy shorelines. In what little light there was from above, along with a scattering of lanterns, I could see rows and rows of docks with large ships in various stages of construction. Some almost complete, others in their infancy. The shoreline was littered with large stacks of wood and enough other materials to build a fleet. All was quiet on the bay, apart from the soothing exhalations of water and a slight breeze that caused sails to flutter and untethered ropes to rustle against their masts.

It was clear Silas and Zarif were making preparations for something significant, and I suddenly swelled with hope that demolishing the mine had thwarted their plans to some degree. When we reached the beach, I slipped off my shoes, realizing that Varro had been barefoot this entire time. He must have portaled to the safehouse so abruptly in his concern for me that he hadn't bothered to put any on. The sand beneath my feet felt softer, finer, and cooler than what I had encountered in most of Artume. The sensations flooded my thoughts with a similar memory from my youth, when my father took me to Erisas Bay and let me collect seashells along the beach while he made small talk with other guild members.

There was a moment, just one, where I thought to convince Varro that now was the time for us to make an attempt at fleeing the Order. There had been no greater opportunity than the one before us now. We were both well-suited for the sea, and with Saryn distracted and Theory far enough away, we might be able to escape this fate and find some way to remove our brands without dying in the process. It would be worth the risk. But I did not speak of those fanciful wishes. The magic shackles branded and hidden beneath our wrists would always prevail. Varro continued to guide me toward a small boathouse whose exterior appeared salt-weathered and suffering decay.

When we entered, he immediately lit a lantern hanging on the wall and then a candle sitting atop a dingy table.

"What is this place?" I inquired, assessing my surroundings.

"Home away from home," he said, turning to face me with an endearing smile.

"Do all the ship workers get these sorts of accommodations?"

Varro laughed. "No, not at all. With their wages and gambling or drinking habits, they'd never save enough to acquire a place like this."

He spoke of it like it was something grand—and grand, it was not. But it did appear to be his.

"So, how did you afford it then?"

"Let's just say my abilities can be used for less violent and more convincing means than what I've been forced to demonstrate in your presence."

He gave me a nefarious grin, and I rolled my eyes at the insinuation. Varro had somehow stolen…acquired…whatever he preferred to call it…a sum of money that allowed him to rent this private boathouse. The center of it was a boat slip cutout, exposing the water to the interior of the structure, where a modest rowboat was tied off. On the opposite side was a meager cot. The space was dusty and dark, but cozy. During the daytime, the two small windows, one on each side, would allow for sunlight. However, I wasn't certain I wanted to see this place in broad daylight. It made the servants' quarters seem respectable.

Varro went to a small chest at the foot of his bed and pulled out a loose-fitting shirt and a pair of pants. The pants were far too big for me, but had an adjustable drawstring, so they would work. He set them on the table, indicating they were for me to change into. He then proceeded to fill a bucket with seawater from the center of the slip and rung out a sponge. I lifted up my nightgown, exposing my naked body to him; but in that moment, there was no sexual energy between us. I was numb, and he was distracted with the task at hand, which was taking care of me. He set the bucket at my feet and knelt down, beginning to scrub the blood gently from my skin. The bucket of clear saltwater turned to a swirl of blood after only one dip of the sponge. He refilled it with fresh water and continued his process of cleansing me. I closed my eyes and relaxed into his touch and the cool sensation of the water dribbling down my legs.

He held my hands in his and cleaned my fingertips and nails meticulously to ensure no evidence remained.

"You don't have to do this, I can just—"

"I want to. And I know you can. I'm very aware of what you're capable of, Moirai," he protested kindly.

Varro continued to cleanse my body, as if performing a ritual. He stood behind me, washing my shoulders and back, then moved the sponge around to my front. My nipples stiffened when he grazed them, then continued to run it down my arm, in between dips of it back into the bucket for more water. When he had thoroughly removed every trace of my victim, he patted me dry and placed the clothing in my hand to dress myself.

After I was fully covered, he approached me. He cupped my face in both his hands and placed the gentlest of kisses on my forehead.

"I know she isn't Versa, but she was still like a sister to you," he said.

I pulled back in confusion. "Who is Versa?" I asked.

Varro's golden skin paled. His eyes widened and his brow furrowed.

"What do you mean 'who is Versa'? Your sister. Versa," he stated flatly.

Suddenly, the scar behind my ear began to itch intensely, and I brushed aside my hair as I ran my finger along it. More confusion set in. "*I have a sister*," I told myself. I *knew* I had a sister. My pulse began to race in sync with my frantic thoughts. *Why is this name so unfamiliar to me? Why does the sound of it feel so foreign?* Tears began to form in the waterlines of my eyes. *Versa*, I repeated, over and over in my head, trying to force the image of a female with the name to mind. But doubt overwhelmed me, because the female I pictured looked just like me.

Varro's hands braced each of my arms and he squeezed, trying to draw my attention back to him.

"Your twin. Your twin, Versa."

By the end of his statement, he was almost shaking me, trying to get me to recollect what had become lost to me.

I yanked myself out of his grasp. "I know," I said in frustration. "I know now. I have a sister. I just…am struggling with the name."

"It's time. You know it is. You must answer the five questions."

"No," I snapped back in frustration. "It's not like that. It…it can't be."

The plan to help ensure my mind was always intact was supposed to be a last resort. He knew even mentioning it would infuriate me, scare me, and possibly send me into a spiral.

"Maybe…" he offered, trying to pacify me. "Maybe you're just exhausted from exerting yourself after days of travelling and, from what I hear, taking down an entire canyon. Perhaps all you need is sleep and a good meal. But you made me promise you that if I ever saw even the smallest of signs, to ask you the questions."

Our plan was a promise sealed by a bargain. If he asked, there was no way I could refuse. It was our only way to measure how much, if anything, was lost due to the Drift.

"Please," I said, almost sniveling, trying to avoid discovering if any more of my memories had become affected.

"You made me swear," he replied solemnly.

Varro proceeded to ask me the questions we prepared with meticulous attention to detail.

Five questions spanning the events of my life.

Five answers I should know.

Five reasons to believe I was still me.

He gave no indication of if I was right or wrong after he asked each one, only proceeded to the next. No expression to drive fear or hope into me that might possibly sway the following answer. No judgement and no reprieve.

When the final answer was given, I awaited his reaction with bated breath.

"You passed," he said, momentarily relieved.

I let out a deep sigh and closed my eyes briefly in acceptance.

Before I could relish in my reassurance too long, however, he added, "You passed, but something *has* affected you. I do not know why you struggled to recall Versa's name, but it is concerning."

Each time he said her name, it became less foreign and more familiar. Like pieces of a puzzle coming quickly back into place; even the memory of the tattoo behind my ear. It's possible these first signs of the Drift had finally touched me, but their effects were waning and impermanent.

Despite answering all his questions correctly, Varro still seemed on edge.

"Do you want to talk about any of it?" he asked sincerely. Discussing how I felt about the people I'd killed in the canyon, Nori's passing, the brutal torture I'd bestowed on her killer, or these early signs of the Drift was the last thing I wanted to do now that I was finally alone with him. All of the pent-up longing, the need for his very presence, and I was teetering on the precipice of my own self-control. What little restraint I had was fading with every passing moment. The sheer scent of my mate was intoxicating—maddening, even.

I reached for the belt at his waist and pulled him toward me. "I have better things to do with this mouth," I teased, while beginning to undo the buckle.

Varro grasped my hand tightly, protesting my pursuit. "Cress," he said breathily, hanging his head reluctantly.

But before he could say another word, I ordered him to shut up and pressed my mouth to his, biting his lower lip and causing him to let out a groan. Varro released his hand from mine in surrender, allowing my fingers to resume their quest. I greedily pulled the leather belt off him and dropped it to the floor, then began to undo the buttons on his trousers in between more kisses. Both of us growing more restless.

Having now fully given in, he placed rough kisses all along my neck. With my hair bunched in his hands he tilted my head, bending me to his will with each fervent kiss. I ran my hand along the outside of his pants, feeling the length of him harden below my fingertips, and squeezed for good measure. He let out a deep and possessive growl, causing my insides to warm. The feeling of his arousal in the palm of my hand made my mouth water; my desire to please him growing as I continued to run my hand across the thin fabric that separated us.

I lowered myself to my knees before him and looked up into the eyes of my mate. His molten blue gaze steeled at the sight of me below him, eager and ready to please. I slowly lowered his pants to the ground, letting my fingertips graze the sides of his muscular thighs. Face to face with his hardened cock, I licked my lips in anticipation. I grabbed him firmly with my hand and began to stroke, causing him to stiffen further against my grasp. Varro reached a hand down and pushed my long hair over my shoulder, gathering both sides in one fist. I leaned forward and teasingly ran my tongue from the base up the shaft, flicking it along the tip before removing my mouth entirely. His hips shifted forward at the absence of my mouth. I looked up at him, watching to see his reaction.

"You're cruel," he said breathily, staring down at me.

"Tell me you like it then," I instructed, goading him to say what he wanted.

Varro grinned and tugged tightly at my hair, as if to teach me a lesson for my games.

"Do you like this?" I said before squeezing tightly and fluttering my tongue along his tip, tasting his arousal.

I paused, looking up again for more confirmation of his approval. His nostrils flared and his jaw ticked.

"Yes," he answered huskily.

"Yes, what?"

"Yes, *Moirai!*"

At his response, I plunged my mouth downward along his entire shaft, working to accept the full length of him into my throat. I braced my hands on his hips, pulling myself deeper with each dip and bob of my head. He bucked against my mouth, causing me to struggle, but I relaxed and resumed my focus on running my tongue up and down in perfect coordination with my hand while using the other to cup him from below. At the feeling of my other hand, his head leaned back, lolling in ecstasy. His chest heaved and muscles contracted while I continued to work him. Occasionally, I lifted one hand to grasp his firm rear end, a masterpiece in its own right. When I began to feel the throbbing of his excitement, I slowed my pace intentionally, dragging out my languid and fluid motions.

The wet space between my thighs ached with a desire for his hands, his mouth, anything to fill the void. I released my mental shields to ensure he knew just how much I wanted him; how much I enjoyed pleasing him this way. There was only so long I'd be able to continue with the charade of delaying his gratification. I tilted my gaze back once more, looking up at him through watering eyes. He ran his thumb across my lower lip, tugging it down and smearing the saliva from my chin as he pulled me away.

"Cress."

"Yes," I gasped, exasperated.

"I'm going to fuck this mouth…" I nodded at his declaration, that ache turning to a throb. "Be prepared to come with me."

Anxious to discover how he'd accomplish such a feat, I turned my attention back to his slick cock. My pace picked up gradually, and his hand still holding my hair squeezed so tightly that it caused a painful sensation. It was quickly countered, though, by the feeling of Varro's Siren Song sending the sensation of a firm touch sliding back and forth across my slick apex. His magic met my own rhythm, and together, we drew forth the most intense pleasure from one another. The likes of which caused me to whimper and cry against him, still undulating in my mouth. The faster he worked me, the faster I worked him. Sounds of our back-and-forth pleasure filled the silence, matched by the sound of the rowboat rocking against the slip.

My knees rubbed against the hard ground, but I was numb to it as my legs quivered and shook with the feelings he wrenched from me, all without a single physical touch. Just as I met my end, Varro thrust forward one last time, emptying himself into my throat and slowly releasing my hair. I slumped back to the floor trying to catch my breath and come down from the exhaustion of bringing Varro to a climax all while trying to manage my own. I didn't think I would ever get used to what he was capable of. I don't know that I wanted to. With his gift, it felt like an infinite number of possibilities were available to us.

Varro pulled up his pants—to my great disappointment—and knelt down to meet me on the ground, coaxing my limp body into his embrace.

"Had I only known that our dreams were pale in comparison to this, I'd have sent you to your knees sooner."

For that remark, I jabbed my elbow into his ribs playfully, causing him to recoil with an amused huff.

"However, I don't particularly enjoy being upstaged Cress..."

There was a sinister edge to his tone; one rife with challenge.

We sat on the ground, his legs on either side of me as my back rested against his chest.

"Watch and learn," he whispered into my ear.

From over my right shoulder, he held his hand out directly in front of me. His raised his pointer and middle finger together side by side and then slowly made a swishing gesture in front of my line of sight. I jerked back into him as the feeling of that same motion unexpectedly grazed my sex. What in three moons?

He then began to use the same two fingers and made tiny circles in the air, sending shivers down my spine and straight to my core. I clasped my hands tightly to the sides of his legs as he continued the spirals, eliciting a moan from me.

"You will sing for me before this is at its end," Varro warned.

His fingertips were like a waltz with precise steps and movements designed with perfect synchronicity, all of which were choreographed for my pleasure. Dragging them up and down, he pressed one forward, which I could feel teasing my entrance. All I could think to myself was I may never touch myself again, because this was otherworldly. In between his torturous hand gestures, he placed kisses along my ear; his hot breath tickling me as he nipped.

As his hand motions quickened, I rasped, "Gods…!"

"Tell them I'm not sorry," he said tauntingly, using my own words against me, giving them a whole new meaning.

Tears pricked at my eyes as I fought the building orgasm. I was damp with the pleasure he had drawn from me, and yet he was unmerciful in his movements. He raised his free hand above my other shoulder, and my eyes widened at the possibilities with two sets of fingers at his disposal.

"Watch," he commanded.

My eyes had already been struggling to stay open in between the fluttering of constant bliss. Yet, somehow, I watched as the left hand proceeded to make the small circular motions above the right hand, which used one finger stroking come hither into my entrance, hitting the most sensitive of spots. The pressure began to build at the two sensations fighting for dominance. The pulsing from my clit created an insatiable hunger inside me. He lifted yet another finger, adding it to the one stroking me with a deeply satisfying pace and filling my aching need further.

Something about watching his craft, seeing the detail of it coincide with the sensations he created through Siren Song, provided even more allure than the act alone. I wanted his gift to be mine so badly. I wanted to lift my hand and, with a simple squeeze of my fist, make him beg me for more. Was he naturally this creative? Was all of this because I had not yet given myself to him, and he needed to find alternative ways to satisfy our desire for one another?

His pace increased rapidly; it felt as if he was truly inside me.

"Sing," he rasped, his body sweating against mine, proving he was just as affected as I was by his actions. My back rose and fell against his chest in swells.

I rested my head back against his chest, closed my eyes, and lost myself fully to the dancing of his imaginary fingers. Sparks radiated all across my body until a cry sprung forth from my lips, followed by three uncontrollable moans. I freed the orgasm from its confines, letting myself crash into a euphoric free fall.

Varro lowered his hands and placed one across my heart, feeling as it practically beat out of my chest as I tried to shed myself of the frenzy he had caused.

"Come here," he said, moving from behind me and standing, offering me his hand to rise.

I was reluctant to take it, unwilling to let our night end, my legs still shaky from his performance.

"I want to show you something," he offered with a wicked smile, and I was delighted at the invitation to continue these private endeavors.

Varro placed a couple of heavy blankets at the center of the rowboat, then helped me down to my seat. He placed himself opposite me, untying the rope that tethered it to the boat house. Using the oar to shove us out of the dwelling and into the darkness of the bay, he made a shushing gesture at me and quietly paddled us out of the main docks. Varro rowed in silence while I studied the various ships under construction. I imagined how this area must be abuzz with workers and trade during the daylight, greatly contrasting the silence and solitude of these hours.

He rowed slower than I knew he was capable of, probably because he wanted to keep the noise to an absolute minimum—however, patience was not a strong suit of mine. Something he knew well. So, I simply rested my hand over the edge of the small boat, letting it submerge into the cool seawater. I focused my energy and generated a current below us, causing our little boat to quickly pick up speed; increasing our pace by at least double.

Even in the moonslight, I could make out his unimpressed smirk as he uttered the words, "Lazy. Some of us are in roles that do require actual physical labor."

"Ungrateful," I scoffed.

Varro rowed until we were so far from the docks that their lantern lights faded into the darkness completely. It was just him and me, the creaking of the rowboat, the moonslight reflecting off the black water with no signs of land or life ahead. I removed my hand from the water and patted it dry on my pant leg.

Leaning forward, he retrieved something from a small pack he had stowed between us. I could see the steel reflecting the moonslight as Varro raised a small knife to his palm and slid it across his flesh.

"What are you doing?" I asked, growing concerned.

"Shh, just wait and listen."

Varro reached over the gunwale as I watched, placing his bleeding hand into the water and swishing the blood around, then proceeding to do the same on the other side of the boat. When he lifted his hand back up, he licked the blood away and healed the wound.

We sat there in silence for what seemed like ages. Just when I was about to interrupt, all of a sudden, a haunting echo rose up from the depths of the sea. A chorus of spine-chilling voices singing in perfect unison. The words foreign, unlike any language I'd ever heard. My eyes widened at Varro as we got pulled into the hypnotic arrangement. He shifted his body closer to me so that we were sitting side by side.

"That is Siren Song," he said, clasping my hand in his and lifting it to place it over his heart. "It is the sweet song of death, and it is my offering to you for our friend Nori. Your last memories of her should not be of her painful cries or his bitter pleas. Let it be this."

Tears were streaming down my face when he removed my hand from his chest and cupped my cheek.

"The Gods will know the purity of her soul; I promise you they will welcome her."

I plunged myself into his embrace, crashing my lips to his, letting the smattering of my tears paint his cheeks. Whether my soul be tainted or damned, I wouldn't go another day in this life or the next without binding myself to this male. The music continued all around us, echoing up from the great depths of the Endless Tides.

I clawed at Varro's shirt, removing it and tossing it into the boat before removing my own. I ached for the touch of our bare skin against one another. I kissed him passionately, over and over again, until I could swallow the aching of grief in my chest and cried no more. Then my grief turned to a ravenous passion that consumed me. I must have him. Our bond was fighting, screaming and gnawing to touch one another. *Just once*, it pleaded. *Just once.*

And so, with no fear or regret, I leaned over and offered myself to my mate with a ragged whisper.

"Take me, I am yours."

I said the words with all the power and resolve of a hundred unconquerable armies. There would be no stopping this; he was the light to my darkness. The Gods had bestowed their ill fates, but this was a destiny of *my* choosing. He did not need to question my will; our bond knew my heart spoke true. He laid the blankets flat at the bottom of the boat, and I removed what remained of my clothing. He followed suit. We both faced each other on our knees, naked as the day we entered this world. All our scars, our histories, washed away till there was nothing but the two of us and the enchanting Siren Song.

"I wish to bind myself to you in the traditions of my people," he began, while pulling the small blade out again and making a cut across his other hand before passing it to me. "You must devote yourself freely," he continued, nodding at my hand.

I ran the blade across my palm without a moment of hesitation, feeling its sharp sting followed by the warmth of my blood pooling in its absence. Varro then clasped our bloodied hands together, combining the essence of our life force. With our fingertips intertwined, he dipped our hands into the water, letting the salty sea water cleanse the blood from our grip. A moment later, more melancholy music rose from the depths, the somber melodies of a friend's elegy slowly transitioning to a hymn of otherworldly devotion.

"This is *our* song," he said, fighting back his own tears.

With our mental shields lowered, I knew his thoughts swirled with every emotion imaginable. The fear of losing me. The fear of the Drift. The pain of being apart. The loss of our friend. The unwavering commitment to protect me. The desire to know my body fully and satiate our bond once and for all. His unerring, unimaginable love. But I imagined the act of listening to one another's thoughts was a fraction of the fulfillment *fideli cœur* offered.

We hadn't even begun, and already I was trembling with excitement and nerves. He healed my palm with a gentle kiss, and then ran the backside of his hand across my chest, gently grazing one of my nipples. He turned his hand and squeezed my breast firmly, almost painfully, while pulling my face to his with the other. Our kisses were frenetic, our hands roaming greedily. The song somehow evolved with each of our zealous movements. I ignored my already swollen and sensitive lips from our earlier engagements and continued to kiss him like it could be our last chance. I inhaled the scent of him accented by the sea air, trying desperately to imprint it in my mind and on my heart forever.

He guided me gently down into the center of the boat and leaned over me with our bare legs intertwined. We were both breathless from the anticipation. Our bond hummed below the surface at the prospect of finally being tethered.

I smiled, letting out a small laugh. "Do you feel that?"

"Yes," he said, followed by more impassioned kisses from my chest down to my stomach, before lowering his face between my legs. Heat pulsed at my core and the sensation of his tongue dragging at a leisurely slow pace along my apex nearly caused me to come undone immediately. His rough, calloused hands squeezed my thighs tightly, pulling me hard against his face as he worked to deliver me a climax.

I panted my words to the sky, to the stars, to every cruel God who was listening, "I lo-I love…you. I love you."

My words were a cry, a whimper and a plea wrapped around the tangled web of pleasure he spun and spun, endlessly.

As if the Gods themselves answered me, Varro was suddenly above me, the tip of his cock placed at my entrance, patiently awaiting my final decision. Still putting me and my wants and needs first. I spread myself wider for him and wrapped my legs behind him before pulling him forcefully into me in response. Taking him. *All of him.* Varro hilted his cock in me, and my back arched with the divine pleasure of our bond reaching out to one another, two dissonant songs slowly harmonizing until they became one beautiful, haunting melody. We both gasped; the sound of our heaving breaths muffled by the Siren Song all around us. Every feeling, emotion, sensation he felt soared through me with lightning speed. In that moment, we were truly one Fae. Our separate forms ceased to be, and there was only unity as the bond eviscerated the past and carved out a future with my mate.

Our bodies moved in concert, and with each stroke, I moaned louder, his sporadic kisses occasionally capturing them against his own breathless groans. He slid back and forth into me with a desperation that engrossed me. I stared at the twinkling stars above as my mate, my fated one, became lost in the sealing of our bond, a primal connecting of our souls, and thought to myself that a cruel fate has never tasted so sweet. And so, I smiled at the Gods in spite of them.

I felt him beginning to reach his climax as I sought to hold on to mine as long as possible. Suddenly, Varro's wings unfurled, and he wrapped my legs tightly around his waist before ascending us into the air to hover above the boat. With one last coda from the Sirens, he erupted with a final thrust, and I shattered into his arms as he held us in flight. My legs quivered with echoes of our pleasure and the bond reverberating through us with deafening magnificence. I do not know how I ever thought I knew lovemaking before a bond. This was how fate intended lovers to feel and, knowing what I know now, I would have wandered Demir a hundred lifetimes in search of it. If they all only knew, they would have never settled for anything less. There could be nothing more than this. Nowhere beyond this.

Our naked bodies slowly descended from the sky back into the boat, and we lay there with only the sounds of our heavy breathing and hearts beating. I curled into his protective arms and spoke for the first time through the bond, mind to mind, *"I have to tell you something."*

CHAPTER

60

Unaccustomed to the feeling of our connected minds, Varro replied aloud, "What's wrong?"

He felt my fear; he could hear it in the way my voice quivered down the bond.

"Before Nori passed, she didn't just show me visions of her assailant…" I hesitated, wondering if I should even speak of it with no confirmations of my own. But I could not keep this secret to myself. The information was too grave, too vital. "She showed me a vision of Princess Embry."

"What of her?" he asked softly, stroking his hand down my arm.

"It was hazy, somewhat unclear. She was engaged in affections with a male. One that I recognized, although it doesn't make sense."

His hand paused its movements. "Whom? Whom did you see?"

I inhaled deeply, my chest already feeling tight from his name sitting at the tip of my tongue.

"Saryn."

Varro leaned away from our embrace and looked at me incredulously.

"What? How would the princess know Saryn?" he asked, looking thoughtful before answering his own question. "Maybe, as Nori was losing consciousness, her ability to accurately convey visions to you in the dreamscape became flawed. She *was* under serious duress."

"I know it makes no sense, but it must mean something. It was the last thing she wanted me to see. I can't explain why, but something isn't right."

We lay there in contemplative silence, him thinking about what I had shared and me staring at the stars, sorting through my grief. Death comes in so many unique forms. Sometimes you see it from a distance, moving toward you at a pace so glacial it's easy to ignore. Other times it hovers above you, mockingly, like the first drops of rain when the sun is still shining. It made me wonder which was better; swiftly, at the hands of an enemy, or slowly, taken by old age.

The finality of Nori's death was profound to me. There were no last words, no vivid interactions, no moment to memorize every detail of her face. Like many Gods, Death mocks the expectations of those it presides over. Varro repeated himself until my attention stirred back to him.

"I will convene with Trace first and bring your concerns to him before we all meet for the sabbath. Say nothing of this to the others."

Varro's instructions were clear, but it was hard to imagine him teaming up with Trace now that we had sealed the bond. Did Varro want to be the one to tell him?

The sensation of the bond had evolved from something erratic to a near continuous flow of energy. It felt reinforced in every way. My body seemed like it had the strength of two now, and though it was easy to settle my mind, there was a constant inclination to communicate through the bond. Before, I never knew how frequently I'd get to see or speak to him, but that constraint had been removed. We parted in the earliest hours of the morning, comforted by the knowledge that even if we weren't able to see each other, we now had access to each other at any time. With it being the sabbath, even the shipyard's occupants would be sleeping in, taking respite from their duties. I portaled back to the castle and made an excuse about my whereabouts to El, citing Gia's personal needs in the middle of the night.

I knew Varro would be busy trying to contact Trace during the day, as unlike me, he must have some idea regarding his whereabouts. Had they met like this before, without the rest of us? It was strange to think of them working together. Every flippant thought or question I had, I wanted to ask him, but I also didn't want to be a nuisance. I knew I'd be seeing him soon enough—even if it still felt like too long.

Things at the castle had seemingly intensified in my absence with more Kingsguards patrolling the halls and stationed at various exits. The gossip mill amongst the servants swirled with news of the missing prisoner that had killed a healer, and I winced each time I caught wind of their misinformed prattling. That healer was my friend! Any information about the prisoner being a Northerner, or working on behalf of the North, were more absurdities planted to stoke the fire of hatred for Cambria. It took every ounce of my self-control not to unload the truth on every one of them. Just once, down the bond, I heard Varro say softly, *"Stay calm."*

When I arrived at Gia's room, she looked like she hadn't slept a wink. Her hair was a disheveled mess, but her soiled clothing was nowhere to be found, so I reasoned she must have discovered a way to safely dispose of it. She sat in front of the mirror at her dresser waiting for me to help make her appearance acceptable. I attempted to brush the tangles from her long blonde curls when I noticed the dark circles around her still-bloodshot eyes. She had clearly been crying since we'd parted. I squeezed her shoulder with one hand, and she unexpectedly reached up to hold it in place with her own.

"Is this our fault?" she sniffled, looking at me for some sort of reprieve.

"I don't know," I said honestly, still grappling with my own guilt and trying to understand why the most innocent of us had to die first. Continuing to create small, intricate braids in her hair, I added, "We have to get to the bottom of this. It can't be coincidence that no guards were present to aid her while she was treating the prisoners." *Treating the ailment I had caused,* I thought to myself bitterly. She would have never been down there treating anyone, trying to make a connection with Embry, if we all hadn't organized her involvement in this whole plan.

A tear rolled down Gia's unusually puffy cheeks. "Cairis hasn't found out any more than I have, other than warning me that Zarif is on the rampage. He has the Kingsguards on high alert, declaring Northern infiltration has breached castle walls, threatening lowborn and highborn alike."

I slammed the hairbrush on the table. "That fucking snake! He *is* the infiltrator. He spreads lies like a plague to his own people. All of this…" I said, throwing my hands up in exasperation, "It's all him. Him and his false king."

Gia shushed me, trying to quiet my voice which had begun to carry. She was already dressed, thankfully, and her hair was as good as I was going to achieve given all my distractions. I was going to tell her about me and Varro when, all of a sudden, I heard his voice yelling frantically down the bond, *"Come! Come as soon as you can!"*

I quickly relayed the message to Gia, who looked at me in a state of utter confusion and shock as to how I suddenly became aware of this message.

"How do you know what Varro is saying…?" Her eyes widened as she turned to face me, and before I could answer her, she declared in disbelief, "You sealed the bond!"

Her statement came out both as a question and an accusation. "Yes," I said. "I'll tell you about it later, but right now we have to go!"

We both exited her room with urgency, making sure that she was seen heading to prayers and me back to my duties per our usual farce, before finding our private places to portal back to the safehouse.

We both exited our swirling gray clouds in the alleyway simultaneously. Anxiety constricting at my lungs, I glanced in both directions, looking for signs of Trace or Varro. We both turned at the sound of abrupt commotion inside. Upon entering the shelter, we discovered Saryn gagged and tied to a chair. His hands and feet were bound tightly with rope, Trace and Varro flanking his sides defensively.

"What is going on here?" Gia yelled in bewilderment. This was an unwelcome sight. Fear began to invade my thoughts as I looked first at Varro and then to Trace, whose nostrils flared and eyes narrowed at my presence. He knew. I don't know how, but he did. And it heightened the uncomfortable circumstances even more. Suddenly, the sound of Cairis barreling through the backdoor broke the tension.

"What in the fuck did I just walk into?" he said brazenly, kicking the door shut behind him.

"That's what I want to know!" Gia added, folding her arms across her chest.

I exhaled deeply, but only because I knew slightly more than them. We all waited silently for someone to begin an explanation that might not result in all of us being in an insurmountable amount of shit with Idris—possibly even the king himself.

Trace's expression was severe, and he remained on guard, knowing what Saryn was capable of. I spoke down the bond with worry, *"Are you keeping him subdued?"*

"Yes," Varro said quickly, mind to mind, before I redirected my attention back to Trace.

"I have been keeping an eye on the safehouse for some time now. I have also been monitoring our fearless leader here," he said, pointing at Saryn. "In doing so, I began to notice some peculiar things that he has never shared with any of us."

"What's that?" Cairis chimed in, just as impatient as the rest of us.

"He has not only been making multiple trips via moonstone to Gods knows where…but he's also been donning pristine Kingsguard's armor along with a face other than his own."

You could hear a pin drop. We had all assumed Saryn had been doing many things we were not aware of while we were embedded. One of which was getting messages to and from the border and helping gather whatever intel he could about incidents that might need our attention. Saryn tried yelling again, the gag muffling his words into something unintelligible, in an attempt to explain himself.

"Why is that concerning?" Gia asked.

"That is why I had not told any of you. It wasn't concerning until our friend Varro here informed me of something Cress shared with him."

Everyone's gaze turned toward me expectantly.

"In Nori's final moments, she sent me a vision of Princess Embry… being embraced by *him*," I said, gesturing at our helpless but lethal mentor.

Gia gasped and Trace's jaw clenched. Saryn's eyes flickered imperceptibly, but I had been watching intently for some reaction as I said the princess's name. Varro bent down close to Saryn's face.

"If you scream, if you make any sort of commotion, I will make you feel the kind of pain that has you begging for Death's cold embrace."

This was one of the few times I had ever seen Varro's demeanor shift so intensely. I could feel the protectiveness of the bond swarming inside of me. He wasn't worried so much about Saryn being a threat to the others in the room as he was worried for me. This was Varro's instinct as my mate taking over his otherwise normally peaceful approach.

Varro removed the gag from Saryn's mouth.

Trace twirled his blade menacingly. "Explain yourself," he commanded.

Saryn panted breathlessly. "What the *fuck* do you all think you're doing! Untie me now. I am a member of the Imperi, and this is mutiny!"

Gia looked slightly concerned, but Cairis was unconvinced—for now.

I stepped forward, taking over the interrogation. "How do you know Princess Embry?" I prodded, trying to break through his mental shields. But after so many years of practice, they were impenetrable.

Saryn gritted his teeth and eyed me angrily. "I don't know her!" he shouted, his spittle landing on the floor between us.

"Don't lie to us!"

"You trust the delusional visions of a tortured and dying female over my word?" he argued.

"She has a name! Say it!" I yelled back at him, furious at his refusal.

"Nori," he said, enunciating each syllable. "You can't trust what she showed you, because it's not real."

I turned my back to him, frustrated with the way this was all unfolding. The thought of more creative means to get answers started to cloud my judgement.

"You want to try and torture a different answer out of me, Cress, go ahead! We've seen your inclination for these methods; you put on quite a show last night… But it doesn't change my answer. I don't know her."

With my back turned to him as he spewed his arrogant denials, I was able to shut out the distractions surrounding everything he espoused, and that's when I heard it. The way his voice slightly raised with the slightest desperation when he said the word *her*.

I turned to face him, cocking my head to the side, assessing him and the silence between us before crouching down to his eye level.

"I think I am going to put on quite a show again, because I'm done speaking with you. I'll speak with the princess instead."

I watched his pupils dilate in confirmation of my threat.

"You dare to torture our only ally…a meaningless royal," he replied.

I stood and began to walk toward the back door before looking over my shoulder and locking eyes with him. "Not a meaningless royal…your mate!"

I turned back to the door, reaching for the handle and keeping my mental shields dropped purposefully as I conjured every sick and twisted thought of what I had planned for her. Making sure Saryn knew what I was prepared to do. Just as I began to step through the doorway, a shout came from behind.

"Stop!"

I turned around, shutting the door behind me, and marched over to place myself nose-to-nose with him.

"Start talking, now, or have a front-row seat to her pain. That's how the bond works, right?"

By now, my peers' expressions had gone from skepticism to impatience.

I instructed everyone but Varro to take a seat. "Friends, we're going to be here awhile. I have a feeling Saryn has much to share with us."

Saryn's story began innocently enough. Many years before our Offering, his fate intertwined unwittingly with that of the southern king's heir. I had thought there could be no crueler destiny than that of mine and Varro's bond; but the Gods must have been especially amused the day they wove Embry and Saryn's star-crossed paths. While he may have broken his vows to us, he had never exposed his true identity to his mate. She had no idea of his role in the Imperi, nor of his magical talents. But she did know he was a Northerner, and loved him despite that.

He described their relationship as simple and easy. And, for a time, untainted by everything he hated about himself. He had fooled himself into believing that peace between the two kingdoms meant another Offering may not be called, and he'd be free to pursue the bond. The occasional smaller missions could easily be disguised as business obligations. I was shocked anyone ever believed Saryn was a merchant of any kind to begin with. He enjoyed a life filled with mundane normalcy—except for the fact that he was secretly courting a royal. There was no reason to believe that her father, King Baelin, would ever allow her to marry a merchant, even a wealthy one.

While Saryn reveled in his secret trysts and the rare joy of having found his mate, there was dissent brewing within the royal family. The ever-ambitious Zarif had allies that reached far beyond the walls of Nasallus. One night, as Saryn secretly exited the grounds outside the castle walls, Zarif sought to add him to that list. He preyed on the weaknesses of others to recruit, and Zarif viewed love as the greatest weakness of all. So began the makings of Saryn's betrayal...

Zarif promised there would be an end to King Baelin's reign, and that unless Saryn cooperated fully, that would include ending the entirety of Baelin's bloodline. The threat on Princess Embry's life was a grave one, but he agreed to spare her, taking her prisoner instead, so long as Saryn agreed to serve the cause as his personal spy in the north. As promised, when the Silent Eve came, Princess Embry was not slain with the rest of her family. But the chain of events that would eventually call for the next Offering were already underway. When Saryn explained that he must return to the North, it was not met with understanding. His brand and oath required he return to Basdie to train us. Zarif and Saryn's meeting was not a pleasant one.

"A sacrifice. A show of personal commitment. You will be my eyes and ears now," Saryn recalled Zarif's cold words before he instructed him to cut out his own eye and place it in Zarif's hand. He winced as he recollected the memory. It echoed the heinous acts Trace was instructed to perform all across Caano and Damas. A sadistic signature of the Hand of the King.

"If you do not return, I will take great pleasure in removing both eyes from your mate before moving on to other, more vital areas..." he'd threatened ominously. Wounded, stripped of his dignity, and fearful for his mate's life, Saryn swore to make progress in the North and bring news of it back to Artume. If he did not bring back something of value, or not return at all, then his mate was as good as dead.

This brought us closer to the present. Zarif did not know the extent of Saryn's gifts; he also did not know the Order to which he was now a traitor, and in the Hand's eyes, Saryn was nothing more than a wealthy northern merchant. So, he gave him the only information he had of value, something he wasn't supposed to be aware of, but also something he had proof of—the moonstones. The entire reason Zarif even discovered the possibility of moonstones in the Ledor Canyon was because Saryn shared with him the information he'd uncovered. With a moonstone of his own to prove he wasn't lying, he had demonstrated enough value to gain trust from the Hand. But that would never be enough to free his mate. Zarif would keep that leverage over Saryn for as long as possible, if not forever.

Suddenly, Trace was standing behind Saryn, whose legs and hands were still bound tightly to the chair. He held his dagger tightly against Saryn's throat. "Tell me why I shouldn't kill you right now; why I should listen to another word. If we don't deliver you directly to Idris, we are *all* guilty!"

Trace had a point. Now that we were aware of Saryn's treachery, anything other than handing him over or killing him ourselves would make us complicit. Part of me feared what would unfold if Saryn went missing and Zarif found out. What would happen to Embry, who was seemingly ignorant and innocent in all of this? Her only mistake being sealing the bond with a member of a secret order from her enemy's kingdom. Briefly, it crossed my mind how sad it was that, despite being mates, she didn't truly know the male who protected her with his life. Other parts of me were beginning to boil over with memories of Saryn's hypocritical ramblings about mates. He, more than anyone, knew how high the costs really were. I had vastly underestimated Saryn's skill. How does one conceal the truth of their own identity, even after the sealing of a bond? The connection between Varro and I was so deep now it was almost intrinsic.

I was abruptly overcome by a realization: If Saryn had divulged information about the moonstones, if he was protecting Embry and secretly working for Zarif all along, then that meant…

I marched toward Saryn and lifted my own blade, hovering it directly above his heart. Trace looked at me in confusion, but didn't speak, his own blade still at Saryn's neck.

"*You* are the reason Nori is dead. Deny it! I dare you."

If he was the person pulling all the strings, he had been moving chess pieces while the rest of us were merely tossing Bones and Stones. If that were the case, then he was the reason we lost her. He could have prevented this, but instead, he sent her into harm's way.

Saryn had the audacity to stare at me with his remaining eye, his face and body covered in sweat from hours of interrogation. But I did not flinch. My blade trembled in eager anticipation as I fought the desire to plunge it deep into his heart and avenge our friend a second time.

"I have been protecting her, watching over her and Embry. It's why Trace kept seeing me portal back and forth from the castle, shifted and in uniform; I had been patrolling the cells. But when we left for Ledor…" His words trailed off in regret.

He looked down at the ground, then back up to face me. "When Zarif got word of what happened at the mines, he went mad, intent on sowing more discourse against the North because we had antagonized his plans." Saryn paused. "It could have been anyone," he swore. "But he chose someone untouched. Defiling a sacred healer would be seen as a high crime. Peasants and local villagers mean very little to the royals, but a gifted healer…" I could hear the sadness and regret in his confession as my hand began to shake with anger. "I'm sorry I was not there to protect her; I didn't make it soon enough." He glanced around at the others. "I am sorry that I failed you all."

A bitter and traitorous tear escaped the well of my eye as I took in the admission. He had been keeping watch on both Embry and Nori in the cells, but was required to escort me to the mines. And it was *my* actions at the mine that angered Zarif into taking such extreme measures.

Trace tightened his grip, holding the dagger flush against Saryn's skin and drawing a line of blood. Varro flinched beside us.

"You're a traitor, a liar, and you failed to put the mission above all. You're an oath breaker. And you deserve to die an oath breaker's death." Trace's words were icy as his apologetic gaze found mine. There was a heaviness to them, laced with his own guilt. Both of us stood there, blades in hand, ready to take Saryn's life. For a moment, there was only him and me. It felt like we were one and the same; fueled by anger and bound by duty. Never more had I understood wanting to live and abide by a code. I cared not for Saryn's explanations and rationalizations, nor how his mate would feel when he took his last breath. I only cared to experience the warmth of his blood pouring over my fist. Suddenly, there was a gentle hand grasping my fingers wrapped around the dagger's hilt. Then, so only I could hear, the soothing voice of my mate.

"Mercy takes longer to forge than hate. Nori would choose mercy."

I hated his poetic proclamations, but the mention of her name broke me from my callous concentration. I lowered my knife, and Trace followed my lead.

"We will deliver you to Theory and Idris; they will decide your fate," Varro declared diplomatically.

"No," Saryn pleaded, emphatically adding, "Zarif doesn't know you're here, he doesn't know what we're capable of together. He's going to move quickly now. We need to act, and it's better for you if he doesn't know what side I'm actually on. My disappearance could set off alarms."

Whether he was begging us to protect himself, Embry, or both, we all knew that delivering him to the likes of Theory and Idris was a fate swiftly sealed. But, the reality of the situation was that Saryn knew Zarif far better than we did. Despite having fed information to the enemy, he had also attempted to protect us along the way. And though he had failed Nori, I did not believe his intentions were to let those betrayals be the undoing of his honor and years of service to Cambria. Saryn, for all his faults, was Imperi through and through.

Gia, still unconvinced, questioned, "I'm as good a shifter as any. Why do we need you? I'm of the mindset that the next step is assassinating both the king and his Hand. We should let Cress and Trace have their way with you."

I was considering her point when Saryn challenged her. "Because I know what they plan to do with the moonstones they acquired, and I also know where that armada Varro's been helping build is headed… If you give a damn about Cambria, then you're going to work with me."

"We'd be crazy to trust you now," Cairis declared, having spoken very little during this whole ordeal, simply observing and taking it all in.

"When this is done you can turn me in, kill me, whatever you like. Just help me get Embry out safely."

"Not even your own mate knows the truth of your identity, nor of your treachery. You're untrustworthy," Cairis reasoned.

"Then I'll make you all a bargain."

At the word 'bargain', each of us lifted our gaze at him in skepticism. If the Imperi blood oath wasn't enough to keep him from betraying us, then perhaps a bargain sealed in magic would be.

"Fine," I said as Varro's voice down the bond firmly yelled "No!"

"You swear on your life to protect each of us, henceforth, putting our lives before your own and…that of your mate," I added for good measure. I could hear Varro's gasp of disapproval through the bond, but it was an eye for an eye. He had already put her well-being above ours, and the mission had suffered. We had already lost one of our own. He shouldn't be trusted. If he wanted that back, then it was us above all else.

To no end, come what may.

I lifted my blade again and freed his wrists of the rope so that he could hold out his hand and seal the bargain with magic. I held my hand in the air between us, waiting for him to place his atop mine and accept my terms. I had made a very similar arrangement with Trace not so long ago, but he had not been asked to put our lives above the powerful bond of a mate, simply above that of his own. One by one, the rest of the Imperi hesitantly placed their hand in the middle. The five of us that remained. Saryn spoke the promise and each of us felt the tug of magic locking his words firmly into place.

As the last rays of the sabbath's sunlight clung to the horizon, I addressed Saryn coldly: "Now, tell us everything you know."

"Don't you think if I could have just shapeshifted my way through the prison, provided her a portal stone, and whisked her away, I'd have done that already?" Saryn snarled at us. "I am telling you, Zarif is capable of more than any of us can imagine. There's no telling what kind of darkness lies within him."

"Well, what *do* you know?" Trace interrogated. We had freed Saryn's hands when completing the oath, but kept his ankles tightly bound to the chair. Varro stood at the ready to render him completely useless.

"He has warded Embry to that prison with very powerful and distinct magic, the likes of which I've only seen Idris display."

"How do you know that?" Cairis probed, working to gain better understanding of just how much or how little Saryn had actually uncovered.

"Trust me. I've tried everything to get her out of there. Before I returned for the Offering, when we arrived back in Artume, and almost every day since," Saryn said, defeated. "She doesn't know it, but I believe if she leaves the confines of that prison while still warded, she is likely to die."

So, Embry was trapped, and beyond just the physical bars of her cell. Zarif had done something to keep her contained, and Saryn had failed to make any progress penetrating it.

Gia's frustration continued to grow. "I know little of wards; how does that even work? More than that, what are our options?"

"I believe she's blood-warded, akin to how we kept you all at Basdie," Saryn answered.

"What does that mean?"

Saryn clenched his teeth in the kind of frustration one sees from a teacher disappointed in their disciples' shortcomings.

"Fuck, Gia, did you read a single book while at Basdie?"

She interrupted him before he could continue to berate her. "I'll have them gag you if you speak to me like that again…traitor," she added with a huff.

"Traitor he may be, but he is now tied to us with his life, so spare me the dramatics," Varro said impatiently, trying to keep us all focused.

Trace spoke calmly from where he had posted himself by the window. "If she is, in fact, blood-warded, then she'll only be free when Zarif is dead. Unless you have something worth trading for her…"

Saryn hung his head, as if he'd thought this through many times already. "I love Embry, but she is not what he has his sights set on. He plans to sail that armada he's building straight to the shores of Cambria, and that is what we should be concerned about."

"With what army?" Cairis snorted, skepticism dripping from his tone. "From what I've gathered, their military is small, poorly trained, and no match for Aeon's."

"Your intelligence is wrong then!" Saryn snapped. "Zarif and Silas have quietly recruited a significant militia, preying on the fear and indignance left in the wake of each Northern-blamed catastrophe. Commoners and wealthy merchants alike are lining up to pledge their allegiance."

"Even if that's true, a vendetta does not a soldier make."

"They're training them to fly, and fly well. Can any of you blind fools guess why they'd want moonstones, an armada, and an aerial army?"

The silence sat heavily between us, each of us lost in our imaginations, thinking through Artume's plan.

Suddenly, Varro's silky voice broke through the awkward contemplation. "You have to have been where you're going in order to portal. None of these Southerners have stepped foot on Cambrian soil...but..." he pontificated, "But if they saw it with their own eyes, then they might be able to successfully portal...from a ship." His last words came out in a whisper of horror.

"Gods..." I blurted out, not realizing I had spoken the thought aloud. "How many? How many, Saryn?"

"Hundreds, possibly thousands if we didn't cut off the moonstone supply quickly enough."

Varro had a worried expression, and Trace's resolve quickly turned into a furrowed brow as I watched him clench his dagger in its sheath.

"If they succeed, then Cambrian forces would be unprepared for such an attack. They've never encountered power such as those stones possess," I surmised, fear mounting with each passing minute.

"Precisely," Saryn confirmed, glad we were all finally catching on. "Aeon's forces will be patiently waiting at the shoreline, thinking the likes of their catapults and volleys of flaming arrows will be enough to push back the armada and deter them completely. But the ships are merely the tactic to get line-of-sight."

Gia, the lesser-experienced of our group when it came to battle tactics, gasped, as if the vision of it was already playing out in her mind. "Will there be enough of them to drive back Aeon's forces?"

Saryn explained that the Artumian Army, even if trained in flight and the use of moonstones, would suffer the same challenges as any Fae who attempted to portal. They would likely try and land a small distance away from wherever the enemy forces congregated, flanking them, and giving them a moment to recalibrate and gather their energy. A portal jump from a ship at sea to the shoreline would be enough to exhaust even the most experienced among them. But for inexperienced fighters—most of whom had spent their lives malnourished—the exhaustion of the act would be nearly instantaneous. It's unlikely any would try to make multiple jumps while airborne, which would only increase their chances of being struck by an arrow.

Success would see them across enemy lines, en masse and mostly uninjured. And that's something Aeon would not be prepared to defend against. There was always the possibility Cambria's fighters could make it to them before they recovered, but more than likely they would still be in shock of what they'd witnessed. Unable to organize quickly enough to confront the enemies bearing down on them from all sides.

Cairis brought up every possible argument or idea he could muster. With each defense, Saryn met him with an equally plausible answer.

"You mentioned Aeon's catapults, but what about when paired with his canons? Could they inflict enough damage before the majority use their stones?"

"I have no doubt that Zarif would keep the armada a safe distance from the shoreline to ensure nothing breaches their defenses. They aren't even warships. They're merely transport boats. It's laughable to refer to them as an armada, but regardless, we should treat them with the same severity."

"Is that true?" Trace inquired to Varro.

"He's not wrong. They barely have the proper supplies to build decent ships. From what I've seen, they aren't designed, built for, or stocked like any warship I've stepped foot on." Varro paused a moment. "Everything makes much more sense now... I can't believe you didn't tell us any of this!" he yelled at Saryn, his voice raising. Another rare demonstration of anger from my mate.

With every further detail Saryn shared, the frustration in the room tipped toward a boiling point. Tensions ran high, sharp-tongued insults were easily strewn about, and the most vexing part of all was the feeling that if we had been privy to these details sooner, we could have prepared, planned better. We could have taken action. Saryn and Theory had instilled in all of us that a good plan was the foundation of achievement, but Saryn had fucked us royally.

Nightfall came, and the room was now illuminated with candlelight, heating the already dry air. The next hour consisted of more arguing, trying to deduce the possibility of how many moonstones were already in their possession, and twice we had to hold back Gia from taking off to go burn down the entire fleet—which was an idea we entertained for a moment; except, the ships weren't the actual problem. The real problem were the moonstones. We didn't know where they were being kept, and as long as those belonged to Zarif, the threat remained intact. Ships or no ships.

Saryn warned us that, as with most rebellions, cutting one insurgent off at the head only grows another. The entire situation frustrated me beyond comprehension. So many had already been maimed or killed to spread their lies. So many minds and hearts poisoned against the North. This battle, however it unfolded, promised to keep Zarif and the king's true motivations concealed beneath a pile of casualties. How they were betrayed by their own royal family. How they were manipulated, their fears preyed upon. Our inability to resolve the matter with diplomacy or even espionage caused me to question our methods. In many ways, I felt caught up in its unstoppable momentum.

All the theater of it, dressing up and acting the part. All of the spying and pretending seemed a waste of effort. Varro could sense the somber hopelessness constricting me, whispering down the bond, *"It's going to be ok."*

Through gritted teeth and fighting back tears, I slammed my balled fists onto the table in front of me. "So, what can we do, Saryn? Tell us!"

"I have ideas, but you're not going to like them."

Trace looked at Varro with concern, and there was something ominous about their willingness to work together.

"The first and simplest part is Nasallus. Gia, you will remain here, tending to the king. There's no chance that spoiled princeling is going to do his own dirty work."

Gia looked disappointed in her role that implied more babysitting than action. Gia's pristine and beautiful exterior betrayed the brutality of her true nature.

Saryn, knowing this, added, "You're finally going to get to put him to the blade. Or, whatever your preference is these days."

Gia's smile widened at that, her eyes alight with the excitement of killing the male who had been putting his greedy hands all over her for far too long. Cairis grinned and nodded at Gia, knowing how much she reveled in this instruction.

"I'd be delighted," she replied sinisterly.

Saryn guided Gia through the approach. When the mission to Cambria was well underway, this would leave Silas at the castle with only the protection of a few Kingsguards. His powerful Hand would certainly be leading the efforts at sea, and this would create the opportunity for her to dispose of the false king, shapeshift into a guard, and make her way to the prison cells to keep watch on Embry till the wards fell and both were safe to escape.

"But how will I know when it's safe to get her out of there? I could accidentally kill her if we make our move too soon," Gia reasoned.

"Once I confirm Zarif is no more, I will alert her down the bond so you two can get out of there."

"Wait, she knows what's going on? You've communicated through your bond?" Cairis asked, trying to understand just how much Embry had known.

"She knows nothing," Saryn declared with heavy sadness. "I haven't spoken to her through our bond since before I returned to Basdie. I was too worried about jeopardizing her safety in doing so." He paused and glanced at me. "She knows *nothing*, and it's better that way."

"But hasn't she tried reaching you?" Gia wondered, having experienced the unique mind-melding herself when she was once bonded. I could see the melancholy overcoming her previously vengeful expression at the memory of her mate this must've drawn forth.

"She has…" Saryn admitted. His gaze remained fixed on me. "No matter how many times she screamed and pleaded down the bond for me to reply, I resisted."

Before that moment, I don't think I had ever seen Saryn appear broken. Even for a minute. But in his eye, there was such deep, unbearable sorrow, that I almost winced at his pain. The thought of hearing your mate beg for a reply, knowing you were alive but not responding… An unspeakable torture. I felt my own bond ripple in response. I glanced briefly at Varro and he looked at me knowingly. A shared understanding of the pain this would cause a mate. One I hoped to never inflict upon him.

Saryn turned back to Gia. "As I said, once I'm sure Zarif is dead, I will relay a codename down the bond, instructing her to call it out as loudly as she can. When you hear her say that word, you get her the fuck out."

He told Gia he did not care who she had to kill or what she had to do, but to escort her far from the castle, emphasizing the need to keep her hidden. If anyone discovered Princess Embry was alive, she would still be at risk. She was not to trust anyone with Embry other than members of the Imperi.

Gia nodded at his grave instructions, then asked, "What name will she call out?"

"Lazarus."

CHAPTER 66

All of a sudden, the shrill blare of horns, punctuated by the booming of drums caused us to freeze in surprise. Shortly after that, townspeople began ringing bells outside of their homes which carried through the windows of the safehouse. Cairis peeked his head out the front door and informed us that villagers were quickly scattering about. Varro interrupted the chaos with, "They are nautical signals; something must be happening in the bay."

We exchanged panicked glances. It was nighttime, there should be nothing but moonslight and twinkling stars. Why would there be anything happening at such a late hour, especially as the sabbath came to a close?

"I'll be right back," Varro said, exiting through the back door and portaling with no further explanation.

With the threat of Siren Song removed, Saryn used his magic to singe the remaining ropes around his ankles, freeing himself from the chair. He didn't make any abrupt movements, slowly raising his hands; a sign he meant us no harm. Within mere moments, Varro returned through the back door looking flustered.

"They're on the move!" he said, exasperated. "They're boarding and loading ships quickly. We need to go; we don't have much time."

We stood in stunned silence, knowing we had only discussed Gia's part in the plan. We weren't ready to deploy ourselves, but there was no time left to debate the best approach. Each of us shifted about nervously, waiting to see who felt confident enough to take command of the situation. Trace's voice cut through the stale air.

"We split into two groups and board separate ships. We sail with them to Cambria while seeking the location of the stones. As soon as we eliminate the option of their secret weapon, we figure out how to deal with the impending aerial assault."

"But how will we get word to one another?" Cairis asked, his question laden with doubt.

"Them," Trace said, pointing at me and Varro. "They can speak mind-to-mind. If we put them on separate ships, we will still have the ability to communicate—so long as one of them doesn't wind up dead."

"What did you say?" Saryn said, looking at the group with confusion and mounting outrage.

"You are mates, are you not? I suspect you've been speaking to one another in silence all night." Trace's words were calculated, almost cold.

"Yes," I said through gritted teeth, knowing that the advantage of our bond *was* something we could exploit.

Saryn let out a disbelieving laugh and shook his head.

"Glad I'm not the only one who has been concealing something important."

His words made no difference to me. I may have kept the truth of my mate from my mentor, but I had not betrayed the Imperi or my kingdom like he had.

Saryn added, "And from the lack of surprise on all your faces, it appears I am the only one not in on this little secret."

Ignoring his poignant sarcasm, I confirmed Trace's deduction.

"He's right. Gia, you return to the castle. I'll sail with Cairis, and Varro goes with Trace."

"No," Varro chimed in. "I'm the strongest in the water, Cairis is the weakest…should it come to that… He goes with me. Trace, you take Cress."

The sound of bells continuing to ring outside was a constant reminder of time running out. We had no intentions of being in the water for any of this mission, but if something went wrong, then the fall below consisted of nothing but the Endless Tides, which was less than ideal for Cairis. However, I didn't imagine Varro would be so willing to put my safety in the hands of Trace after the previous betrayal. I tried to dismiss the thoughts of his former disloyalty and reminded myself of the bargain he and I had made, now firmly in place.

Having felt my confusion through the bond, I heard Varro say, *"It's okay, I trust him."*

"Let me come with you or take up post on another ship," Saryn requested.

Trace turned his attention to him. "If you value your king and his people at all, make haste to Cambria. I don't care if the portal jumps almost kill you."

I watched Trace squeeze the hilt of his sheathed dagger, nerves mounting.

"These ships will easily reach Cambrian shores by morning if they sail through the night. Ready as many able-bodied citizens as you can. Lead them to where the mouth of the Ledor River meets the Endless Tides."

My mind raced to the memory of a map I'd seen in my father's office. The mouth of the Ledor River emptied into the Tides directly below… House Corliss. Varro's home. And the people closest to defend Cambria would be Riverland Fae. My people.

I swallowed the lump in my throat as my resolve turned to fierce protectiveness, and I watched as Varro's eyes widened at the realization that his home would potentially be under siege.

"We'll figure something out," I tried to reassure him silently, letting my bond soothe his anxious pulse as best it could.

Saryn tried to argue with Trace's decision-making. "No, I need to be wherever Zarif is. Unless he's dead, I stand no chance of freeing Embry."

Trace's tone was seething. "This isn't about your fucking mate. This is about *our people*. Go now and warn them. When you see us off shore, you can join us—if you're still alive."

Trace assigning Saryn to return to Cambria via moonstone was no small task. Saryn, as experienced as he was, would still be risking his life to cover such a distance. There was no time for him to take breaks. Knowing this, he offered no arguments, just nodded in grim acceptance.

"We need to go," Varro reminded us. The ships would not wait for stowaways.

I walked over to Gia who was shifting back and forth nervously at the thought of all of us abandoning her in Artume. I clasped her hands in mine and said, "No mercy."

"No mercy," she repeated, looking up at me through her lashes.

Whatever lay ahead for Silas, I almost felt pity for him. Gia wasn't like me; my methods swift and methodical. I had a suspicious feeling that there was going to be nothing quick about what she had in store for him. She pulled me into a tight hug and began to make her exit when Saryn yelled out for her.

"She's my mate!"

Gia, looking over her shoulder, nodded back at him in silent understanding. That remark alone was the most vulnerable I had ever witnessed from Saryn. Varro, Cairis and Trace began to check their weaponry, rifling through a trunk of additional accessories Saryn had kept for us in the safehouse. Many of us couldn't remain as armed as we'd like in our previous roles.

Saryn walked over to me, looking ashamed. All of these expressions were wholly new to him. Vulnerability. Fear. Embarrassment. The stoic façade he had always shown us had melted away. "Don't make the same mistakes I've made," he warned.

Perhaps it was a good thing my mate and I would be on separate ships. I had to trust in his training and abilities to protect himself. Anything other than my full confidence in him would lead me down a path we could not afford.

"The mission above all," I recited.

He nodded, cracking a brief smile at the echo of his words to us at Basdie.

"Focus, Cress. You will know what to do when it's time. If you must, take them all into the darkness with you."

His words were a sharp reminder of the dormant power within me. Sleeping. Waiting to be called upon whenever needed.

My lips began to quiver with the fear that I had been holding at bay until this very moment, reminded that there was no guarantee a mating bond would protect me from the Drift. It was all conjecture and scribbles in dusty, old journals.

"But what if I can't find my way out of the dark?" I asked Saryn, seeking out the kind of guidance only an experienced mentor could provide.

"We all enter the darkness, eventually. We'll meet you there, someday."

Saryn was right. Death came for us all. What I feared most was the notion that not knowing oneself was a fate worse than death.

Varro's voice broke through the intensity of mine and Saryn's conversation by demanding that I quickly changed into attire more befitting of a shipworker. The blue garment of a servant would do nothing to camouflage my appearance.

While I changed, Saryn made himself a small pack of supplies—mostly food and water—for the journey that would push his body to the brink. In the alley behind the safehouse, we witnessed Saryn unfurl his wings for the first time in our presence. They were black toward the ends, and a bluish color nearest to his back, with sharp edges and spiked talons at the top near his neck; aggressive and violent in every aspect. A complete amalgamation of so many other wings I'd only seen in drawings. They were so unique, so distinctive, but not attributable to any one area or peoples, leaving lineage concealed. I should have expected nothing less of the enigma that was Saryn.

He explained he was going to attempt as many jumps as possible while airborne, allowing him to make up ground. With that, he disappeared through a cloudlike ring, leaving the rest of us to fend for ourselves as a team. Thus began our sprint to the shipyards.

CHAPTER 64

The scene we arrived to was disorderly and chaotic, to say the least. The cover of night was lit dimly by torches and lanterns, making it difficult to fully assess the situation. Only a few ships were seaworthy, and numerous Fae pushed and shimmied their way through the crowd to board them. From what we could see, there were far fewer uniformed Kingsguards moving about, which made no sense. Was there not enough time to provide armor for protection? The scene before us consisted mostly of males, with a handful of females, all dressed in regular attire boarding the ships with urgency.

"Where is the military? Where are the Kingsguards?" Trace questioned with concern as he observed the bay.

"I don't know," Cairis said quietly through gritted teeth, sounding just as puzzled.

The sound of sails being hoisted meant there was no more time to delay. Varro pointed at the ship nearest to us. "I've worked with the captain and the crew of this one, so there should be no questions if Cairis and I board there."

"We'll take the far one. Locate the stones as quickly as possible, and send word to Cress of any possible leads."

"What if we don't find them before we arrive?" Cairis asked.

"Then defend Cambria," Trace declared, as if it were that simple.

Cairis did not look satisfied with Trace's response. He turned to me instead. "You have a devastating power inside you, Cress. Be prepared to use it."

Just like the others, Cairis knew about the Drift. Maybe he assumed now that Varro and I were bonded it was a non-issue. Hopefully, that was true, but now was not the time to sow any more doubt.

Varro grabbed me and pulled me tightly into him, kissing the top of my head as I wrapped my arms around him just as tightly.

"He will have your back, I know this," he said in spite of Trace's envious gaze.

He seemed intent to convince himself of this rather than ease any of my own wariness—but after everything else I'd put him through, I could give him that. Trace gave Varro a nod, and then we reluctantly parted ways, heading toward the ship at the distant end of the wharf.

I patterned my footsteps closely behind Trace's, trying to mirror the swift confidence of his movements and block out the distractions of the bustling docks. The night air ushered in a breeze, leaving a chill on my skin. Or, perhaps, it was the blood leaving my extremities to power my thundering heart as each step took us closer to possible confrontation. Trace grabbed a dirty cloth from a ledge and continued to pace toward our destination. He handed it to me.

"Pull your hair back and cover it in this."

"Why?" I said, fumbling with what might as well be a rag in my hands.

He halted abruptly and turned to face me, causing us to practically collide. Our faces were so close that our lips almost touched, and immediately I stepped back.

"To conceal your beauty." He paused, assessing my reaction, of which I gave him none. Not getting what he wanted, he explained, "You look too clean, not like a commoner. Put it on now, and keep your chin down when we board."

"I'll just glamour them," I retorted.

"No magic," he demanded. "If anyone so much as suspects you're glamouring them, we're fucked. Now, do as I say, Cress."

Trace's firm command reminded me of how he used to speak to me. Below all those overbearing words used to reside a warm affection, but now, it was all impatience and worry.

I did as he instructed and wrapped my hair tightly under the fabric, concealing my long tresses. For good measure, I bent down, pretending to lace my boot as I dragged my fingertips through a puddle of silt and clay. When I stood, I ran my hands across my cheeks to weather my appearance further. Trace looked pleased that I was finally thinking like an Imperi.

We waited in the queued masses, preparing to board. All around us their clothes were ragged and their body odor indicated they had not been graced with a bath in some time. I glanced up briefly, taking note of a few Kingsguards already aboard the ship who were overseeing the operations. When we reached the top of the plank, I tried to conceal my fear that we would somehow be stopped, but no one gave Trace or me a second thought. It appeared the only consideration for boarding was to be able-bodied and prepared to fight.

Once aboard, many acted unsure of where they should take up position or what they should do. I felt Trace grab my hand and tug us away from the congestion of Artumians. Feeling the rough callouses of Trace's hand against mine flooded my mind with memories once more. He did not release it till he had led us to the stern and beneath the decks, into a dark corner of the ship's belly where he located some large wooden crates.

"Tell him you're okay," he muttered.

"I don't need to report to him every minute," I argued, annoyed that he felt the need to instruct me.

"Then tell him *we* are in," he rephrased.

I did as he asked, but not because he'd requested it. It only made sense to let Varro and Cairis know we had successfully boarded, and I'd wanted to know if the same went for them.

"We're boarded and safe. Are you all okay?" I sent my thoughts to him and awaited his reply.

When he sent me confirmation, I notified Trace that all had gone according to plan. The look on his face when I shared this information from my mate was one of annoyance, despite the necessity of it.

"May I remind you that you volunteered me for this. It was your idea, putting us on separate ships so you could use our communication to relay updates."

"I did not volunteer you to be on a ship alone with me. That was your *mate's* doing," he retorted.

"You know Cairis can't swim worth a damn!" I argued, feeling the familiarity of our banter lurking at the corners of my memory.

"Maybe you should have taught him during all that time at Basdie after I left. Or were you using the pools for something else, Cress?"

His insinuation only twisted the knife deeper; but I knew that blade was buried deep in his chest—not mine.

"Why are you doing this now?"

"Well, if there's a chance we might die, I suppose I should stop pretending I'm content with your choices."

"I had no choice in how or when I discovered my mate, but you had all the choice in the world when you denied me of your time and affection."

Even in the darkness of the ship, I could make out his sour and defeated expression. His throat worked before he spat out a retort.

"The Gods made you for him, Cress. Would you really have defied them for me?"

No path in life had ever been easy for Trace, he had been conditioned to the loss of choice long before the Imperi stripped us of it fully. My silence gave way to his next remark.

"Five questions."

"No," I replied sternly. The weight of this game held new meaning since knowledge of the Drift and what Varro and I had bargained.

"Please."

"I don't have questions for you."

"That's fine. Just answer mine."

The sound of more Fae cramming in all around us was not enough to dissuade Trace, who somehow seemed intent on focusing on everything but the mission ahead.

"Fine, if you promise to drop this afterwards and focus on the mission, I will answer your questions."

He jumped at my proposal. "If you could travel anywhere in our homeland, where would you go?"

"What kind of question is that in a time like this?" I asked, more than confused, taking special note of how he made sure not to say Cambria aloud.

"Just answer."

"I don't know," I said, rushing my thoughts toward a response. "I'd like to see the golden fields of wheat Nori spoke of from her home. Nothing but vast miles of waving golden hues."

Trace paused, as if he were focused on committing my answer to memory.

"If you had a child, what would you name them?"

Gods send me patience to not murder him. What in the three moons of Demir was he asking this for? Was this some strange thing he did to distract himself from nerves? Did he believe this plan was all going to shit, and figured we'd might as well spend our last hours making pointless conversation?

"I would never bring a child into this world, knowing what I know now," I claimed through gritted teeth.

"If that weren't the case, is there a name you ever liked? Don't most young females think of these silly things?"

"I've left those thoughts behind. But if you must know, Avila. I would have liked to have a daughter named Avila."

I did not like these questions at all. In a time where I needed mental armor, questions like these were taking my head to vulnerable places that would only serve to distract me, if not get me killed.

"If you could see anyone again, who would it be?"

I didn't even have to think before I whispered the words with a quivering lip, "Versa, my sister."

Tears pricked at my lashes, and my hands balled into tight fists as I fought back the anger I'd kept at bay; the place where I had tucked my old life away.

"What's your biggest regret?"

I stared at the floor, lost in a haze of memories. Why did Trace insist on picking at this wound? I answered him without meeting his gaze.

"I regret not taking my sister and disappearing the second word of the Offering arrived. I regret not fighting for my own freedom before it slipped through my grasp." I looked up from the floor to meet his tired hazel eyes. "I regret surrendering my only lifetime to the king, to the Imperi." So much sorrow, and yet, among all the pain and heartache, the Gods revealed to me a gift. My mate. And, as much as I regret losing my sister, having Varro is something I will forever be thankful for.

A tiny smile of understanding crept across his face, and I hung my head in despair at the full weight of my answer.

"You don't believe in multiple lifetimes?"

His question had more of an edge to it than I expected. It didn't seem like one he had planned.

"No, I don't. The Gods are too selfish for that."

"You never really spoke of the Gods when we first met, but it seems that has changed. Why?"

"I am angry with them now. It was easy to ignore them when my life was simple. Once you need them, you realize how little they listen, how rarely they answer, and how eons of existence have made them cruel."

There was no one to discuss this subject with as of late, but it had been weighing heavy on me for a while now. Every time something bad happened, I found myself cursing the heavens for it. Ever since being called to the Offering, I had felt betrayed by them; but perhaps my silence and lack of acknowledgement induced their indifference.

"Do you?" I asked back, not caring that in some small way I was engaging in his game.

"With every waking minute I have in this lifetime, I hope to the Gods there is another waiting for me," Trace answered earnestly.

For him, I guess, I hoped that to be true. So much of his life he wished to erase. Perhaps, even meeting me.

All of a sudden, a burly male at the front of the boat began to shout, garnering the cramped passengers' attention. "No Fae can claim the sea, as no Fae can grasp every grain of sand. We shall sail the Endless Tides and meet the North at their doorstep and repay them in kind for their vicious deceit."

Cheers began all around us as he roused the crowd. Trace and I joined in the jeers just to blend in appropriately.

"They have slain your queen!"

More angry shouts erupted.

"They have maimed and slaughtered our people!"

The inspired crowd heaved their fists and stamped their feet in agreement, jostling the boat.

"They've burned your homes and villages!"

I fought to suppress my feelings toward these falsehoods, as each bold claim demanded a rallying cry.

"Some say they defiled the innocent and most gifted amongst us!"

His claims had me swallowing the lump in my throat as I held back tears, utilizing every ounce of restraint in my body to not burn this entire ship with them all trapped inside. I felt Trace's hand on my shoulder, trying to quell the rage I'm sure he could feel emanating off of me.

"To Cambria!" the man shouted, and in answer everyone responded, "To Cambria!"

In that moment, I knew the lies had fully corrupted the people of Artume. Their motivation, though borne of deception, made them no less dangerous. There wasn't time to undo the ignorance that incensed such riotous emotions within them. The ship began to shift indicating we were beginning our journey, and I felt Trace lean in to whisper in my ear.

"I'll be back; I'm going up top to assess as best I can. Stay here."

He stood and tiptoed his way through the pervasive mob to make his way above. I disagreed with his decision, but kept it to myself and tried to trust his instincts.

While Trace was away, I stayed quiet and monitored my surroundings. I was seemingly surrounded by untrained commoners. Many of them bickered amongst themselves, trying to keep their courage and spirits up by sharing stories of how terrible the Northerners were. I closed my eyes and listened intently. No one uttered a single word of moonstones or any sort of organized plan of attack. I sent a message down the bond.

"We've set sail, and you?"

"Yes," Varro replied quickly. *"We've seen no signs or mention of moonstones. Have you?"*

I confirmed the same for him. No luck in identifying the whereabouts of the stones.

The sway of the ship intensified as we left the bay and headed out into open water.

"Any signs of Zarif?" I asked.

"*None. I don't believe he's on our ship. This one is full of commonfolk and very few Kingsguards.*"

"*How's Cairis holding up?*"

"*Well enough. I think he would have preferred to trade spots with Saryn.*"

I felt his amusement along the bond, like a joyful tickle, and it made me smile.

Trace had been gone for what felt like too long, and I was on the verge of seeking him out myself until I witnessed him squeezing past everyone to make his way back to me at the end of the ship.

"What did you see?" I whispered, eager for any information.

"It's pretty dark out, I can't be sure how many other ships sail with us, but I don't think it's as many as we thought."

"Well, that doesn't sound so bad," I replied.

"Maybe. But you're not going to like the next part."

My stomach sank.

"We're sailing directly into a storm. I hope you're ready to get your sea legs, since you always claimed you were meant for this."

Trace's warning caused a sinking feeling in the pit of my stomach. But not because troubled waters were ahead.

"Storms are a bad—"

"Omen amongst my people," he cut me off. "Yes, I know. But you don't believe in that sort of thing."

My silence conveyed my worry, because the last time he'd said this, the mission at the Canary Veil went off the rails and two of us almost lost our lives.

"Don't worry about the storm. You should be more concerned with how many seasick Fae we are about to be surrounded by."

Hours passed by with the deafening sounds of giant waves battering the sides of the ship. Water rushed down the steps from the deck, and the constant flickering of lightning through the cargo hatch portended the booming thunder. All around us, passengers held their stomachs and groaned in agony. Buckets were passed around as quickly as possible, many of which arrived too late.

The acrid tang of vomit was quickly overpowering; it was enough to make me retch a few times myself. With my hair already a sweaty, matted mess, Trace reached over and pulled the fabric covering it away. For a brief moment, he leaned in close to me and I inhaled his scent selfishly. It was a sweet reprieve from the horrific smell now surrounding me. He handed me the fabric again, instructing me to tie it around my face like a mask to mitigate the stench as much as possible.

I angled my body into his so he could hear me. "I should go up there and see if there is anything I can do to help."

"If you're thinking of using your magic, don't. You must save all your energy for what is to come. You can't waste a single ounce of your power."

"You're right," I said in resignation.

I leaned back against the wall, trying to ignore the heavy rocking of the ship as I sent a message to Varro.

"Is your ship as bad as ours?"

"Sailors, the Artumians are not," he replied quickly, confirming his shipmates were just as inexperienced as ours.

The fact that these ships were so hastily built also had to play a role in their poor performance. The number of times I gave Trace a concerned glance had become too high to count. Each time, he would look at me and offer a comforting nod, as if to say we were going to be fine. But it did not feel fine—it felt like we were going to capsize and drown at any moment.

"Any chance you could call your Siren friends to see if they could do anything about these waters," I joked to my mate through our connection.

"Ha, it doesn't work like that. In fact, they'd prefer if we all ended up paying them a visit, I assure you."

My silence back to him made it clear that I found this idea more horrifying than amusing.

"That's not going to happen, Cress. Just stay focused and keep your lunch in your stomach."

"I'm already exerting more magic than I'd like to keep the sickness at bay, and the smell isn't helping."

Each time I focused in on these silent mind-to-mind conversations with Varro, I could tell it irritated Trace. But I wasn't going to avoid speaking to my mate just because it bothered him. We could all be heading towards our demise.

I didn't recall dozing off—the very idea seemed inexplicable—but I awoke to Trace squeezing my hand till I roused.

"The ship is slowing," he said in a hushed voice. The violent sway had ceased; perhaps the storm had finally passed. "I'll go topside and report back," he continued.

"I'm coming with you this time." If for no other reason than to escape the rank smell permeating the air in our current position.

The look on my face left no room for argument, and I was grateful we needn't bicker about it since a raised voice would only draw unwanted attention.

It was nearly impossible not to accidentally bump into someone or step on the occasional foot as we progressed toward the stairway. I whispered apologies as I passed by others who were still sleeping, or simply unconscious after hours of uncontrollable vomiting. If this was supposed to be Zarif's army, he had planned poorly.

As Trace and I stepped out onto the decks, the smell of fresh air and the chill of the wind was more than welcomed. I took in long, deep breaths. It smelled of seafoam, but all around us there was dense, gray fog. We walked to the edge of the ship and leaned against it, trying to make out our location through the mist blanketing us in all directions.

"It's only very early morning; this fog should clear shortly. No chance of it thwarting Zarif's plans," Trace concluded regretfully.

"We need to get eyes on our surroundings. Do you think one of us could fly above the fog?"

"No, we can't risk that," he said.

"Then let subtler means prevail," I said, not pausing to seek his approval. I began to sharply focus on the air surrounding the ship, when Trace clasped my wrist tightly.

"Don't. You can't waste any energy. Not yet."

I ignored him, tugging my wrist away. Slowly, I pushed the fog farther north—as if it were something I could touch with my own hands—ever so gently giving it the nudge it needed. Trace turned the opposite direction, and my heart sank when I heard his horror-stricken voice.

"Gods be merciful…"

I quickly wheeled around—and that's when I saw it too. Bows of multiple large ships penetrating the fog, one after another. On each ship, a Cambrian crest adorning the sail had been slashed through with black paint, representing that they were now under the control of Artume. So many ships, more than I could count quickly, all marred with black-slashed sails. They were not warships. They were merchant ships.

"They've commandeered Cambrian trade ships," I uttered aloud, knowing Trace already understood the severity of the situation.

My eyes focused further as the ships came closer, and I could then make out the countless numbers of Fae all standing in military formation on the decks, wearing full Kingsguard armor.

I quickly conveyed everything we were seeing down the bond to Varro. He confirmed that he and Cairis now had eyes from a different angle, evaluating the same situation.

"They have the stones. They have to. We're on the wrong damn ships," Trace said quietly, slamming his fist into the wooden railing.

Varro responded with the same assumptions. *They didn't have enough time to build all of their own ships. Maybe they never planned to. They've taken possession of every merchant ship from the North that anchored at Nasallus' trade port.*

The fog had migrated far enough away by then that all of the ships were visible, but I had no idea what was awaiting us on the shore. Had Saryn made it? Were Aeon's people ready and waiting? Maybe catapults and scores of archers were pointed straight at us. All I knew for certain was that Artumian and Cambrian ships were lying in wait just off the coast of the Riverlands. Saryn could not have known about the plan to steal all of those ships, and now they'd transported double—if not triple—the amount of infantry.

"I see him!" Trace said abruptly, pointing in the direction of one of the acquired ships anchored at the front of the new arrivals. I squinted my eyes to make out Zarif's tall, slender figure standing at the front of a ship, barking commands to his military leaders.

At the same time, I heard Varro say, *"We've got eyes on him."*

More passengers were emerging from below deck every minute, but Trace and I stayed focused on our target.

Suddenly, Varro informed me that he was going in for a closer look. I abruptly gasped out, "No," not realizing I had spoken it aloud until Trace grabbed my arm, asking, "What? What's wrong?"

"Varro is in the water," I explained, shakily. "He's swimming toward the other ships to get us more intel."

Without a moment's hesitation, Trace instructed me to focus on the sea and watch for Varro to breach the water. He'd keep an eye on Zarif.

I stared for the longest time at the rippling of the waves, my eyes scanning desperately for his white hair to peek through the dark blue. Finally, I saw him emerge beside the ship farthest from Zarif's. He floated there briefly, looking for a place to crawl aboard. I wanted to reach out, to speak to him, but distracting him was also the last thing I wanted to accomplish. He'd have to be extremely quiet and careful to remain undetected. Once aboard, his soaking wet appearance could easily set off alarm bells. This seemed like a terrible strategy.

"Cress, look at this," Trace said alarmed, drawing my attention away from Varro and back to Zarif's ship.

"Do you see the male with the large box in his hands? He's stopping every few feet. Those have to be the stones. I think he's handing them out to the Kingsguards," Trace surmised, though we could not be certain. The distance rendered our superior vision inexact, but Trace's observations seemed keen, nevertheless.

"I've got this one covered, look to see if any similar activity is taking place on the other ships," he instructed.

By now, the upper decks of our ship had become noisy with angry and anxious passengers ready for a fight. My eyes scanned the other ships, looking for any suspicious movements, when I finally spotted another male carrying the same sort of box shuffling about the deck between soldiers.

"Trace," I whispered. "I think they are distributing them on all of those ships."

"Why not ours?"

"Because these people are nothing more than a distraction. The real threat is on those ships over there."

My breath hitched at the thought of Zarif being willing to sacrifice even more Artumian citizens for his cause. He had never cared about them. They were only sent here to die. He knew they were weak, untrained, with nothing but vengeance and vitriol to fuel them toward a task that would surely get them killed.

Varro's message to me was filled with worry. *"Stones are present, soldiers are receiving them now."*

I relayed the confirmation to Trace, solidifying our understanding of the situation.

"What do we do?" I asked, fear mounting in my voice.

"I don't know, Cress," Trace replied, sounding irritated with his own lack of answers. "I haven't seen what defenses await them at the Cambrian shore, and I don't know whether we should be more concerned about the fliers on our ship or the portalers on theirs."

As I felt the warmth of the sun on my skin, the true gravity of the situation struck me.

"The fog is clearing fully." I looked around frantically, gauging what remained of it.

"I told you it would," he replied, not understanding the threat at hand.

"Trace! Once they can see the shores, they can portal. We have to stop them."

At the far northern end of the coast, the fog had begun to fade. At this angle, only the passengers aboard our ships could see what it had unveiled. All along the Cambrian beach were rows and rows of scattered male and female citizens alike. Not nearly as organized as a true military formation, but there were numbers, nonetheless. The fog slowly peeled away, further revealing the disappointment of what Saryn had been able to amass. A small show of force from the Riverlands, greatly outnumbered by the army aboard these ships.

From what I could see, they had managed to place a handful of catapults a few hundred feet apart on the beach. Archers stood in rows with bows and arrows at the ready. Tears began to swell, clouding my vision as I witnessed youths running along the beaches carrying supplies at the behest of their elders.

"…Children," I said.

Trace's reply was plain and cold, but the weight of it was not lost on me.

"They will defend their homeland the same as anyone else—any way they can."

There were no battlements, no impenetrable walls. No Kingsguard or armies to support them. A handful of cavalries lined up behind the archers. This was a quickly strewn-together local militia of Riverland folk, at best. Saryn had emphatically urged the locals to take up arms before carrying on to Erisas Bay and Tinsilor in search of aid. Their enemies greatly outnumbered them. That was more than clear. And as I watched the fog continue to disappear—faster and faster—I felt panic seeking to corrupt any ounce of a logical thought from my head.

What can I do, I kept asking myself over and over. I felt my hands sweat, and my shaking got worse, as no solutions presented themselves to me. Whenever I confided a problem to my father, no matter how mad or complex, he would tell me that calm waters were clearest. Lost in the emotion of my situation, I had dismissed his advice more than once.

But now, I heeded it. I closed my eyes and fought to suppress the panic. I took in a deep breath through my nose, letting the scent of the sea air engulf me. I focused on slowing my heartbeat and thought of the comforting sparkle of the ocean on the horizon line. My skin felt cold despite the strengthening sun, and though its light did not warm me, it illuminated the shadowed corners of my mind.

From its recesses, a memory from Basdie crystallized, clear and magnificent. Varro's silky voice saying, "She had to have been a mirage, but I could not bring myself to stop sailing toward it."

I flung my head back as my eyes opened wide toward the sky, then I lowered my chin, staring at what little remained of the fog, my purpose suddenly fixed.

"They can't portal to what they can't see," I said to Trace in revelation.

I spent no time explaining. No time pondering if it would work. It had to. There was barely time to instruct the others. Via the bond, I quickly relayed to Varro, "*Get back to your ship with Cairis, stop the fliers at all costs. I love you.*"

Before he could respond, I did my best to shut out the noise of any reply he'd send and turned my attention to Trace. "Don't stop me. Whatever happens. Just stop the fliers. I know what to do."

The worry on Trace's face turned to resolve as he placed his hand on the hilt of his blade and nodded at me with confidence. As Trace walked away toward those receiving weapons, I turned my attention back to the shoreline.

I had only ever used the power of dark wielding for destruction. Volatile and violent in nature. What I was about to attempt, I had never done before. The idea was speculative, at best, only loosely grounded in what I'd read in all my hours of studying magic. Failure meant the Cambrian troops would surely suffer a resounding and utter defeat. I would use the darkness to make an ally of the light. It had to work.

I studied the waves upon the sea, noting their chaotic movements. I closed my eyes and felt the sea breeze brush tendrils of my hair gently across my skin. I absorbed the energy of the sun's comforting rays, settling the goosebumps along my chilled skin. I had to know these elements like they were all one in the same. I needed to allow these elements to become a part of my being, incorporating their essence until I could impart my influence upon them. But harnessing them would not be enough to wield them so quickly, so immensely. Only the might of memory could forge such masterful magic. Remembrances, sweetly layered with nostalgia, swirled in my mind in a storm of emotion.

I navigated the memories of my past, remembering my father's hand on my shoulder as we both looked out at my first sunrise on the water. His pride at me standing by his side was evident, the heir to all he had built. I remembered the roughness of the rope in my hands as he taught me to tie knots properly. I remembered when the captain stepped aside and father let me put my hands on the giant wheel, basking in the immense power I felt from steering the ship. Power that came from controlling something bigger than myself, rather than being controlled by it.

I anchored into that control so deeply that when my eyes opened again, I saw the patterns of the wind; I saw the rays and speckles of sunlight for what they were. Nothing more than paint awaiting its canvas. I stretched out my hands in front of me, keeping them low and unnoticeable. I knew Trace would end anyone who tried to distract me, and so I drowned out the shouts of the commoners-turned-soldiers surrounding me so that only the song of the rolling sea accompanied my painting.

The moment that the fog lifted completely, I could see the sandy beach ahead, the very land that those seeking to portal to would set their sights on any minute now. The sun above it heating the sand. A cool breeze would distort the scene properly. I gathered all my power, pushing the chilled, ocean air directly inland, creating the refraction that distorted the coastline. I held my hands there, steadying myself as I continued to keep a flow of moisture-filled air pulsing into the beach, until finally, silver, mirror-like sparkles rippled all along it. I held it steady, for fear of the distortion not holding long enough.

In the distance, I heard the yelling of orders and rustling of soldiers' wings unfurling. I had to hold the mirage for as long as it took. Long enough to send as many of them as possible into the oblivion of their misguided portals. Small batches of soldiers began to take flight, conjuring their cloudlike circles before them; eyes set on Cambria's shores for the first time ever.

A calamity of battle cries surrounded me. Commoners looked on as their armored peers began the siege. I shoved aside their distractions, praying and willing all my energy into this veil I had pulled over the shores of my homeland and its people. I prayed to the Gods that this shining blanket of deception would be enough to thwart my enemies' attempts. One by one, their small groups entered their portals, and I held my breath waiting to see if any actually arrived on the shores of the Riverlands.

Moments passed by and not a single soldier arrived on the beaches. I felt my chest tighten, constricting with the joy that it was somehow working, but also the anxiety that sustaining this was becoming practically unbearable. After a few more waves of soldiers attempted to portal ashore, I could hear the sounds of chaos erupting. Leaders aboard our ships ordered the passengers to fly ashore. I had no idea where Trace, Cairis, or even Varro was while I ignored every plea he sent through the bond for a response.

I could spare not a single ounce of energy for him or anything else. I had to keep this mirage from dwindling. Angry Fae took to the skies, and I hoped the forces of Cambria, plus the Imperi would be enough to quell them. The boom of cannon fire thundered in the background, and catapults sprang into action in the distance. Cambria hurled all the artillery it could muster in the direction of the Artumian fliers. Inexperienced at evasive flight maneuvers, bodies crashed into the sea all around the ship. Just because these Fae had wings, it didn't mean they had been trained correctly on how to use them. They'd become complacent since the last war, just like our own people.

Zarif had sent more than half his fighters into their portals, and not a one had made landfall yet. I had no idea where I'd sent them. The great unknown of portaling missteps could have resulted in them landing somewhere else entirely, or leaving their bodies and consciousness mangled in between space and time. Either way, they weren't at their destination, and that brought me peace as I struggled to keep the mirage intact.

I felt the elements slipping from my grasp, pulling away from me, and yet I sank my mental talons in deeper, clinging to them as best I could. Every second I held on only exasperated me further. How long until Zarif conceded that his army could not successfully portal ashore? Maybe enough of them had been lost in the attempt that the remainder would simply take flight? I clung to the idea that every one of them I managed to send to oblivion with this golden facade was one less for my people to fight.

I fought as hard as I possibly could, but my fingertips had gone numb and my legs felt heavy, like they could no longer hold up the weight of my own body. My skin burned as if stricken by fever, and I began to sweat profusely. The memories that nourished my power began to dim, suddenly a blurry mess despite my efforts to call upon them. Like a novice artist who mixed too much water with her paint, the colors merged and lost all definition. There were no longer clear pictures of my family's faces. No recollections of my youth. It was a torrent of chaos, swirling violently until the energy was drained wholly from my body, reducing my power to a fraction of what it once was.

Yet I continued, eyes fixed on my creation, releasing all that I could until my eyes began to flicker. And when the darkness took me, I fell to the ground, overcome by the feeling that there was nothing left to give.

CHAPTER 66

First, there was darkness. Then, there was light so bright that it stung my eyes.

"Cress. Cress!" I felt firm hands shaking my shoulders. Smears of color dominated my blurry vision until his face came into focus. Trace was hovering above me; his wings unfurled but tucked tightly around us, protectively.

"Stay with me, wake up."

His voice was frantic as he cradled the back of my neck. When I fully opened my eyes, I struggled to speak his name. There was smoke in the sky behind him, and my ears were ringing so badly that I wanted to cover them.

"Drink this," he said, pressing a small canteen of water to my lips. As soon as the liquid hit my tongue, I began to gulp down the water in large swigs, unable to get enough to satiate me. I felt so utterly tired, and my head was pounding with pain. The sounds of fighting, of war and death still reverberated around me and my eyes prickled with tears.

"Did we win?" I asked him through a cracked voice, fear mounting that we had not done enough.

Trace put my arm over his shoulder and slowly began to lift me to my feet, not letting go until I was stable.

"Not yet," he said. "But you gave us a chance."

My eyes squinted, scanning the beach. It seemed some of the Artumian fighters had made it ashore and were engaged in battle. Bodies littered the shoreline, pools of red blood spreading wide and far. Above us, soldiers were engaged in aerial combat—even Cambria had chosen to bring the fight to the skies. I felt the faint patter of the bond begin its tingling below the surface of my skin again, and then the echo of Varro's voice became repetitive pleas.

"Speak to me. Speak to me. Speak to me."

The words were desperate in my head, like he had been repeating them for hours. How long had he been calling out for me?

"I'm alive. I'm with Trace."

A relieved silence followed.

"I'm okay."

"Thank the Gods. Saryn's reinforcements have started to arrive. Cairis and I are doing our best to fight off as many as we can."

Though my head was still pounding, the sound of his voice was medicinal, offering me clarity and strength.

Bloodshed and destruction littered the shore of my homeland, making anger begin to simmer through the exhaustion.

"Where is Zarif?" I asked Trace, seething.

"Last I saw, he was commanding from his ship; now, I don't know. I've been too busy putting down as many fliers as I could until I saw you on the ground."

"He's a fucking coward!" I declared, staring at the ships anchored a safe distance from the wreckage and carnage he'd caused.

"I'm done waiting." I unfurled my wings and Trace took a step forward, but before he could try to stop me or talk me out of it, I shot straight up into the air.

I soared through the sky, dodging the remaining sloppy airborne skirmishes. I arrived abruptly on the deck of Zarif's ship, my landing rough as I touched down in a crouching position. Standing up straight, I kept my wings tucked tightly, defensively. Zarif was pacing angrily at the front of the ship, yelling orders at the remaining soldiers.

One of them took notice of my arrival and swung at me with his blade. I ducked the strike, then disarmed him and claimed his blade in one swift motion before ending his life. I barely took notice as his body hit the deck, bleeding out. I was singularly focused on the evil that had caused all of this. I would hurt him for Nori. I would make him suffer for Cambria—and moreover, I would end him for the future of his own people.

I heard Trace land loudly behind me, and as more attackers tried to engage me, he intervened, taking their lives swiftly. Zarif had not chosen wisely when he'd selected his protectors. When he finally turned to face the both of us, he did not appear concerned, perhaps still trying to reconcile my familiar face. But when he spoke, it was not to me.

"You're either a traitor or a deserter, and I care not which. The punishment for both is death."

Zarif smirked arrogantly, the expression resonating from his two different-colored eyes void of any fear.

In an attempt to alter his smug confidence, I yelled, "I'll have you know that Lady Gianna is slaying your pathetic excuse for a king as we speak. You're going to have to find a new master to serve."

Trace gave me a sly smile and added, "Perhaps the God of Death." He lunged forward and attempted to land a hit with his sword, but Zarif's skill was unlike anything we'd anticipated. It was hardly describable, much less fathomable. His body abandoned its corporeal form and adopted a spirit form, then abruptly rushed to a nearby Kingsguard, inhabiting him.

I heard Trace mutter, "What the fu—" He spun around to face Zarif's new form. The Kingsguard, now inhabited by Zarif, bore the same two-colored eyes as his true self. He barely gave myself or Trace a second to process what we'd witnessed before arcing his sword in our direction. His skill was far superior to what we'd encountered when boarding the ship. Trace and I circled him, closing in from different angles. The second I lunged, narrowly missing him with the tip of my sword, Trace followed with an offensive maneuver of his own.

Soon, the Kingsguard's body dropped to the ground, stunned, while a blur of what appeared to be Zarif's spirit form transferred to the next nearest enemy combatant. Each time he settled into his host's form, their posture and mannerisms immediately changed. The thrum of the bond pulsed persistently below my skin as my confidence began to wane.

While Zarif searched for an opening to attack, I hailed Varro through the bond.

"Come as soon as you can. Zarif is something…something we've never encountered. I can't explain, just hurry!"

The moment I had met Zarif, I knew there was something sinister about him. Saryn's remarks about not knowing what he was truly capable of echoed in my memory. Zarif's ability was unnatural in every sense of the word. There was not a single mention of this kind of magic in any of the books I'd read amongst the dark wielding journals. And our mentors never spoke of anything remotely close to *this*.

Would we even be able to kill him? Would he always have the ability to leave any body that we mortally wounded? Trace and I continued to press forward with our assault, hoping he would make a mistake. But he was too adept, moved too quickly, even for the both of us. It was as if he knew each move we'd make, even before we did. This formerly frail-looking male was a skilled, capable killer. Still, his ability surely had a price, just like mine. All power comes with a cost, especially tainted magic.

Suddenly, the bond's hum overwhelmed me as my mate arrived, his stunning teal-and-green wings appearing next to me. Blood was splattered across his bare chest, but it wasn't his. Thank the Gods and moons above that he was alive, and seemingly unharmed, if not furious.

Trace and Zarif's blades clashed, each combatant expertly defending against the other's blows. Then, with dizzying speed, Zarif's blade plunged for Trace's chest. Trace was too fast, though, turning sideways to avoid the strike. Still, a trickle of blood flowed from Trace's arm where Zarif's blade had nicked him. Trace took two steps back to assess his wound while Zarif, seizing the opportunity, leapt out of his current Kingsguard's body, fleeing to the far end of the ship, seeking a new host. I heard my mate gasp and whisper something to himself. Suddenly, three guards rounded the corner, all with blades at the ready. Each of us sized them up and prepared to engage.

The piercing reverberations of metal striking metal filled the air. *"Which one is he?"* Varro frantically said, mind-to-mind.

"Look for two-colored eyes," I replied quickly.

"I've got him!" Trace yelled from farther away.

I dropped to my knees, slicing deep across my enemy's stomach. His entrails spilled forth onto the wooden deck with a disgusting, wet plop. I almost vomited at the sight, but I knew Trace needed help. I leapt up, grabbed the lit oil lantern hanging nearby, and threw it to the deck nearest Zarif and Trace. The glass shattered and oil spilled everywhere, causing the flame to expand quickly. If Zarif didn't swap again, Trace might be able to maneuver him into it. I had no idea if fire would kill him, but it was worth a try.

Varro had dispatched his Kingsguard, and now we both stood on the perimeter of the deck, the heat of the blaze pushing us farther outward as we lost visibility of Trace. My energy was still shockingly low from performing the mirage, but I used what little remained to create a pathway for us to approach them. Trace continued to duck and dodge, while Zarif struck out with precision and guile, clearly having the upperhand. When Trace saw the opening in the flames, he yelled to Varro, "Stop him!"

I did not understand the exchange until I saw the body Zarif presided over begin to shake and tremble, clutching at his throat, his airway obviously constricting.

"*Kill him quickly*," I thought, as Varro's Siren Song suffocated him from within. Just as I hoped I'd seen the last of the convulsions, Zarif's spirit sprung forth from the dying body and rushed straight toward… me. I retreated quickly, preparing my wings to take flight, but the specter closed the distance between us with unnatural speed. I shrank back in preparation for impact when, suddenly, Trace intercepted Zarif's form, causing the two to collide. Immediately, Trace's body plummeted to the ground.

Without hesitation, Varro turned his Siren Song toward Trace in an attempt to restrain him. Trace's body writhed on the deck, convulsing. In an instant, I was by Trace's side, assessing him as his body seized violently against the floor. His hazel eyes were gone, replaced by blue and brown. His gaze was absent any recognition, and his teeth ground back and forth as spittle foamed at the corner of his lips.

"You're hurting him!" I yelled at my mate, helpless to what I was witnessing.

Varro walked closer, still exerting the full force of his power.

"I can't let up or he'll escape!"

"But you're killing him!" I pleaded.

Varro argued back, "What would you have me do?"

I grabbed Trace's hand in mine, unsure if the male I knew was even still inside this body. He yanked and tugged against my grasp as Varro struggled to suppress him.

Zarif's form tremored in and out of Trace's body, appearing for a split-second before being pulled back inside. Each time it hovered above his body, Zarif's raspy voice screamed violently, clamoring to be freed. I feared what would happen if he did escape; would he possess me next? Would anything be left of Trace?

That's when I saw Trace mouthing words between Zarif's untamed noises. I leaned in closer, afraid that if I got too close, I would be Zarif's next victim. I knew of no magic in my arsenal to end this. Tears pooled and clung to Trace's lashes as he succumbed to the pain.

"Do."

Snarls and monstrous noises erupted from Zarif's spirit, trying desperately to escape.

"It."

"Do it," Trace repeated. "*Do it.*"

Again, and again, he repeated those two words. Only those words.

My mental shields had been obliterated; Varro heard every rampant thought spinning through my mind in that moment. I looked up at him, tears now welling in my eyes, knowing he was preparing himself for this burden. Before I let him consider it for even a moment longer, I yelled down the bond, "*Noooo!*" forcing him to hesitate, forcing one brief moment of distraction. Long enough for me to draw my own dagger and jam it into Trace's ribs, directly below his heart.

The convulsing quickly came to an end as we both witnessed Zarif's transparent spirit roll out of Trace's limp body. It curled on its side into the fetal position, facing away from us, clutching its chest before taking on its Fae form again. The pallor of Zarif's skin, now grey, was mostly flesh and bone. A feeble body that had once possessed such rare and destructive magic. Varro ran over to the corpse, ensuring he was good and dead, while I pulled Trace's limp body into my arms in a panic.

I slid my blade from his ribs and placed my hand over the wound, channeling all the magic left within me.

"Why isn't he healing?" I cried to Varro, who hurried to my side and knelt on the ground.

"Place your hand on him too," I commanded my mate. "Help me heal him."

Trace's eyes were hazel once more, but all the light in them had gone out. They were glassy and hollow.

When he tried to speak, red gushed from the wound and over my hand, and all that came out was a hacking, bloody cough.

"Why isn't it working? We have to save him!" I shouted. Fae could survive a wound like this one, if healed quickly. But nothing we did was working, and I knew we were losing him.

"Stay with us," I yelled at Trace. Furious tears falling down my cheeks. "I demand you stay."

I held Trace's head in my hand while the other still pressed the wound to no avail.

He rolled his head to face Varro, who looked horror-stricken that I had chosen to end things myself. His throat worked to hold back the emotion I could feel emanating through the bond.

Trace finally choked out a few bloodied words, keeping his empty stare fixated on Varro, "Gods, let me have her in the next life."

His head lolled back toward me and I witnessed him close his eyes, leaving my face as the last thing he saw in this cursed world. And I screamed to the heavens.

"I rescind the bargain! Send him back!"

I pounded my fists on Trace's bloody chest, yelling through tears. I watched as the last of his glamour withered away, revealing the scar his father gave him on his brow, his arms now covered in blood-red tattoos.

"Send him fucking back!"

I cradled his heavy body into my chest and began rocking back and forth, my words a mantra of nothing more than, "Forgive me, I rescind the bargain, forgive me."

The roar of cannon fire faded into the background. My head was filled only with the ringing in my ears, and my own pleas.

In my periphery, I saw the arrival of Cairis and, finally, for the first time since the battle began, Saryn. They were surrounding Zarif's body but well aware of the other body in my clutches just paces away.

His skin was turning cold, and I imagined this was what Nori had felt like, though I never got to hold her in those final moments. Guilt consumed me. It was drowning me from within, and I struggled to continue my pleas to the Gods as a sob wrenched forth from my chest. I wanted to die. I *deserved* to die, for all the lives I had taken that day. For all the lives I had taken in the mines. I felt like a curse upon this cursed place. Trace had only died because I made him bind himself to me, to put our lives above his own. I wouldn't allow myself to believe he chose this. A distinct moment of clarity struck me as I held Trace's lifeless body, his blood soaking through my clothes: I was the one who dealt him a fate he could not fight.

CHAPTER
67

S aryn was lucky to be alive, lucky that Idris hadn't ended him the moment he learned of his treachery. Instead, Idris insisted that Saryn return with us to Artume, to rendezvous with Gia and the princess. His decision seemed illogical to me, but I had a suspicion I was about to see his calculations unfold firsthand as Princess Embry lunged into her mate's arms.

"Lazarus," she cried, happy tears beginning to roll down her cheeks as Saryn embraced her. Idris had spared him any restraints as a courtesy, but had instructed Varro to subdue him at any indication of escape.

"Lazarus…" Idris repeated slowly, letting the syllables roll off his tongue with a velvety-smooth cadence. "I haven't heard your born name in a very, very long time."

Idris folded his hands idly in front of himself. "Not since you took your oath. And yet, here we are, the heir to the southern kingdom saying it with such wanton passion."

Embry pulled back from Saryn's embrace, but held his elbow tightly, protectively. "I don't care what name you call him," she seethed. "More importantly, who are you and what are you doing in my kingdom?" she retorted confidently, as if she had already ruled these lands her entire life. Every day in those cells was one where she awaited the chance to take back what was rightfully hers and avenge her parents.

Idris let out a small and uncharacteristic snort of amusement. I knew whatever he was about to say next was not going to show any deference to her royal standing.

"I am the only thing standing between Saryn and Death's door." He paused, assessing her reaction, and when she didn't blink or flinch, he added, "I could also be the reason that the histories say Artume's last living heir never made it out of her cell alive."

I began to shift my stance defensively, uncomfortable with Idris' threats. The cramped space of the safehouse, plus the shuttered windows, made me feel uncomfortable given the number of very powerful individuals all confined in close quarters with emotions running so high.

Embry stepped forward to protest, but Saryn's grip was firm, tugging her back to his chest. "You don't intimidate me," she spat, fearlessly.

"Princess, do you know what the sentence for treason is?" Idris stalked around her, like a wolf circling its prey.

Down the bond, Varro commanded me not to intervene, but I ignored him, choosing instead to see how this transpired before deciding whether or not to get involved. I'd seen enough useless death for ten lifetimes, and I wasn't about to stand by and watch this female die. And for what? Loving the wrong person? Being born into royalty of an enemy kingdom?

When silence was the only answer to Idris' question, he continued with his icy declarations. "Your mate is oathbound for the rest of his life in servitude of King Aeon. And yet, his actions belied that oath. Aligning himself with the enemy." He made a disappointed *tsk tsk* as he waited for Saryn to respond. He didn't, but Princess Embry did.

"Please, whatever he has done or said, look at the result. We have won a great—"

"Won, your grace? Losses on both sides are likely in the thousands, including two members of the king's own Order—*loyal servants*," he enunciated, "until their last breaths."

I shifted uncomfortably back and forth, trying to stanch the flood of painful images rushing through my head.

Saryn spoke in defense of Embry more than himself. "In war, difficult decisions must be made, and—"

"And you were trusted to make them honorably, in service of our king," Idris argued, raising his voice.

Saryn hung his head in defeat and mumbled something inaudible under his breath.

Idris ignored this and continued calmly, "Make no mistake, he chose death the moment he put you above our cause. He has only himself to blame for the punishment I'm required to bestow."

Finally, Embry broke away from Saryn's grasp, and as he lunged forward to restrain her, Varro sent him swiftly to his knees. Saryn quickly turned his gaze to Varro, his eyes pleading and seething all at once.

"No!" she shouted at Idris, who appeared entirely unfazed by a plea he had already anticipated. "You can't. He is my mate! You'd be killing us both—*please*, just spare him."

Idris lifted his hand and grasped the bottom of Embry's chin delicately, inspecting her beautiful features—not endearingly, but rather as a polite insult to her youth. "A sweet flower you are… I care not for the foolishness of love and mates. A kingmaker hasn't the time for such whimsy."

He dropped his hand from her face, but she showed no signs of defeat. Idris turned his back and slowly walked away, continuing his pontificating aloud.

"Power, strength, riches. My dear, it is nothing if you cannot provide peace. I have counseled many kings in my lifetime. Those that have sought the former often find their heirs at an early ascension. There is only one thing you have of value."

Embry's fists balled tightly at her sides, pinning her crème dress to her bodice. "You ask for the southern seat in exchange for my mate's life?"

Idris looked slowly over his shoulder.

"Peace takes time to restore." Idris walked toward Gia, who was leaning against the wall, appearing tired and disinterested after her own ordeal with slaying the king. He eyed the full length of her stature up and down, like she was a prize horse.

"We have a gifted shifter in our midst. Perhaps one who even surpasses the skill of your own mate. The very one I hear freed you from the confines of your cells and delivered you to safety." He paused, looking back at Embry to witness her reaction. "You did know of his particular talents, right? Or did he keep that a secret from you too?"

"If peace is all you seek, then I offer you the southern throne for fifty years in exchange for my mate's life."

"No!" Saryn yelled. "It's not worth it. Don't do this," he pleaded to his beloved.

I'd never seen Saryn cry, but I could see frustrated tears beginning to well in his eyes at the idea of his mate offering up her throne, all she had left, just to spare him a punishment he'd wholly earned.

Idris ignored Saryn's interruptions entirely and continued to focus his negotiations on the all-too-eager princess.

"Princess, your people's minds are poisoned towards the North. These complex emotions cannot easily be undone. But with one of our own on the throne, we may yet develop the antidote. Still, it would be challenging…" His words trailed off as if he were no longer considering it. "One hundred years in exchange for you and your mate's asylum, confined to the Elorn Mountains."

Instantly, I knew what Idris sought to do. He would keep them both prisoners, warded at Basdie. She was not bartering for freedom—Idris would never grant that after what Saryn had done.

"Don't do it!" Saryn begged. "My life isn't worth losing your throne. You don't know the things I've done."

I could tell he was getting desperate to convince her, trying his best to push her away by any means necessary.

"I'm not who you think I am. I don't deserve you. I don't deserve to live. Please do not give into these demands, Embry!"

She turned to her mate and knelt, meeting him at eye level, now on her knees facing him.

"If you would let me know you, truly know you, a throne is a small price to pay. In a prison cell, in the remotest of mountains, in solitude and in suffering, I would give up everything I have ever known…to *know you*."

Embry's words rippled along my and Varro's bond. An undeniable and relatable truth resounded from them. I felt it. Varro felt it. Even as bitter as Gia was, I knew she felt it. The indescribable tether of having found one's mate was just as much a calling for life as was the duty to one's kingdom or an oath of servitude. The semantics of such nuance can only be known by those who have felt its power over them. It's why Saryn was powerless to his betrayal.

Slow tears began to fall down Saryn's cheeks, matching Embry's as he surrendered to her decision. Embry stood and stepped toward Idris, confident in her convictions.

"You have 100 years with your imposter queen to make peace between our lands. When that time is up, I will be back to claim what is rightfully mine," she said through gritted teeth.

Idris smiled at her and nodded before turning his attention to the rest of us. "Wonderful. It seems we have a coronation to plan. Embry will stay here with Gia this evening to provide thorough details of any essential knowledge before her installment. Tomorrow morning, I will begin transporting her and Saryn to Basdie."

Gia began to fidget, and I could tell her displeasure came from being treated as nothing more than a puzzle piece in the matter. We were all hoping to leave Artume as soon as the mission allowed, but now her fate had been sealed to the aftermath for at least 100 years. I knew she wanted to scream and rip Idris limb-from-limb. Instead, I witnessed her exert composed self-control.

"I know you all wish to properly mourn Trace, and it is my regret that I cannot stay to stand as witness. I do not take the death of one of us lightly. But it is important that I convene with King Aeon and share news of our plans, as well as ensure this traitor is returned to Basdie."

Saryn dipped his chin in shame at Idris' words, the truth of it too heavy to deny.

Before Varro even spoke, I knew he was going to ask the same questions swirling in me as I tried to ignore mention of Trace's passing. "What of the rest of us? Are we to be stationed in Artume?"

"All of you will stay here and see to the coronation efforts. Once successful, Cairis will remain at Gia's side as added protection. She is a valuable asset and your watch over her safety is imperative."

Gia's shoulders relaxed minutely, hearing that she wouldn't be forced to carry on this charade alone. One hundred years was a long time to play such a role. I was eager to hear if Varro and I would also keep posts in Artume. While I longed to smell the lands of Cambria again, to be free of this sand pit, there was nothing there for me anymore. Gia, Cairis—outside of my mate, they were my family.

My hopes were crushed instantly. "Varro and Cress, at the culmination of the ceremonies, you two are to return to Basdie and await your next orders. Theory is likely to greet you." There was relief in knowing we'd be travelling together, that we wouldn't be separated, but nothing about Idris' instruction made it clear how long we would remain that way. What if we were sent off on separate missions? I dared not question Idris or inquire further about the missions in front of Embry. This would have been a grave misstep in his eyes, and since he was already sparing one Imperi life, I needn't press my luck.

CHAPTER

60

I sat on the edge of Gia's bed, running my fingers back and forth across the small piece of folded parchment, like I'd done so many times over the past few days before resigning to not open it. "Just read it already," Gia urged, knowing good and well exactly what it was.

"I can't…I'm just not ready," I argued, letting out a sigh. My fingertips had practically memorized the texture of the paper. For the amount of time I'd held it in my warm hands, it wouldn't be a shock if the heat of my skin had caused the ink and its contents to smear. When Cairis delivered it to me, my heart sank as he conveyed its origins. This letter, which clearly had my name written on the outside, had come from Trace.

Cairis found it while preparing the body for burning. He said it was shoved into the side of Trace's boot. And to think, if he hadn't removed his clothing to give him a proper ceremony, it may have never been found. Whatever words or images lay inside this message could have been burned away to ash along with his body, and I'd have never known its contents. Maybe it would have been better that way? Instead,

I'd agonized over it for days, unwilling to let myself read it, and instead I bathed in my grief and regret while the others worked diligently to prepare for Gia's coronation as Queen Embry. I helped, but found it difficult to focus or assist in any meaningful way. Mostly, I rehearsed apathetically, or found myself nodding in agreement to questions asked of me moments before that I could not recollect.

Even through my grieving and self-loathing, there was one thing I came back to, over and over again. Varro having escaped the battle unscathed was my biggest relief. I told myself these, the losses of Nori and Trace, were losses I would find a way to endure. Somehow. But *he* was the point of no return for me. If I'd lost him, there would be no reason to carry on. But…*he* was my reason. And in between all the planning and commotion, I sought as much refuge in his comforting embrace as possible. Facing so much death and destruction changed me permanently. Mostly it made me more fearful of ever seeing him harmed or losing him. I suffered a few nightmares where he had swapped places with Nori and Trace, and I experienced the losses as if it were him I was losing. These nightmares were difficult to shake. I tried not to let him know how much I thought of losing him now. How it haunted me in my sleep and waking hours.

I was too exhausted from all the sleepless nights to keep up with the façade of being her lady's maid. After a short time, Gia seemed strangely renewed and energized. She kept saying, "I suppose there are worse fates than being a queen?"

I think she told herself this in an effort to bring about some semblance of comfort. But I believed that deep down, this task would be a lonely one. Ruling over foreign lands, foreign people; Fae who had been misled and misguided into a brief but bloody battle with the North before being forced to retreat. Those unable or unwilling to retreat were captured, their bodies destined to illustrate the severity of their crimes against the North. She was supposed to be the spark to a flame of hope. With the usurpers discarded, power transitioned back to those who would support reinstating the peace treaties, adhering to borders, and fulfilling trade alliances. The true heir of Artume atop the throne. Or so the Artumians would be made to believe.

Gia may have been open to the idea of gowns, crowns, jewelry and revelries. She might have relished in presiding over an entire court and kingdom. But she was not a fan of politics, nor keen on economics. I imagined she would struggle in this role, though she wore a brave face. A face that was not her own, only able to find peace in private moments where she could once again transform back into herself. Cairis could protect her physically, but she'd need to find other allies she could trust, even if they could not know her secret.

My mind distracted itself with thoughts of her future, ignoring the paper in my hands.

"You know, Cress, I regret the last words I ever said to my mate." Her regal gown rustled as she made her way to join me on the bed. I scooted over to make room and avoid wrinkling the delicate fabric. "I looked my mate in the eye and lied to him. I withheld any affections, even as my heart broke, and I willingly severed our bond."

I felt unworthy to talk to Gia about her mate. Not when I had one of my own, even in these circumstances. Especially not when our own mentor had put us all in this precarious situation due to his own betrayals. She was the only one of us who had made a clean sacrifice.

"I don't know when he wrote this. I don't even know if it's words at all. He used to sketch; it may not even be a letter," I argued, thinking back to all his detailed drawings when we first met, and the one he'd given me before leaving Basdie.

"If it is a letter…all I'm saying is, were he alive, then maybe he would have said the words himself. But he wrote them to you, perhaps knowing he may never get the chance. In any case, they were his…intended for you. Would you deny him his truth, even in death?"

My chest felt hollow, and a numb tear rolled down my cheek at Gia's suggestion.

"I don't deserve any reprieve that opening this may offer me."

"Then don't do it for you. Do it for him," she coaxed carefully, gently clasping her hand over mine.

The loud sound of horns followed by bells echoed in the distance, indicating the coronation was about to begin. Thousands of Artumians waited anxiously for the return of Princess Embry and to exalt her as their queen.

Gia stood, knowing this would be the last time we saw each other for an unknown amount of time. Directly following her ceremony, Varro and I were to begin the return trip to Basdie. Goosebumps began to form on my exposed flesh. Nerves for her, for me. All of us.

"I never would have guessed that taking the oath of the Imperi meant I'd someday become queen over all of Artume. The mission seems pretty straightforward, right? It's not like I have a war-torn country to preside over or anything…" Gia concluded jokingly, a warm smile turning into a wide, sarcastic grin.

I smiled back and pulled her into my chest, embracing her tightly and taking in her floral fragrance one last time. Looking her over, committing her to memory, before she shifted into the stunning and youthful Princess Embry.

"Treat her kingdom and people well, despite their transgressions, Gia. Lead them with strength and mercy."

The irony was not lost on me that often she and I began a mission with the words "No mercy". But this mission was different. The Artumians were not her enemy.

"I have every intention of it," she confirmed. "I would hand this sandcastle back to Embry as soon as she would have it."

My cheeks pinched into an amused smile at her referring to Nasallus as a sandcastle. It was fragile in so many ways.

"Watch this," Gia said, lifting the hem of her dress up and pivoting into a twirl, the luxurious fabric concealing her body and face. The form that greeted me when she stilled was a perfect image of Embry, down to the most nuanced details. It was no wonder that even a heart of ice like Saryn's had been melted by this kind of beauty.

"Cress…"

"Yes," I replied as she began to make her way towards the door.

"Your mental shields really are shit sometimes. When you see Saryn again, it may be easy to hate him, but ask yourself: if it had been Varro, would you have done the same?"

Unwilling to wait for my reply, she reached for the handle and made her exit into the hall as chimes of bells beckoned her to the southernmost balcony, where the citizens of Artume would crown their new queen.

The door shut softly behind her, and I plopped back onto the bed and resumed fiddling with Trace's note, willing forth the courage to unfold it. My fingers trembled with terror as I began to peel apart the parchment. I steadied my heartbeat, and focused on silencing my mind and heart to the bond, fortifying this moment in deep, utter privacy.

Dearest Cress,

I don't deserve you. I have known this since the moment I laid eyes on you and every day since. I never could have fooled myself into believing otherwise. Not before I knew your true identity, and not a moment since knowing you were fated to another. And beyond that, I know now you are destined for a greatness that does not involve me at your side. He would lay down his life for you, but I would have taken the lives of everyone that stood between us and our happiness. My love for you is tainted. You deserve better than the kind of love I can give. But let me dream. Even for just this moment. Let me dream.

If I could...I would rewrite the stars in the image of our happiness. In another lifetime, this is our story. The story that never was...

Somewhere in the infinite universe, I'm living a different life. I was born into a caring family. I trusted deeply and loved fiercely. I didn't know death, pain and violence. You chose me, not a mate. You chose me. The way you chose him. I don't want some invisible rope tying us to one another. I want you to know me and choose me because I'd choose you, and I'd never need fate to bind us.

In this lifetime, it's ours. It's a beautiful one, too, and as we stand at the edge of the golden wheat fields outside of Nori's home, know that the amber waves are pale in comparison to your beauty. Miles of it as far as the eye can see until we spot the tips of tiny, green, iridescent wings poking up between the hues of yellow. Their wispy edges barely breaching the top of the tallest grasses. You scoop up our daughter Avila in your arms, and she looks at me giggling. Behind us, I hear your sister Versa chasing after her own daughter.

I will see you in another lifetime, Cress. So, when a stranger approaches you at a tavern in the middle of nowhere, I hope you're good and sober. Because I'll never let you out of my sight from that day forward.

—Never yours, but always waiting.

Trace

CHAPTER 60

I cried until there were no more tears. My mourning of Nori and Trace colliding. Both of their lives cut too short, both their lives so different from what they wanted for themselves. My patient and loving mate awaited me in the giant courtyard and my tear-stained kiss would be a stark reminder to him of how much pain I was in. For the deaths I'd felt somehow responsible for. I folded the letter and left it on the table, hoping for Trace's sake that the Gods would grant him such a beautiful life someday.

But I knew that this was the only lifetime I could be sure of, and Varro was more than deserving of my devotion. I would not waste a moment of it. He was my other half. The thought of it brought me immense gratitude and calm. And, even though I would love him with everything I had till my dying breath, that didn't mean I couldn't hope for someone else to get everything they ever wanted.

I exited Gia's room and quickly made my way down the hall. A few nobles were still rushing toward the festivities. With my head turned the other direction, I accidentally bumped shoulders with someone, knocking an item from their grasp. I bent down quickly to pick it up, as expected of a servant who'd made such an error. I lifted it to the tall, thin female who had sharp but stunning features. She was dressed impeccably, with a capelet laying over her lean frame.

"I'm so sorry," I uttered, trying to keep my chin dipped as was the etiquette. The last thing I needed was any trouble with a noble as I was trying to make my final exit from this Gods-forsaken sandcastle.

Her melodic voice startled me almost more than her words. "Do not be sorry, our feet carry us on the whims of fate. Don't you think?"

She smiled and quickly resumed her strides before I could make heads or tails of her strange reply. I turned to study her momentarily from behind when I noticed the eerie pattern across her capelet, almost moth-like. A peculiar attire for the dry heat of Artume. I disregarded it and began my swift exit to meet Varro, assuring him down the bond that my delays were nothing to be concerned about.

⸫⸫⸫

"You had me worried," he said, pulling me into a tight embrace and kissing me atop my head, his usual greeting. We were shoulder to shoulder with Fae as far as the eye could see, all clamoring to witness their new queen.

"I sent word not to be. After all you've witnessed, you think I can't handle myself?" I teased.

"I have always known you could handle yourself, my love."

We began to make our way north in the opposite direction of the balcony. Suddenly, the crowds around us started to cheer in jubilation. Their bodies pushed against ours like herds of animals. Varro held my hand tightly as we tried to squeeze our way through the masses moving in opposition of us. It took much longer than one would expect to close such a short distance to the exit, but Gia must have been putting on quite the show to garner such a display of support.

When we finally put space between us and their bodies, I turned to look back at my friend in all her glory. I was easily reminded that their passionate displays of support were not for her, but for the lost daughter of their once beloved King Baelin. Gia waved graciously at the crowds below, occasionally touching her hand to her heart and then lifting it in the air, as if to give it to them. Her people.

Gods, she was magnificent at this. I would miss her guidance, confidence and friendship. I saw Cairis standing stoically by her side, scanning the skies and the crowds below, protectively. Just as Gia never thought she'd become a proxy queen, I doubt Cairis ever thought the bastard son of a High Lord would ever find himself guarding the southern throne. Seeing the pair close together brought me a sense of calm as I turned away and made my final strides away from Nasallus.

Varro led us through the empty streets. A strange sight to take in as we made our way back to the safehouse. Two strong horses awaited us; my mate had taken care of preparing supplies for the long trip ahead.

"I'll give you a moment to change inside. I can't imagine you want to chafe those stunning legs of yours on the saddle." Varro drank in my figure, reminding me that this barely-there servant's dress would be less than ideal for the ride.

"Don't you want to come inside with me?" I teased, trying my best to seduce him.

He strolled up to me with a rakish smile and a gleam in his eye. He grabbed my hip sharply and tugged me toward him. He leaned in, speaking in a smooth, hushed voice, despite there being no one nearby to hear him.

"The next time I fuck my mate into oblivion, I want it to be as far away as possible from this sandpit."

I laughed. "You love the sand. You live for those shores," I reminded him playfully.

He pushed a strand of hair behind my ear, then nipped at my earlobe before remarking, "Yes, but *you* do not. I can't have any distractions from all the things I'm going to do to your body."

I claimed his mouth, kissing his unrefined declaration right off his lips. His warm hand cupped the back of my neck, deepening the kiss. He fought to tear himself away from our embrace and exert his usual self-control.

When I came out of the safehouse a short time later, ready to begin the long journey north, I mounted my horse where it waited next to Varro's.

As the horses trotted slowly, side by side out of the city, I turned to face my golden mate, admiring the curves of his rigid and muscular arms. "You know, Idris made a big mistake in drugging us when he transported us to Basdie."

"And why is that?" Varro mused.

"I struggle to recollect my way back to it. Could be difficult returning. Could cause delays…" I gave him a sly look with one raised eyebrow.

He played along. "Yes, I, too, struggle to remember the path to the Elorns. Perhaps if we stop along the way, someone may be kind enough to point us in the right direction." Varro's smile widened, his eyes sparkling at the proposition of an extended trip ahead of us. "Is there anywhere in particular we might find ourselves having taken an unfortunate detour?"

I stared ahead at the open, empty desert trail ahead of us and said, mind to mind, *"I think I have a few ideas, if you're willing to get lost with me."*

"With you, I hope I'm never found."

EPILOGUE

Varro's POV

It has been twelve days since I lied to my mate.

Every one of those days has been a struggle to conceal my thoughts and fears from her. Cress did not pass the test of five questions. Not entirely, at least. At the time, I did it to protect her until I could further assess how much of the Drift she truly suffered from. I considered the possibility that this disease of the mind could wax and wane. If she just needed time and distance from the events in the Ledor Canyon, then bringing her unnecessary worry was the last thing I wanted. In hindsight, I'm glad I withheld the truth. Shortly after she struggled to pass the test, we were sent into the chaotic chain of events that led to her wielding more of her power than ever before.

If a lie is to protect someone, then it becomes a secret. And if it was to protect her, was it really so bad? I justify this to myself daily as I wrestle with my conscience.

Cress has a secret of her own. She does not know I am aware that Trace left her a letter. When Cairis discovered it while preparing the body for burning, he came to me. Out of respect. He said he did not feel comfortable giving it to her behind her mate's back. Especially since he was aware of their previous relations. While I appreciated Cairis' intent, I would have never withheld that letter from Cress. I believe firmly in the power of our love. Trace is dead. He wasn't and isn't a threat to our bond.

If anything, I wanted to believe the relaying of that letter would only serve to soothe the overpowering grief and guilt she felt for his sacrifice. If it remedied the wound in any way, I'd want her to have it.

Cairis confirmed for me that he had delivered the note, but she has never spoken of it. Never even acknowledged its existence. I nor Cairis read it. For all I knew, she burned it, or hasn't read it yet, but part of me believes she has. After we left Artume, there was a weight lifted off her shoulders. The grief for him and Nori was kept at bay, and all of the internal self-hatred she'd punished herself with eventually faded from her thoughts. I never brought up how easily I could hear and feel those thoughts. The way she loathed herself. I just loved her harder on those days. The more time that passed, it felt as if the burden of it had finally lifted. Her plague of nightmares seemed to pass as well.

This is why I couldn't bring myself to introduce any sort of dark cloud over what little inner peace she had just found. I also knew that, with Basdie as our final destination, I couldn't promise her continued peace of mind. Saryn was there—unless Idris broke his word and dealt him the punishment we had expected. Cress and Saryn had never fully come to blows over Nori. Add Trace to the death toll, and I feared for our mentor immensely. While she could not directly blame him for their loss of life, she would be the first to reason that he is directly at fault for the mission going so poorly.

How Theory would react to all this would be another volatile component of our arrival. Unless she had already been assigned to another mission, I was uneasy thinking of how she'd react to Saryn's treason. Needless to say, I was not eager to return to Basdie as quickly as Idris would have liked, and taking Cress up on the accidental detours was a welcome distraction from the Imperi. But it would not be distraction enough from the Drift.

I worry the other Wielder's journals that proposed a mate as a viable solution to the Drift were either sorely mistaken or simply did not have a large enough sample size to make such a bold conclusion. With all our time travelling by horseback and making camp, sometimes in tents, other times at various inns, I made a point to ask her all about her life. Just like we did before heading to Artume, I focused on committing the details of my love's lifetime to memory as if it were my own. I encouraged her to ask more questions about mine as well, so it didn't seem so one-sided and intentional. I didn't want to possibly alert her to my true motivations and expose the storytelling for what it really was.

There were two reasons for my actions. Selfishly, the more I knew, the more I could watch for inconsistencies, memory lapses, even go so far as to challenge her with different questions in the future. Unselfishly, I wanted to know her as deeply as she knew herself. I wanted to see her the way she saw herself in her youth, before the Imperi, and how she saw herself today. What if her long-lived life did not come with preservation of the mind like mine would? I would remember for her. I would carry the weight of both our memories. If someday I was the only confirmation she had of a past, then I would be that anchor for her.

These were heavy worries to carry, even for me. Sometimes I would rise earlier than her in the mornings and wander the forest nearby, trying to chase the anxieties from my waking mind. Being connected as deeply as we were, it was hard not to accidentally slip in and out of one another's mental space. This is why I preferred the nights we stayed at an inn. With other travelers around, she and I knew it was the Imperi standard to keep our shields up at all times. She never questioned why our bond was quieter during these stays.

One evening, the sun had begun to set and there wasn't another inn on our map for miles ahead. A map that we would mysteriously lose before ever arriving in the Elorns; not easy to claim you've been lost with a map in hand. Cress led us a ways off the beaten path, seeking a water source for the horses. When she found a shallow creek amongst a lush bed of moss along the forest floor, I was more than content to make camp there. She pitched a tent while I made us a fire. By the time we had completed our typical chores, the twilight sky was barely visible through the heavy canopy of trees.

We may have been farther inland from the sea than I'd prefer, but at least it wasn't the mountains yet. Our previous detour had taken us as far as the plains. Cress insisted on seeing Nori's homeland with her own eyes. I had to admit, the fields of wheat were quite a sight to behold. I have fond memories now of Cress walking through the endless tall grasses, dragging her fingers along the fluffy tips of the awns. She seemed more restored than I'd seen her in some time, and I was glad I didn't protest the longer trip. "Your skin is just as gold as these fields," she had remarked.

Lost in thought of those memories, my attention was stirred when a bare-footed Cress suddenly climbed over my seated waist, straddling me.

"Well, hello there," I said, pleased at her compromising position. She rolled her hips forward—the wicked little thing. My cock hardened and began to strain against my pants. There was no hiding the arousal she drew from me. I am reminded of so many nights in Basdie, before she knew I was hers, before she ever gave herself to me, that my hand and selfish thoughts of her were my only route to relief.

"You know, with the company of only the forest creatures, we can be as loud as we want," she said teasingly.

"When has that ever stopped you before?" I pushed strands of her hair behind her shoulder and began to inspect that delectable neck of hers.

"You're right." She paused, then slid her hand between her thighs, running her fingertips along the length of me, above the fabric. "But I want to make sure the Gods can hear us loud and clear. After all, they made us for each other, right?"

Her breath fanned against my lips, and at the end of her question, she squeezed my member for good measure.

Cress's eyes darkened, and gone was the sweet and innocent female

I first met; what remained was my Moirai. The flames of desire flickered in her gaze, and when she showed this side of herself, it took all of my self-control to not punish her for being so unmerciful with her affections.

My voice dipped low. "Do not tease me so, or I'll be forced to subject you to a song you won't so easily recover from."

She tightened her grip, grasping it firmly, forcing a deep grunt from me. That's it.

It's time she understands that first and foremost, I am of the Sea, and there is a reason rumors run rampant regarding our kind… And the unrelenting way we like to fuck.

I grabbed her hand tightly and pulled it away, pinning it behind her back. I watched as her pupils dilated, and in that very moment, I knew, she knew, that there would be nothing soft or gentle awaiting her, and that she incited this. She had lit this flame in me. And I would make her burn…

I rolled the frame of my body to the side, flipping her over onto her back. Now, I held the upper hand as I pinned her body to the ground. Her gasp of surprise as I made the swift, fluid motion to this position was only the first of surprises I'd wrench forth from her.

"You wish for the Gods to hear us?" I said before biting the edge of her earlobe, tugging it playfully with my teeth.

"Yes," she panted, already caught up in the frenzy of anticipation.

I ran my hand down the center of her stomach, pushing past the top of her loose pants and cupping her slick sex with my fingers. I watched her back arch with want as I pressed my fingers in ever so slightly.

"I fear your ecstasy may draw their envy."

I slid my fingers up and down, refusing to give her the full penetration she so desired.

"How will they know you're not in agony? How will they know when you call out…that it's in pleasure, not pain?" I pondered, beginning to roll my thumb in small circles over her most sensitive spot, causing her to whimper. Gods that sound she made; I lived for that sound.

"Please," she begged, trying to coax me into granting her more of what she craved.

"Tell them, fated one. Tell the Gods who makes you cry out to the heavens."

Just as I commanded her to answer, I plunged my fingers in deeper, using my free hand to squeeze her full breast.

She gasped willingly, "Moirai!"

I slid up her blouse and hovered my body over hers. Cress sighed disappointedly as I removed my hand from her pants, sensing the loss of my touch. The soft swells of her breasts were cupped in each of my palms as I lowered my mouth and traced circles around her rosy peaks. Her hips pressed up into mine, and with each flick of my tongue she began to moan, her skin abuzz with goosebumps as the cold air met my saliva.

I dragged my teeth across her nipple, biting down until she bucked her hips into me from the collision of pain and pleasure.

Trailing kisses across her stomach, I made my path painstakingly slow. I slid my hand back down; this time finding her wetter for me. Lifting my mouth from her skin, I smiled to myself and asked, "They can't hear you, Cress. Who do you cry out for?"

Just as her lips began to utter an answer, I shoved two fingers deep inside of her once more, at the same time using all her thoughts swarming around the sensation to amplify them tenfold. As she attempted to call out "Moirai," I heard the crack in her voice, the moment Siren Song and my labors gifted her a feeling beyond any she could have ever conjured for herself.

The sound of the word barely trembling from her lips had me fighting my own temptation to erupt, but I would find the control. I would find the way to languish in the sensual torture of my mate. For she had no idea the way her mere gaze, her mere touch, did things to me I was not proud of. Not in control of. I had surrendered my body, mind and heart to this female long ago, and I'd gladly spend the rest of my days trying to show her how this tether between us was an obsession I'd faithfully serve at the altar of.

I continued to work her with the rapid plunging of my fingers in and out, the motions dancing in unison with my unique ability. She began the chorus of whines that let me know my mate was finding her climax—but this would just be one of many.

There would be no time for recovery.

As her muscles relaxed and she crumpled from the weight of her orgasm, I slid her pants off fully. While she lay there, attempting to catch her breath, I relieved myself of my shirt and pants. The cool air hit my pecs, sending ticklish delight all across my body. I stared down at my mate relaxing in the aftermath of her bliss, and it made me eager to take her there again and again.

I lay down next to her, coaxing her against my body as I curled around hers. The sheen of sweat across her body was a sign of our illicit exertions. When I was done with her, she was going to need a dip in the nearby waters. She eased into my caress and I kissed her shoulder gently, once, twice, making her think that this is how it would be, but my kiss turned to a nibble, and then a bite. Her muscles went taut as she reacted to the sharp sensation of my teeth against her sensitive skin.

I pressed my chest flat against her back and nudged aside her long hair, giving me access to her neck. I placed firm kisses there and gripped my cock behind her ass, ensuring it was rock hard for her. She felt my motions and nudged her rear further against my groin. This angle was my mate's favorite, and for that reason, I liked to withhold it from her. If I gave her what she wanted every single time, then it wouldn't be special. I grabbed her thigh, lifting her leg to rest it over my hip. Placing myself at her entrance, I teased her from behind.

My tip already glistened with the excitement of our previous actions, and I used it to lubricate her further, sliding myself in mere inches. I held myself there, knowing this would drive her absolutely wild. I forced myself to remain very still, waiting for her annoyance to peak. Expectedly, she began to rock her hips back and forth against what little I gave her. Knowing there was so much more to be had.

I leaned in and whispered, "Whose song makes you come? Tell me. Tell the Gods."

I had barely finished my words before she pushed herself back fully, taking all of me inside of her. Deep and fast.

"Moirai!" A shrill cry and yell melting into one loud answer. Cress continued to writhe against me. I held still and let her find the rhythm and pace of her preference. While she ran her heat up and down my rigid cock, I let myself, for one brief moment, focus on my own lust. My head leaned back, and my eyes squeezed shut tightly. When I opened them again, I ran my hand under her arm and squeezed her breast as I relished in how the curves of her body looked fucking amazing rolling against me.

The cadence of her moans swayed over me like waves in the sea, and I knew I wasn't going to last if I continued to let her ride me at this angle. The position wasn't untenable for me, but the sounds she made would be my undoing. Before she could meet her climax again, I pulled myself from her entrance and rose to my knees, tugging at her hips and re-positioning her on all fours in front of me.

I hated this position because I couldn't see her stunning face, but I also knew there was no better way to work her to the brink where I could control every stroke and thrust. She arched her back and perked that fine ass of hers towards the sky. Waiting for me. Baiting me. Begging for me to take her to the edge of our devious desires and beyond.

I licked my fingers and ran them across her sex, causing her hips to buck. I wanted to make sure she was still good and wet for me. If not, I'd need to delay this for a moment longer, but her pussy was dripping for me. I stroked it a couple of times more before placing myself just inside her entrance. I ran my hand down her spine and, in one motion, gave her a swift spank, the sting of which caused her to contract tightly around the head of my cock. Before she could react any further, I thrust into her forcefully, claiming her fully.

Mine.

Instinctively, she began to undulate, taking me in over and over to the hilt. There was nothing to stifle her moans, nothing to muffle her cries to the Gods as she called out for me, her Moirai. I gripped her ass tightly, watching as my cock sheathed inside of her, the view of which would be forever etched into my memory. I did everything in my power to focus my Siren Song on the details of her unfettered thoughts.

Females experienced sex so differently than males. Oftentimes, their distractions and overthinking clouded the potency of the sensations they could be embracing. But when Cress was with me, she was free of all that. Fully immersed in herself, listening to her body and letting it tell her what she wanted. Being brave enough to take it. To demand nothing less than the highest form of her own pleasure. It was the surrender to this clarity that allowed me to so easily latch on to the thoughts and intensify the orgasm for her. It also meant I knew exactly when she was about to come. And because of this, I aimed to sync my release with hers.

The quaking of her inner muscles caused my cock to pulsate as I fought to hang on a moment longer—just a bit longer, and my beautiful mate would shatter beneath me. Only then would I allow myself the same release. We moved in unison. Made for one another. Crafted by cruel Gods, meant to wander unfulfilled and incomplete until our two bodies joined like celestial objects in the sky. Permanent and intertwined in each other's orbit for all eternity and what little life this cursed world would grant us.

"I love you!" she bellowed out loudly, ushering forth my climax, wrapping it tightly around her own as she let out another shaky declaration of "I love you."

A breath rushed out of me as we both met our end, and all the muscles in my body loosened. I gently slid myself free from Cress, and we both crumpled to the ground. Facing me, I held her close to my chest. Our heavy panting mingled with the sounds of the nighttime insects; she had longed to hear them ever since returning to Cambria.

We lay there quietly in the vulnerability of our circumstances. Knowing our destination and what we'd left behind, the invisible shackles we would always wear, much like the invisible tether I welcomed between us. Cress's forehead rested near the crook of my neck and I kissed it gently. The overwhelming euphoria faded and beneath it was nothing but a fragile secret I could no longer keep. Fear rushed in, armorless, and I surrendered my heart to everything I had kept at bay. Mind to mind, I confessed.

"I have to tell you something."

PRONUNCIATION GUIDE

Aeon: A-on

Alcar: Al-car

Artume: Are-tomb

Aster: Ass-tur

Asterius: Ass-tear-e-us

Astrid: Ah-strid

Avila: Av-uh-luh

Baelin: Bay-lynn

Basdie: Baz-dye

Blackthorn: Blac-thorne

Brynmawr: Bryn-marr

Caano: Kay-no

Cairis: Care-iss

Cambria: Came-bree-uh

Ciaran: See-air-an

Corliss: Core-liss

Cress: Kress

Cressida: Kress-ah-duh

Damas: Duh-mas

Doorlae: Dor-lay

D'eliar: Dee-el-e-ar

Demir: Duh-meer

Eladir: El-uh-deer

Elorn: A-lorne

Embry: Em-bree

Ennae: Een-yay

Erisas: Air-ugh-sus

Evenus: Ev-ugh-nuss

Fenix: Phen-icks

Fideli Cœur: Fih-day-li Cur

Gaia: Guy-ugh

Gia: G-ugh

Gianna: G-on-ugh

Gris: Gree

Huxley: Hucks-lee

Idris: Eye-driss

Ilithyia: Ih-lith-e-uh

Imperi: Im-peer-ee

Islan: Ees-laun

Kasparov: Cass-par-aaf

Kaya: Kai-ugh

Lazarus: Laz-ugh-russ

Ledor: Lee-door

Lorc: Lork

Lorne: Lorn

Magnus: Mag-nuss

Miran: Mere-un

Mirtith: Mur-teeth

Moirai: Moye-rye

Nasallus: Nuh-saul-lus

Niall: Nigh-ull

Nix: Nicks

Nori: Nor-ee

Nyla: Nye-luh

Orni: Or-nye

Oscillius: Awh-sill-e-us

Saryn: Sair-in

Sav: Saav

Seraphine: Ser-ugh-feen

Shira: Sheer-ugh

Silas: Sy-luss

Talok: Tal-ock

Taran: Tear-un

Tinsilor: Tin-sill-or

Theory: Theer-ee

Tiernan: Tier-naan

Trace: Tray-se

Varro: Var-o

Versa: Verse-a

Vesper: Ves-purr

Wendell: Wen-dull

Wick: Wic

Zarif: Zair-if

ACKNOWLEDGMENTS

Readers. First and foremost, always the readers. Welcoming you into the world of the Forgotten Fae has been one of the most unforgettable adventures of my entire life. I am constantly raw and on the verge of tears with how you have embraced me and my writing. On the darkest day, you are the light. In the wildest storm, you are the calm. My gratitude for you is endless, and I am blessed you have let me carve out a small piece in your world to invite you into mine.

To my husband, book two has taken our partnership to an entirely new level. I value your input, feedback, and our process immensely. I am so lucky that besides being my champion, you have shown how much you believe in this journey by being willing to join it. Whether doing developmental editing, providing free voice acting, or by being by my side at events…this adventure is ten times better with you in it. I have never needed a mating bond to know you're the one, but there is some-thing strange and serendipitous about how this part of our life feels meant to be.

Dad, I miss you all the time, and writing stories is still carrying me through my grief. That may never end and I'm okay with that. Because each day I feel myself becoming closer to the grand storyteller that you were.

To my friends and family, your enthusiasm for my author journey is unexpected, and every small show of support is immeasurable in my heart. Thank you for believing in the dream. Not everyone has the luxury of being surrounded by unwavering positivity. To the PM Book Babes aka the OG Night Owls, you guys are my rock and I would have never imagined you'd be the ones by my side, but I should have known all along after all our late-night hours together trauma bonding.

To my besties, KP and Dani. You're the first people I want to share updates and news with. Your opinion always matters. You've never doubted me. You have always believed in where all this is going and I'm so grateful to have authentic friends like you along for the ride.

To my indie author crew, near and far. I am constantly in awe of everything we do to encourage each other to keep pushing, keep writing. Being a dreamer amongst dreamers is a far less lonely place.

To my beta readers, Kelsey and Becky, you dove in with eager optimism, and though I broke you, built you up again and broke you once more, I am grateful that you embraced the vision from its earliest stages.

Publishing continues to be a team effort and I have somehow been fortunate enough to partner with some of the best. Noah, Travis, Jade, Kevin, Sarah, Beth, and Krafigs Design…you knocked it out of the park again! And Rachel, my proofer, cheerleader, and more importantly a true friend who has fought for me at every turn. Your mark on me is permanent. I only wish that all authors were lucky enough to have someone like you in their corner.

To the ladies who call themselves the Raven Trilogy…Kim, Arianna and Lynnette. You guys make me smile, you make me laugh and you should know that it's readers and fans like you that are the reason new authors keep writing and climbing. There are others of you, I wish I could name you all. You're in my email and DMs, and your posts, chats and hype are a lifeforce unto its own and I just want to say thank you. If you're wondering, is she talking about me? Yes! Yes, I am. Keep showing your support for the stories and authors you love. You're changing lives. I promise your impact is real.

ABOUT THE AUTHOR

Lexy Night has always looked to the stars. Growing up, feeling like maybe this planet wasn't where she was supposed to be, it became practically impossible to ignore the indescribable pull of the cosmos. The next closest thing to that are the stories and adventures we can envelop ourselves in, making us feel like we lived a thousand lives in a single lifetime. Whether you find your peace between the pages or the notes of a song, she hopes you find the feeling of home.

Born and raised in Kansas (there's no place like home) she loves Midwest hospitality and is a big Chiefs football fan. When not writing, Lexy can be found snuggling her dogs, cosplaying, attending fantasy balls, binging movies/series, and playing board games. What she enjoys most are giggles with her bookish friends and exploring national parks (and the world) with her husband. Her favorite content genres are Sci-Fi and Fantasy, and she has always appreciated the villains more than the heroes.

You can find more updates, social links, and what's coming next from author Lexy Night at LexyNight.com.

9 798990 863835